About the

New York Times and *USA Today* bestselling, award-winning author **Lisa Childs** has written more than eighty-five novels. Published in twenty countries, she's also appeared on the *Publisher's Weekly*, Barnes & Nobles and Nielsen Top 100 bestseller lists. Lisa writes contemporary romance, romantic suspense, paranormal and women's fiction. She's a wife, mum, bonus mum, an avid reader and a less avid runner. Readers can reach her through Facebook or her website: lisachilds.com

Carol Ericson lives in southern California, home of state-of-the-art cosmetic surgery, wild freeway chases, and a million amazing stories. These stories, along with hordes of virile men and feisty women, clamour for release from Carol's head until she sets them free to fulfil their destinies and her readers' fantasies. To find out more about Carol and her current books, please visit her website at carolericson.com, 'where romance flirts with danger.'

USA Today bestselling author **Julie Miller** writes breathtaking romantic suspense. She has sold millions of copies of her books worldwide, and has earned a National Readers Choice Award, two Daphne du Maurier prizes and an *RT* Book Reviews Career Achievement Award. For a complete list of her books and more, go to juliemiller.org

Fake Dating

Fake Dating:
Undercover

LISA CHILDS

CAROL ERICSON

JULIE MILLER

MILLS & BOON

First Published in Great Britain 2023
by Mills & Boon, an imprint of HarperCollins*Publishers* Ltd,
1 London Bridge Street, London, SE1 9GF

www.harpercollins.co.uk

HarperCollins*Publishers*
Macken House, 39/40 Mayor Street Upper,
Dublin 1, D01 C9W8, Ireland

Fake Dating: Undercover © 2023 Harlequin Enterprises ULC.

Agent Undercover © 2015 Lisa Childs
Her Alibi © 2019 Carol Ericson
Personal Protection © 2019 Julie Miller

ISBN: 978-0-263-31962-0

MIX
Paper | Supporting
responsible forestry
FSC™ C007454

This book is produced from independently certified FSC™ paper to ensure responsible forest management.

For more information visit: www.harpercollins.co.uk/green

Printed and Bound in the UK using 100% Renewable Electricity at CPI Group (UK) Ltd, Croydon, CR0 4YY

AGENT
UNDERCOVER

LISA CHILDS

With love and appreciation for my dad – Jack Childs.
You will always be my hero!

Chapter One

Special Agent Ashton Stryker's heart pounded fast and hard with anticipation and a rush of adrenaline. He was about to meet the greatest threat to national security in his career with the FBI's antiterrorism division. Ash's responsibility was to neutralize that threat.

A bell chimed, announcing his time up with the woman across the table from him. She may have said hi. He wasn't certain; he hadn't been paying any attention to her. His target was farther down the long table, smiling at the man whose hand she shook before he moved on to the woman to her left.

Had she passed anything to him in that handshake? Ash wasn't close enough to see, but there were other eyes on her. Other agents had her under surveillance, too.

Ash stood up and took the next chair down the table. He was getting closer to her. The bell chimed again, announcing the beginning of the next five minutes.

"How can you look like that and be so socially awkward?" the woman across from him asked.

His focus on his target, he only spared the woman a glance. She was probably old enough to be his mother—maybe his grandmother—with iron-gray hair and small reading glasses hanging from a chunky gold chain around the neck of the sweatshirt embroidered with cats. "Excuse me?"

"You haven't said anything to the women before me," she said. "Of course when you look like that—the epitome of tall, dark and handsome—you probably don't have to say anything. You could grunt and women would go home with you."

He felt like grunting with frustration and impatience, but then she might take that as an invitation. "I'm sorry," he said. "This is the first time I've come to one of these things—"

"It's called speed dating," she said. "You only have five minutes, so you have to talk fast."

"I would rather listen," he said. It was what he did. Listening was how he had found the threat. He'd picked up chatter on wiretaps and other surveillance and then he'd found the post himself.

"Oh—" the older woman fanned herself with one of the drink menus "—you look like that and you'd rather listen. No wonder you've never come to one of these things before. You haven't had to. Why are you here tonight?"

Obviously he couldn't answer honestly. Ash was no rookie when it came to going undercover; he'd had some dangerous assignments over the years, going deep undercover in terrorist camps and militia groups as well as a motorcycle gang.

But he had never gone speed dating before. A couple of chairs earlier, someone had run a stiletto heel up his pant leg. Another woman had tried to give him her room key. There was danger here, too. So Ash had to be careful to not blow his cover.

"Why?" the woman asked again, her voice sharp with impatience that he hadn't answered yet.

She definitely reminded him of his grandmother, at least as much as he could remember of the austere woman from whom his father had run away as a teenager. After he'd gotten married and had Ash, he'd come back to visit, but Grandma hadn't approved of Ash's mother any more than she had her own son.

Because the woman was kind of intimidating and because it was easier to sell a cover if you told as much of the truth as possible, Ash replied honestly, "I want to meet someone."

The woman emitted a wistful sigh. "You will," she assured him. "You will."

He glanced down the table again to where the threat chatted easily with the man across from her. He was bald with no neck and an ill-fitting suit. Was he a buyer?

"Ooooh," the woman across from Ash said as if she'd just learned something momentous.

Had he given himself away?

He turned back to her and found her studying him through the thick lenses of her small glasses.

"You already have your eye on someone," she said, and she pointed down the table at the threat.

Ash swallowed a groan. He had given himself away. So he offered the woman a sheepish grin. "Am I that obvious?"

She shrugged. "I'm observant. I don't think she's noticed you at all, though. And in my opinion, you could do better than that pale little blonde."

It could have been the crimson shade of her tight dress or the pale yellow of her hair that made her skin look translucent. But he knew it wasn't—even while he admired the fit of that dress and the bright shade of lipstick on her wide mouth and the shimmer of her light hair.

The woman snorted derisively. "She looks like she hasn't been out in the daylight for years."

Ash knew why Claire Molenski looked that way. She *hadn't* been out in the daylight for years. And if he had his way, he would be locking her back up again soon.

He just had to catch her before she and her greed put into motion an economic and security catastrophe of epic proportions.

CLAIRE'S HEAD WAS THROBBING, and the smile felt frozen on her face. Her lips were so dry that they were now stuck to her teeth, so she couldn't pull them down again. *This is what you wanted*, she reminded herself.

A new life. A life that wasn't so lonely and empty.

She doubted she was going to find that new life in the dining room of the Waterview Inn, though. Most of the guys were much older than she was and some, from the deep indents on their ring fingers, were not as eligible as they claimed. In fact, when she sneezed, one pulled out a handkerchief for her and whipped out his ring as well, which rolled across the grape-leaf-and-vine-patterned carpet.

She giggled as he chased after it. But then that strange feeling assailed her—as if everyone was staring at her. She looked around the room but noticed no one overtly studying her. Maybe she was just paranoid because she hadn't been out in public for a while—for a long while.

That was the whole purpose of coming here. She could have just signed up for online dating. But she'd wanted to go out and actually meet real people—people with personality and character. Only she hadn't yet met anyone she cared to date. The bell dinged again, so she drew in a deep breath to brace herself for the next man to take the chair across from her.

First she looked at his hands, which he'd braced on the table in front of him. The ring finger held no telltale indentation. So she glanced up, and the breath she'd drawn escaped in a gasp of surprise.

Very pleasant surprise. This man wasn't too old for her. His hair was thick and black, and his eyes were a piercing blue. So piercing that he seemed to peer right through her. Had it been his stare that she'd felt earlier?

"Hello," she said. "My name's Claire."

So many of the other men had remarked that it was odd that such a young woman had such an old-fashioned name, but he just nodded, almost as if he'd known her name. But she had never met him before; he was the kind of man a woman would never forget meeting.

So she was definitely just paranoid.

"What's your name?" she asked when he didn't freely offer it.

"Ash," he replied almost reluctantly.

She floundered around for something clever to say, but her mind was blank. Maybe it was because he was so damn good-looking; maybe it was just because she had no idea how to date anymore. It had been too long.

She had read some books about how to flirt when dating. But none of what she read came to her mind. It remained blank, which was a novelty since she was usually unable to stop thinking.

"What do you do for a living, Claire?" he asked.

Several other men had asked that same question, but she actually wanted to tell him the truth. "I work with computers," she said.

"A programmer?"

She was more like a deprogrammer, but she didn't want to explain that. Legally, she really couldn't. So she just nodded. "Yes, it's boring. What about you?" she asked. "What do you do for a living?"

"Government job," he replied. "It's boring, too."

"Politics?" she asked. With that face, she could see him smiling at voters, kissing babies, shaking hands…

He shook his head. "That probably wouldn't be boring."

"Probably not," she agreed. "So you have a desk job, too?"

"Sometimes," he replied.

He had that whole mysterious thing going on, which had probably worked well for him with some of the other women. But Claire wasn't looking for complicated. She'd already had enough of that in her life. She was looking for simple and open and honest and fun—which was why none of the other men had worked for her, either.

Finally the smile left her face. She didn't have the strength to make the effort to fake it anymore. "I'm sorry," she said. "I shouldn't be here."

Maybe she wasn't ready. Maybe she hadn't done enough research. Maybe it was that feeling of being watched—even if she was totally wrong—that unnerved her.

"Aren't you available after all?" he asked.

Again she felt as if he asked a question to which he already knew the answer. She shook her head and tried to shake off her uncharacteristic paranoia. "That's not it," she said. "I'm just not ready…"

She pushed back her chair and stood up as he stood up, too. He towered over her in height and breadth with his impossibly wide shoulders and chest. His black sweater and dress pants made him look incredibly handsome and incredibly imposing. She definitely wasn't ready—especially not for him.

She couldn't believe someone like him would have even come to a speed dating event. He had to have women throwing themselves at him constantly. He didn't belong here, either. But she would leave it up to him to figure that out.

"I have to go," she said, and now panic was joining the paranoia, pressing down on her chest so that she struggled to draw a breath.

"Are you okay?" he asked.

"I need some air…" She whirled around so quickly that she knocked over her chair before rushing from the room.

His deep voice called after her, "I hope it wasn't something I said…"

A woman Claire passed on her way out laughed. "That's not likely…"

Claire heard nothing else but the sound of her own pulse pounding in her ears. What about that man had made her so nervous?

She hadn't even waited for the bell to ding before leaving him. For some reason she hadn't dared. Maybe it was the feeling he already knew things about her that she hadn't told him that had unnerved her. Or had it been the way he had looked at her—as if he could see right through her?

Or maybe it had just been the way he looked—too handsome. Dating him would be like going from a bicycle to racing motorcycles. If she was going to start dating, she needed to start on the bicycle with training wheels.

She had taken a room in the hotel for the night in case she'd had too much to drink and hadn't wanted to risk her life or anyone else's by driving. But she had barely taken more than a sip of her glass of wine, so she could drive herself home. She would feel safer in her apartment than this hotel. As she crossed the lobby, she felt as if even the eyes in the portraits were following her. She didn't need to go up to the room since all her overnight things were still in her oversize purse. So she headed straight for the front doors.

Night had fallen since the speed dating event had started. Even with the streetlights, the parking lot was dark. This hotel was outside the city of Chicago, so it had no parking garage and no valet service. She had to find her own vehicle but at least the lot was just out in front of the hotel.

She was reaching inside her bag, digging for her keys, when someone grabbed her. A strong arm wrapped tightly around her, binding her arms to her sides, as the man lifted her off her feet. She parted her lips to scream, but a big hand clamped down hard over her mouth, muffling her cry for help and nearly smothering her.

Or maybe it wasn't the hand but the handkerchief it held against her mouth and nose that smothered her—with the sweet, cloying scent of chloroform.

If she didn't fight fast and hard, she would soon lose her chance.

And maybe her life…

Chapter Two

"I lost eyes on her." A voice emanated from Ash's earpiece. It was a two-way radio that transmitted what he said and what the other agents said. "She's gone…"

Claire Molenski had stepped through the front doors of the hotel and disappeared into the darkness. Ash had followed her from the dining room, but at a discreet distance that had only drawn the attention of the older woman who had earlier noticed him staring at Claire. The woman had winked at him, either teasing him or encouraging him. Ash had waited only a few minutes before exiting those lobby doors and stepping into the lot.

"Where the hell has she gone?" he asked the question more to himself than to the other agents who could hear him through their earpieces. He hadn't been far behind her.

"We lost the visual on the subject," another agent remarked.

Ash cursed. How had she slipped the surveillance so easily? The woman was a bigger threat than even he had realized. And from the minute her name had come to his attention, she'd had his full attention. He'd known this woman was going to be dangerous.

He stepped deeper into the shadows of the dimly lit parking lot. And he heard something. Something muffled and soft—like a crying kitten—was just loud enough to draw his attention. There were plenty of strays in the questionable outskirts of Chicago.

But was it a trick? A lure?

He moved carefully between the parked cars, keeping low so that no one noticed him. But he noticed a dark shadow, probably of a man, bent over as he lifted something from the asphalt. Lights flashed on as a car started, dispelling the shadow to the image of a hulky bald-headed man. The light shimmered off the pale blond hair of the woman that the man carried.

Claire.

Her head lolled back, her eyes closed. She was either unconscious or dead. That cry Ash had heard must have been her last weak attempt to scream for help. Had he heard her too late? But if she was dead, why was the man carrying her? To dispose of the body?

Ash reached beneath his sweater and drew his gun from his holster. He could have spoken into the radio and signaled for help. But then he might have also made the man aware of his presence. And if he was going to overpower him, he needed the element of surprise.

So he crept through the rows of parked cars as the driver of the vehicle with the lights honked and rolled down his window. Ash had thought it was an accomplice. But the driver called out, "Is everything okay? Is she okay?"

"Just had too much to drink," the man murmured, his accent so thick the words were hard to comprehend.

The driver hesitated yet, his car idling in the lot. He must have realized what Ash had—that the situation wasn't right. At the very least it wasn't what the man claimed. Ash had only seen Claire take one sip of her wine and no more. Had it been drugged?

Maybe that was why she had rushed off the way she had. But she had been clear-eyed and coherent then. Whatever had happened to her had happened after she'd stepped through the doors of the hotel and out of Ash's sight. It had happened so damn quickly that he'd nearly lost her—and still might.

"Why don't we call hotel security?" the driver suggested.

The man slung Claire over one arm and pulled a gun with his other. He pointed the barrel through the open window of the car. "Why don't you mind your own damn business?"

Chivalry forgotten now, the driver sped off—tires squealing as the car careened out of the lot. The car had drawn the attention of other agents, who ran across the lot toward the man.

Ash stepped from the shadows, the barrel of his gun pointing at the man's heart. Claire was slung over his other shoulder, and so small that Ash wouldn't hit her if he fired. Or at least he hoped he wouldn't...

"She is my business," Ash said. "So you can put her down now or you can take a bullet."

The big man scoffed. "You will shoot me?"

Ash shrugged. "Either I will shoot you or one of the other FBI agents will."

All around them, guns cocked. Ash hoped all of those guns belonged to fellow agents. But some could have belonged to this man's associates. Would he have attempted this abduction alone? Which country or group might they be from?

"Put her down," Ash said.

"I could kill her," the man threatened.

"If that was the plan," Ash said, "she would already be dead. But then she wouldn't be worth anything."

The threat she posed would have been eliminated, though. Ash's assignment accomplished. But that gave him no sense of relief—only regret. Anger surged through him, heating his blood despite the cool night air. He had no intention of letting this man, or anyone else, kill Claire Molenski.

The man turned his weapon on Ash, pointing the barrel at him. "Then I will kill you—"

Before he could fire, someone else took the shot, and the big man crumpled to the asphalt. Ash lunged forward and caught Claire before she could hit the ground, too. She was incredibly light and small, more like the weight and size of a child than a woman. But there was nothing innocent or vulnerable about her. He had to remind himself of that; he had to remind himself that she was the danger.

But because of what she knew—and how many nefarious groups and governments wanted that knowledge—she was also in danger. Some people or countries weren't able or willing to pay for the information she had; instead they would torture her for it.

Ash had seen men three times her size break. Claire Molenski wouldn't survive. So just watching her wasn't going to be enough to keep her safe. But protecting her, like she needed protection, would make it harder to gather enough evidence for her arrest.

HER HEART POUNDING WILDLY, Claire awoke in a panic. She had no idea how long she had been unconscious, if it had been minutes or hours since she'd been chloroformed.

Where had she been taken? She blinked her eyes wide, trying to clear her fuzzy vision and her fuzzy head. But the room was dark.

She reached out and breathed a sigh of relief that

her hands weren't bound. Her fingers skimmed across silky material, and she recognized the soft surface on which she was lying. She had been carried to a bed. She skimmed her hands down her body and breathed another sigh of relief that she still wore her dress. Maybe nobody had hurt her.

Yet.

But then a lamp snapped on, and she blinked against the brightness of the light shining in her eyes. "What— where am I?"

"Your room," a deep voice replied.

She couldn't see him—not with the light filling her vision field with spots. Who was he?

And why was he lying to her?

This wasn't her room. Her bed wasn't this soft and smooth. Her mattress was old and lumpy, but since she was rarely home, she hadn't seen the reason to replace it. Or to make the bed, either. Her sheets were never smooth. They were always rumpled, usually kicked to a tangled mess at the foot of the bed, as she rushed to get to the office. She was pretty much always at work—before the sun rose in the morning until after it set again at night.

"Why did you grab me?" she asked, her pulse still racing. While she wasn't bound, she *had* been abducted.

He replied matter-of-factly, "So you wouldn't hit the ground."

"I wasn't going to fall…" She blinked again, and her eyes adjusted to the light enough that she could make him out standing over the bed.

He was tall—taller than she had even realized when she'd talked to him across the table earlier. And he was so broad. No wonder he had overpowered her so easily in the parking lot in the dark. If only she'd seen him coming, maybe she could have outrun him.

Then she remembered the heels she'd been wearing; he would have caught her and easily once she had twisted her ankle. She wiggled her toes, grateful that her shoes were gone. Maybe she could run now.

"Why?" she asked, her fears growing even more. "Why would you bring me here?"

"This is your room," he repeated. "The one you rented at the hotel."

"Oh…" She had rented a room. But she had changed her mind about using it. Obviously he'd had other plans.

"Why did you drug me?" she asked, although she was afraid that she knew the answer.

Was he the kind of man who didn't take rejection well? With the way he looked, he probably wasn't often rejected. Did he intend to take what she hadn't been willing to offer him?

"I didn't drug you," he said.

"Someone grabbed me in the parking lot," she said, "and put something over my mouth and nose…"

"Chloroform," he replied again so matter-of-factly.

"So you admit to using it on me?" she asked, and anger joined her fear. And again she was grateful her hands weren't bound because she would fight him. She would hurt him as badly as he intended to hurt her.

"No," he said. "I recognized the smell. That's why I brought you back to your room, so you could regain consciousness."

"What do you intend to do to me?" she asked, her heart continuing to pound wildly with fear.

He sighed and pushed a hand through his dark hair. "I wish I knew…"

"Then why did you grab me?" If he had no plan…

"I only grabbed you after your abductor had been shot," he said, as if his crazy explanation made perfect sense.

"Abductor?" So now he was trying to place the blame on someone else.

He nodded. "I don't know who the man was."

"Was?"

He nodded again but grimly this time, his strong-looking jaw clenched. "He's gone."

"Dead?" Her voice squeaked with the question. "You killed him?" Maybe there had really been another man… before he'd died.

"No," he said. "Another agent shot him…before he could shoot me."

"And then you brought me back here," she said, as if she was following his preposterous story. The man was obviously deranged. No wonder he'd followed her out of the hotel and tried to grab her.

And she had thought getting to know someone in person first would be safer than dating someone she'd only met online. Maybe dating at all was a bad idea. But how else was she ever going to meet someone who could share her life—her hopes, her dreams?

Somehow she suspected that having a relationship wasn't going to be an issue for her anymore—unless she could somehow overpower this muscular man and escape him. She tried to peer around him to determine how far away the door was.

Or maybe she could yell…

Weren't hotel room walls notoriously thin?

She opened her mouth to scream, but his palm slid across her lips, silencing her. And he joined her on the bed, his thigh hard and warm against her hip. She tried to struggle, but he easily held her down—pushing her into the mattress. And she noticed that his sweater had ridden up, revealing a holster and a gun. He was armed.

Tears stung her eyes as fear overwhelmed her. What was he going to do to her?

"I'm not going to hurt you," he said, almost as if he regretted that he wasn't. "I've been watching you..."

So she hadn't been paranoid.

"I'm trying to stop you from doing something that's going to put your life and the country in danger," he said. "But obviously I'm too late. You're already in danger."

She had realized that back in the parking lot. She'd been scared then. She was terrified now.

"Have you put the country in danger, too?" he asked.

She moved her lips against his palm, as if she was trying to answer his question. As if she could actually answer something so absurd...

She only wanted him to move his hand so that she could scream. If he didn't want her making any noise, he wouldn't risk shooting her. Would he?

If she screamed, hopefully someone would hear her and come to her aid. It was her only chance to escape this man and his madness.

But he didn't move his hand. In fact, it covered her entire face, his fingers covering one ear and his thumb the other. She could still hear him, though—still hear his ridiculous questions.

"Did you already endanger national security?" he asked.

"How?" she murmured the word against his palm.

Who did he think she was? He must have mistaken her for someone else. Maybe it was dawning on him because he stared down at her through narrowed eyes as if determining if he should trust her. He moved his palm slightly.

She could have screamed. But he could still shoot her before help arrived. And then he could shoot whoever might have been chivalrous enough to help her. So she spoke quietly instead. "Who do you think I am?"

His mouth curved into a slight smile. "You're Claire Molenski."

Her pulse quickened before she reminded herself that she had given him her first name. And he'd had time while she was unconscious to go through her purse and find her license. Oh, God, if he had seen her license, he also knew where she lived. He could have taken her keys, too, for her car and her house.

But why?

"Who are you?" she asked.

During their speed dating round, he had only given her his first name but that might have been as made up as his other wild stories.

"Ash," he said. "Special Agent Ash Stryker."

That name definitely sounded made up to her. But then he tugged on the chain that disappeared beneath the neck of his black sweater and pulled out a big shield. She had seen enough of those the past several years that she realized the shield was real.

And so was Special Agent Ash Stryker.

Dread overwhelmed her and she groaned. "No…"

Triumph flashed in his light blue eyes. "You didn't think we would trace the online auction back to you?"

"Online auction?" He might have been telling the truth about who he was and what had happened, but none of it made any sense to her. All she understood was that somehow her life was turning upside down—again. And she didn't know how to turn it right side up. "What do you think I'm selling?"

He just stared at her, obviously convinced that she knew, so that he wasn't even going to bother to answer.

Annoyance flashed through her. She had been too

young before to fight for herself. She wasn't going to go down this time without a fight.

"Do you think I'm selling my body?" she asked.

His lips quirked again, as if he was tempted to grin. "That might explain the speed dating and the hotel room..."

He flicked his gaze down her short, tight dress, as if he were actually considering buying. And heat flashed through her now, making her skin tingle with excitement. But then she reminded herself that he was an FBI agent, and a cold chill chased away the heat.

"But an FBI agent," she said, "*especially* an FBI special agent wouldn't waste his time investigating something that a vice cop would handle."

He arched a dark brow and asked, "Do you know much about Vice?"

"No." She sighed. "But I do know about the Federal Bureau of Investigations."

He didn't ask why; he would have read her file. The FBI probably had a volume on her by now.

"So, Special Agent Ash Stryker," she addressed him. "How are you going to ruin my life this time?"

Chapter Three

The woman was trouble. Ash had known that before he'd even met her. But she was even more dangerous in person than he had expected her to be.

Because he hadn't expected his reaction to her—his very physical, very male reaction to her beauty. Her skin was porcelain—all pale and smooth—and too much of it showed beneath the short skirt of her tight red dress. Damn, she was sexy. She knew it, too, and was using it to her advantage with that flirtatious comment about selling her body.

Hell, if she was really selling, he might have been tempted to make an offer. She was that beautiful. But she was also that treacherous.

"I have never met you before," he reminded her. "So I have had no part in ruining your life."

Was that why she had betrayed her country? Out of spite over her arrest years ago?

"You're such a *suit*," she uttered the slang word for FBI agent with total disdain. "Even without the suit, I should have realized you were an FBI agent. I knew something wasn't right with you."

Her remark had his pride stinging. He was good at going undercover. Nobody else had ever suspected he wasn't who he was pretending to be—even when he'd gone deep undercover with motorcycle gangs and militia groups. But maybe he had been more out of his element speed dating than he had ever been anywhere else.

"Actually, everything's right with me," he said. "You're the one in the wrong."

She shook her head, and her silky blond hair skimmed across her shoulders, which were bare but for thin red spaghetti straps. "I haven't done anything wrong."

"I believe that's what you said last time—"

"It was true last time, too," she insisted.

"You hacked into a bank," he reminded her since she seemed to have forgotten what she'd done. "And cleaned out someone's account."

She defensively crossed her arms over her chest. "I had my reasons."

"Do you have reasons this time, too?" he asked. "Because the only one I can think of is greed."

"You thought that was my reason last time, too," she murmured with even more disdain—as if she thought him an idiot. "But I didn't keep that money. I gave it all away to charity."

"It wasn't your money to give," he pointed out. "And *I* didn't have anything to do with your last arrest." He hadn't even been an agent then. He had probably still been a marine at that time. The Bureau had recruited him out of the service to become an agent. He had been surprised that either of them—the marines or the Bureau—had wanted him, given his background.

She sucked in a sharp breath, and her eyes widened with fear again. When she'd regained consciousness, she had seemed genuinely afraid. Despite what she'd started with her online activity, she obviously hadn't expected that she'd put herself in danger.

"Last arrest?" she repeated his words. "Is there going to be *another* arrest?"

Not unless he could find some more concrete evidence against her. It wasn't enough that knowledge only she possessed had been offered for sale. She was smart enough now that the online auction couldn't be traced directly back to her...except for that knowledge. He would have only been able to arrest her if he could have caught her in the act of selling the information. That was why he had come to the speed dating event, to pose as a buyer.

But somehow he must have spooked her before he had even been able to put in his bid. Then having to rescue her in the parking lot had completely blown his cover. Now it would be harder to find evidence against her. Now that she knew the FBI was on to her she was going to be even more careful. But maybe he could convince her to confess—if he could bluff enough that she thought the Bureau already had enough evidence for an arrest.

"You tell me if I should take you into custody," he suggested. "Have you already sold it?"

"Sold what?" she asked, acting as confused as she had when he had mentioned her online auction earlier.

Claire Molenski was as good an actress as she was a hacker because he was almost starting to buy her act. But only almost. From going undercover himself, he knew how easy it was to assume a role. He usually had to assume one of guilt because he was acting like a criminal. She was assuming one of innocence because she was acting like a victim. As if she had been unjustly persecuted before and now.

But it was just an act. Just an act...

Someone's phone rang. It wasn't his; he always kept that on vibrate. So he reached for her purse and pulled out her ringing cell.

"Maybe this is your buyer."

And maybe here was his evidence. If this caller made an offer for her information and arrangements for an exchange, Ash had her. Instead of triumph, though, he felt a flash of disappointment.

CLAIRE DIDN'T CARE that he had a gun. She grabbed for her phone anyway. She wasn't worried about him intercepting a call from a buyer. She still had no idea what he thought she was trying to sell. She was actually worried that he might intercept a call from someone from the dating service she had joined.

She didn't want a man answering her phone and scaring away a potential match. She had spent too much of her life alone; she wanted to share it with someone now.

But he ignored her attempt to grab for it and clicked on the talk button. "Hello."

She groaned. She had only given out her number to a couple of promising prospects from the dating service— to guys that the service had matched her with for compatibility. She hadn't needed five minutes or a dating service personality test to determine that she was totally incompatible with this man.

These potential matches wouldn't be too promising either after Ash got through with them, especially when he continued speaking, "This is Special Agent Stryker..."

She swallowed another groan. Uttering it would do her no good—just as explaining her hacking nine years ago had done her no good, either. She had still been arrested. She'd been convicted. She'd been sentenced. While she hadn't spent any time actually behind bars in the juvenile detention center with which she'd been threatened, she had been locked up—in a classroom studying to be an even better hacker. And then in a business that specialized in internet security.

"It's your boss," Stryker told her.

She'd worked for Peter Nowak for years, but the former CIA agent still intimidated the hell out of her. Her hand trembled slightly as she reached out for the phone, but Ash Stryker ignored her and continued to listen.

"Give it to me," she insisted.

But he shook his head, still denying her access. To her phone or to the help she would be able to seek with it? She wasn't sure how much help Peter would be, though, if he also suspected her of whatever the FBI did.

She could call a lawyer, though, like she should have last time. But she hadn't wanted her father to go broke trying to pay her legal fees.

Ash replied to whatever her boss had said with "We'll be right there." Then he clicked off her cell phone and pocketed it.

"Why are you speaking for me?" she asked. "Am I in your custody?" Had she already been arrested but she had been too drugged to understand her rights? She really needed to call a lawyer this time.

"Your boss said the building was broken into—"

She shook her head, not buying this story of his just as she hadn't the first stories he'd told her. "We have an excellent security system at the office." Peter had designed it himself. "We also have armed guards. There's no way anyone got in—"

"The alarm system was compromised," he said.

She shook her head, unable to believe it. "But there are guards—"

"One of them was shot."

She gasped as her heart pounded. She saw those

guards every day as she passed them on her way in and out of the office. "No! Who? Is he all right?"

"Nowak is at the hospital with the man."

"Then we need to go there, too," she said.

"He told us to go to the company instead."

"But why would he want me to go there?" She wasn't in management. She had nothing to do with the details of running the company or the office.

"Your personal office was the only one that had been broken into," Stryker said. "We're going there right now to make sure nothing's been taken."

"My office?" She shook her head in denial. "That makes no sense."

"Someone tried grabbing you in the parking lot," he reminded her. "Since they couldn't get the information from you directly, they must have tried getting it from your office."

She wanted to scream in frustration at his stubbornness. But apparently he wasn't the only one with the wrong idea about her. "So a man was shot over something someone thinks I'm trying to sell?"

The guard was shot because of her?

She leaped up from the bed, but the aftereffects of the chloroform must have included dizziness. Feeling faint, she nearly toppled over, but he caught her.

If what he'd claimed earlier was true, he had already caught her another time that night.

"We need to go," he said.

"To the hospital—"

"Are you all right?" he asked as he held her up, his hands warm on her shoulders.

Her legs were too rubbery for her to stand without support. But she insisted, "I'm fine." Or she would be once the room stopped spinning. "I want to go check on the guard."

"Your boss said the man is in stable condition. He will be fine," he assured her. "We need to go to your office and make sure nothing's been taken."

She hadn't left anything of value to anyone else in her office. But there were things of value to her there, things she couldn't replace. And she would be of more use at the office than she would be pacing a hospital waiting room. She wasn't even sure she knew who had been wounded, but it didn't matter. She still felt somehow responsible. Why had someone broken into the company and then only into her office?

"Okay," she said and pulled away from him. Her skin tingled from where his hands had grasped her shoulders when he'd been holding her upright. She needed distance from him. "Let's go!"

"You're in an awful hurry," he said. "But then you wouldn't want someone to *steal* what you're trying to sell."

Beyond irritated with him, she gritted her teeth and replied, "I am not selling anything."

"You want me to believe you were at this hotel tonight because you really were *speed dating*?" He sounded horrified at the prospect.

Heat rushed to her face, which had probably turned as red as her dress. "I really was..."

He glanced around the hotel room. "Is that why you rented a room?"

Her face got even hotter. "I rented a room in case I'd had too much to drink." And she felt as if she had, thanks to the chloroform making her head fuzzy and her legs weak. Or maybe Agent Stryker had made her legs weak. It really wasn't fair that the FBI agent was so ridiculously good-looking. "I didn't rent a room because I thought I'd get lucky."

There had been nothing lucky about meeting Agent Stryker. And while she wanted to meet someone else, she hadn't expected much from the speed dating experience. She certainly hadn't expected to fall in love in five minutes.

On the floor next to the bed she noticed her shoes and her purse. She stepped into the uncomfortable heels. Then she grabbed up her purse and reached into the oversize bag to search for her keys. "I'll drive myself to the office."

He held up her keys; she recognized them because the rhinestone wristband attached to the chain caught the light. She'd bought the wristband key chain so she could slip it over her wrist and always have her keys accessible. Yet she kept tossing them into her bag out of habit.

"We'll take my car," he said as he walked toward the hotel room door. He didn't wait to see if she followed him. He just opened the door and stepped into the hall.

That same feeling of helplessness washed over Claire like it had nine years ago when nobody had believed her about the hacking. Or maybe they'd only cared that she had and not *why* she had.

She didn't want to ride with him. "But *my* car has the permit for the company parking lot," she said as she hurried after him.

"My car is FBI," he said. "That gives me a permit to park wherever I want."

She pulled the hotel room door shut and mouthed his words behind his back. Sure, she was acting childish, but he was just so arrogant and infuriating and...

He chuckled, so he must have somehow witnessed her juvenile behavior. Did he have eyes in the back of his head? "Are you coming?" he asked.

She wanted to say no, but since he had her keys she had no choice. Unless she hailed a cab…

Maybe she should hail a cab. And call a lawyer.

But first she had to go to the office. Had to make sure nothing had been taken. Had to try to figure out what someone had been looking for.

But he had her keys—not just to her car but to her office, too.

"Yes," she finally, reluctantly, replied.

"Come on, then," he said, as if she was a child that needed his direction and protection. "You need to stick close to me."

He had just uttered the words when a door creaked open and a dark shadow filled the hallway ahead of him. Reminded of the man accosting her in the parking lot, Claire shivered with foreboding. She glanced back at the hotel room, but she'd closed the door. And like her keys, Ash probably had the card to the room; she couldn't re-enter without it.

So she hurried up to close the distance between them. But he held out a hand to her as if shoving her back. He used his other hand to withdraw his gun from his holster. She shook her head in protest.

If he pointed that gun at some unsuspecting hotel guests, he was going to scare them to death—like he had nearly scared her when she'd awakened to find him leaning over her.

"Ash…" Maybe she should have called him Special Agent Stryker, but for some reason his first name was what had slipped out of her lips.

Regardless of what she'd called him, he lifted a finger to his lips, silencing her.

The shadow stepped through the stairwell doorway and into the hall. The shadow belonged to a man—a big man—and like Ash, he carried a gun. He pointed the barrel at Special Agent Stryker.

"FBI," Ash called out.

The man didn't care. He cocked the gun and pulled the trigger. But Ash fired, too.

Claire screamed and ducked as bullets struck the walls of the hallway, tearing through the blue-and-green-striped paper to burrow into the drywall. Or pass through into the rooms of those unsuspecting guests.

"Stay down!" Ash ordered her.

Then a bullet must have struck him because he staggered back. But he kept his body between hers and the shooter, using it to protect her as he returned fire.

She screamed again but she wasn't worried just about herself or those guests; she was worried about him. Had he been hurt badly?

Chapter Four

Ash cursed as the force of the bullet propelled him back. He nearly knocked over Claire, who stood behind him like he had directed her. Maybe he should have told her to run. But the man with the gun stood between them and the stairwell and the elevators.

She had no place to run.

Even if he passed her the key card to the hotel room, she wouldn't be safe inside the room—at least not for long. A man this big could easily knock down her door. The only way to keep her safe was to eliminate the threat to her safety.

So Ash fired again. But this was a kill shot. The big man crumpled to the carpet like the guy in the parking lot had crumpled to the asphalt.

"It's okay," Ash told her as he turned back to Claire. "It's over." For now. But how long before someone else tried to abduct her? And why?

Why not just pay what she asked for the information? Unless she was telling the truth…

She moved as if to look around him, but he used his body to block her view. She didn't need to see what he had done to protect them. But instead of moving around him, she moved toward him—her hands reaching out toward his chest.

"Are you all right?" she asked, her voice cracking with concern.

He nodded. But he wasn't entirely convinced that he was all right because he was beginning to believe her and doubt himself. She had been so concerned about the security guard and now about him. Maybe she wasn't the mercenary person he thought she was.

"But you were shot!" she exclaimed, her palms patting his chest as if she were searching for the wound.

He caught her hands and pressed them more tightly against his vest. "I'm fine."

She shook her head. "You must be hurt."

"The protective vest took the bullet," he assured her. He had only felt the impact of the too-close shot. And he would probably have a bruise on his chest from the force with which the bullet had struck the vest. He pulled her hands away from his chest, and she tugged them free of his grasp.

"Thank God you're wearing a vest." Her breath shuddered out with sincere-sounding relief. "But of course you would be wearing a vest."

"Of course." But there had been times that he hadn't been able to when he'd been undercover. He couldn't have risked someone noticing the vest, no matter how thin and indiscernible the Bureau vests were. He also hadn't been able to wear a wire then, either. He had been totally on his own. But that hadn't been anything new to Ash.

"Maybe I should be wearing one, too," she mused, and she must have finally caught sight of the man he'd shot because she shuddered in revulsion.

"He wasn't shooting at you," he said.

Her green eyes widened in skepticism. "Really? I was right behind you."

"He wouldn't have hit you." The guy had been aiming only for Ash.

"Why not?" she asked.

"You're too valuable."

She laughed like he'd heard her laugh during the speed dating event, like he had told her a not-so-funny joke like those other guys must have. "Yeah, right..."

Was her self-deprecation real or feigned? He believed it was real, because he was beginning to believe her. He had conceived his opinion of her from her file—from the things she'd done in her past. He of all people should have known better than to think a person's past defined the kind of person he or she would become.

"The information you have is valuable," he clarified. "They want to know what you know."

"But you think I'm offering that information for sale," she said. "So why wouldn't they just pay me for it?"

"Some people would rather get the information for free," he said.

She glanced toward the man lying on the floor and shook her head. "That's not free."

No. Like the man in the parking lot, this guy had undoubtedly been hired to abduct Claire, but whatever they'd been paid hadn't been enough. The mission had cost them both their lives.

Ash rubbed his chest where the bullet had struck the vest right over his heart. If not for the vest...

During his years with the Bureau, Ash had had some dangerous assignments, but now he wondered if this mission would be the one that cost him his life.

HE HAD KILLED a man, but the police hadn't questioned him. Of course Special Agent Ash Stryker hadn't stuck around to talk to them, either. He'd whisked Claire out of the hotel as if nothing had happened.

But the gunshots still rang in her ears, and she trembled in the aftermath of the close call. Maybe he was right. Maybe the man hadn't been shooting at her. But she'd thought Ash had been hit, which had been entirely too close for her.

She had actually touched him, just to check his chest to see if a bullet had struck his heart. But he'd been wearing a vest. She'd felt the hardness beneath the softness of his sweater. Maybe she should have checked beneath the vest, too. At the thought of pulling up his sweater and peeling off that vest, her pulse quickened. Would his chest have dark hair that would be soft to her touch? Or would his muscles be all sleek and smooth beneath her palms? Her breath caught at both images.

"Is something missing?" Agent Stryker asked.

Her face heated with embarrassment that he had caught her daydreaming about him when she was supposed to be checking her ransacked office to see what could have been missing. Why would someone break into her office?

The power was on her computer but her files were untouched. Nobody would have been able to bypass her security passwords, though. And once they'd sounded the alarm and shot the guard, they wouldn't have had time to even try to figure it out.

What were they so desperate to steal from her?

She reached for the snow globe paperweight that sat next to her monitor. She shook it and watched the flakes float onto the pond, a tiny figurine of a father skated around with the tiny figurine of his daughter perched high upon his shoulders. Her breath shuddered out in relief. "It's okay."

"You were worried about a paperweight?" he asked, his blue eyes narrowed with skepticism.

"Have you ever seen anything like it?" she asked as she held it out toward him.

He shrugged. "It's a snow globe."

"It's special," she said with a soft sigh as sweet, old memories rushed over her. "My father gave it to me."

"Is he dead?"

She gasped at the horror of such a loss. "No!"

He reached for the paperweight, engulfing the delicate glass globe in his big hands. "I don't see what's so special about it," he said as he studied it more closely, "unless you hid a flash drive inside it."

Afraid that he might smash it onto the floor to look for something hidden inside, she grabbed for it, her fingers sliding over his as he gripped the globe. "Don't break it! My father had that specially made for me." To commemorate a perfect day. Of course it had been just the two of them…

Maybe she shouldn't have gotten so upset when her mother left them since she had never really spent that much time with them anyway. And Claire probably wouldn't have if her father hadn't gotten so upset. He had been in so much pain that she'd had to lash out. She sighed again, but this time with regret.

"He's not dead," Ash reminded her.

"Does he have to be?" she asked. "Why can't something he gave me be important to me while he's alive?"

Ash just shrugged again.

Her heart sank as she had a grim realization. "Your father's dead."

He jerked his head in a quick nod, as if he was embarrassed to admit it.

"I'm sorry."

Now he shrugged off her sympathy. "It happened a long time ago."

She doubted that would have lessened his pain very much. If something happened to her father, she would miss him forever. "That must have been tough on you and your mom."

"My mom died with him," he said.

Her hands still covered his, over the snow globe, so she squeezed, offering sympathy and comfort. "That must have been horrible for you. To lose them both…"

For a while she had felt like she had, too.

Ash focused on her now, as if he'd picked up on the tone of her voice. "You lost your mom."

"Yes," she said but then hastened to add, "but not like you did, though. She's alive. She's just gone. When I was sixteen, she left my dad and went to live in England with a man she'd met online."

His eyes widened, and then he nodded with sudden realization. "That was when you hacked into that bank."

"It was the bank that he used and the only money I took was from his account," she said. For some reason she wanted him to know that greed hadn't motivated her. But was it any better that spite had?

He chuckled. "And if I remember right from what I read in your file, you donated that money to a charity called Family First."

She couldn't chuckle. Even after all these years, she was still kind of bitter. Probably too bitter. "I wanted to hurt him."

"Instead you're the one you hurt," he said. "Because he pressed charges."

And yet her mother had stayed with the man. Clearly Bonita Molenski had made her choice when she'd left them, but still it had hurt Claire that her mother had cared so little about her that she would have let her go to juvenile detention. But then the FBI had offered Claire another option.

"You've definitely read my file," she mused. Either he'd read it a few times, or he had a photographic memory. She glanced around her ransacked office. "It hasn't been all bad, though. I actually enjoy what I do."

"You do?" he asked doubtfully, as if he couldn't understand why.

She laughed at his skepticism. "Yes, I do. I've not only been given permission to hack, I've been encouraged to do it. It's fun."

Or it had been until she had realized that her job was pretty much all she had. Of course she'd spent time with her dad when she hadn't been working. But he was finally over her mother and had moved on, so it was time she did the same. That was why she'd joined the dating service—one she'd trusted to make sure that none of the participants were already married like her mother had been. That hadn't been the case at the speed dating event, though. But maybe, like Ash, some of the others hadn't been there to date, either.

He sighed and released the snow globe to her hands. "You're not selling a flash drive with inside information on how to get around security firewalls."

So that was what he'd thought she was selling. "I would never sell that kind of information," she assured him.

After her arrest all those years ago, she had learned to control her impulsiveness and consider the consequences of her actions before she acted. Ironically, learning that had actually made her a better hacker.

Knuckles rapped against the glass wall of her office. "Hey, Boss, what happened here tonight?"

She turned her attention to her young assistant, who leaned now in her open doorway. His bleached white-blond hair was all mussed up as if he'd been sleeping and his eyes were red-rimmed as if he'd been out partying before he'd fallen asleep. Maybe Martin Crouch wasn't as young as she thought—he just dressed and acted young. Peter Nowak must have called him in to help her look through her ransacked office.

"The building was broken into and Harold was injured," she said. As soon as they had arrived at the company, she'd learned the name of the injured guard. Ash had checked in with the hospital again and had assured her that Harold was out of surgery and in stable condition. Fortunately, he would fully recover.

"Is—is he going to be okay?" Martin asked.

He must have been as shocked and horrified as she was. Despite checking security for banks and the government, the company had always been safe and secure—probably because most people didn't realize exactly what kind of computer consulting they did.

"Yes, he is," Ash answered for her.

Martin turned his attention to Ash and asked, "Are you a police officer?"

Claire opened her mouth, but before she could reply, Ash answered for her again. "I'm Claire's boyfriend."

She sucked in a breath of shock at his outrageous claim. Nobody would actually believe that they were dating—not a former lawbreaker and an FBI agent. But maybe Ash didn't intend to tell anyone that he was an agent. Her boss knew but national security relied on his ability to keep secrets.

Martin's bleached blond brows arched in surprise. As her assistant, he knew how many hours they worked and how little time she had for a relationship. "Really?"

"We met through a dating service," Ash replied with a pointed stare at her—probably so that she would back his story.

"Really?" Martin asked again, and he turned toward Claire now.

Technically Ash hadn't lied, but she wondered why he hadn't told more of the truth. Like what he really did for a living. Could he suspect Martin of being involved in offering that information for sale? He suspected her, though, and had revealed that he was an FBI agent. But maybe he'd only done that because she'd nearly been abducted.

Aware of the danger, she followed his lead and replied, "Yes, really. Ash and I met at a speed dating event." Like Ash, she left out the part that it had been just that evening.

"How come you didn't mention anything to me about meeting someone?" Martin asked, sounding hurt, which surprised her.

He was her assistant but not her confidant. She didn't share everything with him. She lifted her shoulders in a slight shrug. "I wanted to see how it worked out before I said anything."

She was damn sure a relationship would never work out between her and the FBI agent. He thought she was a criminal, and she thought he was too uptight and judgmental.

"So you're okay?" Martin asked. At first she wasn't sure what he was talking about—her and Ash—or the break-in. But then he added, "Nothing was taken?"

She tightly clasped the snow globe and shook her head. "Nothing."

"That's good," he said. "Do you want me to help you clean up?"

"No, but thanks for asking, Martin." She was surprised

that he had, though, because she rarely let him touch anything in her space even though he was her assistant.

She hated that someone else had been in her office, touching her things, moving and throwing them around the small area. She didn't need everything to be neat; she just needed it to be where she'd left it so she would know where to find it again. At least they hadn't broken the globe or, as far as she could tell, anything else.

"It's so late," she told Martin, "that you should just go home." Like she just wanted to go home…

Martin glanced to Ash again. Either he was concerned about leaving her alone with this strange man or he was seeking permission from Ash to leave.

He was her assistant, though. He was supposed to defer to her. Usually he did—when he wasn't preoccupied with whatever games he was playing when he should be working instead.

Ash assured him, "I'll take care of her."

Was he offering that assurance as an FBI agent? Or as the boyfriend he was pretending to be?

Easily accepting Ash's claim, Martin nodded and headed for the door. He was probably eager to go back to bed. Or maybe to the party…

Ash waited until her assistant was out of earshot before he asked her, "There really is nothing missing? Not even a flash drive?"

She glanced at the contents of her open desk drawer before closing it again. It had been a long night. She should have been tired, too. "Maybe a flash drive…"

He tensed, his spine straightening so that he stood even taller, making him even more imposing since the muscles in his arms stretched the sleeves of his sweater. His jaw was rigid with tension. He was an FBI agent on full alert.

She laughed at his overreaction and couldn't resist teasing him. "It's okay. I have those photos on my hard drive at home. I don't think the thieves are going to find them nearly as special as I do, though."

He didn't laugh; he didn't even smile. His handsome face still tense, he asked, "Personal photos?"

A pang of panic struck her heart as a terrifying thought occurred to her. "You don't think they'll use those photos to go after my family?"

After all, those men had been so determined to abduct her that they had given up their own lives. In order to get to her, they might use someone close to her to influence her. Could what she did for a living actually put her father and his bride at risk?

Chapter Five

Ash didn't offer Claire false reassurance because it was possible that someone might use her family as leverage to get her to reveal her secrets. And if he continued being honest with her, she might begin to trust him enough to tell him everything she knew. Because even though he now believed she hadn't offered that security information for sale, she probably knew who might have.

Could her assistant have had something to do with it? He hadn't looked bright or mature enough to come up with such a plan, though. But then Claire had only been sixteen when she'd hacked into that bank system.

"Tell me about your assistant," he said even though he already had checked out everyone who worked for Nowak Computer Consulting. That was how Claire Molenski had become his main suspect.

She glanced up from straightening her desk and laughed. "You can't seriously suspect Martin of anything?"

"He's your assistant," he said. "So he must work closely with you, checking security on the same high target sites that you do."

She gestured around her small office. There was only one desk and only one chair. "I work alone."

Nowak Computer Consulting was the only company

who'd had access to all the sites that had been offered up for sale at the online auction. So Ash had thoroughly studied it. As well as talking to Peter Nowak, he had scrutinized the building floor plans and scoured security footage. He knew the layout probably better than Claire did. Just a few steps from her office was the bull pen of cubicles where the assistants worked.

"But he's your assistant, so doesn't he assist you with the projects you're working on?" he asked. Company protocol claimed otherwise, but Ash knew people whose assistants did more of the work than they did.

"No," she corrected him. "As my assistant, Martin brings me coffee and lunch and dinner, if I'm working late." She sighed. "Which I usually am."

Maybe Ash had made too many assumptions about Claire Molenski—although he hadn't been wrong about how much time she spent at the consulting company. He'd thought it was because she legally had to, but maybe it was also because she wanted to. "He doesn't help you with any of your projects?"

"He helps with whatever tasks I give him to handle," she said. "But he doesn't have the clearance to work most of the projects I work."

Because she had the highest clearance at the company. Peter Nowak had reluctantly admitted that to Ash when he'd interviewed the man. The former CIA agent trusted his star hacker, but Ash trusted no one. That was why Claire Molenski was his number-one suspect.

SHE WAS HIS number one-suspect—of whatever he suspected her. The suspicion was back in his piercing blue eyes as he stared at her. She hadn't helped herself by defending Martin. But there was no way her assistant could be guilty of anything that had people getting shot at and killed.

"Who does have the clearance level you have or an even higher level?" he asked.

"My boss." Peter Nowak had been a CIA agent before he'd started his computer consultation business, though. That was why some of the biggest banks and financial institutions in the world as well as the US and several other governments had entrusted him to ensure their internet security. He was good at what he did, and he was beyond suspicion.

So she wasn't surprised when Agent Ash Stryker didn't even blink those surprisingly long, black lashes of his. He had no suspicions about Peter Nowak. His suspicions were all about her.

"None of the other hackers have your level of clearance?" he asked.

Maybe he was willing to consider another suspect. But she didn't have anyone to offer him.

"I don't know," she said. "But I suspect that you know."

"You," he said, confirming her fears. "You have the highest clearance besides Peter Nowak."

She sighed as weariness overwhelmed her. It had been a long day before someone had tried abducting her from the parking lot of the speed dating hotel. "I thought so." That was why she worked so many hours—nobody else could work on the projects she worked. "Since Leslie retired…"

"Leslie?"

"Leslie Morrison retired last year. I was his assistant when I first started working here," she explained. "Leslie taught me everything I know, a lot more than I learned in college." Her professors had been behind the new technology, while Mr. Nowak's company had been beyond it—far beyond it.

"So Leslie is a better hacker than you are?"

She shivered at his coldly suspicious tone. She hadn't offered up Leslie to defray guilt from herself. She wasn't guilty, and neither was Leslie. She slammed her desk drawer shut. "Leslie isn't a hacker anymore."

"I'm sure he still knows how to hack, though," Agent Stryker persisted.

She shook her head. "Hacking isn't like riding a bike. Technology changes so quickly that you have to constantly be hacking to be any good. If you're away from it too long, you're going to be so far behind the security systems and software that you won't be able to hack into anything anymore."

And she'd done it again—deflected guilt off someone else and back onto herself. He was looking at her that way again, as if he was imagining himself slapping cuffs on her, while just a short while ago she'd been imagining herself undressing him.

It really was unfair that he was so good-looking. The FBI agents who had arrested her the first time had been old, or at least they had seemed old to her sixteen-year-old self. Their hair had been gray and receding while their waistlines had been expanding.

Why couldn't Ash Stryker look like that?

Why did his black hair have to be so thick and soft looking? So soft looking that she was tempted to run her fingers through it…

She had been right to join the dating service. It had been entirely too long since she'd been with a man. That had to be the reason why she was so physically attracted to Ash. It had to be the only reason.

"Are you done here?" he asked.

She glanced around the small office. She had organized it again—as much as it was ever organized. It didn't look neat, but at least things were back where she had left them. She shuddered at the thought of someone touching all her stuff. Had they touched her globe, too? If not the intruders, the crime lab who'd investigated and collected evidence might have. They'd left fingerprint dust all over, too, which she'd had to clean up. She hated cleaning.

She reached for the globe again, tempted to take it home with her. But she wasn't sure she was going home. And with security increased at the company, nobody would ever be able to break in again. The globe would be safe. But was she?

"What if I tell you that I am done?" she asked. "Will you take me back to the hotel to get my car?"

"No," he said, and his deep voice held that no-nonsense, matter-of-fact tone that so infuriated her.

His reply confirmed her suspicion that he was actually going to bring her in for questioning. He might even arrest her. She didn't understand exactly what crime he suspected her of, but she had offered him no other suspects.

She drew in a deep breath and stood, ready for him to slap the cuffs on her, ready to relive all her nightmares from nine years ago...

IT WAS LATE.

Too late to question her any further. So Ash wasn't taking her back to the Bureau. For one, he was beginning to believe she really didn't know any more than she'd already told him. And secondly, she was exhausted.

Her slight body slumped down in the passenger's seat of his Bureau-issued black SUV. She was nearly asleep, but she fought back a yawn and told him, "You didn't have to drive me home."

He heard the surprise in her voice; she hadn't expected him to bring her home. She had suspected him to arrest her. Earlier that evening, he would have thought that was because she had a guilty conscience. But now that he was beginning to get to know her better...

He wasn't sure what to think of Claire Molenski anymore. She was smart, but he'd already known that. She was sexy; that he hadn't known. He hadn't known how his body would react to hers. While she shivered slightly despite the heat blowing out of the vents, his skin was hot, his body tense.

That could have been just because of the adrenaline. He had nearly lost her a couple of times. He had to be vigilant because it wasn't a question of if there would be another attempt to grab her. It was a question of when.

And that made him wonder about her guilt.

Maybe her only crime was being too smart. But then who had offered her knowledge for sale? He had been so certain she was the threat that he hadn't really considered other suspects. Only Nowak Computer Consulting, or "No Hack" as it was known in inner circles, had the means to infiltrate those sites.

"You could have just brought me back to my car at the hotel," she said.

He could have. Or he could have handed her off to another agent to drive home. He didn't do security detail. His specialty had always been putting himself at risk, going undercover rather than protecting other people.

"No, I couldn't," he said. While he worked with good agents, damn good agents, he hadn't wanted to trust anyone else with her safety. "There have already been two attempts to abduct you." He suspected there would be more—many more—since so many radical groups and subversive governments wanted the information she possessed.

"Me," she murmured.

"Yes, you." They hadn't been after him…except to kill him and get him out of their way.

"They were after me," she said, as if she were strangely trying to reassure herself of that fact. Then he understood her reasoning when she added, "So Dad and Pam will be safe…"

"Pam?"

"She's my dad's new wife," Claire explained. "And a very sweet lady. Like my dad, she was a single parent for years, so she never had enough money to travel. Because of that they're taking a long honeymoon to visit all the places they've always wanted to see. They won't be home for months."

She jerked her head in a sharp nod. "So that's good. They'll be safe…"

Even as his focus stayed on the road, checking for a tail, he could feel her gaze on him. But again he wouldn't offer her any false reassurance. He would leave that to her. It sounded as if she was doing a good job of convincing herself that her loved ones weren't in danger because of her.

But then she sighed and admitted, "But someone could still track their credit cards." Now she played her own devil's advocate. "They could pull up their travel itinerary and find them—"

"I'll put a protective detail on them," he offered as he steered the SUV into the lot of her apartment complex. "We'll make sure they're safe."

She reached across the console, grasped his arm and

squeezed. "Thank you. But they're not even in the country right now."

"It's okay," he said. "No matter where they are, we can still protect them." At the moment he was more concerned about her safety, though. Ever since he had suspected that she was the threat to national security, he'd had a detail on her apartment, so it should be safe.

But several agents had been watching her earlier that evening, and she had been drugged and nearly abducted...

He worried that she may not be safe anywhere. While the only security he specialized in was national security, he would do his best to keep her and her family safe.

She breathed a heavy sigh of relief. "Thank you for protecting them. They deserve to be happy."

"What about you?" he asked, as he turned off the engine.

When he had been thinking like an FBI agent, he had only been concerned about her professional life. Now he was thinking like a man around her, and he wondered about her personal life. He hadn't missed her assistant's shock that she might have a boyfriend.

Didn't she date very often?

When had he had his last date? He couldn't remember one where he'd been himself and not undercover and just dating for information.

"What about me?" she asked. The lights had shut off inside the SUV, but in the dim glow of the parking lamps, he could see her pale brow furrow in confusion.

He turned fully toward her. Despite the console between the bucket seats, they were close. And with her fingers clenching his forearm, they were touching. He stared into her face, into her eyes that sparkled in the shadows. And he asked, "Do you deserve to be happy?"

She snatched back her hand from his arm and turned away from him. As she pushed open the passenger's door, she replied, "I served my sentence."

He wondered now if that had been too harsh. "I'm not talking about that," he said as he hurried around the SUV to her side.

To protect her...

He glanced around the dimly lit parking lot as he led her toward the door to the building that housed her unit. There were several buildings in the complex. And in that building there were several floors, several apartments. Someone could have slipped past that security detail he had on her place. He shouldn't have brought her back here.

"What are you talking about?" she asked as she dug inside that mammoth bag of hers for the keys that he pulled from his pocket. She took the ring from his hand and quickly found the key that opened the door to the lobby. It was nothing fancy—worn terrazzo floors and chipped plaster walls. But it was close to her office. He wondered if that was why she'd chosen to live here.

He waited until they stepped inside the elevator before he replied to her question. "I was just wondering if you are..."

She arched a blond brow. "Are what?"

"Happy."

She leaned wearily against the mirrored wall of the elevator. The image of her in that tight, sexy red dress reflected around him as if she were surrounding him. Ash struggled to draw a deep breath when he felt like panting as his pulse quickened.

"I thought I was," she said. "Until I saw how happy my dad and Pam are."

Now he knew why she had been at that speed dating

event and it hadn't been to sell security secrets as he had suspected. She had posted online that she would be there, which he'd thought was her way of opening the bidding for information. But she had actually been there to find her happiness. She had really wanted to meet someone and she didn't need to tell him for him to know that she hadn't been looking for him. It was clear that after that arrest in her teens she didn't have any trust or affection for FBI agents.

Not that he could have dated her had she been interested in him. He had no time for a personal life and no inclination to make time, either.

The elevator was old, but it was fast and came quickly to a stop on the fifth floor. He breathed a slight sigh of relief that it had saved him from having to comment on her statement.

She stepped out of the elevator and headed down the dimly lit hall. Uneasy, Ash pulled his gun from his holster as he walked beside her. And when she stopped and extended the key toward the lock on her door, he covered her hand with his to turn the knob.

She glanced up at him, her green eyes wide with sudden curiosity. And she asked, "Are you?"

"Am I what?" he said, distracted by her closeness and by that uneasy feeling that he hadn't had enough agents watching her apartment.

Her mouth turned up slightly at the corners as she replied, "Happy…"

Instead of answering her question, he pushed open the door. Then he pushed her behind him for protection as he saw the total devastation. It was worse than her office had been.

And he worried that whoever had searched her place was still inside—waiting for her.

Chapter Six

Her heart pounded quickly with fear as the FBI agent pointed his gun inside her apartment.

"Stay back," Ash directed her like he had in the hotel hallway. He had been right then: there had been a threat—a man with a gun who'd shot at him.

But she heard no shots now, so she peered around him. "What's wrong?"

"Someone broke into your place."

Even though the heat and strength of his hand covering hers had distracted her, she'd felt the lock turn as the key had disengaged the dead bolt. She glanced at the door frame. It was old with paint peeling, but it wasn't damaged beyond normal wear and tear. "Nobody broke in."

"But it's been ransacked."

Heat rushed to her face with a tide of embarrassment. "No. It already looked this way…"

Except that she hadn't noticed before how messy it was until she saw her place now through his eyes. She had left clothes and books and junk mail strewn all over the furniture and even the floor.

"It did?" he asked. He seemed horrified.

Not only was he an all-too-serious FBI agent, he was probably also a neat freak. If he had actually been at the speed dating event to meet a potential match, it wouldn't have been her. They had nothing in common. So it was probably good that he had only been there to stop her from betraying her country. His thinking her capable of treason was yet another reason they were not at all compatible.

"With as much as I work, I don't have time to clean," she said in defense of her mess.

"You could hire a cleaning lady," he suggested as he reholstered his gun.

But then she'd have someone touching her stuff, putting it away so she'd have to look for it. She leaned down to pick up some clothes from the floor and, like she had at the hotel, she mouthed the words back at him. And as she straightened up again, she saw the grin on his face reflecting back from the glass of her darkened window.

He must have caught her. Again.

"It's not like I spend a lot of time here," she said and flinched at the defensiveness in her voice. She didn't have to make excuses to him. It was none of his business how messy her apartment was.

"So shouldn't it be cleaner, then?" he remarked, his blue eyes twinkling with amusement. At her expense.

She tossed the armload of clothes at him. But his reflexes were quick and he dodged all but the black lace bra that draped over his shoulder. He hooked his finger into the strap and held it up between them as he teased, "Couldn't make it to the bedroom?"

Her face heated even more so that it was probably more maroon than red now as her embarrassment and anger increased.

"You really want to think the worst of me," she said. "You want to think that I'm a hacker and a wh—"

He moved quickly—so quickly that he pressed a finger

over her lips before she could utter the ugly word. "I never called you that," he said.

His gaze skimmed down her body. Now her skin heated and tingled all over—just from how he looked at her. What if he actually touched her?

Of course it had nothing to do with him. Personally. She was probably just unnerved because it had been so long since she'd dressed like this, since she had even attempted to have a social life. She wasn't sure she knew how to anymore. The last time she'd dated she had been a teenager. Then there had been that one boy in college. But he'd been a boy.

There had never been a man.

And Ash Stryker was definitely a man. He wasn't her type at all. But…

She stepped back, so that his hand fell away from her mouth. "I'm not selling anything," she said.

"I know," he replied, sounding almost regretful.

Had he wanted her to be the hacker or had he wanted her…? That was unlikely—especially after he'd seen her messy apartment.

"I don't get this whole online auction thing that had you ready to arrest me," she said.

Fortunately he hadn't been as ready as she'd thought he was since he had brought her home instead of to jail. But then he would have needed evidence to arrest her, and he wouldn't find anything to tie her to a crime she hadn't committed. But what was the crime?

"I may have rushed to a conclusion," he reluctantly admitted.

Since he could admit that he'd been wrong, maybe he wasn't as uptight as she'd thought him. And maybe he wasn't the only one who'd made assumptions since she had been equally as quick to label him as uptight.

"Did you rush to a conclusion or a conviction?" she asked him, her pride still stinging that he'd been so quick to think her a traitor.

He sighed. "There wouldn't have been any conviction without hard evidence."

"I don't understand how there could be any evidence," she said. "I don't even understand exactly what's being offered for sale."

"A way around the firewalls," he said. "The access to secure government data could shut down the country or at least cripple it. The economy—"

"I understand that," she said. "Obviously. That's why I do what I do."

"I thought you did what you do because it was part of your sentence and probation."

"It started out that way," she conceded. "But I served out that sentence and my probation a while ago."

And now she was compensated for the work she did. She was actually compensated very well. She really could afford a cleaning lady; maybe she should hire one. Not because he had suggested it, though. She leaned over and picked up a few more things.

"What I don't understand," she continued, "is how someone thinks they could get around a firewall. Once I find the flaw in a security system, I fix it. I make it go away before anyone else has a chance to find it. That's what I do—that's what Nowak Computer Consulting does."

"Could someone have hacked into your computer and be piggybacking—"

She laughed. "*Nobody* can hack me."

"What about Leslie Morrison, your old trainer?" he asked. "If he taught you so much…"

She winced over a twinge of regret. She had cast suspicion on Leslie even though she hadn't meant to. "He's retired. I already explained to you that to be effective, you have to be active—"

"So it's not Leslie," he agreed.

The twinge of pain eased with relief that he so readily agreed with her. Leslie was happy being retired. He would not appreciate the upheaval of an FBI investigation. Had Special Agent Stryker agreed too easily though? Was he only humoring her?

"But the thing about hackers," he said, "is that there's always a better one. Maybe someone in another country…"

First he'd insulted her integrity; now he was insulting her skills. "If someone else could hack into those firewalls, why are people trying to abduct *me*?"

"I'm not the only one who thinks you're the seller," he suggested. "Someone else does, too."

"But I'm not," she said emphatically, "so what's the point of abducting me when I won't sell them any information?"

"They're trying to abduct you because they don't intend to *pay* you," he said.

Her head had begun to pound a while ago, so she pushed her fingers against her temples to relieve the pressure. "Then how do they intend to get the information? Despite what you think, I won't freely betray my country." She hastened to add, "I wouldn't have done it for money, either."

"Torture," he replied matter-of-factly as if he was quite familiar with it. Because he had been tortured? Or because he had tortured someone? "If you won't tell them freely, they will torture the information out of you."

"But there is no information anymore," she said. "I

made sure that there is no way around any of those firewalls."

"Then they'll kill you." Maybe he was only trying to scare her.

If so, his mission was accomplished. She shuddered with fear and with cold. She wanted to take a hot shower, and then she wanted to go to bed—even though her sleep would undoubtedly be interrupted with nightmares of abductions and shootings. "Well, I'm home. I'm safe. You can leave now."

She wasn't just scared; she was also exhausted. So exhausted that, earlier, she had briefly entertained some crazy thoughts about Ash Stryker. About undressing him.

If only he wasn't an FBI agent…

"You're not safe here," he told her.

Then why had he brought her home? To search it? He hadn't touched anything besides her bra, though.

"We established this is my mess," she said, gesturing around at the cluttered apartment. "Nobody broke in here. I will be fine." Maybe. Once she had a shower and some sleep. If she could sleep…

Not only was her skin tingling but her pulse was racing. She preferred to think that it was only because of the threats to her safety and not because of Ash Stryker. She couldn't be reacting to his nearness. She couldn't be reacting to him. It was just a reaction, just shock from everything that had happened that evening.

He touched his ear and she realized he was wearing some kind of undetectable radio device. "You're not safe because a suspicious vehicle just pulled into the parking lot. The agent who's been watching your apartment thinks there's at least one armed gunman." As he said it, he reached for the weapon in his holster.

"Someone must have followed us from the office," she said.

He shook his head. "Nobody followed me." He didn't sound defensive or offended—just very confident in his abilities. "They must have found your apartment address when they broke into your office."

"No," she said. "I don't keep anything with personal information on it in my office." She worked with hackers. She wasn't entirely confident that one wouldn't use whatever she might leave around to hack into her personal accounts. They probably wouldn't have done it maliciously but just to prove that they were as good as she was.

"At the moment it doesn't matter how they got here," he said. "And we're not going to stick around to ask them how, either."

"But we don't know for sure that they're here for me," she protested as he headed toward the door.

"We can't risk it in case they are," he said. "We have to get out of here."

She shivered again with fear and coldness. The evening had grown too cool for her short sleeveless dress that left her arms and legs bare. She glanced longingly at the warmer clothes scattered about the floor and furniture. Instead of hurling them at Agent Stryker, she should have put on some of them. But she hadn't known then that she would have to leave again because the danger she was in had followed her home.

ASH DIDN'T HAVE a moment to lose. The fifth-floor apartment didn't give them many escape options besides the only door. Neither of them was likely to survive a fall from one of the windows—not from this height.

He caught her wrist and tugged her into the hall behind

him. The elevator wasn't a safe option, either. "Where are the stairs?"

She entwined her fingers with his and tugged him down the hall. "This way," she said. "I usually take them."

That explained why she was so fit despite all the hours she clocked at the computer consulting company.

Then she grumbled and added, "Just not in heels."

Maybe he should have let her change, but he doubted they had time to spare. And he liked that red dress. Maybe a little too much...

She pushed open the door to the stairway. As they headed down the first flight, her heels clicked against each step and echoed off the brick walls. But there was another echo, the clang of a door opening onto the stairwell. Someone was coming up while they were going down—to cut them off?

But then whoever was coming for her wouldn't know that she had been warned of the threat. They would think she was still in her apartment—waiting to be abducted. He caught her arm and pulled her to a stop on the landing between the third and second floors. Beneath his palm her skin was like silk.

She shivered. "What—"

He pressed a finger over her lips like he had in her apartment. "Someone's coming up the stairs," he whispered.

Her eyes widened with panic as she finally heard them, too—the other footsteps echoing in the stairwell. They were heavy footsteps, which meant they were probably big men.

"What do we do?" she whispered, her lips moving against his finger.

"This," he said, and he whirled her around and pressed

her back against the brick wall of the stairwell. She gasped just as he lowered his mouth to hers.

Not only did he cover her mouth with his but he covered her body, too. To hide her. To protect her.

That had been his intent. But her lips were soft beneath his, her breath warm, and he found himself really kissing her. He moved his mouth over hers, taking advantage of her parted lips to deepen the kiss.

And her arms moved between them. Instead of pushing him away, as he expected, they linked around his neck. And she clung to him.

Maybe it was out of fear since the footsteps had grown louder. Finally a man passed them, chuckling beneath his breath. Another man muttered a comment, "Man, they can't even wait until they get to their apartment…"

He passed them, as well. The men's footsteps pounded up a couple more flights, and then a door opened and slammed shut on the fifth floor. Her floor.

Ash forced himself to pull away and then step back from Claire. But he kept his hand on her, steadying her as she trembled.

"They'll be back," he warned, "once they find your apartment empty. We have to move quickly."

But his legs were a little shaky as he headed down the stairs. Passion had nearly overwhelmed him. He'd known she was dangerous; he just hadn't realized how dangerous.

She was so sexy that she had distracted him. She had nearly made him forget why he'd kissed her in the first place—since kissing her had felt so damn right. And hot. His pulse still raced, and not because of the threat those gunmen posed.

She stumbled on the last step, and he caught her, his arms going around her again. She stared up at him, her green eyes wide with confusion. Then her pale skin flushed, and she pulled away from him and muttered a curse. "These damn heels."

"You may need to take them off if we have to run," he advised her.

She nodded in agreement.

But then her feet would be bare, and she was already shivering. Too bad he hadn't caught more than the bra from that pile of clothes she'd thrown at him. She could have used a sweater and some pants. Hell, she could have used the bra since it wasn't apparent to him that she was wearing one beneath that tight dress. But he didn't have the bra anymore, either. She'd snatched it back from him.

"Or I can carry you," he suggested. Maybe that would be best—or at least the fastest—if they needed to get away in a hurry. But instead of reaching for her, he reached for the door to the lobby and pushed it open just enough so that he could glimpse outside the stairwell.

Had the gunmen left another man in the lobby in case she managed to escape them? The agents watching her building from the parking lot hadn't been certain how many gunmen there were. Two or three? And they hadn't wanted to storm the building and risk a shoot-out that could endanger other residents.

Despite the late hour, the lobby wasn't deserted. A man paced the worn terrazzo tile. He was tall and muscular, and as he paced, his black leather jacket fell open, revealing the holster and the gun he wore beneath it.

As she tried to peer over his shoulder, Claire pressed against Ash's back, and her closeness warmed his blood and quickened his pulse. She gasped and her warm breath tickled his ear.

"We're trapped," she whispered. "There's a guy out there and those two guys upstairs."

He turned his head, and his lips nearly brushed hers since she was so close to him. He could still taste her sweetness, but he wanted to kiss her again. Hell, he wanted to do a lot more than kiss her.

"Where are we going to go?" she asked. "How are we going to get away?"

"Don't worry," he said. "I'll protect you." But then who was going to protect him—from her?

She sucked in a breath as her eyes widened more with fear. "Oh, no, it's too late..."

That was what he was afraid of—that it was already too late for him to protect himself from Claire Molenski. She was getting to him in a way that no one else ever had.

Her body trembled against his. "He's seen us," she said. "He's coming for us."

But Ash didn't even reach for his gun. As she'd said, it was too late.

Chapter Seven

If Ash wouldn't draw his weapon, Claire would. But when she reached for his holster, he caught her fingers. His big hand completely engulfed hers. She tried to tug free, but he held on to her as he opened the door to the armed gunman who'd been pacing the lobby.

"What the hell were you doing?" the man asked. "You took your sweet time bringing her down here."

Ash was working *with* him. The guy had unruly dark hair that had gone too long without a cut, just like his darkly shadowed jaw had gone too long without a shave. Along with the leather jacket, he wore faded and torn jeans and motorcycle boots. Was Ash not really the FBI agent that he claimed to be? But then she noticed the badge dangling around this man's neck, beneath his leather jacket. He was an FBI agent, too.

She expelled a breath of relief.

"You could have given me a heads-up that they were taking the stairs, too," Ash grumbled as he pushed past the man and continued through the lobby. His hand still clasped around Claire's, he tugged her along behind him.

"I just got here," the other agent replied.

Ash stopped at the lobby door that led out into the parking lot. "Why are you here anyway, Reyes? You're Organized Crime, not Antiterrorism."

"You don't think your terrorists are the only ones who'd like to buy what she's selling?" he scoffed.

"She's not selling anything," Ash replied for her—as had become his annoying habit.

The other agent's dark brows arched in surprise. "You've convinced her not to betray our country?"

"*She* was never going to betray our country," Claire said before Ash could answer for her again. "And Agent Stryker realized he was a fool for making assumptions about Ms. Molenski's character."

Agent Reyes laughed.

But Ash's face stayed tense, his lips not even curving into a slight smile over her comments. "When they realize that her apartment is empty, they're going to come back down looking for her," he said. "We need to get out of here. Now."

The grin slid off Reyes's handsome face. Why were these FBI agents so damn good-looking? It wasn't fair.

"You get Ms. Molenski to safety," Reyes said. "I've got this."

"Alone?" Ash asked with a glance around the lobby.

Reyes shrugged. "It's better than having you stay and shoot them," he said. "Dead men can't tell us who they're working for."

"A dead agent can't ask them who they're working for," Stryker said. "I hope you have more backup." But he didn't wait around to find out; he pushed open the door and led Claire from the lobby into the parking lot.

"Shouldn't you stay?" she asked Ash. "Shouldn't you help him?"

His hand on his gun, he peered around the dimly lit lot as he led the way to the black SUV. There were a few other ones in the lot, and as he passed one, the lights on it blinked on and off. There were other FBI agents around, but Ash replied, "Reyes can take care of himself."

"So can I." She had been taking care of herself for years. And when her father had been so lost after her mom left them, she had taken care of him, too. Maybe she had taken care of him a little too well when she had tried to avenge his broken heart.

Ash stopped at the passenger's door to his SUV, and as he opened that door for her, he shook his head. "You can't. Not against people like this."

Terrorists and criminals, according to what the agents had said moments ago.

He slammed the door and then in seconds he was behind the wheel, starting the engine and turning the heat on full blast. But she couldn't stop trembling.

He was right. Even though she'd fought at the hotel, she had still been easily overpowered, drugged and abducted. If he hadn't intervened, she'd probably be undergoing torture about now—for codes, that didn't even exist, to bypass government firewalls.

He and Agent Reyes dealt with people like this every day, putting their lives in danger to protect others. She respected that, but she wanted no part of it. In her own life or in the life of the person with whom she wanted to share hers, because worrying about that person every time he went to work would be another form of torture for her.

CLAIRE HAD BEEN quiet since they'd left her apartment. She hadn't even been mouthing snarky comments behind his back. He kind of missed the snarky comments. Actually, he just missed her spirit and spunk.

Maybe she was quiet because she was completely exhausted. It had been an incredibly long, dangerous day for her.

And it probably hadn't helped that he'd started out treating her like a suspect. He hadn't been overly sensitive or respectful of what she was going through. Maybe she was quiet because she just hated his guts.

"Reyes is okay," he told her since she had seemed concerned about the offbeat agent. And as if to prove it, he turned on the two-way radio in the SUV, so that she could hear what he heard through his earpiece.

"I'm not sure they were after her," Reyes was saying. "I didn't recognize them."

"Do you know every criminal in the Chicago area?" Ash asked him.

"Pretty much," he said. "I either grew up with them or I've arrested them. Sometimes—hell, usually—it's been both."

"That must make it hard for you to maintain friendships," Ash quipped.

Yet he doubted Reyes had any trouble making or keeping friends; the man seemed to have never met a stranger...until these two men who'd been in Claire's apartment complex. Their voices hadn't betrayed any accents, but that didn't mean they couldn't be from some other country or, as mercenaries, were representing the interests of some other country.

"At least none of them have burned down *my* house," Reyes teased in reference to Ash's comments about arresting his childhood friends.

"It would be a little hard for them to do that from behind bars. And it's not like Blaine lit the match himself," Ash defended his friend. He and Blaine Campbell's friendship didn't go back to childhood, but it went back to the marines where they had forged an unbreakable bond. That was why he'd been letting his friend stay at his place when he'd been on another undercover assignment.

"True, he didn't light the match," Reyes agreed. "But he was too distracted to smell the fire and put it out."

"The fire was the least of his concerns," Ash said. Blaine had put himself on security duty, protecting the witness from the bank robberies Blaine had been trying to solve. He had nearly lost her and his own life in that fire.

"Exactly. That's why he was distracted and nearly got killed," Reyes said. "I hope you're not letting Ms. Molenski distract you like that."

Now he wished he hadn't turned on the radio in the SUV. "You know me," he said. He had worked with Reyes before, even before they had helped Blaine with the bank robbers. They had worked so well together that they had actually become friends. "You know that's not going to happen."

Ash wasn't like his friend Blaine who had grown up with three or four sisters in a house of women and liked to play hero to damsels in distress.

Ash didn't want to be anyone's hero. He never willingly did protection duty. But for some reason he felt as if no one else could protect Claire like he would, as if she actually was his girlfriend.

"I thought I knew you." Reyes chuckled. "The funny thing is that the only information I got out of those two guys was a story about some couple making out in the stairwell—"

Ash clicked off the radio before Reyes could say anything else. The other agent enjoyed joking around too much.

"Don't worry," Claire said. "I know you only kissed

me so those two guys couldn't get a look at me and possibly recognize me."

That was the reason he'd started out kissing her. It wasn't the reason that he had barely been able to stop, though.

"But now it sounds like they might not have been looking for me after all," she continued. "So I could have stayed home." Her small mouth stretched in a big yawn. "And slept."

"I'll take you somewhere you can sleep," he told her. "And you'll be able to rest assured that no one else will be coming for you. You wouldn't know that at your place. Someone must have followed you from there to the hotel, so they had known where you live even before breaking into your office."

"I went to the hotel straight from the office," she said. "That must've been how I was tracked down at the hotel. It's not like I was watching for anyone to follow me."

He was watching for a tail, his gaze divided between the rearview and side mirrors, the road in front of them and her. She kept drawing his attention. Of course he had to check on her to make sure she was okay. But that wasn't the only reason why he was drawn to her.

"But I don't know how anyone found my apartment," she said, "unless they followed us home from the office."

He sure as hell hoped not or he must have been as distracted as Reyes worried she would make him. "I'm sorry," he said.

"Why?" she asked. "For letting someone follow us?"

"No," he said. "No one followed us." Despite his attraction to her, he had been too cautious. They must have found her address another way; maybe the department of motor vehicles had been hacked and her address pulled off her license.

"Then why are you apologizing?" she asked. "For kissing me? Like I said, I understand why you did."

"I'm not apologizing for kissing you." Because it wasn't something he regretted. "I'm apologizing for making the wrong assumptions about your character."

She laughed at his repeating her words—or maybe at his actually apologizing. Honestly it wasn't something he did very often, but that was because he usually wasn't wrong.

Her laughter turned into a ragged sigh. "Unfortunately you're not the only one who made the wrong assumptions about me. How can we make these other people realize that they're wrong, too?"

"Good question," he murmured.

"Can I post a disclaimer somewhere?" she asked. "Swear that I have no secret security information for sale?"

"You could," he agreed, albeit reluctantly.

She heard the reluctance because she turned toward him and narrowed her eyes. "But you don't want me to," she surmised. "Why not?"

"Because then these people might actually find the real seller and get that information they want." Then that catastrophe he'd tried to avert might come to pass.

She shook her head. "That's not possible. I told you the information doesn't exist."

"You think it doesn't exist," he said. "But maybe you're the one making the wrong assumptions now."

She opened but then closed her mouth without uttering a word. She just shook her head.

Maybe she was protesting his comment. Or maybe she was protesting that he'd pulled the SUV into the parking lot of a hotel along the lakeshore in southern Michigan.

He had been driving for a while. She must have realized he was taking her outside the city.

Or maybe she hadn't been paying attention at all because she asked, "Where have you brought me?"

"A hotel."

"Yeah, I figured that," she said. "It wasn't like I was expecting you to take me to your house even if your friend hadn't burned it down—"

"My friend didn't burn it down," he protested. Blaine felt bad enough over what had happened; he actually felt worse than Ash had over the loss. Except for some years growing up, he hadn't spent much time in that house. Few of his assignments, but for this one, had been in Chicago, so he'd stayed in other cities or woods or foreign countries.

Her lips curved into a slight smile. She hadn't missed his defensiveness with Reyes. But then he suspected that she didn't miss much. Her intelligence, in the form of her hacker skills, was legendary.

That was why he had assumed she was the one selling out national security. It was also why so many other people had assumed the same about her. He needed people to keep thinking that, but he didn't want to push her. He had already pushed her enough for one night.

The night was over now, though. The sky was light, the lake beyond the hotel glowing as the sun began to rise. She gestured toward it.

"But why did you bring me here?" she asked.

"Did you want to go back to the hotel where the speed dating took place?"

She shuddered—maybe as she envisioned that man he'd shot in the hallway outside her room. "No. But I didn't want to be this far away from the city, either. I have to work in the morning." She pushed open the passenger's door, stepped out and turned her face up to the sky.

Her skin glowed like the water, like the sky, and her beauty stole away his breath for just a moment. He had to stay behind the wheel of the SUV until he could catch it again.

She turned back to him. "It's already morning..."

"Almost," he agreed as he stepped out, closed his door and walked around to join her on the passenger's side.

She still held on to her door, holding it open. "We should head back to Chicago. I need to go to my apartment and get a change of clothes."

He could see the goose bumps raised on the pale skin of her arms and shoulders. He closed her door and clicked the locks of the SUV. Then he slid his arm around her slim shoulders to guide her away from the vehicle but also to warm her. Instead of settling against him, she tensed and held herself away from him. "This hotel has a boutique," he told her. "We can buy you some things here."

"But we need to go back to the city," she protested.

"We need to get some sleep," he said as he continued toward the lobby.

"I don't need sleep," she said. "I stay up all night a lot when I'm working. You probably do, too."

He had spent a lot of sleepless nights over the years. "But we don't know who is after you," he said. "We don't know who or how many." He had a grim idea, though. Anyone and everyone. "We're going to need some rest so that we're both alert to the danger you're in."

"Both?" she asked.

He nodded. "Of course."

She fell silent again, except for a few comments about trying to pay as they bought some things from the boutique and checked into a suite. It was just one bedroom, a bath and a sitting area with a pull-out bed. But it was clean and freshly painted with soft carpeting beneath his feet. She waited until he closed the door behind them before she spoke again.

Then she asked, "Why 'of course'?"

He shrugged. "You're in danger. So of course I'm going to protect you." It wasn't his usual job, though. But he'd protected himself well enough over the years that he figured he could protect her, too.

"But less than twenty-four hours ago you wanted to arrest me for treason and now you're going to protect me?" She shook her head. "I don't buy it."

"Buy what?" he asked. Did she think he really meant her harm? That he had no intention of keeping her safe?

"You don't want me to put out the word that I'm not selling that information," she said. "You're using me."

"How's that?" he asked.

He knew how he'd like to use her—since she was still wearing that damn sexy red dress. Something of what he was thinking—of what he was lusting—must have shown on his face because she slapped him.

Her palm just struck his shoulder, though, not his face. And maybe she'd only meant to shove him back since he'd stepped closer to her than he'd realized. Close enough to kiss her again.

He wanted to kiss her again.

"You want to dangle me as bait to draw out all these dangerous people," she said, the usual brightness of her green eyes dimmed with accusation and hurt.

The woman wasn't just brilliant at hacking. She was smart. Period. She could read people as well as she could read computers.

"I might not have worded it quite like that," he said.

But he couldn't deny it. She wasn't a threat to security, but he could use her to draw out other threats.

"But it's true," she said. She peered beyond him to the door he'd just closed as if she was considering running for it. Running from him. "You expect me to risk my life."

"No," he said. That was suddenly the last thing he wanted—her life at risk. "I will protect you. I won't put you in danger."

"You can't promise that something won't happen to me," she said. "You just said that you don't know who these people are or how many there are—or even how dangerous they are."

He nodded. "I don't know that. But I know *me*. And I know that I will protect you. Or die trying..."

She shuddered. "That's not exactly reassuring. I'd rather we both live."

"That's the plan."

"No, that's your hope," she corrected him. "*I* have a plan."

"Why am I afraid to hear this?" he wondered aloud.

"Because my plan is better than yours," she said. Her sass was back.

And he was intrigued by her sass more than her plan. He would listen to it, though, once he could focus on anything other than her mouth and all the bare skin that dress revealed. And in order to focus, he needed to kiss her again.

But before he could reach for her, she was stepping up to him, winding her arms around his neck and pressing her lips passionately to his.

Chapter Eight

He stood stiffly in Claire's embrace, his body tense and hard as she wound herself around him. Her lips moved over his, but he didn't kiss her back. He didn't touch her.

Claire's face heated with embarrassment, and her heart sank with disappointment. The earlier kiss had just been a ruse to protect her.

And she had just made a complete fool of herself.

She pulled away. But then he was touching her. One hand cupped the back of her head and held her mouth to his while his other hand was on her hip, pulling her tightly against him. He kissed her.

He kissed her like Claire had always wanted to be kissed. He kissed her with an intensity and passion that had her toes curling in her high heels. The hand on her head tangled in her hair while the hand on her hip squeezed.

Heat overwhelmed her—heat of passion, not embarrassment. She opened her mouth and invited him in, and he deepened the kiss. She wanted more than this, though. She wanted to strip off his sweater and vest, as she'd imagined earlier, and she wanted his naked skin sliding over hers—nothing separating them.

Even as she trembled with need, she summoned her strength and willpower and pulled free of him. She stumbled back a couple of steps—maybe because of the heels or maybe because her legs shook and threatened to fold beneath her.

"And here I thought I wasn't going to like your plan," he murmured.

So he liked kissing her?

He panted for breath, and his eyes had dilated so that only a thin circle of blue rimmed his pupils. Maybe he really liked kissing her.

"That was your plan, too," she said.

"To kiss you?" He shook his head. "That definitely wasn't part of my plan. I just had to improvise earlier tonight."

"And now?" she asked.

"You kissed me," he said.

She had started it. "We have to get used to kissing each other," she explained, "if you really intend to go undercover as my boyfriend."

He narrowed his eyes at her. "What are you talking about?"

"You told Martin that you're my boyfriend," she reminded him. "Isn't that your *cover*?"

"What does that have to do with kissing?"

"I admit it's been a while since I've dated," she said. "But I believe that boyfriends and girlfriends kiss. Has that changed since the last time I dated?"

A deep chuckle slipped through his lips—lips she could still taste on hers. "The last time you dated someone, you were all about the PDA?"

"PDA?" she repeated.

"Public display of affection," he translated for her.

At twenty-five she felt old and out of touch. Since she worked with younger people, she often felt that way, though. But Ash Stryker was at least a few years older than she was, maybe even several years older, and presumably uptight. She shouldn't feel old and out of touch around him.

"We don't have to kiss in public to prove that we're dating," he said.

Maybe not. But she had watched, usually enviously, couples so in love that they didn't even realize they weren't the only two people in the world. Apparently her mother had felt like that when she'd fallen for the man she'd met online since she had left her family so easily.

"You're right," she said. "We don't have to kiss in public." She didn't want to be anything like her mother.

He narrowed his eyes again. "You make it sound like we might have to kiss in private…"

"You've gone undercover before?"

He laughed again, shortly and cynically. "I've gone undercover a lot."

"Then don't you think we should get more comfortable with each other, so that we don't raise any suspicions?"

Martin had seemed suspicious probably because he knew she had no time for dating let alone a relationship. And she hadn't told him about her intentions to cut back on her work and make time. She hadn't wanted to worry him that his hours might be reduced.

"And what exactly do you mean by more comfortable?" he asked with his own suspicions in his bright blue eyes.

"Just kissing," she assured him in case he thought she meant more.

"So you want to kiss me?" he asked skeptically.

Hadn't he noticed that she had thoroughly enjoyed kissing him?

"Why?" he asked. "What are you up to?"

"You're using me," she reminded him. "Dangling me as bait for all your terrorists…"

He flinched—probably because she'd made him sound pretty callous.

"So, in return, you want to use *me*?" he asked. "For kissing?"

She nodded, and her face heated again with embarrassment when she admitted, "I need practice."

"What?"

"Like I said, I haven't dated in a while," she explained, "so I'm out of practice. I don't want to go out with my potential matches from the dating service and totally embarrass myself." Like she just had with him…

"You joined a dating service?" he asked.

She nodded. "Yes, that's how I wound up at the speed dating event. They sponsored it."

"You're really serious about meeting someone?" he asked as if the idea appalled him.

Now, with gunmen after her, might not be the best time to begin a relationship, though. "Yes," she replied.

"And you want to use me for practice?" he asked, but he didn't seem quite as appalled now.

"Yes," she said with a sigh of relief that he understood. "You can help me hone my dating skills."

"Why would you ask me for help?"

"I'm not asking," she pointed out. "If you want me to risk my life, I want something out of this. I will also help you figure out who really offered the information for sale. So you owe me."

He tilted his head as if considering her proposition. "You can figure out who?"

"I can hack the hacker," she offered. "I'll find the person while you use me to flush out the terrorists." She would have anyway, but he didn't need to know that.

"And you'll use me for dating tips?"

"Not tips," she said with a derisive snort. "I doubt you date any more than I do. I just want to use you for practice."

"Why me?"

"You'll be posing as my boyfriend anyway," she said. "And I won't get emotionally involved with you."

"You won't?"

"You're an FBI agent," she said. "You're not my type any more than I am yours." She held out her hand. "Do we have a deal?"

He looked down at her hand and studied it for a long moment before he reached for it. But when his hand closed around hers, he didn't shake. He pulled her forward into his arms. And he kissed her again.

He kissed her as thoroughly as he had before, using his lips and his tongue and all his considerable skill. Maybe she was wrong about how much he dated. Maybe he found more time for it than she thought…because he was a damn good kisser.

He literally stole her breath away. He had her pulse pounding and her skin tingling. But before she could completely lose her mind, he pulled back and turned away from her.

"You can have the bed," he told her as he flopped down on the couch. "We need to get at least a few hours of sleep. Then I'll drive you to your office so you can start looking for who really offered that information for sale."

Dumb with desire, Claire only managed a nod of agreement. Then she forced her legs to move, to carry her through the doorway to the bedroom. Her body, which was all tense and needy, didn't want to go to bed alone.

"Claire…"

His deep voice stopped her. But she didn't dare turn

back to him because she might ask for more than his kisses. She might join him on that couch and beg him to make love to her.

"Yes?" she asked and hoped he didn't hear how her voice cracked with desire.

"You really don't need any practice..."

IF THE WOMAN got any better at kissing she was going to be lethal—to his self-control and to his sleep. While he'd lain on the couch a few hours, he hadn't slept at all. His body had been too tense, too achy with desire. He'd been relieved when she'd come out of the bedroom, dressed in something other than that damn red dress, and told him she was ready to go to work.

He would have rather she'd said she was ready to go to bed—with him. But kissing was dangerous enough. He couldn't make love to her or he would be risking her life and his because he would be too distracted to protect her.

Hell, he was probably too distracted now.

While she worked at her desk, he'd taken a seat on the credenza behind her so he could watch her work. But he just watched her. She was so beautiful—her skin so flawless and such a pale ivory, her features so delicate and perfect. And her hair was such a bright, pale yellow. It kept sliding across her face and tangling in her lashes. She pushed that stray lock behind her ear but it kept escaping.

The next time it escaped, Ash pushed it back for her, skimming his fingertips across her silky cheek. Then he hooked that errant lock behind her delicate ear.

She shivered and looked up at him. "You're making it hard for me to work."

Did she feel it, too? Did the desire burning inside him burn inside her, too?

He cleared his throat before asking, "I am? So you haven't found anything?"

She shook her head, and her voice was sharp with frustration when she replied, "No. I haven't. But I don't work well with someone hovering over me."

"I could have told you that," her assistant murmured from the doorway of her office. He shot a resentful glare at Ash and asked, "Don't you have a job?"

"Martin!" Claire admonished him.

Ash shrugged off the kid's comment. "Of course. But it was more important to me to make sure that Claire is safe today after the break-in last night."

The kid's face flushed a deep red. "How are you going to keep her safe? Are you a cop?"

She'd been right when she had said that people might be suspicious of their sudden *relationship*. Her assistant obviously was. Or at least he was suspicious of Ash.

"I'm not a cop," Ash said. While some FBI agents had begun their careers in local law enforcement, he and Blaine had been recruited from military. So he wasn't lying until he added, "I'm just an overprotective boyfriend."

"But Claire's not in any danger," Martin said. Then he turned to her. "You're not, are you?"

"Of course not," she assured the kid. "Ash is just what he said—an overprotective boyfriend." She smiled at him with her lips, but her gaze was sharp with a warning he had already heeded.

He slid off the credenza, leaned over and pressed a kiss to her forehead. "I'll feel better once the police find out who broke in here last night and why."

"Probably for the bank stuff," Martin said. "Who wouldn't want access to bank accounts?" His face flushed—probably as he realized he had violated Nowak

Computer Consulting protocol. He wasn't supposed to talk about clients.

Was that how the auction had been traced back to Claire? Because of this kid running his mouth?

Resisting the sudden surge of anger at the thought of Martin putting her in danger, Ash instead agreed, "Who wouldn't?"

Getting into a bank account was what had gotten Claire in trouble. Though given the facts, he could understand why her hurt sixteen-year-old self had acted so rashly and resentfully.

Claire glared at him.

Martin uttered a nervous laugh. "Sorry, Claire, I forgot about—"

She waved a hand in dismissal. "It's okay."

"What are you working on?" he asked. Then he glanced at Ash again. "Or trying to work on?"

"Just checking my files," she said, "making sure nobody accessed anything."

She'd already known last night that no one had.

"Was anything accessed?" Martin nervously asked.

"No." But she touched the snow globe on her desk as if trying to assure herself that it was all right. That nothing had tarnished that memory with her father.

The assistant nodded. "Of course. Who would be able to get past your security?" He glanced at Ash again, as if wondering how he had.

Ash wasn't sure how he had gotten Claire to trust him. Actually he wasn't entirely sure that she did. But at least she'd agreed to work with him.

For a price.

Kissing practice.

That price might be more than he could afford to pay and still retain his sanity.

"Since you're done here, sweetheart, let me take you to dinner." They'd come in to the office late, so it was already close to six o'clock.

With a sigh she signed off her computer and nodded in agreement. "That sounds good."

"You're leaving already?" Martin asked, clearly as shocked as he'd been when Ash had claimed to be her boyfriend. "You never leave this early."

"I did yesterday."

"It's fortunate that you did," Ash said. "What if you'd been here when the office was broken in to?" He shuddered as if imagining the horror.

Claire must have imagined it as well because she shivered. A man had been shot; she could have been, too.

Except that she was worth more alive than dead—until she refused to offer up the information. Then she would die.

Ash couldn't let that happen. Maybe he had been a fool to use her as bait. What if he was already too distracted to protect her?

Claire grabbed up her big purse from the floor next to her desk. It was too big to fit into a drawer. "Let's go," she said. "I'm starving."

Or maybe she just wanted out of the place where a man had been shot. She dug in her purse while he and Martin cleared out of her office. Then she pulled out her keys and swiped a card from the chain through the automatic lock on the door. A red light flashed.

"You can go home, too," she informed Martin. "Last night was a late one."

"I came in late today like you did," he said. "I think I'll stay a little while longer."

Ash slid his arm around Claire's shoulders and escorted her toward the elevator. "Good night," he told the kid.

His reply was another glare from Martin. Of resentment? Jealousy?

Ash waited until the elevator doors closed to ask her, "Does the kid have a crush on you?"

She laughed. "Of course not. I'm pretty sure he thinks I'm ancient."

At twenty-five? Ash nearly laughed at the absurdity of anyone thinking that she was ancient. He doubted that Martin did, either. "If he's not jealous," he said, "then what's his problem?"

She shrugged. "I think he just doesn't trust you."

This hadn't been his smoothest undercover assignment. But still...

"Why not?"

"You showed up right after the building was broken into for the first time," she pointed out. "You don't think that looks suspicious?"

He sighed. "Damn suspicious."

She opened her mouth as if to say more, but he didn't trust security. So he kissed her.

Or maybe he kissed her just because he wanted to. He had wanted to since the moment she'd stepped out of the bedroom of the hotel suite. The red dress had been replaced with a long sweater and black leggings. But even with all that porcelain skin covered, she still looked sexy as hell.

He didn't stop kissing her until the elevator dinged and the doors slid open. Her thick lashes fluttered, and she stared up into his face, her green eyes dazed with confusion and maybe desire.

She didn't speak again until he helped her into the passenger's side of the SUV. Then she remarked, "I thought you weren't into PDA. You know there are cameras in the company elevators."

"That's why I kissed you," he said, although it wasn't entirely the truth. He had wanted to kiss her. "After the break-in, I don't have much confidence in your employer's security system. Anyone could be watching the footage from the security cameras."

She shivered despite her sweater. But then it was Chicago and the wind whipped through the streets, gaining in force as it pushed between all the tall buildings. But he suspected it wasn't the cold that chilled her. It was the danger.

"You think someone could have infiltrated our security staff?"

He shrugged. "Or maybe someone already on your staff was bought off. Like Martin…"

She shook her head. "Martin is just a kid."

He dressed like one, but Ash remembered Martin's employee record. He wasn't that much younger than Claire was. He was just immature. "Kids can make huge mistakes," he reminded her as he closed her door and hurried around to the driver's side.

His skin chilled now. It wasn't the cold; it was that sixth sense that told him someone was watching him. And it wasn't just his backup agents.

"You're never going to let me live that down," she groused as he joined her inside the SUV. "I made a huge mistake when I was a kid."

"You're not the only one," he said.

Her blond brows arched. "You did, too?"

He shrugged. "I wasn't necessarily talking about when I was young."

"You've made a huge mistake recently?"

He arched his brows back at her.

"Oh, about me," she said with a laugh. "You thought I was a criminal."

"It wasn't the only mistake I made," he said. As he started and steered the SUV out of her parking space, he peered around the lot. He recognized the vehicles of his backup units. But there were so many other vehicles in the lot.

"What other mistake did you make?" she asked.

He ignored her question for a few moments as he concentrated on traffic. Despite it still being during the rush hour, the streets weren't as congested as they should have been. That sense of foreboding rushed over him again.

"What mistake did you make?" she asked.

He pushed aside his concerns about being watched and replied, "I didn't think going undercover as your boyfriend would raise that much suspicion."

She emitted a self-deprecating laugh. "It probably wouldn't have if I was actually known to have a social life. But work has been my life for years."

Work had been his life, too. But he didn't harbor the regrets she obviously did. He didn't want more. He would never go speed dating for real.

"Sounds like work might be all I ever have," she murmured.

For him that was more a relief than a problem. "I should have known that I'm going to need to treat this assignment as I have all my other undercover assignments."

"How's that?" she asked.

"When I go undercover, I totally immerse myself in the role I'm playing," he said. "I make myself actually believe that I am who I'm pretending to be."

"So what does that mean?" she asked.

"I'm going to *be* your boyfriend," he said. "For real."

But as strange vehicles closed in on them, he wondered if he would have the chance. Or if his assignment was going to end sooner than he'd thought. Than he wanted…

Chapter Nine

Whatever Ash meant about being her boyfriend for real, he didn't look very happy about it. His handsome face was grim as he studied the road and the rearview mirror.

"Don't look so thrilled about it," she murmured resentfully. "It's not like I really want you to be my boyfriend, either."

"What?" he asked. Either he was distracted or he hadn't heard her at all.

"If you don't want this assignment," she said, "you can get a different agent assigned to protect me."

She had his attention then as he shot her a quick glance. "A different agent? What are you talking about?"

"What are *you* talking about?" she asked. "Being my boyfriend for real? I already told you that you're not my type."

"Why not?" he asked.

She wasn't sure he really wanted to know or if he was just humoring her with the question. It wasn't as if he was paying her much attention. His focus seemed to be completely on the roads, which she didn't understand since traffic seemed lighter than it usually was this time of day.

Not that she left the office this early all that often. But leaving later helped her miss the worst of the traffic jams.

"Why am I not your type?" he asked again. Maybe he really wanted to know.

"Because you're too uptight," she said. "That is totally not my type. I want someone laid-back, relaxed, funny…" That was what she had requested from the dating service for her potential matches.

"And you think another agent might be more your type?" A muscle twitched in his cheek as he tightly clenched his jaw. She could almost hear his teeth grinding.

No wonder he hadn't protested her calling him uptight. There was no doubt that he was.

"Maybe Agent Reyes," she suggested. "He's funny. Relaxed. Good-looking…"

"Maybe he would be more believable as your boyfriend," Ash readily agreed.

Hurt struck her like a stomach pang at how easily he would dump her—even as her fake boyfriend. She'd decided before, at the speed dating event, that maybe she wasn't ready for a relationship yet. Apparently she wasn't.

Maybe she was better off just focusing on her job. She hadn't made any progress on finding out who had posted that not-so-subtle auction of security information. But then she'd been distracted—because of Ash.

Maybe it would be better if he dumped her. For some reason she doubted that Special Agent Reyes would distract her as much as Ash did. While the other man was good-looking, he wasn't Ash Stryker.

"So you're going to hand this undercover assignment off to him?" she asked. *Just like that? Without an argument?*

He must have already been tired of dealing with her—of protecting her. Or maybe he really didn't like her stipulation on his using her as bait. Maybe he really didn't want to kiss her.

"I may not have a choice," he murmured.

Finally she realized why he had been so intent on studying the traffic as two big vehicles drew up close to them. One had crossed the yellow line to hem them in while another drove too close between them and the traffic parked alongside the street. It clipped vehicles, tearing off bumpers and crushing driver's sides. She gasped in shock and fear.

Then the vehicle on Ash's side moved closer, and metal rubbed against metal as they brushed. The passenger's window lowered and the gun protruded, the barrel nearly touching the glass of Ash's window.

She screamed as the gunman fired right at his head.

ASH FLINCHED EVEN as the shot glanced off the bulletproof glass. Then he uttered a ragged sigh of relief that he had signed out the SUV equipped with all the latest and greatest in protection.

Claire stared at him in shock. "How did the glass not break? How are you not dead?"

"FBI SUV," he said. But not all of their vehicles were equipped like this one.

The gunman fired again and again, but none of his bullets penetrated the glass. So the driver edged the panel van closer, squeezing the SUV between it and the other panel van. The sides were plain white where usually a company logo would have been painted.

But then these guys weren't likely to advertise who they were working for.

Ash pressed hard on the accelerator. But another panel van had pulled in front of him.

"Hang on!" he warned Claire as he slammed his front

bumper into its rear bumper. Metal crumpled, and the van swerved—but not enough for him to pass it. Not with the vehicles alongside him.

He had already flipped on the two-way radio when that sense of foreboding warned him that something wasn't right. Chicago traffic was never this light. He'd been hoping the Bureau had blocked off streets. Now he understood it wasn't the Bureau at all.

It was whoever was after Claire. Another country? Home-grown terrorists? Or, as Reyes suspected, the Mob?

He touched the radio again—the radio that had been curiously quiet. Had his backup agents been taken out? That foreboding chilled him even more as he worried that was what might have happened, that the other FBI agents had been neutralized.

Murdered...

Claire probably wouldn't get her wish to work with Reyes then—even if Ash was gone. But then if Ash was gone, she would be, too.

"Where the hell is my backup?" he yelled at the radio.

But they couldn't reply to him—not if they were already gone. He couldn't imagine anyone getting the drop on Reyes, but for the information it was believed Claire had, the interested countries and groups would send their best. Maybe their best was better than Reyes.

Maybe their best was better than Ash...

"No need to shout," Reyes replied, his deep voice emanating from the speaker. "I haven't missed a thing."

Relief rushed over Ash, chased by a twinge of discomfort that Reyes had obviously overheard his and Claire's entire discussion.

The agent confirmed his suspicion when he said, "So, Ms. Molenski, you think I'm good-looking?"

She screamed in response as the panel vans closed in, pushing against the sides of the SUV. But the metal was reinforced and strong enough that it didn't crumple. "They're going to kill us!"

Apparently she didn't think the other agent was so funny now and that he was maybe a little too relaxed.

"They're not going to kill *you*," Reyes assured her.

No. Ash was the one who would die because he was the one standing in the way of these men fulfilling their mission, which was capturing Claire.

She glanced over at him, her green eyes bright with fear. Was she worried about him? Did she care?

"They will kill me," she said.

Disappointment flashed through him. She was worried about herself. But then again he couldn't blame her. It wasn't as if she even knew him since she actually thought he was uptight, and she had already wanted to replace him.

With Reyes...

The other agent said, "No, they won't. They need you alive."

"To torture me," she said.

Ash flinched—not because of the attack. Bullets continued to barrage against his window and the tires and sides of the vehicle. He flinched because he really shouldn't have told her about the torture. But he had needed her to agree to his protection—even though he wasn't doing a very damn good job of it.

"Then they'll kill me," she said, "because I'm not going to be able to give them the information they want."

Despite the vehicles pushing against his, Ash took one hand from the wheel and covered hers that was braced against the console between them.

"I will protect you," he promised. Then he snarled at the radio, "Get us the hell out of here, Reyes."

He accelerated, but he couldn't push the van in front of him out of the way. The back of the van began to crumple, though, the doors folding in.

"Take the next right," Reyes directed.

Ash slammed on the brakes and the vans, going faster, passed him, giving him room to do as Reyes directed.

"There's no road," Claire protested.

But Ash twisted the steering wheel anyway and the tires jumped the curb.

"This is a sidewalk," he told Reyes. It was actually a pedestrian walkway. He was just confirming—not questioning—the other agent's directions, though.

No one knew the city like Dalton Reyes. He had grown up on these streets. Ash had just been transplanted here in his adolescence when he'd come to live with his great-uncle after his parents had died.

Despite it being a pedestrian walkway, there were no people walking along it. When Ash had been worried that his backup had been neutralized, they had, instead, been busy clearing the area. Yet even without the people, the walkway was barely wide enough for the SUV to pass through without scraping the building or the fence on either side of it. A sign snapped as the bumper struck it. A press box crunched against the passenger fender.

Ash ignored it all and accelerated, trying to widen the distance between him and those vans. But at least one had turned onto the walkway behind him. Its grill grew larger as it bore down on them. Then it struck with such force that his and Claire's heads snapped forward.

"You okay?" he asked with concern.

Claire's shiny yellow hair was tangled over her face,

hiding her eyes. But he could feel her fear in the tension in her body. In the breath she held. Maybe it was because she was holding her breath that she didn't answer him and, hopefully, not because she was hurt.

The van bounced back off the reinforced rear bumper of the SUV, and then it swerved and crashed into the side of a building. Its tires had gone flat. Ash hadn't heard the shots, but he knew a sniper had taken out the tires.

His backup had been there all along, clearing the area and setting up snipers. But had they had enough time? Was the area completely cleared? Were there enough snipers?

He was driving the SUV up to another street, so he asked, "Which way?"

"Right again," Reyes advised.

Ash wrenched the wheel and made a right into oncoming traffic as he drove the wrong way on a one-way street. Cars sped straight toward them.

Claire's held breath escaped in a scream of terror.

A van also steered toward them—one of those panel vans—and it struck the SUV in a head-on collision. The fenders and hood crumpled on the van and the windshield shattered in a spidery web.

Another van was done. But at least one more was out there. Maybe more...

Ash slammed into Reverse. But the SUV bumper was caught, twisted and hung up on the mangled bumper of the crumpled van. He was stuck. Another van, also driving the wrong way, pulled up behind him. The doors slid open on the damaged van and gunmen jumped out. The barrels of their automatic weapons pointed at the SUV.

Ash wasn't sure how many bullets the glass could

withstand. How many could it take before it weakened and broke?

He pushed Claire's head down below the dash—just in case—as shots rang out.

Chapter Ten

Ash pressed hard on the accelerator and slammed the SUV into the already damaged van and into the gunmen. Then he jerked the SUV into Reverse, running over the men coming up behind them. He smashed the front of that van while dragging the other one along with him. Tires squealed and metal crumpled.

He twisted the wheel hard and spun the SUV around, which finally jerked the van loose from the front bumper. He sped off down the street—the right way. He didn't need Reyes's help anymore. Ash had lost Claire's would-be attackers. And as he headed back toward the hotel, he made sure he didn't pick up any new tails.

"Are you okay?" he asked her again, taking his attention briefly from the traffic to glance at her.

She nodded, but her face twisted into a slight grimace of pain.

"Your neck is okay?" he asked. "You didn't get whiplash?"

She nodded again—more easily this time. "I'm fine, thank you."

"How about you, Stryker?" Reyes asked, his voice emanating from the radio again. "You okay?"

"I'm alive," Ash replied, "so you're not taking over for me yet." And he clicked off the two-way radio. Not only didn't he need Reyes's help, he also didn't need his input during his conversation with Claire.

But there was no conversation. Claire was silent again the entire route to the hotel. Maybe she was afraid that more assailants would try to abduct her. Maybe she had another reason for her silence.

"Are you going to be disappointed about that?" he asked.

"About what?" she asked distractedly as she now nervously studied the street ahead and the street behind them. Her gaze darted around fearfully.

"That Agent Reyes won't be going undercover as your boyfriend," he said.

She turned toward him with a furrowed brow, as though she was totally confused.

"I thought that's what you wanted," he said. He could have listed her reasons why—because the other agent was relaxed and funny and good-looking. Obviously she didn't think Ash was any of those things.

"I thought that's what *you* wanted," she said. "You don't seem really thrilled about this assignment."

"I'm not thrilled," he admitted, "when someone's trying to kill me."

She uttered a short laugh. "Then why in the world are you an FBI agent?"

He had his reasons, but he had never voiced them aloud. Only the people who knew him well had figured out why. But very few people knew him well. Now he fell silent.

They didn't speak again until he locked the door to the hotel suite behind them. Then she turned on him, standing close as if she could intimidate the truth out of him. All she made him do was want to kiss her.

And more…

"You know why I became a hacker," she said. "Isn't it only fair that you tell me why you're an agent?"

"The Bureau recruited me out of the marines," he said.

She stepped closer and narrowed her gaze. "You're doing that thing you do."

"What thing do I do?"

"That thing where you tell the truth but it's not really the truth." She shook her head as if she'd confused herself. "But it's not a lie, either. It's just not the entire truth. You're leaving something out."

Uneasiness lifted the hair on the nape of his neck. He was nearly as on edge as he'd been when he had realized something wasn't right about the traffic. But now he was uneasy because Claire had already gotten to know him better than most people did since she'd figured out his trick.

"The Bureau recruited me," he said. "That's the story of how I became an agent."

"But I didn't ask you how," she reminded him. "I asked you why. Sure, the FBI recruited you, but why did you say yes? It wasn't like my situation where I had no choice. Either I did my job or I did time."

Since she had only been sixteen when she'd committed her crime, her time probably would have just been served in a juvenile detention center, and she would have had her life back sooner. Instead she'd made hacking her life.

Her green eyes widened in shock. "Or is that why you said yes? Because you didn't have a choice?"

"I had a choice," he said. And he'd chosen what he'd always wanted to do. He just hadn't realized how easy it would be for him to achieve his almost lifelong goal.

She sighed in resignation. "You're not going to tell why, are you?"

He shrugged. "There's nothing to tell. Some little boys

dream of growing up to become firemen or policemen or astronauts."

"And you dreamed of growing up to become an FBI agent?" she asked skeptically.

"Yes."

She tilted her head and studied his face. She had more questions. He saw them in her gaze. But before she could ask anything else, her phone rang from the depths of her bottomless purse. By the time she found the cell, the phone had stopped ringing.

"Who was it?" he asked the questions now.

Her brow furrowed as she studied the screen of her phone. "I don't recognize the number."

His pulse quickened. What if it was a buyer? "We need to get a trace on your phone."

"But that online post doesn't give out a phone number," she reminded him. "The exchange details are to be worked out once the bidding is closed."

"But since I'm not the only one who traced that post back to you—"

"Incorrectly," she interrupted.

"Incorrectly," he repeated to placate her and because he felt bad over his accusations. "Someone might try to make contact with you—"

"Without accosting me in a parking lot?" Her phone trilled again. "I have a voice mail." She punched in some numbers and played the message on speaker.

"Claire, it's Leslie. I know you're busy and you turn down my every request for you to come to dinner, but you need to take a break every now and then and come up for air. And food. Please give me a call back. I'd love to catch up with you."

"I bet he would," Ash murmured.

Somehow her old mentor must have heard about the

break-in at his former employer. He had contacts inside the company yet. Maybe a mole…

If he were truly retired, why was Leslie Morrison still so interested in Nowak Computer Consulting?

"Call him back," Ash told her. "And accept his invitation."

Her eyes widened in shock. "People are trying to kidnap me and you want me to go to dinner at a friend's?"

"Not alone," he said. "You'll be bringing your boyfriend along, of course."

"If we can't fool Martin, we'll never fool Leslie," she warned him. "In fact, Leslie may be extending this invitation just to check you out…if he heard about you. He still has friends at the company." Her brow furrowed again. "So he could be calling about the break-in, too."

Ash was pretty sure that he was calling about the break-in—maybe wanting to know how much Claire knew about it and maybe about the online auction, too. Ash had only agreed that the man wasn't a suspect in order to placate Claire. To him, everyone was a suspect—but her.

"Leslie will believe I'm your boyfriend," he assured her.

"Why?" she asked. "Because you're going to make yourself believe it?"

He'd told her how he immersed himself in his undercover assignments. "Yes."

She laughed. "I don't think you know how to be a boyfriend."

He couldn't argue the point. He couldn't remember the last time that he had been anyone's boyfriend. He'd dated but never for long. A relationship wouldn't have survived his being gone for months on end for undercover assignments, so he had never even tried.

"You're more a bodyguard than a boyfriend," she said.

He flinched at the description. He didn't do protection duty. He did *undercover.*

"Isn't a good boyfriend protective?" he asked. "Doesn't he make sure his girlfriend is safe?"

She laughed again and shrugged. "Since, as an adult, I haven't had a real boyfriend, I wouldn't know."

"Well, you're about to find out," he said. He stepped closer, tempted to show her with his lips and his hands. Instead he clasped her hand around her phone. "Call Leslie Morrison back and accept his invitation to dinner for you and your guest."

"We won't fool him," she warned even as she began to dial the phone.

"We will."

Her lips curved into a half smile. "Because you think you can fool yourself into believing you're my boyfriend."

Ash was worried that he was fooling himself—because this assignment was unlike any other he ever had. Except that it was probably even more dangerous...

THE FOLLOWING DAY Claire had called in sick to work—something she had never done before. Of course that had been mostly because she hadn't dared violate her probation. But even though she hadn't been at work, she had been working—on the laptop with the backup hard drive she'd pulled from her voluminous purse. She always carried a lot of hardware and software with her.

She turned toward Ash and glared at him. "You should have let me keep working," she said. But she wasn't sure if she was irritated that he'd made her stop to come to Leslie's dinner party or if she was irritated with how sexy the man looked in black slacks and a blue sweater that matched his eyes and was loose enough to hide his weapon.

"Were you making any progress?" he asked.

No. She'd been too distracted while confined in that small hotel suite with him. She'd been too distracted with thoughts of his kisses and concerns that he hadn't kissed her again. Why hadn't he kissed her again?

He leaned closer to her, as if he was considering it now as they stood on Leslie's front porch, the doorbell they'd pushed echoing softly inside the craftsman-style house.

But then Leslie's nine-light front door finally opened. "Claire!" he greeted her with delight. "You're more beautiful than I remember."

Her face heated with embarrassment that she had been caught dressing up. From the hotel boutique she'd bought a shimmery green dress that she'd thought flattering. But she'd gotten more of a reaction from Leslie than she had Ash. He kissed the air near her cheek, then turned to her date.

"Speaking of beautiful," her former mentor murmured.

Claire fought back a laugh at Ash's reaction. Of course it was minimal—just a faint widening of his blue eyes. But she loved that he'd been caught off guard by Leslie's flirting. At over six feet with a bald head, her former mentor often caught people off guard with his orientation.

"I'm Leslie Morrison."

"Ash Stryker." He held out his hand.

Leslie clasped it in both of his. "I'm so happy to meet you."

"Thank you for inviting us to dinner," Ash said.

"I've been trying to get this one to come over since I retired," he said. "But she kept saying she was too busy.

Now I know why…" He winked. "Dinner is almost ready. Fortunately for you I cooked instead of Ed."

"It smells wonderful," Claire said as she followed Leslie inside the warm and colorful home.

Ash leaned forward and pressed his lips to her neck. "You smell wonderful," he whispered.

She shivered in reaction to his closeness and to his warm breath on her bare skin. So now he was going to play the part of her boyfriend…?

"Ah, I remember being that in love," Leslie murmured wistfully.

Another man stood in the dining room, cradling a baby in his arms. Like Leslie, he was also burly but sensitive. His voice soft with hurt, he asked, "You're not in love anymore?"

Leslie slid his arm around the man and the baby. "I'm more in love with you, with our family, our home than I ever thought possible."

Her old mentor had everything he wanted; Leslie Morrison posed no threat to national security. Claire had never doubted him. And now she had no doubts about what she wanted in life.

She wanted the loving partner, the children, the home…although hers wouldn't be nearly as clean and decorative as Leslie's. And her food might be take-out instead of the wonderful Cornish hens and stuffing he'd served.

"You're quiet," Ash mused as they left Leslie and Ed waving after them from their front porch. "Are you upset?"

She was unsettled but mostly from the way he'd acted in front of Leslie and Ed. Loving…

He had always had a hand on her. Either on her hand or her leg or, like now, her back, as he escorted her to the parked SUV. He had immersed himself so completely in the role of her boyfriend that she wasn't sure if he believed it, but *she* was beginning to believe that he was actually her boyfriend.

Or maybe she only wished that he was. But if he was, she would never have the life that Leslie had. She would never have the children and the house; she would never really have him because the FBI would always come first. He would go undercover somewhere else—with someone else—and maybe he would so totally immerse himself in that cover that he would forget all about her.

No. She had been right when she'd told him he wasn't her type. The sooner they found the real hacker and she was no longer in danger, the sooner she could get back to her search for someone who actually was her type, for someone who wanted the same things she wanted out of life.

Who wanted a life…

"Are you upset?" he asked again as he helped her into the passenger's side of the SUV.

She waited until Ash slid behind the steering wheel before she replied, "This was a waste of time tonight."

He flashed her a grin. "Isn't this what couples do?" he asked. "Hang out with other couples?"

"You didn't make me accept that dinner invitation so we could socialize," she said. "You wanted to investigate my former mentor."

She had seen some of what he'd been working on today since they'd both been on computers in the living area of the suite. He had accessed all Leslie's financials; of course he would have had FBI clearance to hack, especially with national security at risk. He had also slipped away for an extended visit to the bathroom during dinner, and she was pretty sure that he'd managed to search the house.

He didn't deny his motivation. He didn't say anything at all as he concentrated on traffic on the drive toward their hotel.

Remembering the other time he had been so focused on traffic, she shivered with fear. She glanced around, too, but she noticed nothing out of the ordinary. But then she hadn't last time, either, until it had nearly been too late.

"I investigated him," he finally admitted.

"Then you must have found out what I already knew. Leslie is no longer a hacker." He was a happily retired man who was enjoying his family.

Leslie had Ed. Her dad had Pam. Claire had nobody but an FBI agent who was using her as bait to draw out terrorists. She needed this to be over soon.

"We should have stayed in the suite," she said, "so I could have kept working on finding the real hacker."

"Have you made any progress on that?" he asked.

She shook her head, frustrated about that and maybe frustrated over how Ash had kept touching her throughout dinner. Without his touch she felt cold. Maybe she should have brought along a jacket. But they were nearly back to the hotel now. She glimpsed the lights ahead.

"I can't find who posted that information sale," she said. "But I really don't believe that someone could bypass firewalls that I've made sure were secure."

He pulled the SUV into the hotel lot and parked it. Then he turned toward her. "Maybe there's a better hacker out there than you are."

The air whooshed out of her lungs as if he'd punched her stomach. "A better hacker?"

He chuckled softly at her reaction and opened the driver's door.

She thrusted open her door before Ash could walk around to the passenger's side. "Maybe there's a better FBI agent than you."

He reached beneath his sweater and drew his gun from his holster. "Maybe there is," he readily agreed. "But lucky for you I'm pretty damn good."

"What—"

She had no time to utter her question as he pushed her down to the asphalt. Then he fired so closely that the gunshots reverberated in her ears.

Light flashed in the darkness as Ash's gunfire was returned. Someone was out there shooting at them. She hadn't seen them, but Ash had.

How many were there?

If it was like the other day, with all those vans filled with all those armed men, she didn't like her and Ash's chances to survive.

He was a good agent, but was he good enough to save them this time?

Chapter Eleven

Ash had fired those first shots as warning shots. He didn't want to kill this time. He counted the shots fired back at him, all from one gun. He hoped like hell that that meant only one shooter.

"Stay down," he ordered Claire as he eased his weight off her.

"Where are you going?" she asked, panic in her voice.

"You'll be fine," he assured her. "There's only one of them."

And he couldn't let that one get away.

She grasped his arm, though, holding him back. "One of them can still kill you."

He chuckled again. "Not me…"

He was a better agent than she obviously thought he was. He wouldn't have lived as long as he had if he wasn't.

"Stay down," he told her again. Then, just as the last shot flashed in the darkness, he ran. And before the shooter could load another clip, he tackled him.

An elbow dug into his ribs; a fist grazed his jaw. He dodged the blows and pinned the man's limbs to his sides, subduing him.

"Who are you?" he demanded to know.

The man replied in another language. But he didn't offer his name. Instead, he called Ash a few. Fortunately for him, Ash was fluent in many languages.

Ignoring the insults hurled at him, he asked in the man's native tongue, "Who sent you?"

He couldn't just assume that it was the country the man was from. He suspected it was someone from the same country Ash was from—America.

"Did Leslie Morrison hire you?" he asked—again in the man's language although the shooter was apparently pretending he didn't understand since he didn't reply.

The guy had begun following them from Claire's former mentor's house. He had been waiting outside for them, so someone must have tipped him off that they would be there. Leslie was the only other person who knew they were coming to dinner. Unless he'd told someone else…

The guy cursed again but admitted nothing. He only struggled harder in Ash's grip and nearly broke free—especially when Ash heard the scream.

Claire screamed, her voice high-pitched with fear.

Maybe this man shooting at them had only been a diversion so that someone else could grab Claire. And Ash had fallen for the diversion.

And lost Claire.

CLAIRE'S THROAT BURNED from her scream. And her face burned from embarrassment when she turned toward the man she'd thought was grabbing her from the pavement to abduct her.

"You're okay," Agent Reyes soothed her. "I'm sorry for scaring you. You're okay." Then he called out more loudly, "She's okay."

She wasn't okay. She was terrified. And not just for herself. She was terrified for Ash, especially when she'd heard men speaking in some foreign language.

He had thought he only had one gunman to overpower. What if there had been more waiting for him?

She waited for him to call back, to assure them that he was fine. She heard a grunt, as if someone had taken a blow.

"Help him," she urged Reyes. "Make sure he's okay!"

Reyes laughed. "He's Special Agent Ash Stryker. Of course he's okay. The man is a legend."

Ash was older than her but not more than a decade—not old enough to have become a legend. Most people usually didn't become legends until after they were dead. She wanted Ash alive and well.

"Why do you say that?" she asked.

"As a marine, he survived his deployments to the most dangerous places in the world. As an agent, he's survived going undercover and arresting the most dangerous people in the world." He pitched his voice lower, and for once the grin left his face as he was totally serious and respectful, "That's why he's a legend."

She shivered with fear for all that Ash had survived. What if he hadn't survived?

Not only wouldn't she have met him but she also might not have survived the recent attempts on her life. When she'd said that he might not be the best FBI agent, she had been acting out of spite and wounded pride. She'd been wrong.

Ash stepped out of the darkness as suddenly as he had disappeared into it. But this time he dragged a man behind him.

Reyes groaned. "You killed another one. We can't question dead men."

"He's not dead," Ash informed him. "He's only unconscious."

The grunt must have been his because she could see no wounds on Ash. He hadn't been shot as she'd feared. And he hadn't been overpowered. Maybe he couldn't be overpowered if he was as legendary as Reyes thought him to be.

"He's all yours," Ash said as he thrust the man's limp body toward Reyes.

"You don't want to question him?" the other agent asked in astonishment.

"I already did."

"What did he say?"

Ash spoke in another language as easily as if it were his native tongue.

"What the hell does that mean?" Reyes asked.

"You don't want to know," Ash replied. "Let's just say it was more about my character than his. He wouldn't admit to who hired him."

"But you think you know," Reyes said.

"He was waiting for us outside Morrison's house."

"You can't think Leslie hired him," she said. Not after Leslie had showed them how happy and content he was with his family. "That man must have followed us there."

Reyes chuckled and then teased him, "You didn't notice a tail? Are you getting distracted like your friend Blaine got distracted?"

Wasn't that how Ash's house had burned down? Because Blaine had been distracted.

"No," Ash replied. "And you damn well know it."

Reyes shook his head. "I know it. But I don't understand how you're not." He gestured at Claire. "With her looking like that all the time."

After being knocked to the ground, she probably looked a mess with her dress all wrinkled and her hair all mussed up. But Ash hadn't been distracted even before he'd knocked her to the ground. He'd been aware of the tail—aware of the shooter in the parking lot before the man had even fired his first shot. No wonder Special Agent Ash Stryker was a legend—or maybe he just wasn't attracted to her—at least not enough for her to distract him.

Ash didn't look at her, but stared at the other agent through narrowed eyes. "Did you see a tail?"

"No," Reyes confirmed. "I was the only one following you."

She hadn't seen him. It was a good thing that she was a hacker instead of an FBI agent. "Are you sure he didn't follow *you*, then?"

The grin left Reyes's face again while Ash laughed. "He's relaxed," he said, "but not relaxed enough to let someone tail him."

"Leslie has nothing to do with this man," she insisted. She refused to believe that her former mentor's life wasn't as complete as it had looked. He couldn't want more— he couldn't want so much money that he would risk his freedom and his family to get it.

Reyes looked at Ash as if seeking his opinion. Ash just shrugged. Reyes made a gesture, and other agents materialized out of the darkness and carted off the unconscious man. "I guess we'll find out."

Ash shook his head. "I doubt you're going to learn anything from him. We need to bring Morrison in for questioning."

"You're going to interrogate Leslie?" she asked, completely appalled that he could eat food the man had spent the day preparing and then treat him like a criminal.

"Not me," Ash said. "I can't blow my cover."

She uttered a soft snort in derision. "Like anyone is really buying your cover."

"I'm not sure this guy would've taken him on if he'd known who he is," Reyes defended the agent whom he obviously idolized. "Or what he is, anyway."

"I'm not sure knowing I'm an FBI agent would have prevented any of these abduction attempts," Ash admitted.

"Then what's the point of this cover?" Claire asked. "You don't have to act like my boyfriend. You could just be my bodyguard."

Reyes whistled between his teeth. "Ash Stryker doesn't do protection duty."

"And this isn't," Ash said. "If everyone believes I'm just your boyfriend, there will be more attempts to abduct you."

Panic clutched her heart and she murmured, "Oh, lovely."

"There will also be a better chance that whoever really offered the information for auction will slip up and reveal himself," Ash added.

He was using her. She'd already known it. But hearing that reinforced her need to protect herself from him. She had to remember that he was only acting as her boyfriend. But the only thing he really wanted from her was to stop the threat to national security.

She shivered.

"You should take her inside," Reyes advised. "She's cold."

"And tired," Claire added. "I'm going to the suite."

"You can't," Ash said. "This place has been compromised. We don't know who he might have told where we are. We can't stay here."

"Good," she said.

She wasn't sure she could handle another night in a hotel suite with Ash Stryker—not after he'd acted so convincingly like her boyfriend earlier that evening. Her skin still tingled from all his touches.

But he wasn't her boyfriend; he was a legendary FBI agent, one who was never distracted or unfocused. She should have been grateful that he was as good an agent as he was, but her pride hurt that she didn't affect him like he affected her.

"I want to go home."

She wanted the comfort of familiarity—of her messy apartment and her lumpy mattress. "Please take me home."

"THIS IS NOT my home," Claire said, glaring at him as he carried her bag and her laptop into the hotel suite. "I wanted you to take me home."

"This is," he said.

She shook her head. "No, it's not. This is not my place."

He chuckled. "That's a good thing. It's not a mess like yours."

She shot him another glare. "Very funny. Is that why you brought me to another hotel—for the housekeeping?"

"Housekeeping is just a bonus," he replied. "This is my home."

She glanced around again and finally noticed that the suite was more lived-in looking than the one where they'd stayed the past few nights. He had more clothes here— some books. The suite also had a kitchenette and boxes of food sat atop the small counter.

"You've been staying here since your house burned down?" she asked.

"Yes," he said. "Whenever I'm in Chicago."

She walked around the room again as if taking an inventory of everything in the suite. "Is this all you managed to save from your house?"

He shook his head. "I wasn't able to salvage anything from the fire."

She sucked in a breath as if horrified. "You lost everything?"

"It's not like I had a lot to lose," he assured her. "I've always traveled light." He had been doing that for a long time.

"But you must have lost your pictures—your mementos—of your parents then." The glare was gone, her green eyes warm with sympathy as she stared up at him. "I'm sorry…"

"I didn't have any pictures or mementos of my parents to lose," he told her.

She sucked in another breath—now she probably was horrified of him, not for him. "You don't have anything to remember them?"

"They died in a fire," he explained.

Tears welled in her eyes. "That's horrible. I am so sorry." And then she was holding him, her arms winding around his back as she offered him comfort.

He waited for the questions. People always asked questions when he admitted that his parents were dead. They wanted details, wanted his emotions.

Claire asked no questions. She only offered comfort. But then she had a great relationship with at least one of her parents, so she must have been imagining how upset she would have been if she'd lost her father.

He didn't want her sympathy because he didn't deserve

it. His hands on her shoulders, he eased her away from him. "It wasn't like that."

"Like what?" she asked. "Two people died, leaving you without a father or a mother. That must have been horrible."

"They weren't good parents," he confessed. "They weren't good *people*. They—and a lot of innocent people—died in a fire they started with bombs."

She gasped. "Your parents set a bomb?"

"Yeah," he said.

"You were there?" she asked, her voice shaking as if it was happening now, as if he was in danger all over again.

He nodded. "But, obviously, I was rescued before it went off."

"That's good…" She breathed a sigh of relief. "How old were you?"

"Eleven," he said. "Old enough to know what they were planning was wrong. I called the FBI." Actually he'd called his grandmother, and although she had already passed away, her brother had answered his cry for help. Uncle George had been an FBI agent. "They got there in time to get me out and some other people, but not everybody…"

"I'm sorry," she said. "No matter what else they were, they were your parents. It was a loss for you."

He shrugged off her sympathy again. "The parents of a special agent with the FBI's antiterrorism division were homegrown terrorists—talk about irony, huh?"

"It's not ironic at all," she said. "It makes perfect sense. Now I understand why you became an agent." And she hugged him again, her arms winding tightly around him. "I'm so sorry."

He tried to ease her away again because her sympathy

was affecting him. His heart was warming and aching with longing—with affection. With...

He jerked away from her. "So it's not exactly home, but I think you'll be comfortable here."

"Are you?" she asked as she looked around again. "It's not exactly homey."

His home hadn't been homey, either. Uncle George had been a bachelor his whole life, a man who'd traveled so much that he'd never spent much time at home until he'd inherited guardianship of an orphaned child. He had retired from the Bureau—many years after he could have—to take care of Ash.

"Are you having your house rebuilt?" she wondered.

He shrugged. "I'm not sure I need a house. If I hadn't inherited it from my uncle, I wouldn't have given up my apartment. But the real estate market had bottomed out then, so it wouldn't have been a good time to sell."

"Your uncle passed away, too?" she asked with another gasp of shock and sympathy.

"He was my great-uncle," he explained. "He lived a long life."

"But it must've—"

Hoping to erase that look of sympathy from her beautiful face, Ash goaded her. "He was a bachelor. That was probably why he lived so long."

And the glare was back, directed right at him. "I know what you're doing," she said. "You're trying to make me mad at you so I'll stop feeling sorry for you."

"That's because there's no reason for you to feel sorry for me," he told her.

"There is a reason," she stubbornly persisted. "You just don't like that I feel sorry for you. That's why you're trying to push me away."

"True," he conceded. "But do you know what I do

like?" Instead of pushing her away, he pulled her into his arms—tightly.

She shook her head.

"Kissing you…" And he lowered his mouth to hers. He had started kissing her to get that aggravating look of sympathy from her face. It was gone now…as he lifted his head slightly. And it was replaced instead with the flushed, excited look of passion.

Now he worried that he wouldn't be able to stop kissing her.

Chapter Twelve

During one of his deployments Ash had been embedded. He'd been unable to move, barely able to breathe. But he had survived. He wasn't certain he could survive being embedded with Claire Molenski—not when he would much rather be in bed with her.

But that would be a mistake. And that was why he'd stopped himself from kissing her those few nights ago. He couldn't afford to be distracted and he knew that making love with her would distract him. He doubted he would be able to get her out of his mind and then he might miss the next tail, the next gun pointing at him out of the darkness.

He had to be careful with her safety. And with his heart.

She was getting to him with her quick wit, with her impressive intelligence and with her heartfelt sympathy. Not to mention with her soft touch and her silky lips…

Right now her hair was clipped on top of her head. She wore fleece pajama bottoms and a hooded sweatshirt. But she still looked sexy as hell to him. She didn't even look at him. Instead, she studied her laptop screen, her face tense with dread and betrayal.

He knew why. It wasn't because she was still searching, but because she had realized what he had before the speed dating event. He was the one to offer his sympathy now. "I'm sorry…"

"You already knew," she said with a sigh.

"I don't know who," he said. "Just that someone at your company is behind the information auction." The access being offered for sale was for clients of only Nowak Computer Consulting, so only an employee of Nowak would know who all those clients were.

"You thought it was me."

He nodded.

"I don't blame you," she said with another sigh. "I would think it's me, too."

"You would rather think it's you," he said. After all the time he'd spent with her, he was beginning to know her character well. "You don't want to believe that someone you work with would betray your company and your country."

She sighed. "No, I don't."

"It could have been someone that you once worked with that still has access."

"Leslie?"

She didn't sound as certain of his innocence as she'd been before. But now he wasn't as certain of Morrison's guilt, either. "He was interrogated."

"And?"

He shrugged. "We can neither confirm nor deny whether or not Leslie Morrison is a suspect."

She snorted. "Sometimes you're such a suit."

He wasn't wearing one now. Like her he had opted for casual, but jeans and a button-down shirt were as casual as he got while on the job. Unless he was undercover…

"If we're going to confirm or deny," he said, "I need to get in a suit again. I need to do some investigating of my own."

Instead of relying on someone else to interrogate a suspect, he needed to be doing the interrogating himself. But if he'd interrogated Morrison, he would have blown his cover.

Her shoulders and back straightening, she tensed. "Are you handing me off to another agent?"

He tensed, too, at the thought of trusting her protection to someone else. "No." But he didn't like what he was about to suggest, either. "We've already established that we're getting nowhere in this hotel room."

Except closer to the bedroom. He wanted her so badly. He had to get out of there.

She smiled. "So we're getting out of here? Are we going to the office?"

"I can't keep you safe there," he said.

"Why not?" she asked. "I need to get back to work."

He pointed at her laptop. "You've been working nonstop. Yours isn't the kind of job where you have to go into the office every day."

"But I can't stay away indefinitely," she said. "I need to go back."

"Not yet," he said.

"When?" she anxiously asked.

"Not until this is over. I already raised suspicion spending that one day in the office with you," he reminded her. "I can't justify my presence and maintain my cover as your boyfriend."

"Not without looking like an overprotective control freak." She tilted her head and stared at him in consideration. "Are you?"

He chuckled. "Only when you're nearly kidnapped every time you step outside…"

Resigned to not going to work, she frowned. "Then I can't step outside."

"We have to," he said, maybe a little more forcefully than necessary since her eyes widened with surprise at his harsh tone. "We're not going to find out who's behind the auction unless we flush out his buyers and hopefully him, too."

She tensed again. "So I'm back to being bait."

"Yes," he said but he was reluctant to use her again, reluctant to put her in danger. He would make sure he had an excellent team watching them—a team that wouldn't let any would-be abductor anywhere near her.

"Okay," she agreed with less reluctance than he felt. "If it gets me out of here, I don't even care." She jumped off the couch and headed for the bedroom. But she caught the jamb and turned back. "Where are we going?"

"Movie…" But that would make it difficult for his team to see would-be abductors in a dark theater. He shook his head. "No. Dancing…"

"I don't dance."

He brought up their earlier bargain. "You wanted to practice dating on me," he reminded her. "Dancing is part of dating."

"Not for everyone."

"What if it is for someone you want to date?" he asked.

She rolled her eyes. "I doubt that it will be. The service I joined makes sure to make only compatible matches. So why would they match me with someone who loves to dance when I don't?"

"How do you know you won't love it, too?" he asked. "Unless you try."

She groaned. "But if I love it, I'll have to change my dating profile."

He mocked her groan. "Then you'll get more potential matches…"

She smiled. "Good point. I will have more potential matches. You'll teach me?"

"I'll teach you." He would teach her how to dance with another man. Regret and jealousy twisted his stomach muscles. It wasn't what he wanted.

He wanted her.

CLAIRE HAD AGREED to act as bait just to get out of the close confines of that hotel suite. She'd been going crazy with wanting Ash. But dancing with him was worse. He was too close, his body touching hers, his hands on her…

"Sorry," she murmured as she stepped on his foot again. "I don't remember the last time I danced."

"There wasn't dancing at your dad's wedding?"

Warmth flooded her along with the happy memories. "Yes, but I only danced once—with my dad."

His hand tightened on her hip as he steered her into a turn around another couple on the floor. The other couple was older, probably in their seventies, but they moved much more gracefully than she did.

Ash had brought her downtown to a piano bar that played more slow songs than she was comfortable dancing to. She would like to blame her inability to dance on being so uncomfortable in his arms. But she felt more than discomfort. She felt attraction—more than she'd ever felt for anyone else.

He leaned down, his mouth nearly brushing her ear, and asked, "Were all of the male guests blind?"

She shivered at his warm breath caressing her ear. He must have thought she was cold because he pulled her closer.

"There weren't a lot of single men there," she said. "The rest were relatives or married or both."

She had barely paid any mind to any of the men there,

though. She hadn't noticed anything but her father's happiness. It was only later as she'd wished him and Pam a long and wonderful marriage that she'd realized she wanted that happiness for herself.

She wouldn't find that with Ash Stryker no matter how she wished that she could. His closeness and his touch affected her, making her ache and long for more. But he had nothing to give her—emotionally.

But maybe she could get something from him physically—like dance lessons. The skill would lead to more potential matches.

"So teach me how to dance," she said.

He steered her around another couple. "You think I know?"

"You told me that you would teach me," she reminded him of their bargain. "And you must know how since you're not stepping on my feet."

The pianist began another song, singing along in a smoky voice, "I could have danced all night…"

Ash bent her back over his arm in a dip so dramatic that her hair nearly brushed the floor. "Maybe I know a move or two," he murmured.

A giggle slipped out of her lips, but she held back another one. She had given him such a hard time about being uptight that she couldn't admit now that he was actually fun. He kept showing her moves—twirling her around so that she felt light-headed and giddy.

And happy.

Ash Stryker made her happy. He seemed happy, too, the grin still on his handsome face. She stared up at him, wanting to rise up on tiptoe and kiss him. She could have explained that she was only playing the part of his girlfriend. But she didn't trust herself to only kiss him—not when she wanted more.

Then he dipped her again, over his arm, and then swung her back up so that her face touched his. Cheek to cheek, breaths mingling. Maybe it was just from the exertion, but she imagined that her panting echoed his. They were both struggling for deep breaths; their hearts beating hard in their chests nearly in as perfect unison as their steps now were.

She wanted to kiss him—deeply. But the music stopped. The other couples applauded the pianist, who was apparently going on break for the first time since she and Ash had arrived. They sprang apart now, awkwardly.

"Would you like a drink?" he asked.

Since she couldn't have what she really wanted, she nodded. "I am thirsty."

They hadn't left the dance floor since they'd arrived. So they had no table and had to push their way through the crowd to the bar.

But Ash, with his naturally commanding nature, summoned the bartender immediately. He handed her a wineglass while keeping a glass of water for himself. That glass of water reminded her of what she'd wanted to forget—that he was on duty. He was only doing his job.

"How do you know what kind of wine I drink?" she asked as she sipped the tart white.

"I saw a wine bottle in your apartment," he said. "I believe it was near the front door."

"I intended to recycle it," she explained, then laughed at his skeptical look. "I do recycle."

"Hopefully your potential match will, too."

"And dance…" She was surprised by how much she enjoyed it. Or was that only because she had been dancing with Ash?

"You can add it to your dating profile," he said. "You're a fast learner."

"How do you know how to dance so well?" she asked. "Did you learn in the marines or the Bureau?"

He chuckled as he led her away from the bar. "I had two left feet at the Marine Ball."

"So the Bureau…?"

He nodded. "Undercover assignment."

"I thought you went undercover among dangerous people," she said as she followed him through the crowd. At least that was what his groupie Reyes had told her.

"Didn't you watch *Black Swan*?"

"You were in a ballet?"

He laughed so hard that his blue eyes twinkled and crinkled at the corners and deep creases formed in his handsome face. Her breath caught with awe at his masculine beauty. And she stumbled again, this time over her own feet.

"No," he said, and the grin slid off his face, replaced by a look of wistfulness. "But I had to get close to a dancer to get some information."

Her chest hurt, maybe over her held breath. Or maybe the pang she felt was of jealousy. She suspected that dancer had been female and beautiful and that Ash had gone undercover as her boyfriend, too.

Had that poor woman known who he really was?

Or had she thought it was real?

At least Claire knew the truth. Ash might have tried to convince himself his cover was real. But Claire couldn't fool herself. She had done that once before when she'd convinced herself she was doing the right thing by hacking into her mother's lover's bank account and giving away all his money. That had cost her her freedom for a number of years. Fooling herself over Ash would cost her her heart.

Maybe forever…

The music began to play again.

"That was a short break," she murmured regretfully. She wasn't sure that she could dance with Ash again. Being that close to him, moving that intimately with him...

Ash reached for her wineglass—probably to put it onto a table and take her back into his arms. But when his hands were busy, another man grabbed her elbow.

"Dance with me," he implored her.

He was tall and dark and handsome. But not as tall or dark or handsome as Ash.

"She's with me," Ash said.

"It's just a dance," the man told him with a brow raised as if he thought Ash was overly possessive. She glared at the FBI special agent, warning him not to blow his cover with an overreaction. Despite what Ash believed, not everybody was trying to abduct her.

"It's just a dance," she assured Ash. But when she'd danced with him, it hadn't been just a dance.

But then the man swept her onto the dance floor, and she realized it was much more than a dance—when she felt the gun barrel digging into her ribs.

"You will not scream, Ms. Molenski," he warned her. "You will not betray any hint of fear or panic."

She wasn't an FBI special agent. When she was afraid, she damn well showed it. She wasn't a robot like this man appeared to be. "I—I can't..."

He moved like Ash had, swinging her around other couples on the dance floor, taking her farther and farther from where Ash stood between the dance floor and the bar. And with every spin, the gun barrel dug more deeply into her ribs.

She needed to scream. But would Ash hear her above

the music? Would he know she was in trouble before the man pulled the trigger?

Before she could catch Ash's gaze, the man spun her entirely off the dance floor. Then he nearly dragged her down a short hallway that led to a back door. He released her to grab the handle of that door.

And she turned to run.

"Come with me," he said. "Or I will shoot."

She was tired of being afraid. She was tired of this man and his empty threats. Rallying her courage, she pointed out, "You can't kill me and get the information you want."

"I'm not going to shoot you," he said. "I am going to go back inside and shoot your boyfriend."

Hoping he was bluffing again, she shook her head. "You can't go back in that crowded bar and just shoot him."

"Watch me," he challenged her. And with his weapon drawn he turned back toward the dance floor.

While she hadn't identified any of them, there were other agents in the bar offering backup protection. But she wasn't sure who they were or if they were really even there. But she'd seen Ash in action before; he might not need backup to defend himself.

But what if an innocent bystander got struck in the cross fire?

She would never forgive herself. "Wait!" she called to the man. "I'll go with you."

She told herself it was because of the danger he posed to everyone else, but she knew the only person she was really worried about was Ash.

Until the man opened that back door and dragged her out into a dark alley…

Now she was worried about herself. She had chosen not to run or scream in order to protect Ash.

Now who would protect her?

Chapter Thirteen

Ash's wounded pride had cost him valuable time. If her wanting to dance with the attractive stranger hadn't made him jealous, maybe he would have reacted faster. Maybe he would have grabbed the guy before he had pulled Claire away from him onto the dance floor.

Just before the guy had walked away out of view with Claire, Ash had noticed the bulge beneath his jacket. The man was armed. And he wasn't another agent. He was a threat.

He was a danger to Claire.

Ash hurried onto the dance floor. But couples crowded the area and the man had kept twirling Claire faster and faster until they disappeared from sight.

Where the hell had he taken her?

The piano bar wasn't that big. That was one of the reasons that Ash had chosen it for their dance date. Probably the other reason was that the pianist played mostly slow, romantic songs. As much as he'd wanted to get out of the close confines of the hotel suite, he had still wanted that closeness with Claire—without the risk of his losing control of his desires.

He had lost control, though, because he hadn't been thinking clearly—his brain clouded with his attraction to her. And now he'd lost her.

He tapped the listening device in his ear and turned on the two-way radio. He hadn't activated it earlier because he hadn't wanted Reyes or any other agent's voice in his head. He'd been having enough issues ignoring his own voice whispering how beautiful and smart Claire was—how desirable.

He also hadn't wanted Reyes or any other agent overhearing his conversation with Claire because he was never sure what he might tell her. He had already shared more with her—about his past, about his life—than he had anyone else. Very few people knew about his parents. But he had told her.

She hadn't judged him as others had based on what his parents had been. That was why, as he'd gotten older, he'd learned to share his past with only the people he trusted. He trusted Claire. Not at first but she had earned his trust with her honesty, her integrity, her caring about others. And when he'd told her about his parents, she had understood and accepted him in a way no one else ever had.

Then he had used her as bait again to flush out threats to national security. Guilt and regret hit him like fists in the stomach. Sure, he had promised he would protect her; he'd even believed that he would keep her safe. But he'd failed her.

"Where is she?" he asked aloud, drawing the curious glances of some of the dancers.

"We lost eyes on her," a voice replied in his ear.

But the woman of one of the dancing couples leaned away from her husband and touched Ash's arm, drawing his attention. He had noticed them earlier, though. While in their seventies, they moved lithely, with grace and a harmony that had come from years of dancing together. Her voice soft with concern, the older woman told him, "Your wife went out the back with that man."

Her husband groaned and tried to spin her away. "Edith, don't get involved—"

Edith dug in her heels, refusing to follow her husband's lead this time, and said, "But she looked so scared. She didn't want to leave with that man."

The woman understood the brevity of the situation, but the man just shook his head, obviously thinking that she was overreacting.

She wasn't.

"You shouldn't have let her dance with another man," Edith's husband advised him. "That's a sure way to lose your woman."

Edith slapped his shoulder. "And acting like a possessive caveman is another way to lose her..."

Ash was already walking away but he heard the older man's comment as he headed off the dance floor. "I've kept you fifty years..."

The older woman giggled as youthfully and giddily as Claire had earlier when Ash had dipped her. He shouldn't have let her dance with another man.

But she wasn't his wife. She was, however, his responsibility. Maybe he shouldn't have taken responsibility for her. Protection duty wasn't his specialty. Sure, he'd always survived his undercover assignments. But he had always gone undercover alone, not even with another agent whose safety he'd had to worry about, let alone a civilian. She was smart and savvy, but she wasn't a trained agent.

"She's out back somewhere," he told the others through the two-way radio. "We need to find her before he gets her in a vehicle."

Or she would be forever lost to him.

THE ALLEY WAS so dark that Claire wasn't even sure where they were anymore. No streetlamps illuminated the narrow space between tall buildings. There weren't even lights burning by back entrances to whatever businesses the buildings housed.

She stumbled, and the man nearly lost his grip on her arm. So she did it again in a desperate attempt to wrestle free of him.

His hand tightened around her arm, painfully squeezing. "Knock it off," he warned her. "You're not getting away from me."

"It's the heels," she said. "I'm not used to wearing them." That much was true. She had learned from Ash how to go undercover. But she wasn't pretending to be someone else, as he often did. This man evidently knew exactly who she was, and that was why he'd grabbed her.

"You looked pretty damn graceful dancing with your boyfriend," the man said.

She had felt graceful dancing with Ash. His lessons had made her graceful because she had never had any grace before. She'd been born a klutz; that was why the snow globe her father had given her depicted her riding on his shoulders instead of trying to skate herself. While the day had been perfect, she hadn't been able to learn to skate as easily as Ash had taught her to dance.

"I'm not graceful," she insisted. "It was all him."

"You were smart to leave with me," the man said. "Your boyfriend will live to dance again."

She was both relieved and regretful. Ash would be so mad that she hadn't called out for help, that she hadn't drawn his attention. But then he would have been shot for certain.

"What do you want with me?" she asked as she stumbled again.

He jerked her arm. "I want nothing from you. I am only doing my job."

Not only did he look like Ash, but he had the same philosophy. He was only doing his job. She nearly laughed, but she was too close to hysteria to risk it. She needed to keep her wits about her. She wasn't graceful, but she'd always been smart.

"Your job is to kidnap me?" she asked. She needed to get him talking. She needed to distract him somehow so that she could get away from him.

"My job is to bring you to my employer," he replied.

Maybe he didn't consider it kidnapping because he wasn't going to ask for a monetary ransom, but she did. And the ransom they wanted was information she couldn't give them.

"Who is your employer?" she said.

"You'll know soon enough," he answered.

Thinking of the torture Ash had warned her about, she fearfully asked, "What does he want with me?"

"You'll know soon enough," he repeated as he jerked her arm again, trying to pull her along as he quickened his stride.

She stumbled again, this time for real. Her ankle twisted, and she fell. Asphalt bit into her shins, and she cried out at the pain.

The man swung toward her with his gun, pointing the barrel at her head. "Stop playing games."

"I'm not playing," she insisted.

"Your whole online auction wasn't a game?" he asked. "You ask for bids but reply to none of the offers?"

She'd been keeping track of the action, too, and had noticed that the seller hadn't accepted any offers. It was almost as if he'd changed his mind. Or maybe he'd realized the FBI was on to him. While Ash may have convinced himself he was her boyfriend, nobody else had bought his act…except maybe for her.

"What makes you think I'm the one selling information?" Claire asked the question she had asked Ash what seemed like so long ago. But it had only been days—days since he'd suspected her of being a traitor to her country.

"What?" the man asked. "Have you changed your mind? Is that why you replied to no offers?"

Cognizant of how close the gun was to her face, she gingerly shook her head. "I am not the one who offered that information for sale," she said. "I would never betray my country."

"Not even for a good price?" he asked.

"Not for any price. The risk is too great," she said. "Not just to the economy and the governments of several countries but personally, too. Giving up that information would cost me my freedom."

"Not giving it up will cost you your life," the man threatened, and he cocked his gun. "Now get up!"

If his employer wanted information from her, he was unlikely to kill her. But he still might shoot her. Like torture, a gunshot wound wasn't something she wanted to experience. So she struggled to her feet, but when she tried to put weight on the ankle she had wrenched, she fell again.

"Stop playing!" he yelled.

"I think I sprained my ankle," she said. Maybe. Or maybe she'd just broken the heel on her shoe. But she wasn't going to admit to that. Maybe if he thought she couldn't walk, he would just leave her in the alley.

Instead, he moved the direction of the barrel of his gun. "Get the hell up!" he yelled, his impatience—what little he possessed—gone. "Or I will shoot your damn leg."

She called him on what she hoped was a bluff and asked, "Then how will I walk wherever you're taking me?"

"I don't know how you will," he said. "But you will or I'll shoot your other leg, too."

"You don't want to do that," a familiar male voice spoke from the darkness.

Conflicting emotions overwhelmed Claire. She was relieved for herself that Ash had found her but also terrified for him. The stranger's gun was already cocked and ready to fire.

"You don't want to get involved," the man advised him.

"I am already involved."

"You're the boyfriend…" The man sighed. "Well, Ms. Molenski, looks like I'll be breaking that promise I made you." He fired before she could even scream a warning to Ash.

It was dark in the alley. The man wouldn't have been able to see Ash well. He had to be okay. And she had assurance that he was when he leaped over her and knocked the man to the ground.

Grunts and groans echoed off the walls of the brick buildings as the two men grappled in the alley. She scooted back as feet kicked out near her and a fist swung.

And a gun barrel…

"Get down!" Ash ordered her as another shot rang out.

She was already down. But she laid flat on the asphalt as more bullets and pieces of cement and mortar ricocheted off those brick walls. Shots echoed all around her as if coming from hidden stereo speakers on full volume. She wasn't sure who was shooting now. The man or Ash.

Ash had to be wearing a bulletproof vest like he'd worn one before. He had to be safe as he struggled to protect her. Why was he struggling alone?

Where was his backup?

Then she realized that the echo of shots wasn't coming just from those fired in the alley. There were shots being fired beyond the alley—out on the street.

Like Ash hadn't come alone to protect her, the stranger hadn't come alone to kidnap her. Their backup was also in a shoot-out.

If the other agents didn't prevail, Ash might have more than this one man to fight. Even as great a special agent as he was, he wouldn't be able to fight them all—not if there were as many as it sounded like there were.

It sounded like a war raged outside the alley. And another one within it.

The men continued to struggle over the firing gun. But then the clip must have emptied out, as the shooting stopped inside the alley. And then moments later the struggle stopped.

The shooting outside the alley also stopped, and an eerie silence fell. All Claire could hear now was her own heartbeat thudding heavily and quickly in her ears.

"Ash…" she called out softly.

But there was no reply from either man. So she rose to a crouch. Ignoring the pain of her already scraped legs sliding over the asphalt, she crawled over toward where the two shadows lay in the alley.

"Ash…" she called out again. "Are you okay?"

Still no reply.

She was close now, right next to those lifeless bodies. She reached out, only to put her hand on the ground, but instead of touching asphalt, her fingers sank into something warm and sticky. A pool of blood.

Chapter Fourteen

Ash struggled to regain consciousness; he had to protect Claire. Had this man's backup gotten into the alley while he was struggling with her abductor? Had one of them grabbed her?

He'd chosen to go alone into the alley and have his backup concentrate on the ends of the alley to make sure that no one could escape with Claire. Maybe he'd made the wrong choice.

He cleared his throat and called out her name. "Claire…"

"I'm here," she said. "I'm right here." And her hand touched his face. But it was wet.

"Are you bleeding?" he asked her.

"No. I think you are."

He shook his head. "No. It must be him…"

The man had stopped struggling. Ash hadn't wanted to kill him; a dead man couldn't tell him who'd hired him. And he was obviously a hired gun working for someone else. But he hadn't been working alone.

"We need to get out of here," he said. "Have you really hurt your ankle?"

"I think I just broke the heel on my shoe," she said. "I can move. Can you?"

He was still lying on the ground. The other man had

fought hard and fired so many damn shots that Ash was struggling yet to regain his breath.

"You're wearing your vest, right?" she asked, her voice cracking with concern.

"Yeah, of course..." But now that the numbness was beginning to wear off, he felt the pain. The sharp, stinging pain.

She uttered a sigh of relief.

"This guy had friends," he warned her. "You might not be safe yet."

"What? You doubted me?" Reyes asked. His voice wasn't in Ash's ear but in the alley as the other agent joined them. "I've been handling stupid thugs like that my whole life."

"You took care of them all?" Ash asked.

"A couple of the guys are on their way to the hospital," Reyes replied.

He heard the sirens now and saw the glint of flashing lights at the end of the alley.

"I don't know if they'll make it," Reyes admitted. "What about this guy?"

The guy in question grunted and moved slightly as he began to regain consciousness. He wasn't dead.

Ash should have been relieved that they would be able to question him. But he felt a pang of regret. Or maybe it was just of pain. He grimaced.

"You are hurt," Claire said, her tone accusatory over his lie but also concerned.

"I'm wearing a vest," he reminded her. But the bullets had been ricocheting off the brick walls. It was why he'd told Claire to get as low as she could. Had one of those bullets struck him somewhere the vest didn't protect?

He had recently almost lost his best friend, Blaine, when the special agent had been shot in the neck. He had nearly bled out and would have if Ash and Reyes hadn't been there. Ash moved his hand across the ground beside him; blood had pooled beneath him.

Reyes dropped to the asphalt next to him. "I think you've been hit, Ash." He touched his two-way and demanded, "Get some medics back in the alley immediately. Stryker's got a GSW."

Claire gasped. "Are you in pain?"

He hadn't been at first. He must have been in shock. But now pain radiated throughout his body, so much so that he wasn't entirely sure where he'd been hit. He tried to move, but Claire pushed him back to the ground.

"Stay still," she said. "Wait for the paramedics." Her voice rising with panic, she shrieked at Reyes, "Tell them to hurry."

He must have looked bad. She sounded more scared for him than she had sounded for herself when she'd thought she was alone in the alley with her kidnapper. From the shadows, he had listened to her talking to her abductor.

But she'd been smart. She had bought him time to get to her. Of course she'd been smart; she was a brilliant woman. And beautiful…

He wanted to tell her that, wanted to tell her how much he admired her spunk and her spirit. But footsteps pounded against the asphalt as paramedics and more agents ran down the alley to them.

Two of the paramedics dropped to the ground next to him while another paramedic and an agent turned their attention to the man Ash had injured.

A male medic flashed a light in his face and shone it over his body. "Sir, can you tell me where you've been shot?"

"I'm fine," he replied because he wasn't entirely sure. "A bullet must have just grazed me."

"You're bleeding, sir," the other paramedic said. "We need to know where it's coming from but we can't see here." They began to lift him onto a stretcher they'd carried into the alley.

"I can't go anywhere," Ash protested. He had to question the suspect even though the man wasn't fully conscious. Ash had slammed the guy's head against the asphalt until he'd dropped the gun. But it wasn't the man about whom he was really worried.

"You have to go to the hospital," Claire told him.

He gripped the sides of the stretcher, trying to lift himself off it, but he still hadn't regained his strength. "No, I can't."

"You have to," she insisted, rising up with the stretcher as the paramedics raised it. She swayed unsteadily on her feet. "They have to check you out."

"I have to protect you," he said. She'd said it was just a broken shoe heel, but he suspected she was really hurt.

"I'll do that," Reyes offered.

"I want to go with him," Claire insisted. "I can ride in the ambulance, too."

"She should ride along," Ash agreed, mostly because he didn't want to let her out of his sight again. "She should get her ankle checked." But the stretcher and the paramedics kept rolling him away. And he wasn't sure how effectively he could protect her in his present condition.

Reyes waved at him and called out, "We'll meet you at the hospital."

Ash respected Reyes as a special agent. He would trust the man with his life, but he wasn't sure he could trust anyone with Claire's life. He had nearly lost her himself; he didn't want to take any more chances with Claire.

He shouldn't have used her to lure out more buyers. He should have focused on finding the hacker who'd offered the information for sale. But that person had to be someone Claire worked with—someone she knew, someone who might also pose a threat to her life.

He finally regained his strength enough to sit up on the stretcher. But it was too late. The paramedics had lifted him into the back of the ambulance and closed the doors.

He had to trust that Reyes would protect Claire. He had to trust that he would see her again.

CLAIRE SLIPPED QUIETLY past Reyes, whose attention was on the tall blond man with whom he spoke just inside the double doors of the emergency room. Fortunately the ER doctor had exchanged her broken heels for a pair of slippers, after he'd wrapped her sprained ankle, so that she could move quietly. She didn't move painlessly, though, since every step had her flinching.

But she had to see Ash. She had to make certain that he was really okay. There had been so much blood in the alley. Some of it was still on her hand, staining her skin. She shuddered as she glanced down at it.

Reyes had assured her that Ash was invincible; that no stray bullet was going to keep him down. Sure, he'd lost a lot of blood. But the bullet wasn't even in him; it had gone through his thigh and just nicked an artery.

Nicked?

She had scoffed at the agent obviously trying to downplay a serious injury. Ash could have bled out in that alley. He could have died trying to save her.

That was why she'd left with the stranger—to protect him. But Ash had been so determined to protect her that it had nearly cost him his life. And still, even as they'd been wheeling his stretcher away, he had been worried about her safety. She had to see him, to make sure he was really okay and to show him that she was.

So she had convinced a sympathetic nurse to give her Ash's room number. After hobbling across the ER, she boarded an elevator to the tenth floor. Her painkillers must have worn off because her ankle throbbed. But she ignored the discomfort and hurried down the corridor to his room.

She could hear the deep rumble of his voice even before she pushed open the door to his room. And she breathed a sigh of relief that he sounded good, strong. Happy even...

Then she saw why he sounded so happy. He cradled a bald-headed baby in his arms while a woman with curly dark hair adjusted the pillows behind his back. Then the woman leaned over and kissed Ash's cheek before dropping a kiss on the baby's forehead.

"You really are an angel," he told her with an appreciative smile.

"I love you, too, Ash," the woman said and kissed his cheek once more.

Pain struck Claire again, but it wasn't her ankle that was throbbing now. It was her heart that hurt, clenching in her chest. She'd thought Special Agent Ash Stryker was all about his career but maybe that had just been part of his cover posing as her boyfriend.

Maybe he was really a family man with a wife and a baby. She gasped as that pain overwhelmed her, and she whirled away from the doorway to duck back into the hall before anyone saw her. But as she whirled around, she slammed into a wall of muscle so hard that she bounced off and nearly fell.

Strong hands gripped her shoulders, holding her upright. "Easy," a man's deep voice murmured.

She glanced up into eyes that were a crisp green with a gaze so intense she was certain that the man missed nothing. He was blond and broad and vaguely familiar. She realized he was the man to whom Reyes had been talking when she sneaked past him. Apparently she had only sneaked past Reyes, not him.

"Are you all right?" he asked her.

She nodded, but the pain gripping her heart hadn't lessened its hold. She flinched, which probably betrayed how she was feeling.

"The doctor said your ankle is sprained," he said. "You're supposed to stay off it, Claire."

"You know my name?" she asked. After what had happened at the piano bar, she should have known better than to trust anyone. But there was something about this man, a protectiveness that inspired trust.

"Yes, I know who you are," he said. Taking his right hand off her shoulder, he pulled a badge from beneath the neck of his shirt. "I'm Special Agent Blaine Campbell."

"Oh." So this was Ash's good friend...

She wanted to talk to this man, wanted to ask him questions, but laughter drifting from the hospital room distracted her. Who was that woman?

She hadn't asked her question aloud, but Blaine replied anyway. "That's my wife and baby in there with Ash."

The laughter grew louder, and irritation replaced her pain. She retorted, "No wonder you burned down his house."

"You've been talking to Reyes," he remarked. Even though amusement glinted in his eyes, Blaine Campbell uttered a weary-sounding sigh.

Since she hadn't actually talked that much to the man, she clarified, "I've been listening to him."

"I wouldn't recommend that," Blaine said with a sharp jerk forward as Reyes pushed him from behind.

"Hey, don't go bad-mouthing me to Ms. Molenski," the dark-haired agent said.

Blaine snorted. "*I* would never do that. Too bad you can't say the same."

"Technically Reyes was bad-mouthing you to Ash," she clarified again.

Blaine snorted again. "Ash and I go back too far for that to get you anywhere, Reyes."

The other man nodded. "Yeah, if you burning down his house didn't hurt your friendship, I guess nothing will."

"Why would you want to hurt their friendship?" she asked Reyes. Not that she believed he really wanted to, he just enjoyed teasing people, especially those he considered friends, like Ash and Agent Campbell. It was clear that he thought as much of Blaine as he did Ash.

"Because he wishes Ash was his best friend," Blaine said. "Ash was the best man at my wedding."

Claire lifted her head, listening to the laughter coming from inside Ash's room. Blaine had really had the man currently flirting with his wife stand up beside him at their wedding?

"That's because he saved your life," Reyes said. "But he didn't do that alone. I was there, too."

Blaine grunted as if just the memory of his close scrape caused him pain. "You were there that time. But Ash saved my life many more times than that during our deployments."

They had both been marines, then.

"Honey," a woman's soft voice called out as she joined them in the hall. She must have overheard them. She touched her husband's arm. She had told Ash she loved him, but that love was clearly in her warm brown eyes as she gazed up at Blaine's handsome face. "You have to talk to Ash. He was already trying to get dressed to leave, so I handed him the baby."

"He didn't freak?" Blaine asked in astonishment. "Ash would be more comfortable holding a grenade."

The woman laughed. "That's what I thought when I saw the look on his face."

He had looked pretty comfortable to Claire. But she didn't know how long he'd been holding the infant. Apparently too long because he called out from the hospital room, "Hey..." His tone was soft and stilted, as if he was gritting his teeth and trying to keep his voice low, probably so he wouldn't frighten the baby. "Someone needs to get back in here."

"You all want to go down to the cafeteria for coffee?" Reyes asked.

"We should leave him alone," Blaine agreed.

Mrs. Campbell shook her head. "Not with Drew. He'll try to take him along wherever he's so determined to go."

"To Ms. Molenski," Reyes replied.

"Ms. Molenski?" the woman asked.

"Meet Claire Molenski," her husband introduced them. "Claire, this is my wife, Maggie."

The woman reached out for her hand, taking it in both of hers. "You're Claire. He was asking about you. He's anxious to see you."

The woman spoke with no jealousy or judgment. Clearly her love for Ash was like a sister's for her brother.

"Hey!" he called out again.

"He's anxious all right," Claire agreed. "Because you left him alone with your baby."

Maggie squeezed her hand. "He really is anxious to see you, to make sure you're all right. He cares about you."

Warmth flooded Claire's heart. But she refused to let hope burgeon. Ash cared about his assignment, about flushing out more bad guys and finding the hacker. He didn't really care about her. He wasn't a potential match.

"Come on," Ash persisted from inside the room. "I didn't volunteer to babysit."

"Let's go inside," Maggie urged, but it was Claire she pressed through the doorway first.

She forced a smile and teased him. "I thought you liked babysitting. Isn't that what you've been doing with me?"

"You've been on protection duty?" Blaine asked in surprise. "You hate that. You've always hated that." He flinched as his wife's elbow struck his ribs. "But I could be wrong."

"You are," Ash said. "I'm not on protection duty. I'm undercover." He carefully held out baby Drew to his mother. "I'm posing as Claire's boyfriend while we flush out the security threats."

"Well, that's way different, then," Blaine said with a grin. "She's in danger, and you're protecting her. That's not protection duty at all."

Ash glared at him. "Why'd you come along? Afraid your wife was going to leave you for me?"

Blaine laughed, obviously confident in his wife's love and loyalty. And Claire was suddenly jealous of Maggie Campbell again, jealous that the woman had the relationship Claire wanted for herself. Maybe it was that jealousy that overwhelmed her or maybe it was just exhaustion and pain, but she swayed on her feet as dizziness overwhelmed her.

"She's falling!" Ash cried out. But his warning came too late.

She was going down, and she was unconscious before she knew if she'd been caught or if she'd hit the floor.

Chapter Fifteen

Ash had failed Claire again. First he'd let the gunman get her on and off the dance floor. And then he hadn't caught her when she'd fainted. He'd tried getting out of bed, but his injured leg had folded beneath him and he had fallen.

Fortunately Reyes had caught Claire. Then he'd carried her back to the emergency room. He'd carried her away from Ash. Maggie, with her usual concern for everyone else, had hurried after them to make sure that Claire was all right.

Ash had wanted to go to the ER, too. But Blaine had helped him back into bed instead and assured him, "Maggie will let us know how she is."

"Why would she have passed out?" Ash asked. "Was she grazed with a bullet in the alley, too?"

"She just sprained her ankle," Blaine said. "But she shouldn't have been walking on it without crutches. The pain probably got to her."

"Why?"

"She's not a marine or an agent," Blaine said. "She's not used to withstanding pain."

"No," Ash said. "I mean why did she walk without crutches? Why didn't she stay in bed and rest?"

Blaine laughed.

"What?" He glared at his friend's amusement. "What's so damn funny?"

"For such a smart, observant guy, you're being pretty oblivious," Blaine said.

He still had no idea what his friend was talking about, but now he just shrugged.

And Blaine laughed again. "You really don't get it?" Then his smile slid away, and sadness darkened his eyes. "I forget that you're not used to it."

"Used to what?" Ash asked, wondering what had made his friend sad. Since he'd married Maggie, he'd been pretty disgustingly happy.

But Blaine didn't seem sad for himself. He seemed sad for Ash. He replied, "You're not used to people caring about you."

Blaine was one of the few people who knew Ash's parents hadn't given a damn about him. They would have blown him up with all those other innocent people if an FBI agent—if Uncle George—hadn't rescued him just in the nick of time.

"You think Claire Molenski cares about me?" He laughed now, knowing how much he infuriated the woman. "I accused her of treason. I've used her as bait to lure out potential terrorists. She hates my guts."

And he couldn't blame her. Had someone treated him the way he had treated her, he wouldn't have cared for the person, either. He would have resented and hated him, but his heart clenched with pain at the thought of her hating him.

"Sure," Blaine said as if humoring him. "That's why she put herself through pain to get up here to see you, to make sure that you were all right, because she hates your guts."

Could she actually care about him? Refusing to even

hope it was true, he shook his head in denial. "She probably was just telling me that she was going home."

To her apartment. To her life.

"It's too dangerous," Blaine protested.

"Of course it is," Ash said. "But that's my fault."

Blaine shook his head. "You're not the one putting her in danger."

"Yes, I am," he said as guilt overwhelmed him. "I could have let her post online that there is no way around the government firewalls, that she'd made certain there wasn't. But then I wouldn't be able to catch everyone willing to buy the information that would get them around those firewalls."

"So that's how you're using her as bait to flush out would-be terrorists?" Blaine sounded appalled.

But then he was the quintessential knight in shining armor. He always had to play hero to every damsel in distress.

Ash was the one who'd put this particular damsel in distress. But Claire had proven she wasn't helpless. She was smart, and she was strong. Or so he'd thought until she'd nearly collapsed onto the floor of his hospital room. Everyone had his or her limit. Claire must have reached hers.

"It was a mistake," Ash admitted.

Blaine sighed. "I understand what you were trying to do. You're always looking for the greater good. Sacrifice one life to save many…"

It was something Ash had had to do as a marine and as a special agent in the antiterrorism division. But he couldn't do it now, not when that one life was Claire's.

"It was a mistake," he repeated.

"You had a solid plan," Blaine said. "You were protecting her."

Panic flashed through him again as he remembered how quickly and easily he had nearly lost her. "I didn't do a very damn good job."

"She's not the one with a bullet hole in her leg," Blaine said.

"Reyes would claim that I got distracted."

Blaine snorted. "Like me?"

Ash couldn't deny that Claire distracted and captivated him. "Reyes likes talking smack."

"Are you sure that acting like her boyfriend is just a cover for you?" Blaine asked.

Ash nodded. "Of course. I made contact with her at a speed dating event. The cover as her boyfriend makes the most sense. It was the most believable." Even to him.

When he'd danced with her at the romantic little piano bar, he had felt like a man dancing with his girlfriend. Or as poor Edith had misinterpreted, his wife. She hadn't been wrong about Claire being scared and in danger, though. Once the shooting had begun, her husband must have realized that she hadn't overreacted at all. And that he hadn't reacted enough.

"I know how you go undercover," Blaine said. They had been assigned to different divisions over their careers, but occasionally they had worked together. And they had known each other too long.

Ash sighed in resignation; he couldn't deny whatever his friend was about to say.

Blaine continued, "You're all in."

He couldn't deny that was how he went undercover.

"So don't go thinking it's real," Blaine advised him, "unless…"

He wasn't sure he wanted to hear this, but he respected Blaine and respected his opinion. So he asked, "Unless?"

"Unless you want it to be."

Ash's heart slammed against his ribs as it began to pound fast and furiously. He forced a laugh, albeit a nervous one. He was calmer when people were shooting at him than being put on the spot about his feelings. He laughed harder. "Don't be ridiculous."

"I'm serious," Blaine said. "I saw your face when she collapsed. You care about her."

He couldn't deny that. "She's my responsibility. I'm the one who put her in danger. So of course I want to make sure she's all right."

Blaine narrowed his eyes as if considering whether Ash was speaking the truth or lying.

Maybe he was lying. To himself...

"I'm not like you," Ash insisted. "I'm not meant to be anyone's husband or, God forbid, father."

"I used to think that, too."

"But we all knew you were wrong about it," Ash said. "We all knew you would be a family man someday. You're too much of the protector. You need someone to protect—a wife, a child. I don't need anyone."

Blaine expressed his doubt with an arched brow.

"I don't need anyone," Ash repeated. "I never have and I never will." Maybe if he kept telling himself that, he would believe it.

CLAIRE HAD LEARNED her lesson about eavesdropping. While Reyes had been helping Maggie extricate herself from a group of nurses oohing over the baby, Claire had rolled her wheelchair down the hall to Ash's room. She had heard the end of his conversation with his friend.

And when Blaine Campbell had turned around and caught her, he hadn't been surprised to see her. He'd known she was there and had wanted her to hear, probably so she wouldn't fall in love with Ash and be hurt when he couldn't return her feelings. Special Agent Campbell really was the protector everyone thought he was. The only problem was that his protection had come too late. When Ash had been injured in the alley, Claire had been forced to admit she was starting to have feelings for him.

But now she had proof—his own words—that she was nothing to him and would never be.

"You've got to stop sneaking away from me," Reyes admonished her as he pushed her the last few feet through the doorway into Ash's room.

"Maybe if you hadn't been flirting with those nurses, you wouldn't have lost her," Maggie said as she joined them.

"I was protecting your baby from being fawned all over," Reyes said.

"By offering yourself up to be fawned over?" the dark-haired woman scoffed.

He grinned. "Hey, it would've worked if your kid wasn't so damn cute."

"The baby is adorable," Claire agreed. She'd thought she only needed someone with whom to share her life—a man who shared her interests and her passions. But now she realized she wanted it all. She wanted what Maggie Campbell had—the man and the child. She wanted a family.

But she knew without a doubt now that Ash wouldn't meet any of her needs.

"How are you?" he asked her.

"Fine," she replied even though she felt completely empty inside with her hope gone. But she forced a smile and added, "Now that I'm off my ankle. How's your leg?"

"Not bad, except for the hole. Guess we won't be going dancing for a while," Ash said.

She doubted that they would ever go dancing again.

"But it'll be fine," he added, as if trying to reassure her.

He was a freaking legend—if she believed Reyes. So of course he would be fine. She would be fine, too, when she got over the stupid crush she'd developed on the FBI agent who had only been doing his job.

"Your leg is not going to heal overnight," Reyes cautioned him. "You're going to have to take it easy."

Ash shook his head. "I can't."

"You have no choice."

He stared hard at Reyes and asked, "What are you telling me?"

"Agent in charge assigned someone else to protect Ms. Molenski."

Anger glinted in Ash's blue eyes as he said, "I'm the agent in charge of this assignment."

"The agent in charge of the Bureau," Reyes clarified. "Chief Special Agent Lynch assigned someone else to protection duty."

Ash glared at him now. "Let me guess. You?"

Reyes shook his head. "I don't do protection duty, either." He pointed toward Ash lying in the hospital bed. "I wouldn't want to get distracted and wind up with a bullet in my leg." He glanced over at Blaine and the man's wife and baby and he moved his body in an exaggerated shudder of revulsion. "Or a family…"

Instead of taking offense, Blaine and Maggie laughed. And Maggie told him, "You're going to change your mind one day."

He shook his head. "Never going to happen."

"Never say never," Blaine warned him.

He hadn't offered Ash the same warning, probably because he knew Ash so well that he knew the man was unlikely to change his mind.

"Who's going to protect Claire?" Ash wanted to know.

"The chief assigned a female agent," Reyes said. "He must've thought Ms. Molenski is so beautiful that she would distract any man."

Claire laughed at Reyes's outrageous flirting. "You're crazy."

"Yes," Blaine agreed. "So it's a good thing he wasn't assigned your protection duty."

"He shouldn't have assigned anyone else," Ash said, his voice gruff with resentment.

"It's a good thing," Reyes said. "Neither of you are in any condition to outrun hired thugs right now. And the agent he's assigning is really good. But she won't be the only one. There'll be backup, too."

But there wouldn't be Ash. After overhearing what she had, she should have been relieved. Instead she was disappointed that she would have no excuse to see him anymore. But not seeing him might make it easier for her to get over her crush.

"I'd like a minute alone with Claire," Ash told his friends.

"Sure," Reyes said. "Say your goodbyes and I'll bring Ms. Molenski to her new safe house."

Another place. Another agent. Claire felt nothing but resignation now. Her life had been turned upside down, but this time it had been through no fault of her own.

He waited until it was just the two of them before he spoke. "I'm sorry."

Had he realized that she'd overheard him telling his friend that he didn't need anybody and never would?

"For what?" she asked.

"For putting you in danger."

"You're not the one who offered that information up

for sale," she said. That was the person who'd put her in danger—somebody she apparently knew.

"But I took advantage of the situation," he said. "I took advantage of you."

He hadn't but she almost wished that he had—that she had more memories of them than just their kissing and their dancing. But if they had made love, she would have fallen completely and probably irrevocably in love with him.

"You saved my life," she reminded him. "I'm fine."

"Put up the posting that you initially wanted to," he urged her. "Make sure that nobody thinks you're the one who offered that information."

She shrugged. "Does it matter?" she wondered. "People will think what they will. I am the hacker who managed to get around all those firewalls."

"But you fixed the security problems," he said.

She appreciated that he believed her. "I hope I did. But there might be a better hacker who found a new way around those firewalls."

She'd been too proud and maybe too arrogant to consider that when he had suggested it before. But she had to admit that it was an actual possibility. There were always new hackers with new methods. She worked with quite a few.

"Don't worry about that," he said. "Just concentrate on staying safe."

"We both know that I won't be safe until the person who really offered that information for sale is caught," she said. Since she probably worked with that person, she should be able to figure out who it was.

"Don't," Ash said as if he'd read her mind. "Don't try to investigate on your own."

"I won't be alone," she said. "I'll have protection."

But she wouldn't have him. She worried that no one could keep her as safe as Ash had. But while he'd protected her life, he had endangered her heart. Without him, her heart might be safe. But what about her life?

Chapter Sixteen

A week had passed without another attempt on Claire's life. Ash should have been relieved, especially since he had been laid up in the hospital most of that week. His leg was healed now, at least well enough that he could walk with only a limp and a twinge or more of pain.

"I can get back to the assignment," Ash told the Bureau chief. He had requested this meeting in the man's office in Chicago. Unfortunately the chief had called in Dalton Reyes and Blaine, too.

He wasn't sure who they were supposed to back up. Him or the chief. Since they were supposed to be his friends, he hoped it was him.

"From what I gather, you haven't left it," Chief Special Agent Lynch remarked.

Ash glanced at his friends or the men he'd thought were his friends. What had they told his boss?

"You've been working leads—" his boss reminded him of the reports Ash had been giving him "—trying to track down more buyers and the potential seller of the national security information."

"I've been working from a laptop," Ash clarified, which had frustrated the hell out of him. He'd wanted another meeting with Peter Nowak to see if the former CIA agent was really as above suspicion as the rest of the world seemed to think. He'd also wanted to talk to Leslie Morrison. But most of all he'd wanted to see Claire to make sure that she was healed and healthy and happy. "But the doctor has cleared me to return to fieldwork."

The chief glanced at the letter Ash had given him from his doctor. "Was that in another letter?" he asked. "Because I'm not reading that in this one. I'm reading that you're not completely healed and that you can only return to restricted duty."

"I can return to full duty," Ash insisted. "The restrictions are just a recommendation and totally unnecessary. I'm fully recovered."

"Do you want to return to full duty?" Chief Lynch asked. "Or do you want to return to Claire Molenski?"

Now he glared at the other agents; they had betrayed his friendship if they had told their boss that he had feelings for Claire. But just the mention of her name had his heart rate quickening. "She's in danger."

"Is she?" Reyes asked. "It's been a week with no other attempts to abduct her."

That could have been because Claire had posted that she had no way to bypass government or bank firewalls— if she had actually posted as much. Ash hadn't found any such post, though. Was that because she thought people wouldn't believe it? Or because she'd wanted to continue flushing out terrorists and other radicals?

"She's barely left her office, though," Ash pointed out. "And with the increased security at the consultation company, it would be hard for anyone to abduct her from there."

The chief raised a brow. "And how do you know her whereabouts of the past week?"

"I've stayed involved in the assignment," he admitted what the chief already knew.

Lynch glanced at Reyes and Blaine, his dark eyes narrowed with suspicion. Maybe that was why he'd called them into the meeting. Not because of what they'd told Lynch but because of what they'd told Ash. They had kept eyes on Claire, making sure for him that she truly was safe.

"Why?" the chief asked.

"Because it's my job," Ash explained, "to find who the real risk to national security is. I need to get back out in the field."

"Back out in the field or back to Claire Molenski?" Lynch asked.

He had to see Claire. A week without seeing her beautiful face, without hearing her snarky comments had seemed like never-ending emptiness.

"Claire works with whoever the real risk is," Ash said. "And I've established a cover as her boyfriend. I can resume that undercover assignment."

"You're not in physical condition for protection duty," the chief said as he tapped a fingertip against the doctor's letter.

"I don't do protection duty," Ash said. "I'm undercover. And I'll have backup." He glanced to his friends again.

"They're not in your division," the chief pointed out.

"You're the one who invited them to this meeting," Ash said.

The chief sighed. "A case like this does involve organized crime and bank security. That's why Reyes has already been working it and why Special Agent Campbell should be working it, too."

"I should be working it again, too," Ash insisted.

Lynch chuckled now with amusement. "You sound

like a wounded athlete trying to get back on the court too early." And he was the coach, refusing to let him play.

"It's not too early," Ash said. In fact, he hoped it wasn't too late. There might not have been another abduction attempt in the past week but that didn't mean that one wasn't in the planning stages. Or that the real hacker hadn't decided to stop Claire from finding out his identity.

Because Ash had no doubt that she was trying to find out who it was—that was why she was spending so much time at the office. She hadn't even come to the hospital to see him again, hadn't called. She hadn't even taken his calls when he'd checked in with the agent assigned her protection duty now.

Lynch sighed. "You're a good agent, Stryker, so I'm trusting you to know your limitations."

He knew his limitations. That was how he knew he wasn't the man for whom Claire had been looking at the speed dating event. She needed a man who wanted to be a boyfriend, who wanted to someday be a husband and a father. He'd seen the way she'd looked at Blaine's baby—with longing. She wanted a baby. She wanted a family.

Ash couldn't give her anything she needed besides his protection. And truthfully, he wasn't sure how capable he was of that since he wasn't one hundred percent physically.

"Don't overdo it," Lynch advised him, "and put yourself or an asset like Ms. Molenski in danger."

"I'll be fine," Ash assured him. And he tried to conceal his limp as he walked out of the man's office.

Blaine and Reyes followed him, Reyes grinning as he caught his flinch. "You're fine, my ass," he murmured.

"I've been hurt worse than this before," Ash said and looked to Blaine for confirmation.

"Physically, yeah," Blaine agreed.

"What else is there?" Reyes asked with the oblivion of a man who'd never had an emotional loss.

But Ash's loss had been a long time ago. So he doubted that was what his friend was talking about now. He raised a brow in silent question.

"Claire may not want to see you again," Blaine warned him.

Panic clutched Ash's heart. "Why not?"

"She was there," he said, "when you were talking about how you never needed anyone and never would."

"Why would she care that he was talking smack?" Reyes asked.

"Because she cares about Ash," Blaine said.

Ash shook his head in doubt. If she cared, why hadn't she checked with him to see how he was doing, if his gunshot wound was healing?

"Claire was only playing along as part of the cover," Ash said. And because she'd wanted dating experience so that she could find someone who was an actual match for her.

It wasn't him. They both knew it.

But Ash couldn't forget how well they'd danced together, how perfectly she had fit in his arms. He couldn't forget kissing her, either, the silkiness and the warmth of her lips beneath his.

But he wasn't her boyfriend. He wasn't even her bodyguard. He was just an FBI agent who wanted to make sure she was safe. But he had a sick feeling, an eerie sense of foreboding that she wasn't safe, that she needed him...

So he headed straight to her office. But nobody sat behind her glass walls. The lights and her computers were off. She'd obviously spent a lot of time there though, because take-out containers overflowed her trash can. They'd fallen on the floor.

But the only thing on her desk besides her monitors was the snow globe her father had given her. It glittered slightly in the light shining in from the hall.

"She's gone," a deep voice informed him.

Ash turned toward Peter Nowak and asked, "Did she quit?" He'd met the man a couple of times over the years, most recently when he'd begun investigating the threat. Of course the Bureau chief had been present then, so Ash hadn't been able to ask him the questions he'd wanted to ask him.

The silver-haired man laughed. "No. She just left early today." He lowered his voice. "With her security detail. She's fine."

"Is she?" Ash wondered. "She's nearly been kidnapped a few times. She's been hurt."

Nowak glanced down at Ash's leg. "You, too. But that's part of the job."

He would know. It was an injury that had taken the former CIA agent out of the field.

"It's part of my job," Ash agreed. "It shouldn't be part of hers."

Nowak sighed. "I never intended to put her in danger."

Ash tensed. Was the man making an admission of guilt? Was he the one selling out?

The older man pressed a hand against his suit jacket, over his heart, as if wounded by the suspicion on Ash's face. "Because I gave her the highest clearance. That's all I meant about putting her in danger."

"But she doesn't have the highest clearance," Ash noted. "You do."

Nowak glared, angry now instead of offended. "You

don't want to make an enemy of me, Agent Stryker," he warned him. "I have far more friends in the Bureau than you do."

Was that how he'd been eliminated so quickly as a suspect? Because of his friends?

"I'm not the one who should be worried about my career," Ash said. "You're the one whose company and reputation is at stake right now."

"Exactly," Nowak pointed out. "I wouldn't have risked either. Someone else is behind this, but you're so busy suspecting the wrong people that you haven't found the right suspect." The first time they'd met, the man had defended Claire, had said that Ash was wrong about her.

He'd been right then. And he was right now about Ash being worried. He wasn't worried about his career, though. He was worried about Claire. Maybe she'd left early because she had found the right suspect.

He had to find her before she put herself in more danger than she already was.

CLAIRE HAD SPENT the past week at the office. But no matter how much she'd thrown herself into her work, she hadn't gotten any closer to finding who was behind the information auction.

Nor had she forgotten about Ash…

She had wanted to call him. Or at least take his calls when he'd checked in with the agent protecting her. But she hadn't trusted herself not to betray her feelings for him.

Agent Sally Burnham already suspected that Claire had a crush on her former protector. Mostly because she had one on Agent Stryker herself. When they'd first met, the woman had expressed jealousy over his posing as Claire's boyfriend.

"I wish he was mine," the woman had dreamily commented.

Claire had shared that wish, but she'd only admitted it to herself. Then she'd focused on work. That hadn't been possible today, though, because Martin hadn't showed up.

Martin always showed up. He never called in sick. No matter how hungover or sleep deprived, the young man had never missed a day. Nor had he ever failed to answer his cell when Claire texted or called.

He hadn't come in today, not even late. And he hadn't answered any of her texts or calls. So she had convinced Agent Burnham to bring her by Martin's apartment.

"This might not have been a good idea," Burnham admitted as she peered around the run-down neighborhood. She reached under her jacket, probably for her weapon, but she didn't pull it out.

Apparently Nowak Computer Consulting didn't pay assistants that well if the dilapidated apartment complex was all Martin had been able to afford. Sirens wailed but didn't drown out the loud music and the shouting emanating from several apartments as Claire and Agent Burnham walked down the dirty hallway to Martin's unit. Technically, Burnham walked slowly while Claire limped. Her ankle was healing since she had spent most of the past week with it propped up on a chair.

It was starting to hurt now and she had to be careful to not twist it again on the stuff strewn around the hallway. Empty beer cans, liquor bottles and fast-food bags lined the floor like breadcrumbs leading them farther down the hall.

"We have to check on him," Claire insisted. "Martin sometimes drinks too much."

Maybe he'd gotten alcohol poisoning. Or had been robbed since his neighborhood wasn't the safest.

Her worry increasing, she hurried down to the door of his apartment and lifted her hand to knock. But Agent Burnham caught her wrist and stopped her.

The dark-haired woman had drawn her weapon now, and she held it tightly in her other hand. "We have backup coming," she said. "We should wait."

But the same uneasy feeling that had compelled Claire to check up on her assistant made her reluctant to wait a moment longer. What if he was incapacitated inside and needed help?

She couldn't worry about her safety when another person—a person she knew and cared about—possibly needed her. She tugged her wrist free of the other woman's grasp and pounded her knuckles against the door.

The force of her knock had the door creaking open; it wasn't locked. It hadn't even been shut tightly. She couldn't imagine anyone leaving their doors open in this apartment building in this area of the city. Martin was sometimes distracted and out of it, at least when he was hungover. But she couldn't imagine that he would have forgotten to shut or lock his door.

Then she noticed the splintered wood around the door. The jamb was broken. That was why the door wasn't shutting. Someone had either pried it open or kicked it open in their haste to get inside.

"Martin!" she called out, raising her voice above the din of the music and the shouting.

If there was a reply, she couldn't hear it, so she rushed inside the apartment. It was far messier than hers had ever been—furniture overturned, the stuffing from the cushions fluttering about the room like the snow in her globe.

"Martin, are you okay?" she shouted as she stumbled over the broken furniture.

He wasn't. He lay in a pool of blood on the floor, staring up at her through dead eyes. A scream tore from her throat.

Chapter Seventeen

Despite the loud music and the shouting and the sirens, Ash heard Claire's scream. The volume of it cut through the noise; the terror of it cut through his heart. Ignoring the pain radiating from his leg, he ran toward her.

Ignoring the gun that swung toward him as he burst through the doorway, he rushed past the female agent, holstered his gun and grabbed Claire's trembling shoulders.

"Are you all right?" he anxiously asked her.

She shook her head.

"Where are you hurt?" And why the hell hadn't the agent protected her?

"I'm not the one who's hurt," she said as she pointed a shaking hand toward the floor.

And Ash tore his attention from her to focus on the dead man. "Your assistant…"

The man was obviously dead, his eyes open wide in shock and unseeing in death. Blood stained his bleached blond hair. And his face was a swollen mess of fresh bruises. His fingers had also been broken, and his arms and legs were at odd angles from his torso. He had been tortured.

Claire had to know that Martin was more than hurt;

he was gone. Dead. She trembled while tears streamed down her face.

Ash turned toward the female agent again. "Why did you bring her here?"

"When he didn't show up for work or answer her calls, she insisted on coming here," Agent Burnham said.

"You're supposed to be protecting her," Ash admonished the woman. "Instead, you bring her to a murder scene…" One of the most gruesome he'd ever seen. He shuddered at the pain the young man must have endured.

"I insisted," Claire defended the woman. "If she hadn't brought me, I would've come alone." She was still shaking in shock, but she was also bristling with anger and the feistiness he knew and…

He couldn't even think the word. He wouldn't let himself.

"I'm not in FBI custody," she continued. "You can't stop me from going where I want to."

So she could have seen Ash—if she'd wanted. She hadn't wanted to be with him. Instead she had wanted to come here.

"It's too dangerous," he pointed out. Especially in this part of the city.

He had nearly lost it when he'd heard the address where Agent Burnham had brought her. This wasn't an area of the city where anyone should visit, let alone live.

But Martin didn't live anymore.

"What happened?" he asked Burnham.

"We found him that way," the female agent replied.

Actually it looked like Claire had found him that way; she'd entered the apartment first. He wasn't impressed with Agent Burnham's protection duty.

"Did you even check the apartment?" he asked. "To make sure that the killer isn't still here?"

The woman's face reddened with embarrassment, and she finally moved away from the door. But the studio apartment was small. A killer could have only been hiding in the bathroom, and she checked that quickly.

"It's clear," she announced with a shaky sigh of relief.

"Have you called it in?" he asked.

Her face reddened some more, and she hurried into the hall, reaching for her radio.

"It's too late to help him," Claire murmured. She must have mistakenly thought that Ash wanted Burnham to call an ambulance. "I should have come sooner. I should have come when he didn't answer my texts asking why he was late."

And walked in while Martin was being tortured? He shuddered at the thought of what could have happened to her. That *this* could have happened to her, as well. She could have been tortured and killed.

Ash leaned down and felt Martin's skin. He was ice-cold. He shook his head. "I suspect he's been dead for a while," he said. "Maybe since last night. You couldn't have saved him."

Instead of bringing her comfort, his words brought her more tears. They streaked down her face as sobs slipped from her lips. Seeing her in so much pain brought him pain, too. He closed his arms around her and pulled her trembling body against his.

She wrapped her arms around his neck and clung to him. She was scared and upset and only seeking comfort. He knew that her clinging to him wasn't personal; it wasn't like she'd missed him.

Like he had missed her…

He hugged her more tightly and silently thanked God that it wasn't her he'd found dead on the floor. He didn't care what the doctor had recommended. He was going to be the one to keep her safe even if it cost him his life.

CLAIRE'S HEART KEPT pounding erratically. Maybe it was from finding Martin's body. Maybe it was from being with Ash again. He had dismissed Agent Burnham and had brought her home, or at least to the hotel he called home.

He'd settled onto the couch beside her, with his arms encircling her as if he needed to hold her together.

She had felt as though she was falling apart—until he'd pulled her into his arms. Then she'd been able to hang on to him while her world spun out of control.

"My dad and Pam are safe?" she asked. She knew it wasn't the first time she had asked him, but she desperately needed to know.

"Yes," Ash assured her again. "I checked with their security detail, and there have been no threats to their safety. They're going about their honeymoon completely unaware that anyone is even watching them."

She should have been relieved that their lives hadn't been disrupted. But she wasn't entirely convinced that they were really safe—that anyone was really safe right now.

"I didn't know there was any threat to Martin's safety," she murmured miserably. If only she'd known…

"You could talk to your dad and stepmom," Ash offered. "Then you might feel better—"

"No." She shook her head. "No. Someone might trace the call. I couldn't risk it." She couldn't risk their lives any more than she might have already.

"I can make sure that the call isn't traced," he offered.

She considered it for a minute but then shook her head again. "No, my dad would be able to tell that something's wrong." They had always been so close that he would pick up on her fear and sadness. "He would worry, maybe even cut their honeymoon short. I can't do that to them."

"They deserve to be happy," Ash murmured, repeating back words she'd uttered to him what seemed so long ago. "You do, too, Claire."

Tears stung her eyes and her nose. She blinked to fight them back. She had already cried so much all over Ash that his shirt was probably soaked with her tears. But she wanted to cry again because she had no right to happiness. Not now. "No, I don't."

His arms tightened around her as if he sensed she was about to fall apart again. "This wasn't your fault."

"Martin is—was my assistant," she said. "They used him to get to me." She would have closed her eyes to hold in those threatening tears, but then she would see his body again—his poor, brutalized body. He had been tortured like Ash had warned she would be tortured if he hadn't saved her from every single attempt to abduct her.

A horrible thought occurred to her. "What if someone really believes you're my boyfriend?"

"I hope they believe that I am," he said. "Or I've gotten really bad at going undercover."

She shouldn't have agreed to his going undercover as her boyfriend again. She shouldn't have left Martin's apartment with Ash; someone could have seen them. And if someone had, they would assume that they were together. She'd been leaning so heavily on him and not just because her ankle was still sore even though the swelling had gone down.

"But they could use you…like that…" She shuddered as she imagined Ash's handsome face battered and bruised like Martin's had been. "To get to me."

"Don't worry about me," he told her.

As if she could shut off her feelings and concerns so easily.

"You've already been shot trying to save me from a kidnapping attempt," she reminded him and herself of that horror of crawling over to him in the alley and finding him bleeding. "I can't *not* worry about you."

"Then why didn't you come see me again?" he asked. "I was in the hospital a few more days, but you stayed away."

She'd had to force herself to do that. And to do that, she'd forced herself to remember his words—that he had never needed anyone and never would.

"You didn't need me there..."

He groaned. "You overheard me talking to Blaine. He just told me today that he saw you."

Heat rushed to her face. "Eavesdropping. I shouldn't have, but it wasn't like you were saying anything that I didn't already know. I understand that you're just doing your job. And I also understand how much that means to you."

"I'm not just doing my job this time," he said. "I care about you."

Her heart lurched with hope and something else— something she couldn't admit to feeling, even to herself. "I care about you, too," she said. "That's why I don't want you getting hurt again because of me."

"I wasn't hurt because of you and neither was Martin," he said. "I was hurt because of whoever is trying to sell out national security."

"You could be tortured because of that, too," she warned him.

He shrugged. "It wouldn't be the first time. I'm not easy to torture."

The man was a legend. Reyes had already told her

that, but now she believed it herself. "But I don't want to see you like that."

She reached out and slid her palm along his cheek. Light stubble tickled her skin. She shivered in reaction as desire overwhelmed her.

He lowered his head and touched his mouth to hers. But before she could kiss him back, he pulled away. "I'm sorry. You're vulnerable right now."

She had always been vulnerable with him. Before she'd even known who and what he was, he had unsettled her. "This is what I want," she said.

"This?"

"You…" But she couldn't blame him if he didn't want her back. After all the tears she'd wept, her face was probably all swollen and blotchy. How could he want her?

He didn't lower his head to hers again. Instead his arms tightened and he lifted her. Swinging her up, he carried her to the bedroom.

Worried that he was going to lay her down and leave her, she clung to him and pulled him down with her. But he didn't protest. Instead, he kissed her now—passionately. His mouth consumed hers, his lips moving over hers, his tongue dipping inside to taste her.

To devour her.

When he lifted his head again, she panted for breath while her lungs and her heart ached. He levered himself up, and she worried that a kiss was all he was giving her. Again.

But then he pulled off his shirt, along with his holster and his vest. She skimmed her hands over his naked chest, loving every ripple of muscle and soft, dark hair. Then she reached for his belt, pulling it free so that she could lower his zipper.

He groaned.

Then he was undressing her, pulling off her sweater and her jeans and her underwear until she lay naked beneath him. He kissed her again. Her neck, her shoulder, the curve of her breast. His lips closed over a nipple and gently tugged.

She moaned as sensations chased through her body, straight to her core. She ached there, too, for him. "Ash…"

As if he knew, he touched her there. His fingertips teased her while he continued to kiss her breasts and then her lips again.

"Please," she murmured against his mouth as she reached for him. When she closed her hand over his erection, he groaned. "Make love to me," she urged him.

He kept teasing her with his fingers until she squirmed beneath him. And that ache eased slightly as he pleased her. But it wasn't enough. She wanted more. She wanted him—all of him.

She knew she could never have that emotionally, but maybe she could physically. He thrust inside her, building that pressure again with each deliberate stroke. While he moved inside her, he kissed her, their tongues softly caressing each other as their bodies joined in ecstasy.

He was so deep inside her that she felt as if he was part of her—the core of who and what she was. She wrapped her legs around his waist, arching up to meet each thrust. Just as they had on the dance floor, they moved in perfect unison in the bedroom.

After a few more strokes, they reached release together. Claire cried out as the pleasure overwhelmed her. Ash shuddered and then flinched. As he dropped onto his side next to her, she caught sight of the bandage on his thigh. He was not fully recovered from the gunshot wound.

Who had taken advantage of whom?

"I'm sorry," she murmured. Sorry that he'd been hurt. And sorry that he wasn't really her boyfriend.

She was the sorriest that she had already fallen in love with him.

Chapter Eighteen

"I'm the one who should be sorry," Ash said. "I crossed the line."

And despite all the times he had gone undercover before, Ash had never crossed that line. He had always acted professionally even when he'd been acting like a terrorist or a member of a gang or militia.

But for the first time in his career, he had been distracted from his assignment. He had never been distracted in the way that Claire Molenski distracted him.

His gun was on the floor. What if someone had followed them here from her assistant's apartment? Would he have had the presence of mind to hear someone breaking into the hotel suite? Would he have been able to reach his weapon in time to defend her?

"I just about begged you to cross that line," she said, and her face flushed red with embarrassment.

Or passion…

She was such a passionate woman. She had reacted to his every touch so much so that he wanted to touch her again. But she reached out first.

Her fingers trailed over his thigh, along the edge of his bandage. "I forgot that you're still recovering."

"I'm recovered," he assured her, and he wasn't just

talking about his leg as another part of his anatomy reacted to her touch.

She sucked in an audible breath of surprise. "Is that possible?"

"Apparently so..." He had never wanted anyone again as quickly, but maybe that was because he had never wanted anyone as much as he did Claire.

Her fingers trailed up his thigh to his manhood. He gritted his teeth, but still a groan slipped out. Her fingertips skimmed over him, teasing him.

"Claire..."

"You don't want to make love to me again?" she asked, and she actually fluttered her lashes at him. He'd seen Claire sassy and scared; he'd never seen her flirting. The woman was dangerous. So very dangerous to him...

His heart shifted in his chest, lurching as it swelled with emotion. But he refused to give a name to all those surging emotions. He would only recognize and act on the passion as he made love to her again.

He made love to her thoroughly, kissing her lips and every inch of her silky skin. She writhed beneath him, arching her hips, begging for more.

She forgot his injury again. She forgot her pain and loss. Maybe she was just using him to forget that she'd lost a friend. Ash didn't care.

He would do whatever he could to ease her pain. So he gave her pleasure instead, loving her over and over... until her tears began to fall again. He tensed, but it was too late—his pleasure came—overpowering him so much that he felt close to tears himself.

He was overwhelmed and humbled. And all he could do was hold her close as she sobbed onto his chest.

THE NEXT FEW days passed in a blur of emotion and regret and loss. Claire had spent enough time in the hotel suite—enough time in Ash's arms—crying, making love, falling in love…

Or she had probably fallen in love earlier before they had even made love. Maybe it had happened on the dance floor. Or in the alley.

But it didn't really matter *when* she'd fallen. It didn't even matter *that* she had fallen—because nothing would ever come of her feelings. While Ash had made love with her, he wasn't in love with her.

She doubted that he was even capable of falling in love since he was so convinced that he had never needed and would never need anyone. All he wanted was his career.

Not a wife or family. Not even a real girlfriend…

While she loved Ash Stryker, she knew he wasn't the man for her—not the man with whom she could spend her life. She would never have with him what her father had with Pam. Or Leslie had with Ed.

And she wanted it all.

At the moment none of that mattered, though. She cared about nothing but paying her respects. So she stepped out of the bedroom in a black dress.

Ash glanced up from his computer and his body tensed as he studied what she was wearing. "Where do you think you're going?" he asked.

She tensed then. "This isn't any dancing dress," she pointed out. "So I think you know…"

He shook his head. "You can't."

"I can't *not* go," she said.

"It's too dangerous."

That was what he'd said every time she had attempted to leave the apartment over the past few days. It was too dangerous.

And after seeing Martin's battered body, she hadn't argued with him. She had even ordered her black dress online since she hadn't wanted to go out to buy it. But she had every intention of going out to wear it.

"I don't care how dangerous it is," she said. "I have to do this."

"Why?"

"I need to pay my respects," she said.

But she wasn't even certain who she would pay them to; she didn't know if her assistant had any family. He hadn't talked about his parents or siblings. He had mentioned friends, ones he'd partied with. But she really needed to pay her respects to Martin himself.

"This isn't about respect," Ash said. "It's about regret. You blame yourself for what happened to Martin."

She couldn't deny that.

"What if I do?" she asked. "It makes no difference in this situation. I still need to go to the funeral." Actually, she needed to go even more because she felt so responsible for what the poor kid had endured. It was bad enough that he'd died, but how he'd died...

She shuddered at the horrific memories.

Ash shook his head again in refusal. He had apparently forgotten that she didn't need his permission. She wasn't in his custody, only his protection.

"Martin was my friend," she said. But maybe that was stretching it.

Ash called her on that exaggeration. "Did you hang out at his apartment? Did you go to the bars he went to?"

She said nothing and just glared at him.

"Did you have him over to your apartment?" he asked. "For dinner? To watch a movie?"

"I didn't have to go out with him," she said. "We were work friends. I saw him every day for the past three years." That was more than she'd seen anyone else, even her father.

Ash sighed. "Just because you worked with the man doesn't make you friends."

She laughed at his hypocrisy. "So you're not friends with Agent Campbell and Agent Reyes?"

"I am," he said. "But Blaine and I knew each other longer before we worked for the Bureau. And Reyes and I have a lot in common."

She hadn't known Martin well enough to know if they'd had anything in common. "It doesn't matter if we were real friends or not." After she'd been busted for hacking, she had been too busy to keep old friends or to make new ones. "He was my assistant and I'm going to his funeral."

Ash sighed in resignation as he put aside his laptop and stood up. He only flinched a little as he put weight on his wounded leg. Like her sprained ankle, it was healing quickly.

"This is a bad idea," he warned her.

Maybe it was.

"You're wearing a suit," she remarked. "Are you going to the office?"

He shook his head. "No. I know you," he said. "I knew you'd want to go to the funeral no matter my telling you how bad an idea this is."

"You knew?" He knew her well. But unfortunately, she knew him well, too. So well that she'd had to accept they had no future together.

He sighed again—a long-suffering sigh as if protecting her was such a chore. But then given what he'd been through, it was.

"And you intend to go with me?" she asked.

His lips curved into a slight grin. "What kind of boyfriend would I be if I let you go to a funeral alone?"

"A real one?"

"You must have had some really lousy boyfriends," he remarked.

"I haven't dated for a long time," she said. So she couldn't remember what her boyfriends had been like, but apparently they hadn't stood by her when she'd gotten in trouble for hacking.

Ash nodded in recollection. "That was why you wanted my kisses."

His blue eyes brightened and glistened with desire. He must have been remembering that he'd given her more than kisses. She'd wanted that, too.

But she didn't want this, didn't want him acting like a real boyfriend, because he might get hurt again.

"I already called Agent Burnham," she said. "She can go with me."

The brightness of his eyes dimmed. "Hell, no."

"It wasn't her fault that I went to Martin's apartment." That she'd found him…

"No," he agreed. "It was yours. Just like going to this funeral is your mistake."

Her anger flared like it had when he'd suggested that there could be a better hacker than her. He hurt her pride more than anyone she'd ever known—probably because she cared so much what he thought of her. She needed to stop caring about him. "Fine. It's my mistake. I'll make it alone."

She headed toward the door, but he stepped between it and her, blocking her exit. He was close—so close that she felt his breath when he murmured, "You're not going anywhere…"

Her heart pounded harder as she wondered if he

intended to carry her back to the bedroom like he had a few days ago. He'd made love to her then to distract her from her pain. From what she'd seen.

She wasn't going to let him distract her again—not that he had tried since that first night. She'd awakened alone the morning after they'd made love, and for the most part, except for a glance he shot her now and then, he'd acted as if it hadn't happened. As if they hadn't made love.

That had hurt her pride and made her mad at him, too. "I'm not?" she challenged his order—or at least his right to give her any orders.

"You're not going anywhere alone," he continued. "I'm going with you."

But she wasn't pacified.

She would rather go alone than put him in danger. But she had to do this.

For Martin.

She had already cost the young man his life. It was her expertise that Martin had been tortured to divulge. So, no matter how Ash tried to convince her otherwise, it was her fault.

She shrugged. "Suit yourself, suit…"

She knew Ash well enough to know that he would anyway. If she refused to go to the funeral with him, he would show up alone.

"It's your funeral," she warned him and then flinched at her poor choice of words. It wasn't his funeral. At least it wasn't yet.

He turned the knob and held open the door for her. "I just hope it doesn't wind up being yours."

She waited until she passed him before murmuring, "Me, too…"

She didn't want it to be his funeral, either. Hopefully

he had called in his friends—his real friends—for reinforcements. Because she had a bad feeling that they might need them.

Chapter Nineteen

Ash walked into the funeral home with one arm clamped tightly around Claire. To anyone watching them—and a lot of people watched them—it could have looked as if her boyfriend was offering her emotional support. Instead he was trying to protect her. That was why he held her with only one arm, so that his other hand was free to grab his gun from the holster under his suit jacket.

Claire thought her assistant had been killed to get to her. If that was true, then his funeral would be the perfect place to actually get to her. Because anyone who knew Claire would know that she would have to pay her respects to her young assistant. Even now she moved down the aisle of the funeral home toward the casket sitting in front of the room.

Ash wasn't convinced that Martin deserved her respects. She felt guilty—as though she was the one who'd put her assistant in danger. Ash was beginning to believe that it might have been the other way around.

The kid hadn't possessed the hacker skills that Claire had. According to Nowak's background check in Martin's employee file, he had only hacked in to some video games and a few social media sites, so he couldn't have found ways around bank and government firewalls. He couldn't have been selling his own knowledge. But maybe he'd been selling hers.

After seeing where he'd lived, it was obvious Martin had needed money. When Ash had conducted a deeper investigation into the kid's financials, he had found that Martin had debts, too. Gambling debts. And those kinds of people, bookies and loan sharks, didn't like waiting for their money.

"This was a bad idea," warned the voice in his ear—through the radio device. Dalton Reyes's voice merely echoed the voice already in Ash's head telling him he'd made a mistake. "I recognize a lot of these people..."

From organized crime. Just whom had Martin borrowed from for those gambling debts? Who did he owe? And had they showed up to try to collect from whoever had survived Martin and inherited those debts?

Ash recognized some faces himself—from terrorism watch lists. That posting could have brought out all of them. He suspected one of them had probably tortured Martin. Had the kid admitted that he knew nothing? But before he'd died, had he given up Claire, exposing her as the only one who could have bypassed those firewalls?

"We should go," Ash told her as they stopped at the open casket. The kid looked better now—with his eyes closed and makeup covering his wounds—than he had when Claire had found him. Maybe she'd needed this, needed an image to superimpose over that other, more horrific one in her mind. She didn't need to stay for the services, though. "You're not safe here."

She trembled against him. He felt and heard her uneven breathing. She was crying again. He hated how much pain she was in over her assistant's death, and he hated that coming to this funeral would only cause her more pain emotionally.

And probably physically, as well.

"We don't have enough backup," Reyes warned in his ear. "We have to get the hell out of here."

They had prepared for the possibility of a few suspects attending Martin's funeral, like Leslie Morrison and Peter Nowak; Leslie sat next to his former employer in chairs a couple rows back from the casket. By seeing them together, conversing in hushed tones, Ash realized that Leslie wasn't a former employer. He still worked for Nowak.

Ash had pored over all the employee records, though, so Leslie's capacity wasn't official. What did he unofficially do for Nowak that the two of them looked so guilty to be caught together?

Their faces flushed as they caught him staring at them. Then their gazes went to Claire, and that look of guilt increased. Had their greedy plan put her in danger? Were they concerned that she might wind up like her assistant had? Lying in a casket, tortured and dead?

Ash had to make certain that she didn't wind up that way. The Bureau hadn't prepared for as many suspects as had showed up for the funeral; they were outgunned.

"We need to leave," Ash told Claire. He turned her around before Leslie and her boss could approach her.

He expected her to dig in her heels, like Edith had when her husband had tried to move her away on the dance floor. He expected Claire to argue that she couldn't leave until after the service.

But she offered him no argument. Instead she moved quickly, despite her still-swollen ankle, down the aisle between all those "mourners." She was a smart woman. He should have known that she would realize the danger they were in.

He just hoped that they hadn't realized it too late.

HAD ANYONE REALLY cared about Martin? Nobody cried. The only one who had shed a tear for him had been Claire. But those tears dried as she realized what Ash probably already had. Maybe she had already known, too, but hadn't wanted to face it until now. Until she saw that there really weren't any mourners at the funeral...

Except for Leslie and her boss and a few kids that must have partied with Martin, the rest of the mourners were scary goons in ill-fitting suits. Ill-fitting because the suits couldn't completely hide the weapons beneath their jackets. These guys looked like the men who had already tried abducting Claire. They were hired henchmen. Or buyers.

Martin was the one; he had posted that information for sale. But he hadn't had the actual knowledge. Unlike Leslie, who had mentored her, she hadn't taught the young man everything she knew—probably because she hadn't completely trusted him. And apparently with good reason. But had he been trying to sell her knowledge anyway?

Was he the one who'd put her in danger?

It certainly appeared so as those scary men closed in around her. They reached for her now as she and Ash tried to push through the crowd gathering around her.

The people were like paparazzi, pushing close for a picture. But they didn't just want a picture. They wanted Claire.

For three years Martin had been her assistant, and he had betrayed her.

Was there anyone else she could trust?

Ash.

She clung to him. But he was easing away from her slightly. Then she realized why when he pulled his weapon and blew his cover.

"FBI Special Agent Stryker," he said. "Step back."

Instead of warning the men away, his announcement seemed to free them to pull their own weapons. Screams and shouts of fear rose from the few real mourners.

Claire couldn't scream. Her fear was choking her. But she wasn't afraid just for herself. She was afraid for Ash, too. He was still recovering from his previous gunshot wound. He couldn't get shot again.

She had been wrong. So wrong to insist on attending this funeral. As he'd warned her, it would probably wind up being hers. And his.

She cleared her throat just enough to whisper to him, "I'm sorry..."

She wanted to tell him more. She wanted to tell him that she loved him. She had held those words back before, out of embarrassment, because she'd known that they were too incompatible to have a future together. Now she realized they had no future at all.

But before she could say anything more, gunfire erupted in the funeral home. The shots were close and deafening. Claire covered her ears as Ash covered her body with his.

He wore a vest, but it hadn't mattered last time. He had still been shot. She doubted it would protect him any better this time. He'd taken a bullet in the leg before; she suspected these men would aim for his head. They would want him dead quickly so that they could get to her.

She wanted to apologize again. Most of all, she wanted to profess her feelings.

But it was too late.

ASH WASN'T EVEN certain who was firing. The bad guys or his backup. No matter who was shooting, the bullets were going wild, endangering everyone inside the building. He needed to get Claire out of the funeral home.

He kept low, covering her with his body, and led her toward the exit. But hands grabbed at him. He swung his gun in every direction, but he only fired to stop the other men from firing at him.

He wasn't worried about his own life but Claire's and what would happen to her once he was no longer able to protect her. Even now pain radiated throughout his healing leg, but he ignored it as he pushed forward.

She wobbled on her feet—maybe with fear. Maybe with pain from her healing ankle. He shouldn't have brought her here. But he'd thought he'd had enough backup.

Now in the chaos, he didn't even know who was the backup and who was the threat. So he trusted no one but the voice in his head warning him to get out as quickly as possible.

And Reyes's voice telling him which direction to take like he had when all those panel vans had surrounded him on the streets.

"Go out the side door," the other agent advised. "You won't get out the way you came in—except in a body bag."

Ash changed direction just in time. The bullets intended for him struck chairs near him as he propelled Claire through the sitting area. He saw no side door.

And for a moment he wondered if he should have trusted that voice in his ear.

By his own admission Dalton Reyes had grown up with thugs. While he had arrested several, he'd also admitted that they'd been his friends. So maybe he still had some allegiance with them. Maybe, for the right price, Reyes could be a thug himself.

But then the door loomed ahead, an emergency exit that wasn't immediately visible behind a potted palm. The long fronds nearly hid the escape route. But it had never been more of an emergency than it was now as hands grabbed at Ash, pulling him back as more hands grabbed at Claire, tugging her away from him.

He slammed his elbow back into some guy's nose. Blood spurted. Then he struck another with the barrel of his gun. With a curse and an oath, the guy dropped to the carpet.

But still Claire was being pulled away from him toward that exit. Had Reyes set him up?

Someone Claire trusted had set her up. Maybe nobody could be trusted now with so much at stake.

Ash could rely only on himself. So he lifted his gun.

The man holding Claire pointed his gun toward her head. "I will kill her," he threatened.

Her green eyes widened with fear. But then she nodded slightly—giving Ash permission to fire. The guy probably didn't intend to really shoot Claire. It had to be only an empty threat since it was her knowledge that everyone wanted. Other people stepped back, too afraid to call his bluff.

But then, even if his threat was empty, he could kill her accidentally since his finger was against the trigger. He could pull it convulsively when he was shot. Using his back, the man pushed open that emergency exit door—intending to drag her outside with him.

A siren wailed, announcing to the room that the door had been opened, that Claire was about to be dragged out. Sirens outside echoed the wail of that siren, as additional reinforcements arrived. But they were too late to be much help anymore.

Even if they got inside quickly, Claire would already

be gone. And, with all the armed men around him, Ash would probably already be dead.

Claire's eyes widened again with shock and disappointment. She had trusted Ash to protect her, to keep her safe.

So he trusted himself, and he took the shot. More gunfire echoed.

Chapter Twenty

Blood dripped down Claire's face and throat and soaked her hair. She couldn't stop shaking; her quivering muscles were beyond her control. She had never felt as powerless as she had in that funeral home, as she did now when she couldn't even control her own body.

Her teeth chattered, and goose bumps raised her chilled skin. She was so cold.

She didn't even feel the warmth when Ash slid his arm around her. She felt nothing anymore but shock...

"You're okay," he soothed her. "You didn't get shot." But his fingers shook as he wiped the blood from her face. "It's not yours."

It wasn't hers. It had come from the man holding her—the man Ash had shot. But when that man had fallen, another had tried to grab her. It had been the scariest nightmare of her life, but it had been real.

And if not for Ash, she wouldn't have survived. She was surprised that she had. Unless...

"Are you sure?" she asked him.

He cupped her face in his bloodstained hands and studied her. "Are you hurt?" he asked, his voice gruff with anxiety. "Do you think any of this blood is yours?"

"It must be," she said. "We both must be bleeding..."

There was blood on Ash. Some trailing from the

corner of his mouth, some more from a scratch on his forehead. It was his. He had been hurt and all because she had stubbornly insisted on attending the funeral of the man who'd betrayed her.

She reached up and touched his mouth with her trembling fingers. "You are."

Before she could, he wiped away the trace of blood from his lips. "I'm fine."

"How?" she wondered. "How in the world are we both not dead?"

A man chuckled. It wasn't Ash; his face was drawn taut with gravity. He looked to be almost in as much shock as she was that they had survived.

If they had…

Special Agent Blaine Campbell stepped out of the shadows of the room to which Ash had brought her. She didn't remember where they were or how they'd gotten there. She didn't even remember how they had actually escaped the funeral home. Alive.

If they really were…

"I've wondered that myself," Blaine Campbell remarked. "There were some situations in Afghanistan that I still don't know how we survived."

Ash shuddered. "This felt a lot like those…like we weren't going to make it."

"Are you sure you're all right?" Blaine asked as he studied his friend.

Ash shook his head. "No, I'm not all right. I'm mad as hell."

Claire sucked in a breath of surprise at the anger in his voice and on his handsome face. But she couldn't blame him for being mad at her. She had insisted on going to that funeral despite all his warnings.

"I'm sorry," she said. She was so sorry for putting him

in danger—for nearly costing him his life. If something had happened to him...

"I'm mad at myself," he told her. "Mad that I took you into a situation I knew would be dangerous."

"It was my fault," she murmured.

He shook his head. "None of it was yours. It was your assistant's."

The man who'd been hired to help her had been the one who'd really put her in danger. She felt like crying again, but she had already cried too many tears over Martin Crouch.

"He offered your knowledge—he offered *you*—for sale," Ash said, and fury shook his voice.

"But he's the one who paid the price," Blaine remarked, "with his life."

Not only had he died, but he'd died painfully. She felt no vindication in that, only regret.

"It's over," she murmured.

"No," Ash corrected her. "It's not over yet. It's not over until everyone wanting that information—wanting *you*—has been apprehended."

"You're not going to catch them all," Blaine warned him.

"I have to," Ash said with grim determination. "If I don't, Claire will never be safe."

Remembering all those hands grabbing at her, she shuddered in revulsion. She couldn't live like that; she couldn't live in a constant state of fear.

His hands were steady as he cupped her face and tipped it up so that her gaze met his. His blue eyes were full of anger and determination and integrity.

"I will catch them," he promised her. "I will make sure you're safe again."

"What about you?" she asked. He had nearly been

killed so many times. If he went after those men again, he was going to be the one in danger.

"I'll be fine," he said, dismissing her fears for his safety. "And so will you. Blaine will protect you. That's why I brought you here."

Blaine shook his head. "This is a bad idea, Ash. You can't go after all of them alone."

"I'm not," he said. "I have Reyes and the agents who were backup at the funeral home."

"The ones who survived," Blaine said. "There were casualties. Wounded. It was like freaking Afghanistan. I should be out there with you like I was back then."

Ash shook his head in refusal.

"Reyes is a damn good agent," Blaine said, which he probably only admitted because the other man wasn't there to hear him. "He can keep her safe."

"Reyes is damn good," Ash agreed. "But he doesn't have a wife and kid, Blaine. You do. That's why you need to stay with Claire."

The blond man looked as though he was about to argue. But he was torn. He obviously loved his family and didn't want to risk never returning to them.

"It's safer here," Ash said. "I made sure no one followed us."

Blaine nodded, taking him entirely at his word. "I did the same."

So she was safe. But what about Ash?

She reached out and grabbed his arm. "Don't go," she pleaded. "Don't do this…"

"I have to," he said. And he knelt before her chair again and took her face in his hands. Staring deeply into her eyes, he said, "Remember everything that I'm doing, I'm doing for you."

She shivered at his ominous tone. "Getting killed?" she asked. "You're doing that for me?"

Instead of answering her, he stood up. Then he flipped on the TV she hadn't even realized was in the same room with her before stepping outside the door with Blaine. He'd probably turned on the TV so that she wouldn't overhear their conversation. Her ears still ringing from the gunfire, she probably wouldn't have been able to hear them anyway.

But she did hear the TV. On the flat screen, her boss spoke to reporters at a news conference. "There is no threat to national security. There is no way around government or corporate firewalls," Peter Nowak assured the press and the world. "Since Ms. Molenski checked the security for those sites, they have been rechecked and reworked several times."

She noticed a man standing among the reporters. But he wasn't pushing a microphone toward Nowak or flashing a camera. Leslie Morrison was just listening. As Ash had suspected, the man hadn't really retired, he was the one who'd rechecked her work. He'd probably been doing it for years.

Peter Nowak continued his press release. "She has no access to those sites nor does she have any access to Nowak Computer Consulting. Because of the threats to her personal safety, she has resigned."

Claire couldn't remember much of what had happened during or immediately after the funeral home. Maybe she had resigned. But she suspected that she had been fired instead.

Did Peter think that she had been involved in Martin's scheme? That they had been working together?

Or did he think her entirely responsible?

A door closed, startling her, so that she forgot about

the television. She didn't really care about her job anymore. She didn't care if she lost it.

"Where is he?" she asked as only Blaine stepped back inside the room with her.

"He's gone," Blaine replied.

"Why did you let him leave?" she asked. He was still hurt and had just barely survived their last ordeal. The blood on his face had been his.

"For the same reason that he let you go to that funeral," Blaine replied. "I knew I couldn't talk him out of it."

No, Claire didn't care about her job anymore. But she cared about Ash. She didn't want to lose him. But then she had never really had him.

THE WAR ZONE had moved from the funeral home to the international terminal at the airport. Despite airport security, gunfire erupted. Shots were exchanged. Bullets struck intended targets. The wounded were brought to the hospital, the survivors into custody.

"These were your people," Reyes remarked as he watched the last of the vehicles pull away. He turned the key in the ignition of his Bureau-issued SUV. While it was FBI, he'd had it customized with spinner rims and paint with glitter in it so that it would blend in on the streets where he had to go. "Now we round up mine."

Ash didn't care whose people were whose. He just wanted them all apprehended. He just wanted Claire safe. Nowak putting out that press release might have helped. If everyone believed what he'd said...

Reyes glanced over at Ash and gestured at his suit. "Not sure you're going to fit in."

Ash touched his jacket lapel and thought of how Claire called him a suit. "I don't want to fit in."

"Really?" Reyes asked. "I thought that was your

thing—fitting in, going undercover so completely that nobody would ever guess that you're not the cover."

That was the problem. Even he had begun to believe that he was really Claire's boyfriend. She didn't believe, though. She had kissed him just to gain expertise to kiss other, more compatible men. And she had made love with him only because she'd been devastated and lost over the gruesome murder of a man she had thought a friend. Of course her definition of *friend* was far more generous than Ash's.

Martin Crouch hadn't been a friend to her.

For a moment, back at the funeral home, Ash had doubted Reyes's friendship. But the man had been there when Ash had needed him. Once Ash had swept Claire out that side door, Reyes had rescued them in a vehicle, speeding away with them before any more shots could be fired. He had saved them then. And he'd had Ash's back at the airport.

But where they were going now was an area as dangerous as any Ash had ever been. "I'm not worried about a cover right now," he said. He was pretty sure none of Reyes's people would buy one anyway. "I'm worried about ending this. I want this to be over."

"Is it ever really over?" Reyes wondered. "Once this assignment ends, another one begins—which is lucky for us, I guess. Or we wouldn't have jobs. There will always be bad people in this world, though."

"There are good people, too," Ash said.

Reyes sighed and revealed a cynicism he usually hid beneath his humor. "I've met more bad."

"I've met Claire," Ash said.

Reyes laughed now. "And that little thing outweighs all the bad?"

Ash tensed with shock and fear as he realized that for

him, she did. She mattered so much more than all the bad things that had happened to him. "Yes."

Reyes cursed colorfully. "You can't be thinking about her now," he warned Ash. "You can't be distracted. I need you to be focused. Or we're not going to make it out of here alive."

Ash had to make it out alive. He had to go back to Claire and tell her how he felt about her. He had to tell her that, while he had never needed anyone before, he needed somebody now. He needed *her*.

DESPITE HER SPRAINED ANKLE, Claire had been pacing since Ash had left. It had felt like days ago. She should have told him then how she'd felt about him. She should have told him she loved him, and she should have made him promise to come back to her.

The doorknob rattled. Blaine drew his weapon from his holster and stepped between the door and Claire. With his free hand, he gestured her back—indicating she should take cover in the other room of the two-room suite.

But she shook her head, refusing to budge. Sure, it could have been someone else—someone who might have followed them from the funeral home or might have followed Blaine from wherever he'd come. But it could have been Ash.

And she wanted to see him. She needed to see him. Desperately.

"Don't shoot," a deep voice warned before the door opened to a dark-haired man. But it wasn't Ash.

"Reyes," Blaine said, his voice deep with relief.

But Reyes was alone. So Claire felt no relief—only more fear.

"Where is he?" she anxiously asked. "Where's Ash?"

Blaine tensed, too. "What the hell happened, Reyes?"

Now she noticed that the man wasn't as cocky and carefree as he usually was. His dark hair was mussed, his face bruised. He had obviously been in a fight.

With bad guys? Or with Ash?

After Martin's betrayal, Claire had wondered who she should trust. Only Ash...

But he wasn't here; she was alone with these men instead. Ash had trusted these two special agents and considered them his friends. Were they?

"Biggest roundup of bad guys *ever*," Reyes said like a little boy who'd caught the most fish on an outing with his dad and brothers. Or with the enthusiasm of a man who loved what he did.

Blaine must have thought he looked more like a little boy bragging because he chuckled in amusement.

"You're going to be safe now," Reyes told Claire. "It's over."

"It's really over?" she asked doubtfully.

He nodded.

"Then where's Ash?" Why hadn't he come back to tell her? "Is he hurt?"

Reyes touched his lip. Maybe Ash had been the one who'd hit him. "He wasn't when I saw him last."

"What the hell happened?" Blaine asked again.

"He asked me who a gambler would owe money to on my side of the city."

"Martin was a gambler..." She hadn't thought his little bets had been all that serious. But he must have accumulated some debts with the wrong people. Remembering how horrible he had looked when he'd died, she realized it was very serious. Serious enough that he'd been driven to offer her knowledge for sale to save himself.

"You told him?" Blaine asked. "It could be the person who killed Claire's assistant."

"Ash is convinced it is who killed the kid." Reyes touched his swollen lip again. "I offered to bring him there. But he insisted on going alone."

For her? To make sure Martin got justice? But Martin had started everything, had caused so many other deaths and near-deaths. Maybe Martin had had justice.

Tears stung her eyes. But she wasn't crying for the loss of her friend. Her tears were for Ash. "He's confronting a killer alone?"

"Ash has been my friend since we were just a couple of cocky kids in boot camp," Blaine said.

"Some things never change," Reyes murmured.

As if Reyes hadn't spoken, Blaine continued, "But he's always been a loner."

Because he had learned at a young age to trust no one since his parents had been willing to sacrifice his life along with so many others…

Had anyone ever really loved him like she loved him? She should have told him. But she wondered if it would have mattered. Ash cared more about his job and justice than love and relationships.

He had friends, but when he really needed them most, he pushed them away—like he'd pushed her away. Would he survive this confrontation with a killer?

"You know where he went," she pointed out, "so go there. Save him."

But even as she said it, she knew that by the time they arrived it would be too late. Someone would probably already be dead.

She just hoped it wasn't Ash.

Chapter Twenty-One

Ash should have been afraid or at least on edge as he walked into the business of the most notorious loan shark in the seediest part of Chicago. Maybe he wasn't uneasy, though, because it wasn't housed in the usual strip club or pool house from which loan sharks usually worked. This loan shark worked out of a tea shop.

This tea shop took bets and processed high interest loans with just as much frequency as the others. He also had to show his FBI badge to the two goons posted outside before he was even allowed through the doors. He expected them to reach for the guns holstered beneath their lumpy jackets. Or maybe just slam their already battered fists into him. Instead, they opened the stained-glass double doors for him.

Maybe they had already spotted his backup parked across the street. While he had refused to let Reyes come along for the takedown, he wasn't completely careless or stupid. He wasn't going in entirely alone. Given the size of the goons and their guns, it was good that he had backup close. But the guys just nodded as he passed through the doors he held. Maybe they were so passive because they knew that it was all over.

That was why Ash hadn't wanted Reyes along. It was

more important that the other agent go to Claire and assure her that her ordeal was over, that she was finally safe again. Ash never wanted her to be as scared as she'd been in the funeral home or as shocked as she'd been after it.

He'd been so scared that the blood on her face had been hers, that she'd been hit when he'd killed the man holding her. She had stared at Ash so vacantly, but then it had all been too much for her.

As he crossed the hardwood floor of the beautiful little shop, a woman glanced up from her table at the back of the restaurant. She put down her Bunco cards and slid her cat-eye glasses from the end of her nose until they dangled from the thick gold chain around her neck. She wore a sweatshirt like his grandmother would have worn—one with cats on it made of felt or velvet or something. The sweatshirts were about all he remembered of his grandmother; she hadn't approved of his mother, so he hadn't seen her very often.

He suspected this woman would have liked his mother. They were quite alike—every bit as cold-blooded.

"Did you finally give up on that little pale blonde?" she asked hopefully. She hadn't been at the speed dating event to meet anyone; she'd been there to bid on the information Martin had told her was being sold to pay his debts.

Even though Ash had no intention of giving up on Claire, he nodded. "I realized she had nothing for sale. Have you realized the same yet?"

She uttered a heavy sigh of utter resignation. It was probably why her goons hadn't tried to stop him because *she* knew it was over. According to Reyes, Beverly Holdren had run a lucrative loan shark business for many years. She'd had people hurt but never killed. But Martin's wild claim had made her so greedy that she'd crossed a line she'd never crossed before. "Yes."

"Too bad for Martin Crouch that you hadn't realized it sooner."

She narrowed her eyes and stared up at him as if she needed her glasses back on to see him clearly. Or maybe she was just trying to determine how much he knew.

Since she'd fallen for Martin's bluff, he made one of his own. "We have DNA evidence from the scene." The lab hadn't finished processing any of that evidence collected from the scene. He made a tsking noise with his tongue. "It was a very messy scene."

And it was too damn bad that Claire had been the first one to come upon it. She'd been in shock that day, too. She'd been through entirely too much and part of that had been because of this woman.

"Martin…disappointed me," she said, like a grandmother might talk about her naughty grandson.

But a grandmother would have only scolded or at the most paddled his behind. She'd had the poor kid tortured. Maybe she'd even done some of it herself…

"There was a lot of evidence left behind at the scene," Ash added to his bluff. He had no idea what had been collected. "Once we match that DNA to you and your goons, we will have enough for an arrest and a conviction." A glance outside told him those goons were already being taken into custody. Hopefully they would be able to match their DNA to whatever had been recovered from Martin's battered body.

"Since I'm going to go to jail anyway…" She lifted the gun she must have been holding beneath the table and pointed the barrel at him.

He was so surprised that he just laughed. He had survived terrorists and mobsters and was about to be taken out by an old, gray-haired lady with a gun?

CLAIRE NEVER SAW Special Agent Ash Stryker again. Ash was fine, though; he had brought Martin's killer to justice weeks ago. But Claire hadn't heard that announcement from his lips; she had learned that good news from his friends Blaine and Maggie Campbell.

She wanted what they had. The young couple's love and happiness reminded her of her father and Pam's. And seeing them together had reminded her that she wanted that kind of loving relationship for herself. She wouldn't find that with Ash. He wouldn't open himself up to his friends; he wouldn't open himself up to anyone.

She loved him, but she could love again. Maybe…

Maybe there was someone else out there for her. Someone who would actually return her love. That thought— that hope—had compelled her to try another speed dating event.

Unfortunately it was at the Waterview Inn, the same hotel with the same grapevine carpeting in the dining room where she had met Special Agent Ash Stryker. He had no reason to be there now. He no longer thought she was a traitor to her country. So he didn't have to stop her from selling out national security.

Apparently he didn't have to see her ever again.

The bell dinged, drawing Claire's attention back to the man sitting across from her. His blond hair was thinning and his waistline thickening. But he probably wasn't that much older than she was. Nor was there any mark on his finger from ever wearing a ring. Still he hadn't interested or attracted her—not like Ash had.

The blond man had been talking, but she hadn't heard a word he had uttered the entire five minutes. He hadn't seemed to mind that she hadn't participated in that conversation, though.

He grinned and heartily shook her hand like a politician confident that he had her vote. She wasn't even sure that she'd told him her name. But apparently he didn't care that he knew nothing about her.

Ash knew about her. He knew more about her than anyone else ever had. He knew about her past and what she wanted for her future.

Maybe that was why he hadn't come to see her again after he had arrested Martin's killer. Maybe he'd known that there was no point in seeing her again when he couldn't give her what she wanted. A relationship. A family.

The bell dinged again, signaling the beginning of the next five minutes. Claire barely glanced up to greet her new potential match. So she caught just a glimpse of black hair, blue eyes and chiseled features as he settled onto the chair across from her. He reached his hand across the table and introduced himself, "Hello, my name is Ash Stryker."

She stared at his hand and remembered how it had caressed her body, how it had made her skin tingle. She didn't reach for it. She couldn't touch him again and not want him. Already she ached for him. Or maybe she had never stopped.

"So what's your name?" he asked as if he really had no idea.

She glared at him but said nothing, refusing to participate in whatever game he was playing with her.

"We only have five minutes," he reminded her. "Aren't you going to speak to me?"

"Why?" she asked. "What cover are you going under now?"

Amusement twinkled in his bright blue eyes. "Isn't it kind of presumptuous to discuss going under covers? We've only just met."

She sighed. "No, we haven't."

But she wished that they had. Then she could just enjoy how handsome he was with that thick black hair and those bright blue eyes. She could enjoy how funny he could be, even though he wasn't amusing her much now. And if they had really just met, she wouldn't know yet that they had nothing in common, that they would have no future.

"No, we haven't just met," he admitted. "In fact, it feels like we've known each other forever. Like there wasn't a time that you weren't a part of my life, that you weren't a part of me..."

Surprise had her gasping. She hadn't realized that he felt that way, too—as if they were parts of a whole. That was why she'd felt so empty and incomplete without him.

He reached for something.

She tensed and nervously glanced around the dining room because usually when he reached for something, it was his weapon. But he didn't pull a gun. Instead, he placed a gift bag on the table between them.

"What's this?" she asked. Just as she hadn't reached for his hand, she didn't reach for it, either. She just stared at the glittery red gift bag.

"Look inside," he urged her, and now his eyes brightened with excitement. And in that moment he reminded her of her father, who had barely been able to wait until her birthday or Christmas to give her presents. He hadn't been able to wait to see her reaction to the gift he'd chosen for her that he'd been pretty certain she would love.

Why did Ash think she would love this gift?

Her hands trembling slightly, she reached inside the bag. Her fingertips skimmed over cool glass, and she pulled out a musical snow globe. The music automatically began to play. It was the song to which they had danced last at the piano bar. *I could have danced all night...*

She really could have and wished that they had. Inside the snow globe a dark-haired man spun a blonde woman around a dance floor. Claire shook the globe and sparkling confetti rained down around them.

She couldn't stop staring at it in awe. "Where did you find this?"

"I asked your dad who made that one for him that you love so much," he replied. "Thankfully they were still in business and willing to make this one for me."

He drew her attention from the globe to him, and she asked in shock, "You talked to my dad?"

"Yes, of course," he said in that matter-of-fact tone that had once infuriated her. "I had to ask his permission."

"Permission for what?" she asked, completely befuddled why he would talk to her father. "To make me a globe?"

"I asked for his permission to propose to you." He dropped to his knee on his side of the table. "Will you marry me, Claire Molenski?"

Was she dreaming? She must have fallen asleep while the last man had been talking, and she had dreamed up this perfect fantasy.

The bell dinged.

"Claire, you have to answer me," Ash said. "We're out of time."

Panic attacked her just as it had the last time she'd

met Special Agent Ash Stryker at a speed dating event. She couldn't believe what he was saying, what he was doing. She couldn't believe that any of it was real or really happening. That panic overwhelmed her, making it hard for her to think or even breathe. She needed air. Now. Instead of answering him, she stood up so quickly that she knocked over her chair. Then she grabbed her purse and ran from the room.

"You did it again," a bald-headed man said from beside Ash. "You scared her off." He must have been at that other event.

Ash would like to believe that he wasn't the one who had scared her off that night. But tonight he definitely was to blame. He'd thought she would love the globe... because he had thought she might love him.

He couldn't believe how wrong he'd been. He shouldn't have listened to Blaine and what he'd said about her hobbling up on a sprained ankle to check on him. That hadn't been out of love but out of concern for a fellow human being.

Ash was definitely not the man she wanted. But he'd thought he might be able to convince her that he could be that man. He could give her what she wanted. He had been so wrong...

He picked up the globe and stared at that dancing couple. They looked so happy, so in love as they twirled deliriously around that dance floor. The dark-haired man in a suit, the blonde woman in a red dress.

Ash had wanted to give her that perfect memory like when she'd skated with her father. But maybe he had only reminded her of the nightmare, that they had nearly been killed in an alley behind that piano bar. Maybe he had reminded her that his life was dangerous and since they'd met, he'd brought that danger into her life. He didn't blame her for running from him.

He sighed and shoved the globe back in the gift bag. Then he headed from the room. Maybe he should have run right out of the room after her. Maybe he should have tried to catch her. But even though his leg had healed enough to run, his pride was stung too much to chase her. His heart was hurting. He felt more than disappointment. He felt devastation.

He had been so hopeful that she would at least consider his proposal. He hadn't expected an immediate yes. He'd realized that she would have to think about it, that he might have to convince her.

Hair lifted on his nape as an eerie sense of foreboding overwhelmed him. Somebody was watching him. He stopped and glanced around the dimly lit lobby.

"You talked to my father?" she asked, her soft voice reaching him from the shadows. She stood just outside the doors to the dining room.

"Yes," he replied. Her father had been everything Ash had thought he would be considering he had earned so much love and loyalty from his daughter. Mr. Molenski had been warm and welcoming and even understanding when Ash had explained what a fool he'd been to try to resist his feelings for Claire. "I guess it was presumptuous of me."

"What was presumptuous of you?"

"Meeting him." A man shouldn't talk to a father until he was certain that the daughter returned his feelings. "I met Pam, too. She's very nice." She had been every bit as warm and welcoming as her new husband had been.

"Are they having fun?" Claire anxiously asked. She loved so deeply—her family, her friends, even her work…

Why couldn't she have loved him?

"They seem very happy," Ash assured her. "He was worried about you, though." Until Mr. Molenski had met Ash and gotten his promise that he would make his daughter happy. Too bad he had already broken that promise.

She sighed and stepped from the shadows to join him in the middle of the lobby. "I talked to him a few days ago. I wish I hadn't called him. I knew he would hear it in my voice and worry."

"Hear what?" he asked. "You didn't talk to him until after everyone had been caught and you were safe again. What did he hear?"

"Me," she said with a heavy sigh. "Missing you…"

Maybe he had reason to hope; it burgeoned in his chest again. Maybe he hadn't read her completely wrong. "You missed me?"

She gave a brief, reluctant nod.

"I hoped you would," he admitted.

She glared at him slightly resentfully. "Is that why you stayed away?"

"I wanted to talk to your dad before I saw you again," he said. The minute he saw her again, he knew he would propose, so he had wanted her father's permission first.

"But the protection detail had been pulled off him and Pam," she said, "so you must have hacked into my itinerary for him to find out where he would be now."

He offered her a sheepish smile. "I have some skills, too," he murmured.

"You're a hacker," she teased him. "I could have you arrested for breaking into my personal files."

"You probably could," he agreed. "I also stayed away because it took some time to have that globe made." He had wanted every detail to be perfect.

She reached out for the bag and lifted the globe from it. Tears glistened in her eyes as she studied it.

"It was worth every minute spent waiting for it," she said. "It's so beautiful."

"You're so beautiful…" She was wearing the red dress again; he loved that damn dress. But he loved what was in it even more. "And so smart and funny and sexy…" He couldn't imagine his life without her in it now. The past few weeks had been hell without her—far worse than any deployment or undercover assignment.

She glanced from the globe to him and back. "Did you really just propose in there?"

A grin teased his lips at how disbelieving she was. But then she had overheard that ridiculous claim he'd made to Blaine. He nodded. "Yes, I really asked you to be my wife."

"It's not part of some cover?" she asked. "You're not going to pose as my fiancé because I'm in danger again?"

"I don't want to be your fiancé as a cover," he said. "I want to be your fiancé for real. I want to be your husband for life."

Hope replaced the disbelief on her face, and her lips curved into a slight smile. She nodded.

He grinned as happiness overwhelmed him. It seemed like she was saying yes. "There's something else inside the bag. You must have missed it."

She reached into it again and pulled out a red velvet box. Her hand trembled as she held it. Her voice low with awe, she murmured, "You really are proposing…"

"Yes," he replied.

She popped open the box and stared down at the brilliant round diamond.

"Are *you* saying yes?" he asked hopefully.

"I didn't think it was real," she said.

"This isn't part of an undercover assignment," he assured her. "This is real. My feelings for you are real." And no matter how much time passed, they would never go away.

"I thought you coming here with this globe and that proposal was a dream," she said. "I thought that you didn't need anybody and never would."

He groaned at what a fool he had been to ever think that. "I was wrong."

"Is this wrong?" she asked as she held up the ring. "Do we have anything in common?"

He tapped the glass of the globe, and the music began to play again. "We love to dance."

She nodded.

"We love to kiss."

She smiled.

"I love you," he said. "I didn't know how much I could love someone until I fell in love with you. And yet I love you more every day. With every smile you smile, every word you speak, I love you more."

Her breath caught and tears welled in her eyes. He didn't know if those were tears of happiness or regret that she didn't return his feelings.

Then she said it back. "And I love you. I love how heroic you are, how strong and yet graceful and funny, too. I love you so much."

His heart pounded hard with excitement and happiness. She loved him. "I would say that we have more in common than most people do."

"I'm a slob," she reminded him.

"I love that about you, too," he responded. "And we'll hire a cleaning lady."

She laughed and then she was in his arms, hers winding around his neck and she rose up on tiptoe and pressed her lips to his. "I love everything about you."

He kissed her back but lifted his mouth long enough to ask, "I'm not too uptight? Too much of a suit?"

"I love that about you, too," she said, and her green eyes sparkled with that love she professed. "You're perfect..."

"I am perfect," he readily agreed, "but only for you. I will give you all the love and attention I can."

Her smile dimmed for a moment. "I'll be happy with whatever you can give. I understand how busy you are, keeping the world safe and all."

He grinned at her exaggeration. "You keep the world safe, too."

"You know that I didn't really quit?" she asked. "That I'm still working for the company."

Nowak had only put out the press release to protect her. And it had worked. "I know everything about you."

"I do intend to work less, though," she said as if warning him. "And pretty much only from home, like Leslie does."

"I'm cutting back, too," he said. "I'm going to do more administrative work—concentrate on training and leading more agents to save the world."

She gasped in shock. "What? Why?"

"I don't want to go undercover anymore," he said. "Not unless I'm going undercover with you."

Her smile returned, brighter than before, and she picked something out of her bottomless bag. A key card for a room. She waved it in his face. "Want to go under covers with me now?"

He shook his head. "Not until you give me an answer, Claire. Will you marry me?"

"Yes, I will," she replied ecstatically. "I will marry you!"

He swept her up in his arms and carried her toward the elevators. He couldn't wait for the honeymoon. He had to have her now and every night for the rest of their lives.

* * * * *

HER ALIBI

CAROL ERICSON

Chapter One

The sea crashed on the rocks, and the tide tried to drag her back under but she resisted its pull. She forced open one eye, the lid weighted like a manhole cover.

To keep it open, she focused her dry eyeball on the filmy white curtain billowing into the room from the French door ajar to the balcony. Another wave from the ocean below made its presence heard as it broke and then clawed at the rocky shore. She could almost taste the salt from the sea spray on her tongue.

She licked her lips. The air in the room lay heavy upon her, and she still hadn't managed to open her other eye. She lifted a lethargic arm and rubbed her closed eye, hoping to stimulate it.

She blinked against the stinging sensation and rubbed again, smearing moisture across her cheek to her ear. Had she been crying in her sleep? That deep, dark slumber she couldn't seem to shake?

Raising her hand in front of her face, she wrinkled her nose. Not tears, blood. She hadn't had a bloody nose since she was a kid. She pinched the bridge of her nose with two fingers, sniffing, and her nostrils flared at the tinny smell that seemed to invade every pore.

The odor revived her, stunning her like a prod. She jerked her bare limbs beneath the silk sheets. She bolted to a sitting position, the back of her head hitting the headboard. Pain, all out of proportion to the tap of her skull against the wood, coursed through her body, and she gagged.

As if that bump had awakened every nerve ending in her body, her right hand began to throb. She spread out her fingers, the red cuts on her hand standing in stark relief against the white sheets.

What the hell happened? Why was she bleeding, and why was she naked in her ex-husband's bedroom?

She scrambled from the bed, tripping over something soft on the floor in the semidarkness. Gasping, she fumbled for the light switch on the wall next to the bed and jabbed at it with her thumb.

Her gaze dropped to the floor, and she staggered back, her mouth agape. A scream gathered in her lungs but lodged in her chest, choking her instead. Closing her eyes, she drew in a deep breath. Somewhere deep down inside, she knew vomiting would only make this situation, whatever it was, much, much worse.

Her self-preservation, one of her strongest instincts, took control of her brain and her eyelids flew open. She extended her leg and with her big toe, she prodded the shoulder of her ex-husband, crumpled on the floor.

Her investigatory digit met cold flesh, and the reality rushed in on her, just as surely as those waves were rushing to shore outside that window. She clapped a hand over her mouth and hissed through her fingers, "Niles?"

The *s* hung in the air and only the drapes floating into the room whispered a response.

She fell to her knees and crawled toward Niles's still form. Covering two fingers with the bedspread that hung to the floor, she placed them against his neck. The once-vibrant man, who couldn't seem to sit still for a second, didn't have one ounce of life left in his body.

She sat back on her heels and surveyed the opulent bedroom she'd painstakingly decorated a lifetime ago. What had happened in this room?

She dug a knuckle into her temple. She couldn't remember coming into the bedroom with Niles last night. She'd come back to the house with him in his car after the drink they'd shared at the Marina Sports Bar. He had the file she'd wanted to see in his home office.

He did so much work from home she didn't figure it for a ploy. Niles didn't need ploys. He'd moved on to another woman shortly after their separation. Hell, who was she kidding? He'd moved on to multiple women *before* the separation.

Then what? Had he drugged her? She ran her tongue around her dry mouth. Had he not wanted to show her the file?

She peered at her hands and the cuts on her right palm. Her gaze darted to the bloody wounds gouging Niles's back. He'd been stabbed...to death.

They'd fought last night. They always fought. That was why they'd got divorced. Civilized people divorced. They didn't kill. She hated Niles, but she never wished him dead.

The breeze filtering in from the open door tickled her ear. She shook her head. Not just dead. Murdered. And she'd blacked out...again.

Adrenaline coursed through her veins, and she sprang to her feet. Her head swiveled back and forth, her gaze tripping over her clothes in the corner. Why had she taken them off? She dragged in a deep breath. If she panicked now, she'd get herself into even deeper trouble.

Get dressed. Get out.

As she tiptoed to the jumble of clothing, a building dread accompanied each step. There could be only one reason for her to strip off her clothes: if they were soaked with blood.

She leaned forward, pinching the material of her blouse between two fingers and pulling it free from the pile.

The spotless white silk had her releasing a noisy breath. She grabbed a handful of the black slacks and shook them out—dry as a bone. As dry as her mouth.

Her underwear had been dislodged from her slacks and fell back to the floor. She scooped up her bra and panties and put them on over her cold, clammy flesh. Had she showered at some point last night?

She pressed her nose against the skin of her upper arm—not sweaty, but not exactly fresh, either. She crept into the bathroom and nudged the light switch with the side of her hand, casting a warm glow over the gray tiles with their bright blue accents.

No droplets of water appeared on the floor of the walk-in shower. No damp towels littered the bathroom or hung on the racks. She edged up to the vanity and peered at her reflection in the mirror.

A pair of wide violet eyes stared back at her, and a smear of blood created a line from the corner of her eye to her ear. That was her own blood from the cuts on her right hand. She didn't have a speck of Niles's blood on her. She stuck two fingers in her mouth and then rubbed the red streak from her face.

If her clothes weren't bloody and she hadn't taken a shower, surely she'd be covered in his blood if…? But she'd blacked out.

She spun away from the mirror and scanned every corner of the bathroom. Nothing looked out of place—except her standing here in her underwear.

She whipped a hand towel from the rack and wiped the light switch, and the sink and shower faucets for good measure. Then she rushed back into the bedroom and erased her fingerprints from the light switch in there, too. She didn't have to wipe down the entire house, as she'd been here recently. Hell, she used to live here.

She inspected the bed, squinting at the pillow and sheets, searching for strands of her dark hair and blood from her cuts. Those would be damning, but she couldn't afford to spread even more of her DNA around by going into the laundry room and washing the bedding.

Then she crouched beside Niles's dead body and studied the cuts on his back and the ripped, slightly freckled flesh. She shivered.

She looked at her hand, the thin red lines of the cuts creating a horizontal pattern on her palm. She reached up and buried her fingertips in her hair, tracing over a tender lump on the back of her head. Had she and Niles had some kind of fight? A physical altercation? Could his killing have been in self-defense?

She bunched up her hand into a fist and pressed it against her stomach. Self-defense when she stood to gain 100 percent control of Snap App? Self-defense when everyone knew they had been fighting over the company for months?

Nobody would believe her—not with her past. She couldn't afford to be at another scene involving a dead body.

She picked up the towel and continued wiping down surfaces in the bedroom. With a brisk nod, she dropped the towel to the floor and picked up her slacks next to it.

She slipped into the black pants and gasped, patting the pockets. Her lashes fluttered as she huffed out a breath. She'd left her phone at home last night on the charger. Her battery had been dying lately and she couldn't be happier about it now. She didn't need her cell phone signal pinging in this house at this time.

She pulled her blouse over her head. As she reached for the top button, she grabbed threads instead. Her button had popped off—the oversize multicolored, highly unique button.

With her head pounding, she dropped to her knees and ran her hands across the wood floor and underneath the dresser. Her fingers stumbled across the button and she slid it across the floor and dropped it into the pocket of her slacks. Then she stepped into the high heels placed next to each in perfect alignment.

She scooped up the towel and gave the room a final look over her shoulder from the bedroom door. She froze. *The knife.*

What if the knife had her prints on it? Her head swiveled from side to side. What knife? She hadn't seen a knife anywhere.

Her gaze slid to Niles's body. He had stab wounds on his back, but what about his front? If she rolled him over, she could leave more evidence of her presence here. If she didn't, she could be leaving a murder weapon with her prints on it.

She kicked off her heels and approached Niles. She feared him now more than she ever had alive. Still gripping the hand towel, she pushed at his inert form enough to tilt it on its side. Before he fell back to the floor, she'd determined there was no knife beneath him—nothing beneath him except more blood. This had been angry overkill.

It hadn't been her anger that had killed him. But then she'd blacked out.

She grabbed her shoes in one hand and shuffled out of the room backward, as if she expected Niles to jump up and point an accusing finger at her, and then turned and jogged down the curved staircase, sweeping the towel along the banister for good measure. She and Niles had come back to the house for some file, and she still had every intention of leaving with that file.

She scurried into Niles's home office and scanned the clean surface of the mahogany desk. She and Niles hadn't even made it far enough to get the file. But she knew exactly where they were.

With the towel still clutched in her hand, she dropped her shoes and crouched before the desk drawers, pulling open the bottom one. She shoved the hanging files aside and then snatched a letter opener from a pencil holder on the desk. She jammed the point into a circular release at the bottom of the drawer and slid open the false bottom.

She released a sigh. The labels indicated the file folder she wanted was on top of some other folders and a few other items. Niles must've got it ready for her. She removed the folder, replaced the false bottom, closed the drawer and wiped down everything.

Gripping the folder in one hand, she turned away from the desk and tripped to a stop when she saw two crystal tumblers on the counter of the wet bar. She yanked the towel from where she had it draped over her shoulder, rinsed out both glasses, wiped them down and put them back on the shelf behind the bar.

The computer had to be her next stop, to check the footage from the security cameras. Covering the mouse with a tissue from Niles's desk, she navigated through the security software.

She drew in a quick breath as her mouth dropped open when she realized the system had been disabled. Had Niles done that earlier? Had his killer? Had she?

Now she needed to sneak out of here…and find herself an alibi.

CONNOR DUG HIS feet into the sand and squinted at the surfers battling the heavy surf—and each other.

He pulled out his video camera, zoomed in and started

filming the Cove Boys and their antics in the water. Summer might've ended but the rowdy group of surfers who ruled the cove with a belligerent localism never stopped when they thought outsiders were riding their waves.

Connor caught the Cove Boys dropping in on others' waves, cutting them off, yelling and making rude gestures. This footage would help with the lawsuit.

The Cove Boys' aggressive behavior had its desired effect as, one by one, the harassed surfers came to shore in defeat.

A couple approached him, their boards under their arms. The man reached back and yanked down the zipper of his wetsuit. "Are they always like that?"

"Yep." Connor held up his video camera. "But we're trying to stop it. Some local surfers who don't like the reputation of the cove are bringing a class action lawsuit against these guys—and I just captured some solid evidence."

"Good. It's about time someone did something about these guys."

Out of the corner of his eye, Connor saw a surfer clambering from the surf and coming at him. He turned, widening his stance on the wet sand, his muscles tense.

Jimmy Takata, one of the Cove Boys, threw down his board. "What's up, Wells? What's the camera for?"

"Whaddya think? You guys can't stop even when your attorney tells you to lie low."

Jimmy lunged at him, and Connor dropped the camera on top of his bag and raised his hands. "You wanna go there?"

"You're playing with fire, Wells." Jimmy leveled a finger at him. "Your old man doesn't rule this town anymore, and he did a crap job when he did."

Connor's eye twitched behind his sunglasses. "Aren't you kinda old to be playing beach bully, Jimmy?"

"Never too old to protect your own. Besides, you're not a cop anymore, so stop trying to recapture your glory days." Jimmy guffawed as he scooped up his board and waded back into the water.

Connor crouched and stashed the camera in his bag. Then he hitched it over his shoulder and scuffed his bare feet through the dry sand to the line of cars on the road above the beach.

He slid behind the wheel of his truck and tossed the bag on the seat next to him. Gripping the steering wheel, he let out a breath. If he could help break the stranglehold the Cove Boys had over the best surfing spot in San Juan Beach, it might go a little way toward restoring the town's former luster.

It seemed a million years ago since his father patrolled this small beach community as its police chief and the residents could trust each other and trust authority. Then the drugs moved in and all that ended—along with his father's life.

Connor swallowed the bitterness that flooded his mouth and took a swig of the warm water from the bottle in his cup holder. He'd leave this place, as others had, if it weren't for the land and his father's dream. Didn't he owe that to him?

Someone rapped on his window and he jumped. He peered through the glass at the couple from the beach and powered down his window.

The guy stuck his hand into the open space. "Thanks, man."

"For what?" Connor jerked his thumb toward the beach. "They're still out there intimidating people."

"Yeah, but if that lawsuit prevails and those idiots are slapped with an injunction, they're going to think twice about their localism—and your video footage should help."

The woman held out a business card. "If the attorney needs witnesses, give me a call. We'd be happy to help."

"Thanks." Connor plucked the card from between the woman's fingers. "I'll give this to the lawyer filing the lawsuit."

With a wave of his hand, Connor cranked on his engine and pulled away from the gravelly shoulder, spitting dust and sand in his wake. After a few miles, he made a turn to the east, away from the coast and the town of San Juan Beach.

The narrow, two-lane road wound into the low-lying hills and the early-fall temperature rose several degrees as he escaped the sea breeze. The hotter the better. His grapevines needed the warmth.

On the way to the house, Connor pulled over and jumped out of the truck. He cupped a bunch of grapes in his palm and sniffed—the sweet had started to overpower the tart— right on time, even though this crop wouldn't be the harvest for the wine. He had to wait another year for that.

Good thing he was a patient man.

As he made the last turn, he hunched over the steering wheel and squinted at the white car in his driveway. Someone had ignored the no-solicitors sign posted at the entrance to his property—probably another one of those Realtors. That shiny cream-white Lexus looked exactly like a Realtor's car.

His jaw hardened, and he threw the truck into Park. He pushed out of his vehicle at the same time a woman emerged from the Lexus.

As she floated toward him, her hands held out, Connor blinked. Her perfume wafted toward him and enveloped him in her spell. When she reached him, she wrapped her arms around his waist and rested her head against his shoulder, her chestnut hair lifting in the breeze, his capture complete.

Her warm breath caressed the side of his neck as she whispered in a husky tone, "I'm in trouble, Connor. And I need an alibi."

Chapter Two

Connor's body, still hard and strong, stiffened. She knew he wouldn't be putty in her hands, but she'd hoped she wouldn't have to bring out the big guns.

He stepped back, and she unwound her arms from around his waist. She didn't want to be clingy.

Narrowing his blue eyes, he folded his arms across his unyielding chest. "What now?"

She gazed over his shoulder at the empty road bordered by grapevines and pasted a smile on her face. "The vineyard looks good. I can't wait for the first bottle."

He snorted, "Are you really trying to butter me up? You should know better."

"I need to ease into this." She squeezed his rock-solid biceps. "Can we talk inside?"

"Hang on."

He turned back toward his truck, opened the door and ducked inside, giving her a spectacular view of his backside in his board shorts. From the look and feel of Connor's muscles, she wouldn't be surprised if he worked this vineyard single-handedly, but he must still be spending time at the beach, given his sandy bare feet and the burnished-gold sheen on his brown hair.

He walked toward her, a black bag slung over his shoulder. As he passed her, he nodded toward the house. "Follow me."

"Hardly the red carpet I was expecting after all this time."

"Maybe it's more than you deserve after all this time."

She sucked her bottom lip between her teeth. She definitely needed the big guns this time around.

As she walked into the house she expelled a soft sigh. "You redecorated."

"This is my house now, not my parents'. What's wrong? You don't like it?"

She ran a hand along the back of the cream-colored leather sofa, which had replaced an overstuffed floral one that had been littered with his mother's handmade pillows. "It's an improvement."

He placed the bag on a granite island that separated the kitchen from the living room, where a wall once stood that had supported a shelf showing off Connor's surfing trophies.

"Do you want something to drink? No wine…yet."

"As much as I could use some alcohol right now, it's still morning and I need my wits about me…all my wits." Or at least the ones she still possessed after last night's blackout.

"I have water, orange juice and iced tea from a bottle."

"Tea, please." She perched on the edge of the sofa, the soft leather almost sighing beneath her weight, and wedged her purse next to her feet.

When Connor exited the kitchen holding two glasses, the ice clinking with each of his steps, she patted the cushion next to her.

He handed her the glass, tossed a coaster onto the coffee table hand carved from a log and took the chair across from her.

Looked like he wanted to keep his wits about him, too.

The two of them had always shared a magnetic attraction to each other, but maybe he'd been able to shut down that magnet after their last contact a few years ago.

"Tell me what's going on." He took a long gulp of tea. "Is it that husband of yours?"

"Ex-husband."

"Right. You're still fighting with him about that multi-million-dollar company?"

"It's much worse than that, Connor."

"Just spill it, Savannah."

"Niles is dead…murdered."

Connor's eyebrows shot up to that lock of brown hair that curled over one eye. "Murdered? Wouldn't that be all over the news? I know I'm kind of a recluse these days, but I do have a TV—cable and everything." He jabbed a finger at the huge flat screen that claimed the space above his fireplace.

"It's… He's… I don't think he's been discovered yet."

Connor jumped from the chair, and the tea splashed over the side of the glass clutched in his hand. "What are you telling me?"

"I found him. At his house. Dead."

"And you didn't call 911?"

"Of course not."

"Of course not?" He threw his arm out to the side. "No, why would anyone call the police upon discovering a dead body, especially the dead body of your ex?"

"Exactly." She took a small sip of tea and avoided his wild-eyed stare.

He stopped pacing and landed in front of the couch, looming over her with iced tea dripping from his hand onto the polished hardwood floor. "What the hell happened to him, Savannah? Why didn't you call the police?"

She shook her glass to rattle the ice. "He was stabbed

to death, and I didn't call because the police would've arrested me."

"Why?"

"Because I woke up in his house, in his bed, and I don't remember how I got there." She closed her eyes and held her breath.

The shocked stillness reverberating off Connor in waves made her more nervous than the agitated pacing. She peeled open one eye and swallowed.

A muscle throbbed at the corner of his mouth, and the fingers curling around the sweating glass sported white knuckles. His blue eyes had darkened to the color of a stormy sea.

Then he blinked, drained the tea in one gulp, wiped his palm on the leg of his board shorts and set the glass on the coffee table. "You'd better start from the beginning."

Warm relief flooded her body and she almost collapsed against the sofa cushions. This was the Connor she'd hoped to see—in control and even-keeled. He hadn't agreed to anything yet, but he hadn't thrown her out on her derriere, either.

Sitting up, she squared her shoulders. "Niles and I met for a drink last night to discuss some business. I had come across something in the books and wanted to see some files."

"Why didn't he just send over the file? Why the meeting, the drink?"

She studied his square jaw, clenched in disapproval. Did she detect jealousy in that question?

"Niles had been wanting to discuss other aspects of the business with me for weeks and figured this was his opportunity to have me at his mercy." She cleared her throat. "I really wanted those files, so I agreed."

"How did the meeting go?"

She ran her fingers through her hair, avoiding the sore spot on the back of her head. "Like all our meetings. We ended up in an argument."

His eyes flickered, but he took a seat on the edge of the coffee table and she eked out a little sigh because he was no longer looming over her.

"Did anyone at the bar notice you arguing?"

"I'm sure a few people did. We exchanged sharp words and may have got a little loud, but there was no knock-down-drag-out."

He rubbed his knuckles across his clean-shaven chin. He'd shaved off the beard since the last time she'd seen him. Bearded or not, the man still pushed all the right buttons in all the right places.

She licked her lips, and his gaze bounced to her mouth and then back to her eyes.

"What happened next? How'd you end up at his house? That house in La Jolla, right?"

"Yeah, that one." She caught a drop of moisture on the outside of the glass with her finger and touched it to her temple. "Niles had left the file I wanted at the house. I had to go with him to retrieve them."

"Go with him? You didn't drive your own car?" He tipped his head at the window, toward the Lexus in his driveway.

"I walked to the bar. It was close to my house and you know I don't like to drive after even one drink."

"Is that what you had? One drink?"

"Two." She held up two fingers in a peace sign and then brought the fingers together. "Scout's honor."

Unless she'd downed whatever was in that crystal tumbler at the house.

"I'm not checking on you, Savannah. I believe you. What

I'm trying to get at is if you were drunk when you left the bar with him."

"Absolutely not. I don't get drunk…anymore."

"So why'd you black out? Do you remember going to his house? Driving in the car with him?"

"I do remember getting into his car. I remember more arguing on the way to the house, arriving at the house and then…" She shrugged. "Nothing after that. I don't remember what we did at the house. I don't know how I lost my clothes and ended up in his bed. And I sure as hell don't know how he wound up dead."

"And you didn't…"

"What?" She jerked her head in his direction.

He swiped a hand across his mouth as if to keep the words from tumbling out. "You're telling me that someone broke into Niles's house, murdered him in a violent manner and you were allowed to sleep peacefully through it all. Why weren't you killed along with Niles?"

"That, I can't tell you." She skewered him with a gaze. "You almost sound disappointed."

Connor pushed up from the coffee table and stalked to the kitchen. "Don't play the poor-me card. I know you too well."

He thought he did, but she'd kept secrets from him before.

He buried his head in the fridge and popped up with a bottle of beer in his hand. "I'm not offering. Someone needs a clear head here, but it's not gonna be me."

"Beer for breakfast?" She held up her hands to deflect his scowl. "Never mind. And I already told you, I have no idea why the killer left me undisturbed…almost undisturbed."

"Almost?" He took a swig of beer and hunched over the kitchen island.

She jabbed her index finger into her chest. "I did not voluntarily take off my clothes for Niles, and I did not crawl into his bed."

"The murderer took the time to strip you naked and place you in Niles's bed? Where was Niles's body?"

"On the floor next to the bed."

"Next to you?"

"On the floor."

He snapped his fingers. "Did you check the security cameras? A place like that, a guy like that—he had to have video surveillance."

"All disabled."

He scratched his chin in an absentminded manner. He must've just lost the beard and missed it, although why Connor's facial hair occupied her thoughts at this crucial moment was a mystery. She squeezed her thighs together and huffed out a breath. No, it wasn't, no mystery.

"Murder weapon?"

"Gone."

"Blood?"

"All over Niles and the floor beneath him, but only a little on me and none on my clothes."

"You had blood spatter on you?"

"I wouldn't call it spatter." She curled her right hand into a fist. She didn't want to show him her palm, but she couldn't hide it. He'd notice it anyway.

Holding her hand out to him and spreading her fingers, she said, "The blood came from some cuts on my hand."

He sucked in a sharp breath, and then skirted the counter and charged toward her. She shrank back when he dropped to his knees in front of her and took her wrist between his fingers.

But she had nothing to fear from Connor.

With a gentle touch, he traced a fingertip over each cut, sending chills down her spine.

"These aren't very deep…and they're on the wrong hand."

"The wrong hand?"

"The wrong hand for stabbing. You're left-handed."

She clasped his shoulder with her left hand. "I knew there was a good reason to run to you. D-do you think someone's trying to set me up for Niles's murder? Because I do. That's what I think."

"Could be. Do you have a motive?" He dropped her wrist and rose to his feet, as her hand slid from his shoulder.

She rolled her eyes. "Take your pick. We were fighting over the business. With his death, I get the whole thing, controlling interest back in my lap. A-and there's something else."

He had returned to his beer and raised his eyebrows as he took a sip.

"Life insurance." She knotted her fingers in front of her. "Lots of life insurance."

"It's natural to assume a spouse would be the beneficiary of life insurance, even after a divorce. It's not necessarily the first thing most people going through a separation think about."

"Niles Wedgewood is not most people. He *did* think about dropping me as his beneficiary after the divorce in favor of his new girlfriend, Tiffany, and his junkie twin brother, Newland, and his sister, Melanie, up in San Francisco, but I convinced him we should leave each other as our beneficiaries until we had the business worked out."

"And people know this?" Connor tugged on his earlobe, a sure sign of worry.

"His divorce attorney knows it."

"How much are we talking?"

She dropped her chin to her chest. "Millions."

"With Niles's death, you stand to get the business and millions of dollars in life insurance money."

His gaze sharpened and his eyes looked like chips of ice, sending a flutter of fear to her belly. She'd better get used to that look—especially if she couldn't produce an alibi for last night.

"Looks bad, huh?"

He nodded. "Did it occur to you for one second to call the police?"

"You know more than anyone why I won't do that. No, it never occurred to me. I need an alibi, Connor. I need you."

"You want me to lie to the police for you. Claim you were here last night."

She leaned forward, planting her hands on her knees. "Mom and I lied for your father."

There it was.

Connor's eye twitched at the corner. "There's no footage of you at the house. You didn't drive your car, so it wasn't parked in the neighborhood. How'd you get home? Taxi? App car?"

"Do you think I'm stupid?" She sprang up from the couch, excitement and hope fizzing through her blood. He was going to help her. "I walked, and if you think that was easy with heels on, it wasn't."

"You walked home, got your car and drove straight down here?"

"I showered and changed first, but I didn't waste much time."

He snapped his fingers. "Cell phone? The police are going to pull your records. They're going to know your phone was at Niles's house last night at precisely the time he was murdered."

"I didn't have my phone with me."

His head jerked back. "You didn't have your phone? Who doesn't carry their cell with them?"

"My battery has been dying on me. I left it at home, charging. I thought I'd be walking up to the bar to meet Niles for a quick drink, a discussion and those files."

"And then you drove down here with it turned on? They're gonna see that, too."

"Foiled again." She held up one finger. "I turned the phone off when I plucked it off the charger. It's off even now."

His eyebrows formed a V over his slightly sunburned nose as he pinned her with a slitted gaze before turning away from her.

The look sent a chill up her spine. Despite her explanation, he was wondering why she hadn't brought her phone with her to the bar...but he'd see she'd been telling the truth about her phone.

"If the police don't believe you...or me, they can track your license plate. There are cameras on the highway between here and La Jolla. If they want to, all they have to do is enter your license plate number and—" he flicked his index finger against his thumb "—they could get a hit, placing your car on its way to San Juan Beach today instead of last night."

"I removed my plates."

Connor swung around, his longish hair brushing his shoulders. "You could've been pulled over for not having plates."

"I figured it was worth the risk for just the reason you mentioned. Did you think I wasn't listening to you all those times you went on and on about police work and new innovations?" She tapped the side of her head. "It fascinated me. I was listening."

"What's your story?" He folded his arms, ready to listen.

"I was upset after meeting with Niles. I made him drop me off near my house, and then I hopped in my car and came down here to see you." She strolled to the window and rested her forehead against the glass. "I was here at the time he was getting stabbed."

"Why would you rush to my place? We haven't seen each other in four years, not since your marriage."

"We were…in love. Everyone in San Juan Beach knows that. I never got you out of my system. Never forgot you. Never stopped wanting you back." Her breath fogged the window, and she drew a line through the condensation.

The silence yawned between them until she couldn't take it anymore. She did a slow turn and met his eyes. "Is that…believable?"

"I suppose it could fool *some* people." The frost dripping from every word made it clear she hadn't fooled him. "But we're gonna have to make it stick."

"How? What do you mean?"

"You can't go running back to your former lover and then leave him a few days later to get back to managing your multimillion-dollar company and spending Niles's life insurance money."

"I could if my lover rejected my advances."

"He wouldn't do that."

"He wouldn't?"

"You wouldn't have turned to him in your hour of need if you didn't think you'd meet fertile ground. If I'm going to lie for you, you're going to have to see this through. You're going to have to stick around for a while to give this story legs."

"I can do that—if you'll have me."

He leveled a finger at her. "I'm not going to get caught in this lie. I'm not going down for you—no matter what you and your mother did for my dad."

"I understand. It's in my best interest that we don't get outed—life or death, actually."

"Did you pack a bag or rush to me with just the clothes on your back?"

"Of course I packed a bag. It's in my trunk."

"I'll get it." He held up one hand. "Keys."

She grabbed her purse from the floor by the sofa and dragged her keys from a side pocket. She tossed her key ring to him, and he caught it with his outstretched hand.

"Be right back."

She watched him for a few seconds out the window and then turned, her lips twitching into a smile. It had been time to play her ace in the hole, but she knew she could get Connor to come around to her way of thinking. Even though he'd been a cop once upon a time, he had no regard for the police anymore. No trust in authority. Not much trust in her.

She sauntered toward the hallway and peeked into the first bedroom, the master suite, which Connor had transformed with dark woods and rich jewel tones. She didn't know he had such good taste—unless he'd had help.

She'd come to San Juan Beach with confidence that Connor didn't have a woman in his life. She still had her spies in this town, and they kept tabs on Connor for her. It wasn't exactly stalking—just a healthy interest in the one man she'd love forever, but could never have.

The front door slammed and Connor yelled out her name, as if she weren't down the hall.

She tripped back toward the living room and poked her head around the corner. "What's the commotion?"

"What the hell is this?" He waved a plastic grocery bag above his head.

"I don't know what you have there." She wrinkled her nose as she eyed the bag.

He yanked on the handles, pulling it open. "You don't know what this is?"

Her heart pounding against her rib cage, she crossed the room on shaky legs.

Connor thrust the open bag under her nose, and she staggered back…away from the sight of the bloody knife.

"Savannah, tell me the truth. Did you kill your ex?"

Chapter Three

Connor studied Savannah's face as she peered into the plastic bag at the bloody knife.

Her big violet eyes widened, and her lips parted. Those eyes, a color he'd never seen before in his life, and the long lashes that framed them gave Savannah a look of innocence—but he knew better.

Who thought to leave a cell phone at home and remove a car's license plates without something to hide?

Savannah's bottom lip quivered as she dragged her gaze from the bloody evidence in front of her to his face. "I—I don't... No!"

She spun away from him, clutching her belly. "I didn't put that in my car. You found it in my trunk?"

"I found it in the spare tire well."

"Why were you looking in there?" She glanced at him over her shoulder, her mouth tight as if she blamed him for the presence of the knife.

The knots in his gut tightened. He wanted to trust Savannah, believe her crazy story. God, he loved this woman... once.

"The corner of the cover wasn't lying flat, so I lifted it. The bag looked out of place. What's it doing there, Savannah? Is it the murder weapon?"

"How do I know?" She lifted her shoulders to her ears

and turned to face him. "I'm telling you, Connor, I blacked out when I got to Niles's place."

"The point being, you could've got into an argument with him, continued your argument from the bar even and…"

"Stabbed him multiple times in the back?" She shook her head back and forth.

"Maybe it was self-defense." He tied the handles of the bag together and placed it on the floor by the front door— not that he could leave it there. "Maybe the fight got physical, and he attacked you with a knife. You got it away from him and struck back."

"That's insane, Connor. I didn't have any…" She stopped and touched the back of her head with her fingertips.

"Any what? What's wrong?"

"I have a bump on my head. I was going to say I didn't have any injuries, but I have this lump on the back of my skull and these cuts on my hand."

His feet had been rooted to the floor ever since he'd entered with the knife and a terrible dread in his gut. Now a new urgency propelled him forward.

He took Savannah by the shoulders. "Turn around."

She presented her back to him, and a silky fall of dark hair rippled across her shoulders.

He nestled his fingers in the strands of her hair and slid them up to her scalp.

She winced and sucked in a sharp breath.

"Here?" He traced a large, hard knot on Savannah's head.

"Ouch. That's the spot."

"You didn't have that before you woke up this morning?"

"No. I don't think the skin is broken, and I didn't notice any blood in my hair."

"He could've pushed you, and you fell back against something."

"Maybe that's why I blacked out. Oh, Connor." Dipping

her head, she pressed a hand to her forehead. "I don't know what happened last night."

His hands dropped to her shoulders again and he massaged his thumbs between her shoulder blades. "We're going to figure it out, Savannah."

"And what if we figure out I'm responsible for Niles's death?"

He turned her around to face him and kissed her forehead. "We'll deal with it."

"And what about that?" She pointed a slightly trembling finger at the bag by the door.

"We should get it tested for blood and fingerprints."

She jerked back from him. "Are you crazy?"

"I thought you wanted to find out who killed Niles." He folded his arms and dug his fingers into his biceps to keep from touching Savannah again. That never seemed to end well for him.

"Yes, but how are we going to ID blood and prints from the knife without taking it to the police?" She sliced a hand through the air. "I'm not doing that, Connor."

"I think I can work around that."

"Connections?"

"Maybe a few." His father *had* been police chief in this town for over twenty years, before the sheriff's department took over and swallowed up the San Juan Beach PD. "In the meantime…"

"In the meantime, get rid of it."

"I'll find a place." He aimed his foot at the suitcase he'd dragged in with the knife. "Why don't you unpack and get ready for our first appearance?"

"Our first appearance where?" She twisted a lock of hair around her finger.

"In public. If you showed up on my doorstep last night,

we'd be out and about by now…or at least we should be to prove you're here."

"Makes sense." She tossed her wound-up hair over her shoulder. "Are you sure you want to do this?"

"Like you pointed out earlier, I owe you for what you and your mom did for my dad. You never let me repay you for that."

"Because even though Mom and I lied…and said Chief Wells killed my stepfather in self-defense, it still led to your dad's death."

Connor gritted his teeth. "Self-defense or not, it would've ended for Dad that way. Your stepfather's associates were not going to let anyone get away with killing Manny Edmonds without payback."

"My mom was always grateful for…what your father did."

"My dad would've done anything for your mom." Apparently it ran in the Wellses' blood to do anything for the Martell women. Dad's devotion to Savannah's mother had broken up his marriage to Mom and ended his life. And Connor's own devotion to Savannah had strained his relationship with his mother. How would this latest association end?

"Brunch?"

"What?" Connor ran a hand down the side of his face.

"I'm going to change while you get rid of that knife. Are we having brunch or lunch out to show my presence in San Juan Beach?"

Savannah sure seemed anxious to dispose of what was probably the murder weapon. "I'm not going to dump it."

"Okay, whatever." She strode past him and grabbed the handle of her suitcase, yanking it up. "I don't want to know what you do with it."

"Shouldn't we take a look on TV or the computer to see if Niles's body has been found yet?"

She held up one hand in front of her face. "I don't want to know that, either. Better to feign surprise when the cops come calling."

With a toss of her head, she tipped back her bag and dragged it across the floor to the hallway.

As she veered toward the guest room on the right, he called out, "Master suite. We're back together, remember?"

Without a word or backward glance, she changed course and wheeled her bag into his bedroom.

He bent over and snatched up the plastic grocery bag by one handle. As it dangled from his fingertips, he stared at the spot where Savannah had disappeared into his bedroom.

He'd wanted Savannah back in his life for so long and now she was here in the flesh—needing him, sharing his bedroom, willing to engage in a pretend romance with him.

Turning, he grabbed the front door handle. How could this possibly go wrong?

SAVANNAH SMOOTHED HER hands across the cotton skirt that hit her midthigh. How many more ways could she feel guilty for dragging Connor into her mess?

Mom had dragged Connor's father into her messes, and here she was, carrying on the famous Martell tradition. She and Mom had lied about the night her stepfather was shot and killed, all right, but it wasn't for the benefit of Chief Wells.

Savannah could never tell Connor the truth about that night; he would never look at her the same way again. He'd blame her for his father's death. And because she had to keep this secret from him, they could never have a relationship—not a real one.

When she heard the front door open, she grabbed her

purse from Connor's bed, and swung it by her side as she marched into the living room. "Ready?"

He spread his arms wide and his gray T-shirt stretched across his chiseled chest. "As long as it's casual."

"Is there anything but casual in San Juan Beach?"

"You haven't been here for a while. A couple nice places popped up along the strand, still casual dress, though."

The cell phone that had been charging on Connor's kitchen counter dinged, indicating a new text message. She swallowed. "I'd better see who that is."

Connor nodded.

She slid the phone across the smooth granite surface and tapped the incoming message. The words on the screen screamed at her. She read them aloud for Connor's benefit. "'Have you heard? Call me.'"

"Who's it from?"

"It's from Dee Dee Rodriguez. She's Niles's admin assistant at the office."

"You'd better call her."

"So it starts." She went to her contacts and called Dee Dee's number.

Dee Dee didn't even wait for the first ring to end. "Savannah, have you heard about Niles?"

"No. What happened? What's wrong?"

"He's dead."

"What are you talking about?" She lifted her eyebrows at Connor. Did she sound convincing? She put the phone on speaker, so he could hear everything, steer her in the right direction.

"Niles is dead, Savannah. Murdered."

"Murdered? Is this a joke, Dee? It's not funny." *Feign disbelief.*

Connor nodded.

"Would I joke about someone's murder?"

"I—I don't believe you. Why haven't I heard anything?"

"I just found out. The police are here." She lowered her voice. "They were asking about you."

Savannah licked her lips, her gaze darting to Connor's face. "What happened, Dee? Who found him? I was just with him last night."

"All I know is that his housekeeper found him this morning. I don't know how he died. If…if you saw him last night, it must've happened after that, or this morning before the housekeeper arrived."

"Oh, my God. This is terrible. I—I'm going to turn on the news or look it up on my computer."

"I'm not sure the news is out there yet. Where are you, Savannah? I'm sure the police are gonna head to your place."

"Probably, although Tiffany is closer to Niles than I am now—in every way, including physically. I'm not even in San Diego. I went south to San Juan Beach."

"Oh, my God. Are you with that hottie from the picture you showed me?"

Heat clawed up Savannah's chest and she turned away from Connor. "Yeah, I'm down here with Connor."

"Lucky girl, unlucky Niles. Stay safe. Maybe there's some kind of hit out on both of you."

Savannah chewed her bottom lip. If that had been the case, she'd be dead, too. "I will. If the cops ask you about me again, you can tell them I'm in San Juan and would be happy to talk with them."

"I will. It's gonna be crazy at the office."

"I can't imagine anyone's going to get any work done, so why don't you all just take the rest of the day off?"

"Well, we can't just… Oh, right. You're the boss now, aren't you?"

"Tell everyone there to take a mental health day."

"Will do."

Savannah ended the call and spun around. "How did I sound?"

"Convincing. Now, get on your laptop like you said you would."

She dropped her purse on the floor where she stood and returned to the bedroom. She pulled her laptop from a zippered pouch on the side of her suitcase and brought it into the kitchen.

As Connor hovered over her shoulder, she powered on the computer and did a search for Niles Wedgewood. Her hand trembled as she clicked on the first link that popped up. "Local news outlet already has the story, but no specifics."

Connor leaned in closer, his warm breath stirring her hair. "Just a snippet—body believed to be that of Niles Wedgewood, cofounder and CEO of Snap App, discovered in his ocean-side mansion in La Jolla. No further details at this time."

"The police are going to call me, aren't they?"

"Homicide detectives. They'll probably want to interview you face-to-face, especially once they find out you were the last person to see him alive."

"I'll be ready." She snapped down the lid of her laptop and rubbed her hands together. "Now, let's go eat and make my presence known in SJB."

Savannah bounced along in the passenger seat of Connor's truck as he pulled onto the road from the property he'd inherited from his father. She rolled down the window and inhaled the scent of the air sweetened by grapevines.

"I think I can detect the aroma of wine already."

"This time next year, I hope to have my first harvest."

She tapped on the window. "I didn't notice a name for the winery. Have you thought of one yet?"

"I suppose the easiest choice would be San Juan Beach Winery."

"That's a mouthful and kind of boring." She drummed her fingers on her knee. "I'll think of something clever."

"Did you think of Snap App?"

"I did. Catchy, isn't it?"

"It is." He turned the truck west toward the coast. "I'll take you to one of the newer places if you're up for seafood. There's a steak place, too, and they both do a breakfast or brunch or maybe even lunch."

"Seafood. I'm trying to rid my diet of red meat."

"Ethical or health?"

"I do love animals, but it's for health reasons."

He gave her a quick glance up and down. "You? You're as fit as you were in high school, when you were a soccer star."

"Soccer star?" she snorted. "Our team was awful."

"Yeah, but you were the best one on that awful team." He nudged her shoulder with the heel of his hand.

"You always were biased."

"I know. In my eyes, you could do no wrong—even when you did wrong."

Savannah tucked her hands beneath her thighs and sealed her lips. She'd done more wrong than Connor had known about, but why dredge up old skeletons? The new ones were keeping her busy enough.

She cleared her throat. "How much help do you have on the vineyard?"

"I have a chemist working for me, who drops by a few times a month. I have a couple guys who work the land daily, and I hired a marketing person who's going to help design the bottles, labels, logos—that kind of stuff."

Savannah wagged a finger in the air. "Don't let her

choose the name of the winery. I have dibs on that—I mean, since we're back together and all."

"Don't take liberties."

"How long do you think we need to play kissy-face?" She dropped her gaze and pleated her skirt with restless fingers. A girl could hope.

"Kissy-face? You mean how long should we pretend to be a couple?"

She lifted her shoulders. "Same thing."

"We'll play it by ear. Let's see what the homicide detectives have to say. Let's see if you're their prime suspect." He gripped the steering wheel at the top with both hands, his knuckles blanching.

"Oh, God. Don't even go there. I don't want to think about it—any of it." She tipped her head, resting it against the window.

"Have you tried to remember what happened after you got to Niles's house?"

"I won't." She hadn't remembered the time before, either.

Connor's head jerked to the side. "Why so sure?"

"I—I don't know. That time last night just feels like a black hole. Besides, if I was roofied, I'm not going to remember. I don't think any victims after they'd been slipped Rohypnol ever remember what happened, do they? It's usually forensic evidence, rape kit, even CCTV and witnesses that help piece things together and lead to a conviction, not the victim's testimony."

"Typically, but why would Niles drug you?" Connor dragged a hand through his hair, tucking one side behind his ear. "He wasn't after you, was he? Wanting to get back together?"

"No way. He'd already moved on to a new girlfriend."

"Then why drug you?"

"I'm thinking it wasn't Niles who drugged me. Maybe somebody slipped something in both our drinks."

"At the bar?"

She nodded. "This the place?"

"How can you tell? The fishnets in the front or the giant swordfish?"

"Don't be a smart-ass." She punched his thigh with her fist and met rock-hard muscle. Being a vintner agreed with Connor—the longer, sun-bleached hair, the casual attire, his more relaxed attitude. The fact that he hadn't tossed her out on her bum after her outrageous story was a testament to that new attitude.

Although if she were honest with herself, she'd known Connor wouldn't turn her away. He never had even when she'd deserved it.

He swung the truck into a parking place around the side of the restaurant that fronted the ocean. "Tourists are out in force. That's the thing with these new restaurants. They do cater to the tourists."

"Is the food any good?"

"Would I take you out for bad seafood? It's decent."

"Maybe we should've gone to one of our old haunts with the old local crowd, like the Black Whale."

"Too risky. Too many direct questions. We need some time to ease into this."

When he turned off the engine, Savannah slid from the truck, yanking down her skirt as her sandals hit the asphalt.

Connor had come around to the passenger side. "Should've waited for me to help you out. The truck sits kinda high."

"I'm not going to hurt myself falling out of your truck." Connor might not be a cop anymore, but he hadn't lost his protective instincts. Thank God.

He took her hand. "It's showtime."

She was going to enjoy this role more than most of the ones she played. She squeezed his hand and bumped his shoulder with hers.

He opened the door for her, and she stepped into the restaurant, her breath hitching at the panoramic view of the ocean from the windows across the dining room. "Wow, no wonder this attracts the tourists."

"Hey there, Connor." A slinky hostess floated toward them, and Savannah moved in closer to her man, even if it was pretend.

"Hi, Cher. Do you have a table for two? No reservation."

"You don't need a reservation here, Connor. We have a no-show in the back, and that table has your name on it."

"Thanks, Cher."

As the resourceful Cher led them to the table with Connor's name on it, she twisted her head over her shoulder and winked at Savannah. "We're hoping to serve his first bottle of wine here someday soon."

"I can't wait for that myself. We're trying to come up with names for the winery right now."

Cher's eyes popped and a little stumble marred her sashay. She recovered nicely and pulled out a chair for Savannah. "Well, let us know when you decide. Enjoy your meal, you two."

Seated across from Savannah, Connor raised one eyebrow. "Laying it on a little thick, aren't you?"

She hunched across the table and grabbed both his hands. "We're back together. You're the man I ran to in the middle of the night, knowing you'd take me back."

The light from the window glimmered in his eyes as he studied every detail of her face. Could he see the truth there? She would always turn to Connor Wells in a crisis because he'd always be there for her.

He raised one of her hands, turned it over and pressed a kiss against the pulse throbbing in her wrist.

"Can I get you something to drink?" The waiter cleared his throat and asked again, "Drinks?"

Savannah tore her gaze away from Connor's and jerked her hand out of his grasp. The connection between them still sizzled, even under the current circumstances. It would never go away, but this was all still make-believe and she'd kept too many secrets from Connor to ever make this anything more than playacting.

"Since it's still before noon, how about a mimosa?" She ran a finger down a plastic drink menu. "The pomegranate mimosa, please."

"It's one of our most popular. And you, Connor? The usual?"

"That'll do."

Maybe nobody at this tourist trap knew Connor enough to ask probing questions, but they knew who he was. Everyone in San Juan Beach had known the Wells family. Her own mother had always told her to cozy up to Connor. The Wells family not only had position, they had money or at least land, which always translated into money.

She'd cozied up to him, but it hadn't been for power or money—and now she had plenty of the latter, thanks to Niles's death.

As the waiter walked away, Savannah tapped the side of her water glass. "The usual?"

"I've been doing a lot of wine tasting the past few years, and I found one I liked here." He shrugged. "I'm a creature of habit."

Savannah cranked her head over her shoulder at the loud voices coming from the bar. "Football game?"

Connor bolted upright in his chair, craning his neck

toward the bar. "Not sure why they'd be pointing at us if it were."

As Savannah's gaze darted among the faces turned their way, she placed a hand against the fluttering in her belly. Was there news about Niles?

The bartender, Angel Cruz, burst through the low swinging door that led behind the bar and charged into the dining room. "Connor, there's a fire—at your place."

Connor jumped from the table, knocking over his glass of water. "The vines?"

"I don't think so, man." Angel tapped the cell phone in his hand. "My buddy said it's a structure."

"The house? Not the house." Savannah had tossed her napkin on the table and pushed back her chair.

"It's not the house, either. Some building on the property between the house and the vineyard."

"I'll settle this tab later." Connor swirled his finger above the table. "Fire department already there?"

"Yeah, yeah. Go, dude. Don't worry about this stuff."

Connor grabbed her arm and practically dragged her from the restaurant.

When they hit the parking lot, Savannah shook him off. "It sounds like it's under control, Connor, and thank God it's not the vines or the house."

"You don't understand, Savannah." He put his lips close to her ear. "The building that's burning? That's where I hid the knife."

Chapter Four

Connor raced back to his house, his truck flying over the asphalt. He'd be able to talk his way out of any speeding ticket right now.

Savannah sat beside him, twisting her fingers in her lap, worrying her bottom lip with her teeth.

She'd been mostly quiet after he told her about the knife in the burning building. She hadn't seen him put it out there, had she? Not that she had an opportunity to set a fire before they'd left for lunch.

He flexed his fingers on the steering wheel. "How the hell does a fire just start? There's nothing in that building like a heater or water heater or gas cans. It's just a storage area for now."

"A storage area that currently houses a murder weapon."

His hands jerked and the truck swerved. "What are you saying? There's no way anyone saw me hide that knife." Including Savannah.

He squinted at the white divider line on the road in front of him. "Besides, I thought your theory was that someone set you up for Niles's murder. How would that jibe with someone trying to destroy the murder weapon in a fire?"

"Destroy it? Is that what someone's trying to do? Maybe they're trying to expose us...me." She flicked her fingers at the window. "Firefighters swarming the place, putting out a fire, discovering a knife where a murder victim's ex-wife happens to be staying."

"I get you." He rubbed his aching jaw. "Why do you think I hightailed it out of that restaurant so fast? But intentional? How would this...arsonist even know you were here? How would he know I put the knife in the shed?"

Crossing her hands over her chest, Savannah said, "I don't know. What if the firefighters find it? Are they going to put two and two together when the news gets out?"

"Don't worry about it." He squeezed her bare knee, and then snatched his hand away.

How far would they take this pretense? He'd never been able to resist Savannah, despite his mother's warnings.

Like mother, like daughter. Mom always knew Dad had a soft spot for Georgie Martell, Savannah's mother, and when Dad wound up shooting and killing Georgie's husband to protect Georgie and Savannah, that had been the last straw for Mom.

As Connor turned onto the road leading to his property, Savannah tugged on his sleeve. "It looks like they're finished already...and there's a cop here."

"The sheriff's department always shows up with the fire department." He powered down the window and stuck out his arm.

The sheriff's deputy jogged to the truck. "You the owner?"

"Yeah, what happened?"

"Fire in that small wooden structure, not too much damage but you'll have to replace the roof."

"How'd the fire department get here so quickly?"

"You're lucky. Someone saw the smoke from the road and called it in."

"Cause?"

The deputy spread his hands. "Looks like arson."

Connor swore and Savannah stiffened beside him. "Now, who the hell would want to burn down my storage shed? Kids?"

"Maybe." The deputy swept his arm forward. "You can go ahead. They're wrapping it up, and the fire chief is going to want to speak with you."

"Got it, thanks." Connor pulled away from the deputy and rolled up his window against the smoky air. "Arson."

"This is freaking me out." Savannah scooped up her purse from the floor and hugged it against her chest. "Why would someone set fire to the very shed where you just hid the knife that killed Niles?"

His gaze flicked to her face. "You're sure you weren't followed here?"

"I—I don't think so. Like I said, I ran home first to change clothes and throw some things in a bag. It was still early morning when I drove down here, almost dark. I think I would've noticed the headlights of another car dogging me on the road."

Connor rolled up the window and stepped on the gas pedal. "Don't be obvious."

"You mean we shouldn't run straight to…wherever you hid the knife and pull it out in view of the firefighters and deputy?" She rolled her eyes. "I think I can handle that."

He slid her a sideways glance. "I think you can handle a lot."

He pulled in front of the house, and an average-sized man who seemed overpowered by his gear tromped up to him, his heavy boots stirring up little clouds of dust with every step.

Connor mumbled under his breath, "The fire chief. Let me do the talking."

"It's your property." Savannah turned away and shoved open the passenger door.

Connor scrambled from the truck and thrust out his hand. "Chief, I'm Connor Wells and this is my property."

"Chief Murray." After shaking Connor's hand with his own gloved one, Murray jerked his thumb over his shoulder. "Arson. Crude Molotov cocktail. You know anyone who'd want to start a fire at your place?"

"Not a clue." Connor shoved one hand in the pocket of his shorts. "I'm just glad he decided to torch my storage shed instead of my vines."

Savannah had joined him and draped her arm casually around his waist. If she wanted to continue the pretense in front of the fire chief, who was he to complain?

"Yeah, that's unusual. Someone wanting to do you the most amount of harm would've started with your grapevines." Murray tipped his hat back from his forehead. "Maybe it was kids pulling a prank."

"In my day, pulling a prank would be playing ding-dong ditch, not setting fires."

Savannah pinched his side—hard. "That's probably what it was. They figured this was a worthless building with nothing much inside, so they wouldn't get in so much trouble if they were caught. I mean, as opposed to setting fire to the house or the land, which could've spread."

This time Connor nudged her sandaled foot with the toe of his shoe. If she kept going on and on about how worthless the shed was, she could raise the chief's antenna.

Connor cleared his throat, as much to stop Savannah from opening her mouth again as from the smoke lingering in the air. "I wouldn't say completely worthless. The shed isn't empty. Was anything inside damaged?"

"Singed a little, scorched…and now waterlogged, but the fire mostly damaged the roof, where the arsonist tossed the incendiary device." Murray stepped aside and waved his arm. "We've put it out completely, if you want to have a look inside, but don't go in yet. The wood's still hot and we're going to rip off that roof before we go."

Connor put his hand on Savannah's arm as she took a step forward. "Stay here. I'm just going to take a quick look."

He approached the blackened shed, water dripping from the roof, and one wall caved in. Ducking his head, he peered inside, his gaze wandering to the wine barrel where he'd stashed the knife.

A hand clapped on his back and Connor jumped and spun around.

Cole Miller, a friend of his, held up his hands. "Whoa, sorry, man."

"You're good. Just startled me."

"Yeah, who wouldn't be on edge? When I saw that we were riding out here to your property, I was hoping we wouldn't find the vines on fire. Glad it's just this storage shed."

"I had the same thought when Angel over at Neptune's Cove told me there was a fire at my place—anything but the vines."

Cole hit the side of the shed with his hand. "Anything important in here? You have insurance, right?"

"Nothing much. I'm starting to collect some casks for the wine and some other stuff I'm going to need to construct my wine cave, and yeah, I do have insurance. I'm gonna need it to replace the roof and at least one side—unless my deductible is too high."

"Let me know if it is. My brother's still doing construction, and he'd be happy to give you a deal on the job." Cole squinted over Connor's shoulder. "Is that Savannah Martell over there looking hotter than the sun?"

"She's back."

"For you?"

"What else?"

"No telling with that girl." Cole blinked. "I mean, you know. Sorry, man. I'm glad if you two are back together."

"We are, and don't worry about it."

Cole coughed. "Did the deputy tell you we found some footprints around the perimeter of the shack? Flip-flops."

"Really? An arsonist wearing flip-flops?" Connor lifted his own foot. "Has to belong to the guy—or girl—who started the fire. I haven't been out here in flip-flops."

Another firefighter approached with an ax balanced on his shoulder. "We're going to start working on the roof now, Mr. Wells."

"Maybe I'll talk to the deputy to find out if the guy left any more clues." He nodded to Cole. "I'll catch you later."

Seeing his direction, Savannah, who'd been practically hopping from foot to foot, beat him to the deputy. When Connor reached them, she was asking about evidence.

The deputy answered, "We did find footprints around the shed—flip-flops."

"One of the firefighters told me that. They're not mine."

"Not mine, either." Savannah pointed to her sandals. "Does that further point to teenagers?"

The deputy shrugged. "San Juan is a beach town. A lot of people wear flip-flops—some all year long."

"But to set a fire? It's looking more and more like kids to me."

Connor interrupted to shut her up. "Did you find anything else?"

"The jar used for the Molotov cocktail was one of those ones that people use to preserve fruit. My grandma used to do that, and I recognized it from a piece of glass."

The sound of a blade splitting wood cracked through the air and Savannah grabbed his arm.

"They're taking the roof down. Do you need me for anything else, Officer? I'm going to make some calls to my insurance company and maybe my friend's brother to find out if he can do the repairs."

Savannah dug her fingers into his biceps. "We're not going to stay out here and watch them demolish the roof?"

"You can keep an eye on them if you want, Savannah. I'm going to make those calls, if there's nothing else."

"One more thing." The deputy adjusted his equipment belt. "How come you never applied to the sheriff's department after the San Juan PD went away? I'd heard you were a good cop."

"That was six years ago. I'm surprised you remembered." The familiar knots tightened in Connor's gut.

"I never forgot that story about how those drug dealers went after your father, the chief, when he killed Manny Edmonds. That was some crazy stuff for this small town."

Connor's jaw tightened. "That situation didn't have to end with my father's murder. He'd been warning the sheriff's department about Manny for years, and nobody listened to him."

The deputy took a step back and a bead of sweat formed on his brow. "Didn't know that."

"It's ancient history." Connor rolled his shoulders and patted the phone in his pocket. "I'm going to make those calls now. Are you going to watch the demolition, Savannah?"

She nodded, her lips pressed into a thin line.

Connor pulled his phone from his pocket and strode toward his house.

Savannah didn't like being reminded of that ancient history, either, as Manny had been her mother's husband, and Connor's father had killed Manny to protect the Martell women.

His father had admitted to him later, and only because

Connor had overheard a conversation between him and Georgie, that the kill hadn't been in self-defense. He'd killed Manny in a fit of pure rage over what he'd been doing to Dad's town…and what he'd been doing to Georgie Martell, which seemed the stronger motive. And Georgie and Savannah had lied to protect him, claiming Manny came at him with a weapon. They'd even planted Manny's gun in his hand.

Connor slammed the front door behind him and perched on the edge of a stool at the granite island. If he were honest with himself, his father's admission had done as much to sour him on police work as his death had. It had destroyed Connor's trust in authority in general and his father in particular.

He wiped a trickle of sweat from his face and placed the first call to his insurance company.

About forty minutes later, Connor stepped onto his front porch, and Savannah, standing several feet from the shed and talking to Cole, waved her arms over her head to signal him.

Cole always did have a thing for Savannah.

Connor stepped off the porch and joined them. "All done?"

"Yeah, Chief Murray was just going to get you. Any luck with the insurance company?"

"They're going to send out an adjuster tomorrow."

One of the firefighters called out from the rear of a fire engine, and Cole waved back.

"Looks like we're all done." Cole touched Savannah's shoulder. "Welcome back, Savannah, and my condolences on your ex-husband's…death."

"Thank you, Cole." She patted his hand, still resting on her shoulder.

Cole tromped back to his truck, his gear making him look a lot bigger than he really was.

Connor took a step forward to stand beside Savannah, his shoulder bumping hers. "You told him?"

"Wouldn't I? I talked to Dee today and she told me. He'd think it odd once he found out about Niles…and he will find out. Everyone will."

"You're right. Quick thinking." In fact, all Savannah's instincts so far had been right on—as if she'd rehearsed them. He rubbed two fingers against his temple. "Everything go okay out here otherwise?"

As she waved at the departing sheriff's deputy, a tight smile on her face, she said, "They knocked down the roof, tore out the damaged wall, but didn't touch anything inside."

"They didn't divulge any more clues to you as to who set this fire?"

"Nope. All they have is the piece of jar from the Molotov cocktail and the flip-flop prints. Doesn't exactly narrow it down."

"But doesn't point to anyone following you here and trying to draw attention to the hidden knife. It didn't work anyway."

"Speaking of the hidden knife." She tapped his shoulder. "Shouldn't we check on it?"

The dust from the last emergency vehicle to drive through the gate settled, and Connor hacked out a breath that seemed to have been trapped in his lungs ever since they drove onto the property.

"Let's look." He turned and walked toward the damaged shed, with Savannah hot on his heels. As he ducked inside, his nostrils twitched at the smell of the soggy, burnt wood.

Savannah followed him in and stood in the middle of the space, hands on her hips. "At least with that entire wall down, we don't need a flashlight, and it's not unbearably hot. It must get dark in here at night."

Connor grabbed a large screwdriver from a pile of tools on the floor, covered with ash, and pointed it at the wine cask at the end of a row. "I put it in there."

He took two steps toward the hiding place and jimmied the spigot off the front of the cask. A flutter of fear whispered across the back of his neck before he thrust his hand inside.

"Well?" Savannah whispered the word in his ear, even though they were the only ones in the shed.

His fingers grasped the knife's handle, crinkling the plastic bag around it. "Still here."

"Thank God." She grabbed a handful of his T-shirt. "Let's get it out of here before the insurance adjuster and the construction workers descend tomorrow, or before the arsonist decides to come back and toss another homemade bomb at it."

Connor eased the bag out of the cask. "I think I can find another place for it."

"We can't just destroy it? Get rid of it?" Savannah clamped down on her bottom lip with her teeth.

"It has blood on it, evidence. It might have the blood of the killer on it. You'd want to know that, wouldn't you?" A muscle ticked at the corner of his mouth.

"Of course, unless..."

He cinched his fingers around her deceptively fragile wrist. Savannah had always been one of the strongest women he'd known. "You said you couldn't have done it, even though you blacked out. No blood on you, no evidence, only those superficial wounds on your hand."

"That's *not* what I was going to say." She twisted her arm out of his grasp. "Maybe my blood *will* be on that knife because the killer used it to cut my hands."

"Either way, I don't want to destroy this evidence if it is the murder weapon. We don't even know if it is." He cocked his head. "Did you hear that?"

"No. I can't hear a thing over that giant fan the fire department left to dry the water."

Connor cupped her elbow and steered her out of the shed. As they stepped outside, a dark Crown Vic rolled up and a man in a suit jumped out of the passenger side of the vehicle before it even came to a complete stop.

Savannah murmured out the side of her mouth, "Who the hell is this?"

A cold dread dripped down Connor's spine, as he clutched the plastic bag with the knife in front of him.

The man in the suit adjusted his dark sunglasses and brushed some dust from the lapel of his jacket. "Savannah Wedgewood?"

"Yes, Savannah Martell, actually." Her body had stiffened beside Connor's and her fingers pinched the material of his shirt at the side.

"I'm Detective Krieger from the San Diego Sheriff's Department, Homicide. This is Detective Paulson. We're here to ask you some questions about the murder of your ex-husband, Niles Wedgewood."

Chapter Five

The detective's words acted like a sledgehammer to her solar plexus. She'd been expecting this visit, had been almost anxious to get it over with. But not while Connor was standing next to her with a bloody knife in his hands, bag or no bag.

She swallowed and opened her mouth, but her tongue and throat were too dry to form words.

Krieger's bushy eyebrows jumped to his hairline. "I'm sorry. You knew about your husband's death, didn't you?"

"I—I did. His assistant, Dee Dee Rodriguez, told me earlier today." She placed a hand against her stomach. "Just hearing it again punched me in the gut."

"I'm sorry."

She slid her arm around Connor's waist, her fingers touching one edge of the plastic bag in his hands. "This is Connor Wells."

"Mr. Wells."

Krieger stuck out his hand, and Connor released the bag and took it.

"We just had a minor catastrophe on my property—a fire."

The other detective stepped around the sedan, planting his black wingtips in the dirt. "Yeah, we saw the fire engines on our way in. Much damage?"

"Just a storage shed, nothing important and no injuries." He waved the bag toward the house. "Would you like to come inside to conduct this interview?"

"Thanks." Krieger gestured for his partner to follow Connor first, twisting his head around to survey the scorched shed.

Savannah swallowed hard and tried to avert her gaze from the plastic bag swinging from Connor's fingertips.

Krieger's gaze slid to Savannah's face. "Quite a day."

"Oh, that." She flicked her fingers toward the shed. "Nothing compared to Niles's death."

Krieger bowed his head, and she moved in close behind him as if to block the shed from his view and his mind. The way Connor was waving that bag around had her heart skipping beats. He couldn't excuse himself to hide it, but he'd better watch it or that knife would come flying out of the bag and land at the detectives' feet—and then they'd be in real trouble.

She stumbled on the first step and bumped into Detective Krieger's suited back. "Sorry."

"Are you okay?"

"Rattled. Like you said, this *has* been quite a day."

The detectives' hard-soled shoes clattered on the wood floor as they maneuvered around the living room to take their seats.

"Something to drink?" Connor pulled out the trash drawer and placed the bag with the knife inside.

Krieger declined and Paulson requested a water.

Savannah didn't dare look at the detectives and check if they'd noticed Connor throwing away the bag. Why wouldn't he pick up some damaged items from the shed and dispose of them in the trash?

She smoothed her sticky palms against her skirt as she sat on the edge of the couch. The detectives had claimed the two chairs facing the couch—like an inquisition. They just needed the bright light.

Connor returned to the room with a glass of water for Detective Paulson and one for her. "Here, babe. Your throat's probably scratchy from the air outside."

Connor was jumping right in with their little deception. He used to call her babe when they were together. She tapped her fingers at the base of her throat. "You're right. It is."

She took a sip of water and then folded her hands around the glass, balancing it on her knee. "What can you tell me about my ex-husband's murder, Detective Krieger? Dee Dee, Niles's assistant, didn't have much information and I read only a small blurb online."

"He was stabbed to death, Mrs... Ms...?"

"You can call me Savannah, but I did return to my maiden name, Martell." The cuts on her palm tingled. "Stabbed. How horrible."

"I gather you were the last person to see him. You two had a drink last night at the Marina Sports Bar?"

"We did, yes."

"Purpose of the meeting?" Krieger's gaze shifted to Connor and back.

"Business."

"You still own Snap App together. Is that right?"

"We do." She wasn't going to point out the obvious fact that the company belonged to her now—lock, stock and barrel.

"Your meeting was about Snap App?"

"It was."

"Cordial?"

The corner of her lip twitched. "Not really, but no different from any other discussion Niles and I had—married, separated or divorced."

"What was the reason for the divorce?" Again, that subtle shift of attention from her to Connor.

"Infidelity—his."

Paulson cleared his throat. "What happened when you left Niles, Savannah? Where did you go? What did you do? When did you last see Niles?"

So, Paulson was the one to get to the nitty-gritty. Would he be the one to slap on the cuffs?

"We left the bar together. I got into Niles's car with him to finish our discussion, he drove me to the corner and then I walked home. That's the last time I saw him." The ice in her glass tinkled as her hands trembled.

Paulson's gaze dropped to her glass. "You walked home from the bar?"

"I walked *to* the bar, also. It's less than a mile to my house, and I wanted to clear my head. That's when I decided to come down here to see Connor—and that's what I did."

"You didn't see your ex or hear from him after that?" Paulson hunched forward, so far that Savannah could see the freckle on his earlobe.

"I didn't, but there's something I don't understand." She tucked a strand of hair behind her ear. "Was Niles murdered in his home?"

"In his bedroom."

She placed the glass on the coffee table and pinned her hands between her knees. "We had security cameras at that house. I know because I hired the company and oversaw their work. Wouldn't Niles's murderer be caught on tape?"

Krieger shook his head. "The security cameras were disabled."

"Oh." Savannah covered her mouth with her hand.

"We're not even sure the killer is responsible for disabling the security system, because Ms. Rodriguez thought

Niles was having problems with the system. Did you ever have problems with that system?"

"Not when I lived there."

Paulson drained his water and tapped the glass with one finger. "Mr. Wells, what time did Savannah arrive at your house last night?"

Savannah's heart pounded so hard the buttons on her blouse trembled. Surely, Paulson and Krieger could hear it beating.

"She came in around eleven o'clock."

Paulson asked, "Were you surprised to see her, and at that time of night?"

"No." Connor reached over and stroked Savannah's wrist with the pad of his thumb. "We'd been talking about getting back together. Her meeting with her ex last night was the final straw, I think. The thing that finally convinced her we belong together."

She grabbed Connor's hand and kissed the back of it. How would she ever repay him for this?

Paulson scratched his chin. "So, you two were together from about eleven o'clock last night until now?"

"Except for the few hours I went to the beach this morning," Connor said.

Paulson scooted forward in his seat. "What time?"

"Around eight to ten. Left Savannah sleeping. Wait." Connor ran a hand through his longish hair and the ends flipped up. "You're not looking at Savannah for this, are you?"

"What? Are you?" Savannah knotted her fingers together. "Wh-why?"

Krieger raised his shoulders to his ears. "Exes, acrimonious divorce and business deals. It's natural we'd look at you."

"Not natural to me." Savannah jumped up from the

couch, grabbing her water, which sloshed over the side of the glass.

Connor pushed to his feet and placed his hand at the small of her back. "You'd better show the detectives your hand, Savannah."

Her head whipped around and her eyes widened. Was he trying to get her arrested? "M-my hand?"

Krieger and Paulson exchanged a look that made her stomach flip-flop.

Paulson stood up first, and Savannah tilted her head back to look at him. Funny, she hadn't noticed how tall he was when he was the silent partner. Now that he was grilling her, he towered over her like an ogre.

Connor grabbed her right hand and uncurled her fingers, displaying the horizontal cuts on her palm.

Krieger's eyebrows, which seemed like they had a mind of the own, cocked in two different directions. "What happened, Savannah?"

"Oh, this?" She stared at her hand. "I was straightening up a bit before I left last night and my butcher block of knives tipped off the edge of the counter. I stupidly made a grab for the knives and cut myself. Pretty dumb move, huh?"

"It's quite common for someone to get cuts on their own hand while they're stabbing someone." Paulson crossed his arms.

"Only one problem with that, Detective." Connor planted a kiss in the middle of her palm amid the cuts. "Savannah is left-handed. She wouldn't have stabbed her ex, but she really wouldn't have stabbed him with her right hand."

Paulson's chest seemed to deflate. "We're going to want you to come to the sheriff's station in La Jolla in the next few days to give a sample of your DNA. Can you do that?"

"Of course."

Krieger put one hand in his pocket as if to strike a casual pose. "Would we find your DNA in the house, Savannah?"

"DNA? Blood? No. Hair? Maybe." She flipped her hair over one shoulder. "I've been in that house a few times recently…for business. I don't think it would be odd to find some evidence of my presence, but blood? There would be no reason for my blood to be there."

She hoped to God they wouldn't find any from these cuts.

The detectives asked her several more questions, handed out their cards and asked her not to leave town and to report to the station in La Jolla the day after tomorrow in the afternoon.

She assured them she would, and both she and Connor walked them to the front door.

Her muscles still clenched, she watched them descend the porch, and just when she thought she could breathe again, Paulson made a half turn.

Tapping his chin, Paulson raised his eyes to the sky. "Wells. You *are* the son of the former police chief of this town who shot and killed the drug dealer Manny Edmonds, aren't you?"

"That's right. Shot and killed him in self-defense and then paid the price when Manny's goons murdered him."

"Hmm." Paulson took a few more steps, stopped and twisted his head over his shoulder. "And Manny Edmonds was your stepfather, wasn't he, Savannah?"

"That's right."

"You were present when Chief Wells killed him."

"I was."

"Hmm. Okay. Thank you."

Paulson stopped again, his hard shoes scraping against the gravel as he pivoted. "One more thing."

"Of course." Savannah could barely squeeze the words past her lips.

"Do I have your permission to search the trunk of your car?" Paulson linked his hands in front of him as if he'd just asked her for a cup of tea.

She stretched her lips into a smile. "Of course. I'll get the keys."

Her shoulder banged against Connor's as she spun toward the house, but she avoided meeting his eyes. Why did they want to look in her trunk? Thank God Connor had found that bag…and too bad he'd been waving it around under the detectives' noses.

She dragged her keys from her purse with shaky fingers and took a deep breath. She couldn't allow Paulson or Krieger to see her trembling hands.

As she stepped out onto the porch, she stabbed the remote with her thumb and the lights of the Lexus flickered once and the trunk popped. "It's open. Help yourself."

Paulson lunged toward the car and flipped up the trunk. Half his body disappeared inside, and Savannah knew he was lifting the cover to the spare—where Connor had found the bag.

She forced herself to breathe—in, out, in, out—Connor's body vibrating beside her.

Paulson extricated himself from the trunk, glanced at Krieger and gave a quick shake of his head. "Okay to look inside the car?"

"Absolutely. It's unlocked."

Paulson rummaged around her car for several minutes, and then emerged, the tight politeness of his face somewhat askew. "Thank you. That's all."

Detective Krieger nodded and waved. "Thank you for your time. Sorry for your loss."

"No problem. Let me know if I can be of any more help."

Savannah gritted her teeth as she watched the two detectives walk back to their vehicle.

Connor touched her shoulder. "Let's go back in the house. We look weird standing here staring at them, making sure they get back in their car and drive off."

"But that's exactly why I *am* staring at them, just in case Paulson stops and asks another one of his casual questions dripping with suspicion and innuendo, or decides he wants to see what's in that plastic bag you were swinging around." She peeled her hands from her upper arms, where her fingernails had created crescents in her flesh.

Connor held the screen door open for her and she stepped into the house, massaging the back of her neck. "Why do you think he wanted to search the car? The trunk? How did he know?"

"Maybe he didn't know about the knife." Connor's shoulders twitched.

"You don't believe that any more than I do. Someone tipped them off. The same someone who put the knife there."

"Might've been an anonymous call."

Savannah rubbed her eyes. "How do you think it went otherwise? Do you think I'm their number one suspect?"

"Maybe not number one, thanks to your alibi, but definitely a suspect."

She dropped onto the couch cushion and leaned her head back, staring at the ceiling. "Why do you think Paulson threw in those little jabs at the end? Is he implying that there's a connection to my being at the site of one killing and Niles's death?"

"Why would he imply that?" Connor peered into her face from above. Placing two fingers at each of her temples, he rubbed in little circles. "The death of your stepfather has nothing to do with the death of your ex-husband."

She hoped it didn't.

Closing her eyes, she said, "The two of us involved in two separate violent deaths—must look odd."

"He's just trying to rattle you."

Connor stopped his massage, and she opened one eye. "Why would he want to do that?"

"Because you're a suspect and he wants you to know you're a suspect, and he wants you to understand that he's looking at you, has already looked into your background."

"And finds it suspicious." She tapped the side of her head. "Keep rubbing. I suddenly have a ferocious headache."

"Probably because you haven't eaten anything all day. Do you want to go back to Neptune's Cove and continue our lunch date?"

"We do want the locals to think we're back together and inseparable, don't we?"

"That's the plan."

That plan sounded like heaven right now. Too bad it was all tied up with Niles's murder.

Connor's fingers trailed down her face and the column of her neck before squeezing her shoulders. "Okay, let's try this again."

Did he mean lunch or their relationship? Because being back in Connor's realm felt good, felt natural. But she'd left him because of the lies and the lies hadn't gone away. In fact, they'd been compounded by more lies. She didn't want to start a relationship based in deception, even though that had been the only way her mother ever started a relationship.

She wasn't her mother and never would be. She also couldn't afford to tell Connor the truth.

She ducked away from Connor's touch and staggered

to her feet. "I'm starving and I could use that mimosa now more than ever."

As she reached for her purse, her cell phone, tucked in the side pocket, rang. She pulled it out and glanced at the display. She met Connor's urgent stare and held up the phone. "It's just Letty, Niles's housekeeper."

She answered the phone. "Letty, are you all right? I heard about Niles today."

"Did you?"

Savannah drew her brows together. "Dee Dee called me and I just talked to the police. Have they spoken to you yet? Do you know anyone who would do this to Niles?"

"As a matter of fact, I do. It was you, Savannah, and I have the evidence to prove it."

Chapter Six

Savannah jerked her head up, her eyes widening in her pale face. Connor's stomach dipped. What bad news could Niles's housekeeper be telling her? He mouthed, *"What's wrong?"*

She tapped her phone's display and a woman's slightly accented voice came over the line. "Well? What do you have to say?"

"I—I don't know what you're talking about, Letty. I had nothing to do with Niles's murder. Why would you even think that?"

Connor's hands convulsively clenched into fists. Why would Niles's housekeeper think Savannah killed him?

"Oh, you forget, Savannah. I was in that house for the fights. The cheating. The lying," Letty snorted. "I don't even blame you. I felt like killing Mr. Niles myself a few times. He didn't treat me any better after you left."

"Letty, don't even say something like that." Savannah shot him a glance and licked her lips. "And during any of those…fights, did either of us get physical? Did I ever threaten Niles? Of course not. Yeah, I wanted the man out of my life, but the divorce was good enough."

"The divorce was not good enough. You still had the company together and would always have to work with him or let him buy you out. I know how these things work. I overheard the two of you enough times."

Connor folded his arms over his chest, biting the inside of his cheek. He didn't need a recap of Savannah's marriage—he'd tried not to think of it over the years. Savannah needed to know what Letty had on her…and what she wanted now.

"Whatever." Savannah flung her arm out to the side. "None of that means anything now. I did not kill Niles and I can't imagine what proof you have that I did."

"I'm not going to tell you that, Savannah, not yet, but I'll give it back to you when we meet…and you hand over five hundred thousand dollars."

Savannah's gaze met Connor's and her lips tightened. "That's what this is all about? I never took you for that kind of person, Letty."

"We all have to do what we have to do."

"Yes, but I didn't kill Niles, so you don't have any evidence."

"You'll see. Come alone, bring the money, in cash, and I won't contact the police about what I found and what I know."

"Letty, this is ridiculous. If you need money, I'll give you money. You don't have to resort to blackmail, which is illegal, I might add."

"So call the police."

Savannah ran a hand through her hair and clenched a fistful of it. "Where and when do you want to meet?"

"Logan, by the warehouses. There's one with a yellow sign out front. Be there at nine o'clock tonight with the cash. I'll turn over your property and we'll call it even."

"I'm only doing this because I don't want the police looking at me. I didn't kill Niles, Letty, and you must know that."

"I know what I know."

Savannah opened her mouth to respond, but Letty had ended the call, and Savannah threw the phone at the couch and screamed.

"What does she have, Savannah?"

"I have no idea. I didn't leave anything there." She paced to the window and spun around. "I can't believe she's doing this. Blackmail."

"Does she have some grudge against you?"

"We weren't besties or anything, but it was Niles she didn't like."

"Why?"

Savannah pleated her skirt with her fingers. "Because he's an ass and rude."

"Why'd she continue to work for him?"

"He paid really well, or at least I paid Letty well, and Niles had to keep the agreement with her when I left."

"Greed. She's doing this because she can. Because she knows you'll pay."

"If it's something ridiculous, I'm not going to pay her a dime." She clapped a hand over her mouth. "How am I going to pay her five hundred grand in cash? I have about forty bucks and change on me and if I run to the bank now and withdraw that kind of money, it's going to raise all kinds of red flags with the police."

"I'll take care of the money. I'd just like to know what she has first."

"I told you, if it's something that can be explained away easily, I'm not paying her anything, and she can go to the police for all I care. She's going to have a helluva time explaining to them why she didn't turn over this explosive evidence when they first questioned her and decided to turn to blackmail instead."

Connor shook his head.

"What?" She narrowed her eyes. "You don't think I should pay her? If it's the money you're worried about, I'm good for it. Haven't you heard? I'm the beneficiary of millions in life insurance money."

He inhaled deeply through his nose. When had Savannah become so difficult? He rubbed the back of his neck. Who was he kidding? After her stepfather died, she'd changed, and he could never figure out why. It wasn't as if she blamed Connor's father for Manny's death. She'd never cared for Manny, but when he died, something between them…shifted, and they'd never been able to set it right again.

Why would this time be any different?

"I don't care about the money. Haven't you heard? I inherited a lot of property when Dad died and I sold off a lot of it to finance the winery." He briefly clutched his hair into a ponytail and then released it. "I'm just beginning to think you're getting in deeper and deeper. Maybe you should just tell the truth."

For once.

Her mouth dropped open. "You're kidding. You know as well as I do the truth isn't enough sometimes—and this is one of those times. Someone incapacitated me and probably Niles, too, and then murdered Niles, leaving me to hold the bag. This is some kind of setup. If I go to the police, you can bet there will be more evidence popping up to implicate me."

"Could it be Letty?"

"You think Letty could've murdered Niles and then tried to set me up for this blackmail scheme?"

He shrugged his shoulders, which ached with tension. "Could be. She's the first one who stepped forward to cash in."

"I know she hated Niles, but murder?" She strode to the couch and swept up her phone. "I don't think she's capable."

"She thinks you are."

Savannah pointed her phone at him. "She doesn't, really. She just found this clue—whatever it is—and figured I'd pay to make it go away."

"And that's exactly what you're going to do."

BY THE TIME Connor found a new hiding place for the knife, cleaned up and withdrew the cash from his bank before closing time, their lunch date had turned into dinner.

He stuffed the backpack loaded with stacks of money under the table at his feet and smiled at a different waiter from the one they'd had earlier in the same restaurant. "I'll have the Widow's Peak pinot."

"And I'll have the pomegranate mimosa…again." Savannah planted her elbows on the table.

Connor raised an eyebrow. "It's not breakfast anymore."

"Are there mimosa rules that I missed somewhere?"

He tipped his water glass in her direction. "You make up your own rules, Savannah. You always have."

"I like the hair." She tugged on her own glossy ends. "Now that you're no longer a cop, you decided to grow it long?"

"Honestly, it's pure laziness. Do you remember Lucy, who used to cut my hair? She left town, and every time someone new cut it, they just couldn't get it right."

"Lazy." She rolled her eyes. "You don't have a lazy bone in your buff bod."

"Tell me how the company's doing. I mean—" he waved his napkin before flicking it into his lap "—outside all the other stuff."

"The other stuff? You mean the murder of the CEO?"

"Yeah, that."

She cocked her head and caught a drip of condensation on the outside of her water glass with the tip of her finger. "Not as well as it should be."

"Really?" He coughed into his napkin. "That's not what I've been hearing...and that's not how the stock is going."

"You're following Snap App's stock?"

"I'd better be. I own a lot of shares."

"Oh, then I'd better work harder."

"Seriously, what's the problem?"

"Earnings seem to be going down."

"Again, that's not what the stock price is reflecting."

"I know."

The waiter returned with their drinks and paused by the table. "Everything okay out at the vineyard, Connor? We heard about the fire."

"Thanks, Brock. It was just a storage shed. Firefighters put out the fire pretty fast, so there wasn't much damage."

"I heard it was done on purpose." Brock glanced over his shoulder. "Any suspects?"

"Not yet." Connor swirled the wine in the glass. "Any ideas?"

"Yeah, I have an idea."

Connor's fingers curled around the stem of the glass. "Are you serious?"

"Dude, I heard you were filming the Cove Boys this morning."

"Who?" Savannah had been listening to their exchange, her head turning from side to side, as if she were watching a tennis match.

"Some localism going on at the cove. You know, pushing out other surfers from different areas." Connor turned back to Brock. "That's right. I was filming them this morning. You hear something?"

"Just that Takata was pissed off and talking trash."

"Enough to start a fire?"

"Maybe." Brock rapped his knuckles on the table. "Gotta get back to work. I'll come back around."

"Thanks, man." Connor tapped his wineglass against the rim of Savannah's champagne flute. "Cheers."

"To what, exactly?" She sipped her bubbly drink and scrunched up her nose.

"We may have discovered our arsonist."

"Jimmy Takata's become some rabid surfer?"

"You know how localism goes. These guys think they own the best waves on the beach and drive everyone out. People started calling them the Cove Boys, and several are suing them."

"And you decided to get involved in it?" She traced the rim of her glass with her fingertip. "Why? You're not a cop anymore."

"The sheriff's department won't do anything about it."

"Not your problem, Connor. Can't help yourself?"

"I hate to see that kind of stuff going on in this town." He took a longer pull from his glass than he intended under Savannah's amused eyes.

"So what happened this morning?"

"I was at the cove, helping out the lawsuit with my camcorder, and Takata didn't like it."

"He threatened you?"

"I don't know if I'd call it a threat, but he got aggressive."

Savannah snapped her fingers. "That could be it, couldn't it? We were so worried that someone followed me here and set fire to the structure to smoke out that… object, and it could just be a local problem."

"We don't know for sure if it's Takata."

"Sounds promising." She stared at him over the rim of her glass. "Why didn't you think of that before, when the deputy asked you if you had any enemies?"

"I don't think of Jimmy Takata as my enemy. If it was him, that's a pathetic attempt at intimidation."

"Maybe, but it is criminal. That can't help his case any."

"I'll call tomorrow and drop his name." He held up his glass to the candlelight. "If I could make something like this at my vineyard, I'd consider that a success."

"Widow's Peak?" She placed a hand against her chest. "Maybe it's some kind of sign. I guess I'm a widow."

"Technically, not. Niles was your ex."

"I wish I hadn't encouraged him to keep that life insurance coverage. It looks bad."

"It all looks bad, Savannah, but in the end, if you didn't do it, you'll be okay."

"You don't believe that."

He took another sip of wine, savoring the blackberry taste on his tongue before swallowing. "Tell me more about the company. You know I couldn't be prouder of you for what you've built."

A rose tinge that matched her drink touched her cheeks. "Thanks, Connor, but it wasn't all me. Niles had a brilliant mind and was able to realize all my imaginings."

"I know." He pinged the side of his glass with his fingernail. "I always thought if I'd had something like that to offer you, I could've made you stay."

Her hand shot out and she grabbed his wrist, "It wasn't like that at all. Things just got…complicated between us. I know your mom hated me—and I totally understood it. My mom had no right to embroil your father in her problems."

Connor's mouth twisted up at one corner. "I don't think my father could've kept away from Georgie if he'd tried, and besides, he was the chief of police. He had a duty to help her."

"You and I both know Chief Wells wouldn't have gone to those lengths for anyone other than my mom."

Savannah still had hold of his wrist, and he slipped it out of her grasp and threaded his fingers through hers. "I'm just sorry it had to affect us and what we had."

"I heard you two were back together."

Connor jerked his head to the side and nodded to Savannah's best friend in town, Lexi Morris.

Lexi dipped down and gave Savannah a one-armed hug. "So glad to see you back here. I heard about Niles. I'm so sorry. So horrible and scary. Are you worried someone could be coming after you, too?"

"I don't think his murder is related to the company, but I do feel safer down here with Connor." Savannah brought his hand to her lips and kissed his knuckles.

"And you." Lexi prodded his shoulder. "I heard there was a fire at your vineyard."

"Just a small one. Nothing much damaged."

"Typical for you two." Lexi rolled her eyes. "Drama dogs you everywhere. I'll be following the news of the murder. I hope they catch the killer. Niles wasn't my favorite person in the world, but nobody deserves that."

"I hope so, too. Are you having dinner with Zach?" Savannah craned her neck, twisting her head to take in the dining room.

"We're finished." Lexi made a face. "I'll tell you about it later. Just meeting a few friends for drinks at the bar, but let's catch up soon. Lunch?"

"I'll call you." Savannah kissed the tips of her fingers and waved them at Lexi as her friend turned back to the bar.

"She didn't seem surprised to see you here, or see us together." Connor took a deep breath. Maybe this was going to be easier than he thought.

"No, she didn't. Didn't even ask when I got here." She pushed her water glass to the side. "Food's here."

Connor dug into his fish and chips, and after Savannah

squeezed lemon over her grilled salmon, she snatched one of his fries and popped it into her mouth. "Mmm."

He pointed his fork at her. "I don't know why you just don't order your own fries."

"It's more fun stealing yours, and if they're not mine the calories don't count." She grabbed another one to prove her point.

While they ate, he asked her more questions about the business. She'd majored in computer science at San Diego State and had met Niles there. He hadn't been worried about Niles at the time because Savannah had assured him she and the computer geek, as she'd called him, were just friends.

But after his own relationship with Savannah had unraveled, Savannah and Niles began spending more time together and she'd come up with this idea for a social media app. They'd put it to work, formed Snap App, made millions and got married, or got married and made millions.

And there had been nothing he could do to stop any of it.

Now Niles was dead and Savannah stood to gain control of the entire company—and that life insurance money.

"Enough about me." Savannah dabbed her mouth with her napkin. "How's the winery coming along? It looks like you have fruit on those vines."

"I need to wait one more year before harvesting the grapes and making wine. The plants need to go through a few growth cycles before they're ready to produce wine."

"You mentioned you have a chemist. Have you decided on the formula or recipe or whatever you call it?"

"Yeah, Jacob is finalizing it now." He tapped his chin. "You missed a spot of tartar sauce."

"Can't take me anywhere." She swiped at her face with the napkin, missing it again.

Connor hunched forward and swept his fingertip across

the spot of white sauce. He brought up his thumb and pinched her chin. "You're as beautiful as ever, Savannah. You sweep in here and spellbind me, wrap me up in a web until I don't know if I'm right side up or upside down."

She fluttered her long lashes, not even denying the compliment like most women would. "D-does that mean you regret helping me?"

He dropped his hand and dropped his voice, pushing away his empty plate. "No. I do owe you. If you and your mother hadn't lied to the police and told them Manny drew his gun on my father first, Dad would've been arrested for murder, or at least manslaughter."

She coughed and gulped down the rest of her water. She glanced at the diners nearest to them, absorbed in their own conversations. "If you hadn't agreed to give me an alibi for Niles's murder, it's not like I would've reported your father. It's water under the bridge now."

"But you still brought it up when you asked for my help."

Savannah dropped her chin to her chest and looked at him from beneath her long lashes. "I regret that. I never meant to call in the favor. I knew you wouldn't turn me down."

Connor clenched a fist against his thigh beneath the table. He couldn't figure out which was worse—Savannah using an old favor to bring him to heel or her understanding that she didn't have to use anything at all to make him come around.

"I'm coming with you tonight when you meet Letty, even though she told you to come alone."

"You'd better stay out of sight. I want to see whatever she's got so I can gauge how worried I need to be."

"You don't need a worry gauge." He drilled his finger into the table in front of her. "The fact that someone thinks she can blackmail you should cause you enough concern—whatever she has."

"It does, believe me. That's why I'm meeting her. How much time do we have?"

Connor rolled his wrist inward. "About an hour, but it'll take us almost thirty minutes to drive up there. I'm not familiar with Logan. What kind of area is it?"

"Sketchy—some residential, some light industrial with a whole lot of abandoned warehouses, and that's where we're meeting."

"Great. Why do you think she picked that spot?"

"It's isolated, no witnesses, and I believe she lives out that way."

"So, Letty might have reinforcements on her side."

"She's not going to hurt me, Connor. She just wants the money."

"Everything you thought you knew about Letty went right out the window when she decided to use this information against you. She could be plotting anything."

"I think she's planning to nab the cash and quit working as a housekeeper. I almost admire her." Savannah buried her chin in her hand.

"What?" Connor bolted upright in his chair. "She's a criminal about to commit an illegal act, already committed that act by calling you."

"True, but that was some quick thinking on her part to jump on a piece of evidence and turn it to her advantage."

"Save your admiration until you find out what she has. Seems like an immoral money grab to me."

"Of course. I'm not condoning her actions, especially because they're aimed at me. I'm just marveling at the realization that you never really know anyone, do you?"

Uneasiness churned his gut. And what about Savannah? Did he really know her? She'd changed from the girl who'd been raised by an economically struggling single mother. The girl who'd mastered everything she did to prove she was as worthy as all the kids who lived in comfort and ease in their idyllic beach community.

Her current wealth had given her a different kind of confidence. The founding of Snap App had afforded her more wealth, several times over, than any of the kids she used to try to impress.

"Well, I'm ready to find out what she has." Savannah threw her napkin on the table beside her plate.

"Let's get the check." He waved at Brock, who was heading for the bar to pick up a drink order.

On his way past their table, a tray of drinks balanced on one hand, Brock slipped their bill onto the table and tapped it with one finger. "See you next time."

Connor put his knuckle on the check. "I'll get this," he said to Savannah. "You don't want to start spending money like you have it."

"I do have it—even without full ownership of the company and Niles's life insurance."

"I know." He pinched the bill between two fingers and squinted at it in the low light. "I'm just kidding."

She nudged his toe beneath the table. "That's nothing to kid about. Once those detectives find out all I stand to gain from Niles's death, they're going to come calling again."

"They may know by the time you go in to give your DNA sample, and they probably put in a request for your phone records already." He pulled some bills from his wallet and placed them on the tray.

"I liked it better when you were kidding." Savannah hitched her purse strap over her shoulder. "Do you think they'll find it odd that my phone was off during the crucial time?"

"Maybe. There's not much they can do about it, though."

He grabbed the bag with the money and hitched it over his shoulder as he stood up from the table. "Ready?"

"As much as I'll ever be."

They said goodbye to a few people on the way out, and Connor kept his explanations of the fire brief.

When they got inside the car, Savannah turned to him. "How are we going to do this? If Letty sees me with someone, it might scare her off."

"You can drop me off at a distance and drive my car in. Just pick me up on your way out. If there's trouble…get to the car and honk the horn."

"Yeah, that's the problem with skulduggery. When you're leaving your cell phone at home, there's no way to get in touch."

As he started the engine he slid a glance her way. Had she expected skulduggery the night Niles was murdered? Was that why she'd left her phone at home?

"Just be careful."

"I know Letty."

"We went through this before. You *thought* you knew Letty. This is a different person you're dealing with now."

"You're right." She twisted around and smacked the money bag with her hand. "Do you want this bag back?"

"Of course. I'm not leaving any evidence with Letty that we paid her off. Any self-respecting blackmailer is going to bring her own bag for the money."

"And if she doesn't?" She tugged her skirt over her thighs. "Then what?"

"That's her problem. She can dump the cash in the back seat of her car. Don't let her leave with the bag."

"Got it."

They discussed a few more logistics on the way to Logan, and when he exited the freeway, Savannah pointed to her right. "Take this street down to the T in the road and then hang a left. You might want to park there and turn over the car to me."

"Remember, park as close to the warehouse as you can. This doesn't look like the kind of area where you want to be loitering."

"You, either." She tapped on the window. "You can wait at that gas station. There's even a convenience store."

"Great. I'll get some coffee and thumb through the smutty magazines."

She squeezed his thigh. "You don't read smutty magazines."

"Who said anything about reading?"

"I give you points for trying to lighten the mood, Wells."

"Just be careful." He swung into a parking space at the side of the service station and turned the wheel over to her.

He watched the taillights until they disappeared as Savannah turned right onto a side street. He strode around the corner of the building and entered the convenience store, where he bought a cup of coffee.

Then he pushed out of the front door and took off in the same direction as Savannah and the car. He had no intention of waiting out this meeting in the store. He'd try to keep out of Letty's sight, but he didn't really give a damn about what she wanted. The woman was blackmailing someone who'd employed her, paid her well and, if he knew Savannah, had treated her well, too.

He picked up the pace as he turned down the side street and spotted the warehouses crouching at the end of the cul-de-sac. As he drew closer, he couldn't see a yellow sign and he couldn't see any cars.

He wove through the first row of buildings and tripped to a stop when he saw two cars parked in front of a hulking warehouse with a corrugated metal roof.

He watched from the corner of another building, but seeing no movement, he crept forward with his heart thumping in his chest. How long could this exchange between the two women take?

As he drew closer to the building with the yellow signage, he cocked his head, listening for voices. The silence caused a ripple of fear across his flesh.

He placed his hand on the metal door, which was standing open several inches, and hunched forward, peering into the cavernous space of the warehouse. The moon filtered through some broken windows, creating a muted spotlight around two figures—one crouching and the other sprawled out on the floor, a dark pool beneath her head.

Chapter Seven

Savannah flinched as her hand brushed Letty's clammy skin while she searched her front pocket.

A soft creak echoed in the warehouse, and Savannah spun around on her knees, placing one hand on the cold cement floor as she listed to the side.

"Savannah! Are you all right? What happened?"

She released a breath and staggered to her feet. "Connor, what are you doing here? Not that I'm not glad to see you. It's Letty. Sh-she's dead."

Connor strode across the floor, stopping short of the dead body between them. "What happened here?"

"I don't know." She wrapped her arms around her midsection. "When I got here, I saw Letty's car out front and then I came inside and saw her body on the floor. It's a gunshot wound. She has a gun in her hand."

Connor crouched next to Letty, his gaze darting from the gun in her hand to the gaping wound at her temple. "She killed herself?"

"That's what it looks like."

"Or that's what someone wants it to look like." He jabbed a finger in the air over the body. "What were you doing when I walked in here?"

Savannah swallowed. "I—I was looking for the evidence she had. I know it sounds sick, but that's what I came here to get."

Connor's jaw tightened and her stomach sank. She plucked at the material of her skirt. "I realize it sounds awful, but I spent several minutes in shock just staring at Letty, and several more minutes trying not to be sick."

"And then several minutes searching her pockets."

She closed her eyes and drew a deep breath. "That's what we came here for, Connor. We were willing to hand her five hundred grand for whatever she has. Just because she…killed herself, I'm not going to leave without it."

"You don't really believe she killed herself, do you? She was just about to score an easy five hundred thou."

"But if she didn't—" Savannah flattened a hand against her belly, afraid this time she really would hurl "—who did kill her and why?"

"To stop the blackmail plan."

"Who'd want to do that…except me?" She swept her arm to encompass the warehouse. "And I just got here."

"Did you find what you were looking for?"

"I found nothing." She poked at an empty duffel bag with the tip of her sandal. "Except this. You were right. She was ready to collect the money."

"Did you look in her car?"

"No. Should we?"

"We're not going to do a search, but let's take a look before we get out of here."

Savannah hoisted the bag with Connor's cash, and he took it from her.

"You didn't leave anything in here?"

"No. I walked in with the bag, saw Letty, rushed over and dropped the bag. I was very careful with what I touched and how I touched it, and I didn't lay a finger on the gun in her hand."

"Okay, you're getting to be an expert at this."

Savannah convulsively clenched her hands at her sides. Connor had no idea how right he was.

He pushed the warehouse door wide with his toe and slipped into the night. She followed.

With his T-shirt over his hand, Connor opened Letty's unlocked car door and did a quick scan of the front and back seats. "I don't see anything. Either she was lying… or someone took it."

The blood rushed to Savannah's head and she swayed, grabbing Connor's belt loop to steady herself. "What do you mean?"

"Let's get out of here." He tipped his head back and studied the outside of the building. "I'm guessing these warehouses are too old and too dilapidated to have any kind of security or camera system."

"I can't imagine why they would, and I doubt Letty would've picked this place if she thought our meeting could be caught on CCTV."

"You drive." He gave her a little nudge toward his car. "Let's go."

She slid into the driver's seat and squeezed the steering wheel with her hands to keep them from shaking. She drove out the way she'd come in, neither of them saying one word until she hit the freeway.

Then she turned on him. "Why would someone kill Letty and then take the evidence she had against me?"

"To have the evidence against you."

She licked her dry lips. "Do you think I'm going to get another blackmail demand?"

"I don't know."

"Or worse? Someone wanted Letty's evidence to continue my setup."

"We don't even know what Letty had and if it was damning enough to send the detectives your way." He smacked the dashboard. "Who knew about this meeting? Do you think she told someone? Does she have a family?"

"She has a husband and some adult children. I doubt her husband knows anything about the blackmail scheme." Savannah shifted her gaze to the rearview mirror. "Do you think someone could be following me?"

"How? You said yourself nobody followed you down here. I know for a fact nobody tailed us to the warehouse. Maybe someone is following Letty. Whoever killed her got to the warehouse before you did. How long do you think Letty had been dead?"

"I have no idea. I didn't touch her, and I wouldn't have known what to look for if I had."

"Did you smell gunpowder in the warehouse? I detected a faint whiff, but it can hang in the air for a while."

"I didn't notice any gunpowder smell—don't even know what it smells like. The warehouse smelled oily to me anyway. It could've been gunpowder."

"You weren't late." Connor drummed his fingers on his knee. "How did someone beat you there and kill Letty before you got there?"

"You're still assuming someone killed Letty." She lifted her stiff shoulders. "Maybe it was a suicide. How do we know what's going through anyone's mind? Maybe she even killed Niles and was regretting everything."

"A few hours ago, you assured me Letty couldn't have killed Niles."

"What do I know?" She pinched the bridge of her nose.

"Not much of anything. You don't even know what happened that night."

She cranked her head slowly to the right and stared at his profile. "Are we back to that? I know I didn't kill Niles. I would've had blood on my clothes, and if you're going to suggest I murdered him while I was naked, I checked the bathroom for signs of a shower. Hell, I even sniffed my own armpits for evidence I'd cleaned up—and I hadn't."

"Look." He placed a hand on her thigh. "Don't you think you should see a therapist to get to the bottom of it?"

His hand felt heavy through the thin material of her skirt, and she tensed her leg muscles. "I didn't black out from any suppressed memory from a traumatic event. I was drugged. There's no coming back from that. No memories are going to return from a drugged state."

"You sound so sure. You have no proof of any drugs. You would've had to have been drugged in the bar, and that's unlikely. I think we agree Niles didn't drug you."

She tapped her fingers on the top of the steering wheel. "Maybe he did."

"You also told me before he had no reason to knock you out, as he wasn't interested in getting you into bed."

"He could've had a different motive."

"A killer is either waiting for Niles or breaks into his house, finds you conked out, murders Niles and proceeds to strip you of your clothes and put you to bed?"

"To set me up." She flung her hand at the windshield. "Just like this thing with Letty."

Connor shook his head. "We need to take a step back from the speculation and focus on Letty's death back there. Assuming she didn't kill herself, how did her killer know about her meeting?"

"My head hurts." Savannah massaged her right temple. "She must've told someone."

"Maybe she's working with someone and that person double-crossed her."

"This is going to look weird, isn't it? The fact that Letty's employer is murdered and then she's murdered? What are the chances?"

Connor held up his index finger. "But Letty's death was made to look like a suicide. The gun's in her hand, a single gunshot to the head. Unless the killer left some evidence or Letty has some defensive wounds, this might go down as a suicide. The detectives might think she had something to do with Niles's death."

Savannah closed her eyes briefly and then focused on the white lines skimming by outside the windshield. She hoped Letty's death was ruled a suicide, to give them a little breathing room. She needed room to breathe.

Later, as Savannah turned down the road leading to Connor's house, she asked, "Those detectives are going to want to talk to me about Letty, too, aren't they, whether or not they deem it a suicide?"

"I'm sure they will."

"If they're going to be looking at her phone records, I'd better tell the cops that Letty called me today to discuss Niles's murder."

"Be as truthful as you can."

Whipping her head around, she said, "I'm not telling them I was there that night, Connor. It's too late for that anyway. I could be charged for…for leaving the scene of a crime, not reporting a murder or whatever they can dig up. That's not happening."

"I said as truthful as you *can* be."

As she brought the car to a slow roll in his driveway, Connor unsnapped his seat belt. "Park to the right of the truck."

Several minutes later, when they were in the house with the door locked behind them, Connor grabbed his phone from the counter, studied the display and held it up to his ear to listen to a message.

Savannah paced, twisting her fingers, and when he put the phone down, asked, "What was that about?"

"Don't worry. Just the fire chief letting me know they were reporting the fire as arson for the purposes of my insurance claim."

Savannah dropped to the couch and aimed the remote at the TV. She regretted it immediately when Niles's handsome face and slick smile filled the screen. "Story's exploded."

Connor walked up behind her and placed a hand on her shoulder. "We knew it would. No surprises."

"Yeah, the surprise is going to be when someone discovers Letty's body."

"I wonder when that's going to happen." He squeezed her shoulder briefly before releasing it. "Those warehouses look like they haven't been used in years."

"Her family will report her missing." Savannah pressed her fingers against her lips. "Why did she get involved in blackmail? She'd be alive right now, home with her husband, if she hadn't got greedy."

"Did you notice if she had a phone on her?"

"She didn't. Was there one in the car?"

"Not on a charger or anywhere else I could see."

She muted the TV as the news shifted to another story. "Maybe she's playing the same game we are—leave your phone home so the police can't trace it."

"Her family's not going to be able to trace her, either, if she didn't have her phone with her. Unless she told someone where she was going, which is unlikely, her body might be there until someone looking at the warehouses sees her car and discovers her."

Savannah dug her fingers into her scalp. "That's horrible. I can't bear to think about it."

"And yet—" Connor folded his tall frame into the chair across from her "—you were willing to leave Niles at his house, dead."

"That's different." She slipped out of her sandals and

wedged her bare feet against the coffee table. "Niles was at his home. I knew someone would be discovering him, and that someone happened to be Letty—bad luck for her as it turns out."

"She sealed her own fate by taking something she thought incriminated you and then trying to sell it back to you."

Savannah rubbed her upper arms, where a trail of goose bumps had sprung up. "So you do believe that's why Letty was murdered and now someone else has that evidence."

"Maybe." He hunched forward, driving his elbows into his knees. "We just have to wait for the other shoe to drop."

"That's encouraging, thanks."

"Or…"

Her head popped up. "Or?"

"We do a little investigating of our own. I still have some connections and a little know-how. You're familiar with the players and have more money than you know what to do with. Let's launch our own investigation, independent of the police."

"If it can help me out of this mess, I'm all for it."

"We'll start a list of…suspects tomorrow morning."

"Suspects? I don't know anyone who'd want to kill Niles."

"C'mon, Savannah. The guy must've had enemies. He cheated on you with other women. Do you think he changed his behavior?"

"I'm sure he hadn't." She drew up her knees and wrapped her arms around her legs. "Niles was the kind of guy who was geeky throughout high school and college, and then became attractive all of a sudden when he made millions."

"That's understandable, but the dude was married—to you." Pushing out of the chair, Connor snorted, "Crazy bastard."

Savannah's cheeks warmed and a smile tugged at one

corner of her mouth. She was glad Connor still felt that way, even though she'd done a number on his head.

He pivoted and leveled a finger at her. "I have one condition."

"Shoot."

"You make an appointment with a therapist and see if you can remember anything about that night."

Savannah swallowed a lump in her throat. "Really?"

"I mean it, Savannah. You lost several hours of your life, and you owe it to yourself to get those back."

"I'd have to admit to the therapist that I was there, in that room with Niles's dead body."

"They're bound by confidentiality, and I can refer you to someone, someone you can trust." Connor folded his arms. "That's the condition."

"All right, but I don't think it's going to do any good. Those memories are gone for good." Just like those other memories buried in her past.

"Okay, then. Investigation starts tomorrow." He swept her cell phone from the counter and held it out to her. "I think it's safe to turn this on now."

She rose from the couch and took the phone from him. "I'm sure it needs to be charged again. I wasn't lying when I said the thing dies all the time."

He jerked his thumb over his shoulder. "The sheets are clean in the guest room. Remember to make the bed every day so nobody gets suspicious that you're sleeping here as a guest. I'm going to see if there are pillows in there."

She watched through narrowed eyes as he headed for the back rooms. Maybe she hadn't expected him to sweep her off her feet and carry her to his room…but she sure wanted it.

Sighing, she hopped up to sit on the stool at the counter and attached her phone to the charger. It buzzed in her hand, and she glanced at a stream of text messages filling up her screen.

A glimpse at the first message told her the news of Niles's death had spread like a cancer. She dutifully tapped each text, reading the messages of shock and condolence, her tongue wedged in the corner of her mouth. Even Mom had sent her a text—a cryptic one, of course.

One of the last messages, one from an unknown number, had a picture attached to it. Savannah tapped it and swept her fingers over the picture to enlarge it.

Her gut twisted and she dropped the phone.

"Savannah, what's wrong?"

She turned toward Connor, gripping the edge of the counter as her world tilted. "Someone sent me a picture of a button."

"A button?" Connor's brows snapped over his nose.

"It's the evidence—Letty's evidence against me."

Chapter Eight

Connor ate up the space between him and Savannah in two long strides and caught her by the shoulders as she listed to the side. He smoothed a hand down her rigid spine.

"Let me see." He reached over her and scooped up the phone, the picture of a colorful button still enlarged on the display. "This is your button? Do you even know if it's missing?"

Nodding, she cleared her throat. "When I got dressed at Niles's, I noticed the button on my blouse was gone. It's pretty distinctive, so I got down on my hands and knees to search for it and found it beneath the dresser. I—I thought I dropped it in the pocket of my slacks."

"You haven't seen it since?"

"I forgot about it. I stuffed my slacks in the laundry basket in my closet when I got home after I left Niles's place." She bowed her head, tugging at the roots of her hair.

"If you never looked for the button, it could still be in your pocket."

Her head shot up, and then the light died from her violet eyes, turning them into dark pools. "You think Letty or someone else planted that button in Niles's bedroom? It's too unique. I bought that blouse in Paris. There's no way somebody found a duplicate for that button."

"Okay, okay. It's the same one." He wedged his hands against the counter, dropping his head between his arms.

The fact that Savannah had been careless enough to let the button fall out of her pocket gave him a glimmer of hope. She'd been so cold-bloodedly precise about everything else—her phone, her car's license plates, her fingerprints. This detail finally pointed to a woman frantic and caught off guard by the murder of her ex-husband.

"There's no text accompanying the picture? No demands?" He brought the phone close to his face and backtracked to the message with no words. "The number says Unknown. I suppose Letty's killer wouldn't be dumb enough to call you from his...or her real phone."

"If he's not blackmailing me, what does he want?"

"What he *didn't* want is for you to have that button back." Connor placed the phone on the counter and rubbed his chin. "But how did he know about that meeting? How did he know Letty had the button?"

"Maybe he's working with her and decided to keep all the ransom money for himself."

"Husband?"

"No way."

He cocked an eyebrow in her direction. "Spouses have murdered each other for a lot less than five hundred grand."

"I don't know. Maybe you're right." She pushed off the stool and stumbled. "It has to be someone she told, because only you and I knew about the meeting with Letty. Nobody followed us. Nobody followed me down here."

"You're sure about that?" He shoved his hands in his pockets, resisting the urge to reach out and steady her. If he touched her, he'd take her in his arms and never let her go—and that wasn't his best course of action right now, no matter how much he wanted her.

"I'm sure. There wasn't much traffic at that time of the

morning, and believe me, I was watching for anyone trailing me."

"I do believe you." He tapped the phone. "Get rid of that message and let's call it a wrap. Your bag is in my room, so I'll give you some time to get ready for bed. It's been one helluva day."

Savannah dug her fists into her eyes and rubbed, smearing mascara and eyeliner across her cheeks. "Are you sorry I showed up on your doorstep? Where Savannah Martell goes, trouble follows. That's what you used to say."

"I did?" He huffed out a breath. "I guess nothing's changed, but I'm not sorry you showed up. Where else would you go?"

An hour later, Connor lay on his back in his large bed and stared at the ceiling. Would he be able to help Savannah out of this mess? Did he want to?

He had to face the possibility that she'd killed Niles in self-defense and had blocked it out. It had to have been self-defense.

He squeezed his eyes shut and rolled over.

A FOOTFALL WHISPERED behind her, and Savannah dropped half an eggshell into the mixture in the bowl.

"Jumpy, aren't you?" Connor reached over her shoulder and plucked out the shell with two fingers. He tossed it into the sink, dripping egg white on the kitchen tiles.

"Don't make a mess in here." She whisked some pepper into the eggs and milk. "You didn't have any bacon or sausage in the fridge. Scrambled eggs and toast okay?"

"Fine, but you didn't have to cook breakfast." Connor ripped a piece of paper towel from the roll and swiped at the spot on the floor.

"I owe you…big-time. A little breakfast barely makes a dent in that debt."

"There's no debt owed here, Savannah." He leaned against the sink, his hands gripping the counter behind him.

Her gaze skimmed over his body, drinking in every inch of him, his board shorts hanging low on a pair of slim hips, his tight abs dusty gold from the sun. She'd fallen for Connor Wells the first time she'd laid eyes on him back in middle school. After Mom's second divorce, she'd moved the two of them from the mountains of Colorado to the sandy beaches of California.

Once Savannah got a glimpse of Connor, all her resentment toward her mother over the move vanished.

Connor had taken to her as well, teaching her how to surf, easing her transition to a new school, a new lifestyle. Life had been good—until Mom met Manny.

Connor snapped his fingers and she blinked. "Earth to Savannah. Where did you go?"

"A little trip down memory lane." She turned back to her eggs and whipped them into shape.

"Ahh, the good old days." He squeezed past her and grabbed a tub of butter from the fridge. "You wanna hop on a board while you're here?"

"Let's see." She placed a fingertip on her chin and rolled her eyes to the ceiling. "I'm under investigation for the murder of my ex, just missed the murder of my former housekeeper and I'm living under the threat of blackmail. Who *wouldn't* want to go surfing? I thought I was the irresponsible one here."

He shrugged and scooped a couple pats of butter from the container and dropped them into the frying pan. "Those things will still be true whether you're riding the waves or not."

"I thought we were going to start investigating today."

"We are, as soon as you call Thomas Bell."

"Thomas Bell?"

"The therapist."

She clenched her jaw as she prodded at the butter now sizzling in the hot pan. Connor was like a dog with a bone.

"That's the deal." He nudged her in the back.

"All right. Leave me his number." She dumped the egg mixture into the pan. "Friend of yours?"

"He is...now."

"Now?" She stirred the eggs in the skillet and then blinked at the congealed yellow mess. "He was *your* therapist?"

"That's right." Connor crossed his arms, widening his stance.

"Oh, I didn't know..." As her cheeks heated up, she shifted the pan from the fire to another burner. But she could've guessed. Connor had lost a lot in a short span of time—his father, his job, his mother...and her.

Although his life was an open book to the people he held near and dear, he wasn't the kind of guy to bare his soul to just anyone. He must've been in bad shape to turn to a professional.

"It wasn't my idea. After Dad was murdered and the sheriff's department started taking over the San Juan PD, they sent me to Thomas as a condition of my employment with them."

"But you didn't work for the SDSD." Connor had quit police work in disgust after Manny's cohorts had killed Chief Wells.

"I was considering it, so I saw Thomas for a few sessions and then I continued with him." He turned away from her and reached into the cupboard for a couple plates. "I never thought seeing a therapist would have any value for me. I was wrong. Thomas is a good guy and he knows what he's doing."

"And yet—" she slipped two pieces of bread into the toaster "—you never went back to law enforcement."

"Thomas helped me with that, too. I came to terms with my decision and realized my life had to take a different direction."

"Now, that *does* sound like therapy talk." She waved the spatula at him.

"Guilty." He held up the two plates. "Eat at the counter okay, or do you want to sit at the kitchen table?"

"Let's sit at the table. It's such a pretty view." She couldn't wiggle out of this therapy thing, but she didn't have to tell Thomas anything. The therapist would have to maintain her confidentiality with his good friend and former patient, Connor, too.

As she buttered the toast, Connor reached around her and scooped half the eggs onto one plate and half onto the other.

"There's marmalade in the fridge for the toast."

"And salsa for the eggs?"

"You know me. Can't eat eggs without salsa."

She *did* know Connor. He'd always been open, friendly, up-front. She'd been shocked by his open manner when she'd first met him. She figured everyone had family secrets, things you just didn't tell anyone—her mom had drilled that into her enough times. But then her mother had so much to hide in her own past.

And now Savannah did, too.

She spun around from the refrigerator, clutching a jar of salsa in one hand and a jar of orange marmalade in the other. "We're good to go."

As they sat across from each other over toast, eggs, juice and coffee, Connor had to spoil the moment.

"Have you looked at your phone yet this morning?"

"Of course."

"Anything more from the blackmailer?" He heaped some salsa over his eggs and offered her the spoon.

"If only we knew for sure he *was* a blackmailer. I haven't heard anything from him...or her. What does he want? Why would he go to those lengths—murdering Letty—to get that button? I could've dropped that button at any time in Niles's house."

"But you didn't. You were wearing that blouse the last night Niles was alive, so you would've had to have lost it the same night—and you told the police you didn't go to the house." Connor tapped her plate with his fork. "If they catch you in one lie, they're gonna look at you even more closely."

She dragged the tines of her fork through the runny salsa on her plate. "What do you think those detectives are doing right now?"

"They might be requesting your phone records. They might be checking the Marina Sports Bar, verifying your story."

The toast she'd just eaten rumbled in her stomach. "Most of that checks out."

"If there's CCTV outside the bar, how's that going to look?" Connor snapped a piece of toast in half.

"It will show me and Niles leaving the bar together and getting into his car, if the camera is pointing that way. I told the detectives we got in Niles's car, so that's not a problem." She shredded the paper towel next to her plate. "The problem is that button, or at least the person who has the button."

"I don't see how he—"

"Or she."

"—or she can use that button to blackmail you now. He'd have to sneak back into a crime scene and plant it."

"That's what Letty would've had to have done, although at least she'd have a reason to be at the house."

"In Letty's case, she could've told the police she found the button at the house, picked it up without thinking and then realized later it was yours and it had significance."

"I suppose so." Savannah dropped her fork, along with the pretense of eating, and dragged a pad of paper toward her. "You wanted me to start a list of people connected to Niles, and I think the first one on that list has to be Tiffany James, his girlfriend."

"First—" Connor fished his phone from the front pocket of his shorts "—you're going to call Thomas and make that appointment."

She held out her hand. "All right, although I don't think it's going to do any good."

"Humor me." He smacked the phone against her palm.

Connor had left Thomas Bell's contact info on the display and she tapped the screen to place the call she'd been dreading. She eased out a breath when it went to voice mail.

"Hi, Thomas. My name is Savannah Martell. I'm a friend of Connor Wells, and I'd like to make an appointment to see you."

Connor poked her arm and circled his finger in the air.

She stuck her tongue out at him. "As soon as possible. You can call me back on Connor's phone. Mine is acting up. Thanks."

She ended the call and shoved the cell back across the table toward Connor. "Happy?"

"Very." He aimed his fork at her plate. "Are you going to finish those eggs?"

"I don't have any appetite at all. How you can eat after what we saw last night is beyond me."

"Really?" He dumped more salsa onto her plate. "Last night when you were going through Letty's pockets, you didn't seem that squeamish."

"I was doing my best not to vomit." She'd had the same

gut-wrenching feeling when she saw Niles's wounds, but Connor seemed to think she was some coldhearted schemer—and he didn't even know the half of it.

"It's a good thing you didn't." He corralled the rest of her eggs with the last corner of his toast. "I don't have much sympathy for blackmailers anyway."

Before they finished cleaning up the kitchen, Thomas Bell called Connor back.

"Thanks for returning Savannah's call so quickly, Thomas. I'll give the phone over to her."

Savannah dried her hands on a kitchen towel and took the phone from Connor. "Hello."

"Savannah, this is Thomas Bell. I can get you in as early as tomorrow, if that works out for you. I just had a cancellation."

"Sure." She licked her lips. "What time?"

"Eleven o'clock."

"I can do eleven." She could do any time. What did she have going on except the fight of her life to prove her innocence?

Thomas gave her the address of his office, even though she knew damned well Connor would take her and probably escort her inside.

She put down the phone. "There. That's done. Now I think we need to go see Tiffany today."

"Won't she think that's strange?"

"I have a reason to see her, one she won't mind."

An hour later, they were on the freeway up to San Diego, and Connor asked, "How come Tiffany didn't live with Niles?"

"Honestly, I think it's because Niles found it easier to cheat on her if they kept their separate residences."

Connor shook his head. "The one time I met Niles, he did not strike me as a player."

"That's because you met him before Snap App's stock went public and the money really started rolling in. All that money sort of made him like a pro athlete—without all the muscles. Once women found out who he was and what he was worth, they threw themselves at him." She shrugged. "He had a hard time resisting."

"Did Tiffany throw herself at him?"

"In the most blatant way possible. Tiffany's a stripper… I mean, an exotic dancer."

Connor's mouth dropped open. "Niles was going to marry an exotic dancer?"

"I don't think Niles had any intention of marrying Tiffany, despite the big ring he gave her."

Connor whistled. "Niles was playing with fire. Once the detectives discover all of this, they're going to have a few more suspects to look at than you."

"Then I'd better make sure they know about Niles's cheatin' ways."

"Especially if Tiffany doesn't tell them herself." He tapped her phone, which was charging on the console. "Aren't you going to call her?"

"I didn't want to give her a chance to say no." She swept her finger across the display on the dash to make a phone call. "But now we're almost there. How can she refuse?"

The ringing of Tiffany's phone filled the car and just when Savannah got ready to leave a message, Tiffany answered, her voice breathless.

"Savannah? Is that you?"

"It is. How are you doing? I'm so sorry about Niles."

Tiffany's voice broke on a sob. "It's horrible. I can't even get out of bed."

"How did you find out?"

"The police came to my front door and told me." Tiffany sniffled. "I can't believe it. D-did the police talk to you? They want my blood or something."

"They did question me and they want my DNA, too. It's not a big deal, Tiffany. I'm sure they're going to ask everyone close to Niles...just to rule us out."

"I'm shocked and just heartbroken." Tiffany paused to blow her nose. "Do you think I can keep the ring?"

Connor rolled his eyes at Savannah, but she wasn't about to judge Tiffany.

"Of course. Niles gave it to you." She maneuvered the car onto the next off-ramp—the one that would take her to Tiffany's condo. "In fact, I need to talk to you about a few things, Tiffany. Can I come over right now?"

"Right now?"

"I'm in the neighborhood, right around the corner, actually."

"Oh. Okay."

The car's speakers amplified some whispering and rustling noises on the other end of the line, and Savannah raised her brows at Connor.

"You can meet me at the pool. It's toward the back of the complex."

"See you in about fifteen minutes."

Savannah ended the call and drummed her thumbs on the steering wheel. "Did that sound to you like she didn't want us in her place?"

"That's exactly what it sounded like. I thought she couldn't get out of bed."

Savannah lifted her shoulders. "Maybe the place is a mess."

Fifteen minutes later, Savannah pulled her car into the parking lot of the sprawling condo complex.

"Exotic dancing must pay well." Connor shaded his eyes as he peered out the window.

"I'm sure you can guess Niles bought the place for her."

Savannah parked where she could find a spot marked for visitors. When she got out of the car, she tugged on the wrinkled legs of her shorts. "At least we're dressed for the pool."

They followed a path through lush landscaping and Savannah inhaled the scent of jasmine as the sun warmed the back of her head. This could all be so pleasant, especially with Connor by her side, if she weren't trying to figure out who was framing her for murder.

They turned a corner and faced a fenced pool area scattered with chaise longues, the blue water lapping at the sides of the pool. Connor breathed out. "Nice."

"Wish we were here to enjoy it." Savannah tried the gate, but it didn't budge. She hung on to the bars and pressed her face between them, spotting Tiffany stretched out in the sun. "Tiffany!"

Niles's girlfriend turned her head, her bleached blond hair piled on top, and waved.

Before she could stir herself, another woman pushed out the gate and held it open. "Friends of Tiffany?"

"We are, thanks." Connor caught it and ushered Savannah through. "You first."

Savannah's flat sandals slapped the cement as she approached Tiffany, whose eyes were hidden behind a pair of huge sunglasses.

"Thanks for seeing me, Tiffany. You'll be glad you did."

She started to nod and then her head snapped back when Connor came up beside Savannah. She scooted her dark glasses down the length of her nose. "Hello there."

"Tiffany, this is Connor Wells. Connor, Tiffany James."

Tiffany held out a limp hand, her long fingernails glittering in the sun. "Hi, Connor. Nice to meet you."

He squeezed her fingers in an awkward handshake.

"Same here. If you ladies don't mind, I'll stake out this chaise longue over here and soak up a few rays."

"So, you're the famous Connor Wells." Tiffany shoved her glasses back up her nose, and a little smile played about her full lips.

"Famous?" Connor grabbed the hem of his T-shirt and yanked it over his head, putting his rippling torso on full display.

Savannah couldn't see Tiffany's eyes behind her sunglasses, but she didn't have to see them to know where the woman had focused her gaze.

"Oh, Niles may have mentioned you a few hundred times."

"Sorry for your loss." Connor stretched out on the chaise longue as if he didn't have a care in the world.

Savannah knew he'd be listening to every word the two of them said.

Tiffany's mouth immediately curved down. "Thank you. It was a shock."

Savannah pulled up the chair between the two recliners now inhabited by Tiffany on one side and Connor on the other. "Do you have any idea who would want to kill Niles?"

"Besides you and me?"

Savannah sucked in a breath. "That's not funny, Tiffany. I hope you're not telling the detectives that."

She waved her long nails in the air. "No, but he was a cheatin' dog, wasn't he? The cops are gonna learn that, even if we don't tell them."

"I had ceased to care about Niles's cheating."

"Did you ever care?" Tiffany shoved her sunglasses to the top of her head and shifted her gaze to Connor, lounging behind her.

Savannah scooted to the right to block her view. "Did

Niles tell you anything about problems he was having, or any enemies?"

"No." Tiffany narrowed her eyes. "Is that what you came here to ask me? Are you workin' for the popo now?"

"Just curious." Savannah bent forward and straightened a strap on her sandal, dipping her hand into Tiffany's bag at the same time. "I really came to see you to make sure you contact Niles's attorney, Chris Neelon. Niles definitely left you something in his will."

"He did?" Tiffany's lips parted. "How much?"

"That, I don't know. That's why you have to call Neelon. I wanted to make sure you knew about Niles's will."

"Do those detectives have to know that?" Tiffany flicked her fingers in the air at a young man in a white shirt and slacks crossing the pool deck.

"It's a murder investigation. They'll know everything like that."

The man stopped in front of Tiffany's chaise longue and flashed a set of white teeth in his brown face. "Pool-side massage, Ms. James?"

"Yes, Diego. Can you set that up and I'll be over in a few minutes?" She glanced at Savannah. "If we're done."

"We're done. Just wanted to let you know about Niles's will and see if you had any ideas who killed him." Savannah twisted around in her chair. "Are you ready over there, sun worshipper?"

Connor opened one eye and rubbed a hand across his chest. "Feels good."

"I can have Diego set up another massage, if you like." Tiffany sat forward and tugged her swimsuit cover-up from her impressive body.

Connor didn't even blink. "We'd better get going. We wouldn't want to disturb you in your mourning."

Tiffany's nostrils flared. "What's done is done."

Savannah pushed up from the chair and raised her hand. "I suppose I'll see you at the funeral—whenever they release the body."

As Tiffany stretched out again like a cat, they sauntered across the pool deck and swung open the gate.

When it clanged behind them, Connor took Savannah's arm. "That didn't tell us much."

"Maybe Tiffany didn't tell us much, but her condo will." Savannah held up the key chain she'd swiped from Tiffany's bag. "But we'll have to make it fast before she notices it's missing."

"You're kidding." Connor dropped his shirt on the ground.

"While some of us were flexing our muscles in the sun, some of us were working."

"We'd better hurry up in case she changes her mind about succumbing to Diego's magical hands." As Connor bent over to sweep up his shirt, he turned his head toward the pool. "Do you know her condo number?"

"I've seen it enough on Niles's papers and correspondence. It's 246."

Cupping Tiffany's key chain in her hand, Savannah strode down the path that led back to the units, with Connor right beside her—as it should be. She'd missed having him on her side. He gave her confidence and an unshakable belief that everything would turn out for the best—even when she strongly doubted that, like now.

They walked upstairs to Tiffany's corner unit, and as Savannah slid the key into the lock, Connor stood behind her, keeping watch.

She pushed open the door and stepped inside, the smoky air making her blink. She whispered, "I thought she gave up smoking. That was a deal breaker for Niles."

"Niles isn't around anymore, is he?" Connor nudged her inside and clicked the door behind them.

Savannah put her hands on her hips and surveyed the messy room. "Why wouldn't she want us in here?"

"Are you expecting to find some bloody clothes? A bloody knife?" Connor smacked a fist in his palm. "Oh, wait. *We* have that."

"Maybe she has my button." Savannah crept toward the hallway leading to the rooms in the back. She paused at the only door that was closed, resting her fingertips on the handle and cocking her head. The hair on the back of her neck quivered for a second before she turned the doorknob.

She gulped when, out of nowhere, the cold barrel of a gun pressed against her temple.

Chapter Nine

The distinctive sound of a safety being released from a handgun cut through the air. Connor reached for his waistband, but he'd left his own weapon at home.

"Savannah!"

At his call, she came stumbling back into the room, a large bearded man prodding her forward at gunpoint.

"What the hell are you doing in my place?"

Connor's adrenaline whooshed and receded, leaving him dizzy. He clenched his hands at his sides. "*Your* place? This is Tiffany James's place, and we came up here to return her keys."

"A-and leave her a card." Savannah took a small step away from the man holding her at gunpoint. "We just saw her at the pool, and I accidentally took her keys."

The man growled, "Why not just go back to the pool and give them to her?"

"She was going to get a massage. We didn't want to disturb her."

Savannah's demeanor had him in awe. She could think on her feet with the best of them.

"With Diego?" The bearded man's voice boomed behind her.

"What?" Savannah twisted her head around.

Connor held out his hand. "Put the gun away, man. This

is a misunderstanding. We're not here to rip you off. Savannah came up here to leave Tiffany an attorney's card. Put the gun down."

The man secured his weapon and shoved it into the waistband of his ripped jeans. "You're Savannah Wedgewood, Niles's ex."

"That's right, and you are...?"

"Denny. Denny Cosgrove, Tiffany's...ex."

Connor's gaze tracked over Denny's tousled hair and bare chest. Didn't look like Denny and Tiffany were ex-anything.

"This is Connor." Savannah waved her hand at him.

At least she hadn't called *him* an ex.

Denny lunged forward with an outstretched paw and squeezed the hell out of Connor's hand. "Sorry about the gun. I thought someone had broken in."

"If we had thought anyone was here, we wouldn't have just waltzed in with the key." Savannah dangled Tiffany's key chain from her finger before dropping it on a table. "Sorry. We'll just leave this here."

"And that card?" Denny scratched his tattooed chest as he eyed Savannah.

"Of course." She dug in her purse and pulled out a card, wedging it beneath the key chain.

Denny slid the card toward him with one thick finger, squinting at the print. "Is this Niles's attorney? Is Tiffany getting something from Niles?"

"I believe so, yes." Savannah slid a quick glance Connor's way. "Have the police talked to you yet?"

"Me?" Denny's face reddened. "Why should they talk to me? I got nothing to do with that murder. I never even met the guy."

"I mean when they talked to Tiffany. If you're staying here..."

"I'm not staying here. Just picking up some stuff Tif has of mine."

"Okay." Connor reached out and grabbed Savannah's hand. "We'll get out of your way."

Denny waved the card at them. "Thanks for this. Tif deserves something after what that guy put her through."

Once outside the stuffy condo, they marched toward Savannah's car in silence. Connor got in the passenger side and waited until Savannah was behind the wheel.

"That's why Tiffany didn't want us at her place. She's still hooking up with Denny and didn't want you to know."

"Denny sure seemed interested in Niles's money, didn't he?"

"Looks like Niles wasn't the only one stepping out in that relationship." Connor buzzed down his window as Savannah started the car. "And Denny is one dude you don't wanna cross."

"He *was* a little eager to pull out that gun."

"It's not just that, Savannah. Did you see his tattoos? He belongs to Sons of Chaos."

"The motorcycle gang? You knew that from his tattoos?"

"They're like any other gang. They get certain tattoos that mark their membership and standing in the organization."

"You think I should mention this to the police when I go in tomorrow to give my DNA?"

"Why not? They asked you before if you knew anyone who would want to kill Niles. Denny looks like a good suspect to me."

"Do you think Tiffany set up Niles? Maybe not for murder, but to fleece him?" Savannah maneuvered the car out of the parking lot of the condo complex and joined a stream of traffic.

"That could've been the plan, but you don't think Niles

is that naive, do you?" Connor rubbed his chin, which had been itching ever since he saw Denny's full beard. "Maybe they were playing each other. He was getting what he wanted out of her and paying her for it."

Savannah wrinkled her nose. "That sounds so…tawdry. And if Niles was compensating Tiffany for her company, why would she want to kill the goose laying the golden eggs? Why would Denny?"

"Maybe they knew about the will and figured she'd get more with Niles dead—or at least get it as a lump sum and then she could be with Denny."

Savannah shook her head. "I can't imagine two men more different than Niles and Denny."

"Niles and I aren't exactly twins, either."

A rosy blush tinged her cheeks. "That was kind of the point."

"Because what we had was so bad?"

"Because I didn't need anyone or anything else reminding me of you after I left."

"Why?"

Savannah shifted in her seat and sighed, "If I couldn't have you, I didn't want to be thinking of you every day."

As the car idled at a red light, Connor brushed his knuckles down her forearm. "But you could've had me. Didn't I make that clear?"

"There was too much guilt for me, Connor." She sniffled. "My stepfather's associates killed your father because he was protecting my mom, and that strained your relationship with *your* mom."

"I always had an uncomfortable relationship with my mom. You know that."

"I'm sure all that happened between our families made it worse, and the fact that you sided with me over her."

"My father was doing his job. He was protecting a citizen of San Juan Beach."

"We both know he never would've been there if my mom hadn't called him personally."

"If I can forgive you, why can't you forgive yourself? You don't even have anything to forgive. You were a barely out of your teens, still in college."

The knuckles on Savannah's hands turned white as she clenched the wheel. "I don't want to talk about this anymore, Connor."

He turned his head and stared at the passing scenery. Savannah's excuses didn't make sense. There had to be more. He'd accepted that she just wasn't that into him, but the heat between them still sizzled. What he wouldn't give to be a fly on the wall in her session with Thomas.

But now he had to settle for a fake relationship with the woman he loved more than anything, the woman he'd lie, cheat and steal for.

"Don't you think it would be a good idea if I dropped by the sheriff's department right now to give them my DNA? Would that make me seem more cooperative?"

"More anxious. They told you to come in tomorrow. If you keep your original appointment, that's cooperative enough."

Savannah flipped a U-turn and Connor clutched the armrest as the tires of the car squealed. "Where are you going?"

"The scene of the crime."

His fingernails dug into the leather of the armrest. "Are you kidding?"

"House is still in my name. I still have keys. Why not?"

"Because your ex was just murdered there and you're a suspect. It might look suspicious."

"If someone sees me. Will the cops have someone watching the place?"

"Probably not. I'm sure they're done processing the crime scene by now. They've taken their prints, their pictures, their evidence."

"Which apparently does *not* include the button from my blouse."

"Too bad we didn't have a chance to look for that at Tiffany's." Connor rolled his tight shoulders. They had too much to deal with too fast.

As Savannah drove through the pristine neighborhood of La Jolla, Connor glanced at her profile. "Are you sure you want to do this?"

"If we're going to conduct our own investigation into Niles's murder, we have to start with the scene of the crime."

"What do you think you'll find there?"

Her head whipped around. "Why are you trying to dissuade me? You said yourself the sheriff's department has processed the crime scene. My name is still on the title of that house, I have the keys and I have every right to go there. What's the problem?"

Connor rubbed his jaw. What *was* the problem? The nagging voice in the back of his brain that kept telling him the killer would want to return to the scene of the crime?

"Don't want it to look bad for you." He lifted one shoulder.

Reaching across the console, she rubbed his thigh. "Thanks, but if there's nobody there to see me, that's not going to happen. Besides, I have a reason to be there."

"Which is?" He held his breath.

"Niles worked from home a lot, and he has company files there. I want them."

"The homicide detectives would've taken his laptop and any other devices at the house."

"I'm talking about paper files—like the ones he was supposed to hand over to me that night before we were both incapacitated."

"Okay, that's your story. Stick to it."

She huffed out a breath. "It's not a story, Connor. I swear, sometimes you act like I'm guilty."

"We don't know what happened that night, Savannah. You…blacked out."

"Sometimes you act like I'm guilty—and that I *know* I'm guilty."

Connor stared out the window as the rolling green lawns and lush, colorful landscaping rushed by. "Did you like living here?"

She huffed out a long sigh. "I did. The house is beautiful."

"If you're still on the title, that means the house is yours, too, right?"

Silence descended in the car as Savannah maneuvered the winding roads uphill, hunching forward in her seat. The hard set of her jaw told him she had no intention of answering his question, even though he knew the answer. With Niles's death, she stood to gain control of Snap App, millions in life insurance money and a multimillion-dollar home in La Jolla. Quite a haul.

"It's right around the next curve." She swung the wheel and slowed the car. "And I don't see any cop cars out front."

Even if he hadn't seen pictures of the house before, the yellow crime scene tape stirring in the ocean breeze was a dead giveaway. The white Mediterranean loomed at the end of the cul-de-sac, and Connor knew the Pacific roiled and scrambled over the rocks just beyond and downhill from the house.

How the hell had Savannah sneaked out of here on foot and walked home?

She pulled into the driveway and cut the engine. "The walk home wasn't bad, especially after I kicked off my heels."

Before he had a chance to answer, she hopped out of the car and slammed the door. By the time he scrambled from the car and had followed her up the walkway, she was yanking yellow tape from the front door.

She dangled it in front of her from her fingertips. "Does this mean they plan to come back?"

"Not necessarily." He snatched the tape from her hand and crumpled it in his fist. "The cops are not going to clean up a murder scene for you. They leave that chore to you."

"I remember." With her mouth tight, she shoved her key into the lock and pushed open the door.

Of course, Savannah and her mother had had to take care of the mess when his father shot and killed Manny in their home. Dad had even taken care of that for Georgie, calling in a cleaning crew from San Diego that specialized in crime scene cleanup; blood, brains, tissue—they did it all. What would Savannah and he find here?

As he stepped over the threshold of the house she used to share with her husband, Connor tilted back his head to take in the vaulted ceiling above the foyer, and squinted into the light. The blue, green and white furnishings that littered the great room looked like a continuation of the ocean and sand at the foot of the cliffs over which the big house loomed. He could see Savannah's stamp on the room—bright, airy and carefree. What secrets lurked beneath this cheery facade?

She shot him a look from beneath her dark lashes. "Do you like it?"

"It's…beachy."

"Appropriately so." She crossed the room to the staircase and put one foot on the bottom step, resting her hand on the banister. "D-do you want to go upstairs and see it?"

"Might as well get it over with." He pulled in a deep breath and blew it out as he took Savannah's hand and marched up the stairs ahead of her.

When they hit the second level, she squeezed his hand and said, "Last room at the end of the hall."

The door to the master bedroom gaped open, one band of yellow tape across the opening. Connor ducked beneath it and crossed into the room, tripping to a stop when he saw the bloodstain on the throw rug that carried over to the hardwood floor.

He whistled. "Niles lost a lot of blood."

"I know."

"Take me through what you remember." He skirted the mess on the floor and sauntered to the French doors that led to a balcony and a magnificent view of the Pacific.

He unlocked one of the doors and swung it open. The white drapes unfurled into the room, caught on a sudden sea breeze.

Savannah had got hung up at the room's entrance, her eyes wide and shimmering pools. "I—I woke up on that side of the bed, the same side as Nile's body on the floor."

She took a stuttering step into the room. As she shuffled around the bed, her sandals scuffing against the polished wood, her gaze darted to the place where she'd found her ex-husband, his flesh punctured and ripped by a knife— the same one hidden on Connor's property.

She thrust a finger at the tousled bed. "There. I woke up there, naked, cuts on my right hand. My mouth dry as a cotton ball, my brain foggy, confused."

"Was the door to the balcony closed and the drapes drawn?"

"No. Just like now, there was a breeze that morning, and

the door was slightly ajar. I was dreaming that I was in the water and struggling for the surface."

"Did you see Niles right away?"

"I didn't see Niles at all at first. It was still dark outside and the room was dark. I—I stubbed my toe on his body." She hugged herself, and dug her fingers into the flesh of her upper arms. "When I flicked on the light, I saw him at my feet."

Connor tilted his head. "Weren't you afraid the killer might still be in the house?"

"I don't know why, but that never occurred to me." She tossed back her hair. "I guess I figured he'd committed the act and taken off."

Connor pulled the rest of the story out of her in bits and pieces. It hadn't changed much from the account she'd given him from the moment she'd landed on his doorstep.

She showed him where she'd found her button and how she'd stuffed it into the pocket of her slacks.

"I guess I missed my pocket and that's how Letty found the button, or it fell out when I finished tidying up."

"Where did you go after you…cleaned up the room?"

"Down to Niles's office." She pulled her light sweater around her body. "I wanted the file Niles had promised me."

"Must've been an important file for you to think about it in a moment of panic."

Her eyes narrowed briefly like a cat's that had considered and then dismissed some prey. "That's why Niles and I got together. That's why I came to this house. I wasn't going to leave it behind." She crooked her index finger. "I'll show you."

Once again Connor ducked beneath the yellow tape crisscrossed over the door. He followed Savannah down the curved staircase, her composure causing a tickle on the back of his neck.

The sight of Niles's blood had shaken her, but if he thought Savannah was going to collapse against his chest in a fit of despair, he'd be dead wrong. She'd been oddly stoic after Manny's death, too.

She strode across the great room and pushed open a door that led to an office, its walls lined with bookshelves, a single large window framing a profusion of color in the front garden.

"We must've had a drink." Savannah flicked her fingers toward the wet bar. "There were two glasses over there, a lipstick stain on one of them."

He drew his brows over his nose. "Is that something you'd do normally?"

"To tell you the truth, not really, especially if I'd already had a drink. But if Niles was insisting, I might do it to appease him, just to get my hands on the file."

"Maybe it wasn't your drink."

"Too late now. I dumped the booze in the sink and rinsed out those glasses."

"What kind of booze?"

She swooped down on the wet bar and tapped a cut glass crystal bottle with her fingernail. "This scotch. It was Niles's favorite."

"Maybe we need to take that with us, see what's in it. If you think both you and Niles might've been drugged, maybe that's the source."

"Good idea." She grabbed the bottle from the shelf and put it on the edge of the wet bar. "So, I came in here, grabbed the file and hiked down the hill and through the backstreets to my house."

"The file was on the desk?"

"No." She raised a finger. "Which was weird. There's a false bottom in one of the desk drawers and the file was still there."

"How'd you know it would be there?"

"I'm pretty sure Niles told me on the way over. We often put important papers in there, papers we might not want to secure in the safe but didn't want out in the open."

"What was in this file?"

"Financials. Stuff we don't want to reveal to the general public. I didn't think it was out of the ordinary for the file to be there."

"You just said it was weird that the file was there."

"That the file was *still* there." She shook her purse off her shoulder and unzipped it. "Whatever happened to us must've happened pretty fast if Niles didn't even have time to remove the file from the desk drawer. When I came down here, I expected the file to be on the desk. When it wasn't, I knew he hadn't taken it out of the drawer yet, and I was able to retrieve it from its hiding place."

"What are you doing now?"

Savannah had moved behind the mahogany desk, holding up a pen she'd pulled from her purse. "I'll show you how it works."

Connor joined her behind the desk, crouching next to her as she pulled open the bottom drawer on the left side.

She shoved aside some hanging folders and inserted the tip of the pen into a minuscule hole in the bottom of the drawer. As Savannah wiggled the pen, her tongue lodged in the corner of her mouth, Connor heard a small *click*.

She lifted a panel from the bottom of the drawer, exposing a cavity that held a few file folders and a flash drive. "I took the file from here."

"Handy. I wonder why he didn't take it out when you got back here."

"I can't tell you. I don't remember." She replaced the panel and sat back on her heels.

Connor leaned over her, grabbed the pen and scooted

the files back into place. As he set the pen on the desk the top sprang free and rolled off the edge. "Looks like you broke your..."

Connor's throat tightened as he eyed the various pieces.

"That's okay. I don't even know where I got that pen. Must be one of Niles's."

Connor prodded the broken pen with his knuckle and then brushed if off the table and crushed it beneath the heel of his shoe.

Savannah's eyes widened. "What the hell are you doing?"

"That might be a pen, but it's doubling as a recording device."

Chapter Ten

Savannah choked and scrambled backward like a crab, away from the shards of pen littering the Persian rug. "A—a recording device? Someone's been listening to me? To us?"

"Or tracking your movements." He stirred the pieces with the toe of his shoe. "It could be a GPS or even a camera. I can't tell, but if the eavesdropper was still listening I don't think we gave it away that we knew what it was. The pen rolled off the table and broke. That's all he knows."

"Oh, God." Savannah clutched her throat with one hand. "It must've been in my purse from the beginning. Someone planted it when I was here, in this house."

The sound of a car door slamming had the two of them locking eyes.

"Now what?" Still on the floor, Savannah crawled to the window and hooked her finger on the edge of the drapes, peering outside. "Damn."

"The cops?" Connor dropped to his knees and scooped up the pieces of the pen or microphone or GPS or whatever it was into his palm.

"Niles's sister, Melanie."

"Does she have a key?"

"I'm sure she does, or she wouldn't be here." Savannah

jumped to her feet and scurried out of the room, calling over her shoulder, "Act naturally."

She hit the foyer just as Melanie pushed open the front door.

Niles's sister jerked back, releasing the door, which swung open and hit the wall. "Savannah, you scared the hell out of me. I saw the car but I thought it was one of Niles's."

"You gave me a fright, too." Savannah descended on Melanie and wrapped her arms around her former sister-in-law's thin frame. "I'm so sorry about Niles."

Melanie returned the hug. "Thank you. It was awful news. Who'd want to kill my brother? Do you think you're in danger, too?"

Oh, yeah. She was in danger. "I have no idea who'd want to kill Niles, but I hope to God I'm not on anyone's list."

Melanie cocked her head. "Really? Who are we fooling? Niles had made some enemies since you two struck it rich."

Connor's flip-flops slapped the floor behind Savannah, and she made a half turn. "Melanie Wedgewood, this is Connor Wells. Connor, Niles's sister, Melanie."

"Nice to meet you, and I'm sorry for your loss." Connor reached around Savannah to shake Melanie's hand.

"Pretty crazy stuff. You never think murder is going to hit your family." Melanie smoothed her short dark hair back from her forehead with one hand. "But here we are."

"What *are* you doing here?" Savannah shoved an unsteady hand in the pocket of her sweater. She hadn't yet recovered from Connor's discovery about the pen, but in a way it wasn't the worst news she'd had all day. Now maybe Connor would believe that someone was trying to set her up, instead of shooting doubt at her from his impossibly blue eyes.

Melanie jabbed a finger in Savannah's direction. "You may have inherited everything Niles had, but I'm still his next of kin and the cops told me I was basically responsible for Niles's funeral…and other things."

"Don't go up there." Savannah put a hand on Melanie's arm. "You don't need to see that. Connor knows about these things, people you can hire."

"Really?" Melanie's heavily lined eyes widened. "I was shocked when the sheriff's department told me they didn't clean up the…mess left behind in a homicide."

"There are companies that will take care of that. I'll look some up for you right now, if you two want to talk privately," Connor offered.

"I don't think Savannah and I have anything to discuss in secret, do we?" Melanie arched an eyebrow in her direction. "But if you want to help me out, I'd appreciate it. I wouldn't even know where to start looking."

Connor held up his cell phone. "I got it."

As he wandered back to Niles's office, Melanie jerked her thumb in his direction. "Dreamboat, if I actually swung that way."

"Speaking of dreamboats, is Faye with you?"

"She had clients she couldn't leave. She never liked Niles anyway."

"She would be here for you, not Niles."

"I never liked Niles much, either, at least not lately." Melanie put a hand over her mouth. "I didn't just say that. I'm a terrible person and an awful sister."

Savannah squeezed Melanie's shoulder. "We all say things during times of stress. I know you loved Niles, even when he was being impossible."

"He messed up." Melanie brushed a tear from her cheek. "He should've treated you better. Maybe should've treated other people better, as well."

"I don't think that would've changed anything, Melanie. We just weren't meant to be a romantic couple. We should've just stayed business partners."

"That would've never worked for Niles. He was smitten with you, although I never got the impression the smit was mutual." Melanie's gaze tracked to the office door, which Connor had closed behind him.

Savannah spun around, flinging her arms out to her sides. "Now it's all a big mess—Niles dead, murdered. I know he had his enemies, but I can't think of anyone who'd want him dead."

"What about that girlfriend of his?" Melanie swept past Savannah and meandered to the sliding glass doors that led to the backyard. "Tiffany. From what I could tell, she was kind of a shady character. Who dates someone you meet while she's dancing around a pole?"

"Niles and lots of other men." Savannah folded her arms and perched on the arm of her favorite recliner. "I can't see Tiffany murdering Niles. She'd be killing her benefactor…"

"But?"

"But what?" Savannah lifted her chin and met Melanie's eyes.

"That sentence had a definite *but* at the end of it."

Savannah raised and dropped her shoulders. "Looks like Tiffany has an ex hanging around—a scary-looking biker dude."

"Maybe that's it." Melanie snapped her fingers. "Jealous biker dude."

"I'll make sure I mention him to the detectives."

"You haven't spoken to them yet?" Melanie narrowed her dark eyes, looking enough like Niles to give Savannah the chills.

"Yes, they came down to San Juan Beach—where I've been staying with Connor—to question me, but they want me to stop by the station so I can give up my DNA and to ask more questions. I'm going in tomorrow."

"Your DNA?" Melanie clicked her tongue. "They don't suspect you, do they?"

"Ex-wife getting control of the multimillion-dollar company, life insurance money, house in La Jolla." Savannah jabbed a finger into her chest. "Number one suspect right here."

Melanie snorted, "Ridiculous. They can ask me. Besides, weren't you with dreamboat in there at the time of the murder?"

"How do you know that?"

"Uh, I asked the detectives." She raised her hand. "Not that I suspected you."

"I was with Connor."

"Done deal." Melanie brushed her hands together.

Connor exited the office, tilting his phone back and forth in front of him. "Called a company for you, and they're coming out tomorrow, unless that doesn't work."

"You *are* a dreamboat." Melanie blew a kiss in Connor's direction. "Thank you so much."

"While you're here, you're welcome to take anything, Melanie." Savannah waved her hand around the room. "Niles has some family pics and some things from your parents."

"Wow." Melanie blinked her eyes and dabbed at the corners. "It's just my brother Newland and I now in our immediate family, and Newland's no use while he's battling his demons. That hurts."

Savannah wrapped Melanie in another hug. "Take as much time as you need here. Are you talking to the detectives while you're in San Diego?"

"I spoke with them on the phone, but they wanted me to come in for another interview, a face-to-face." She sniffed and shook her finger at Savannah. "And you'd better believe I'm going to tell them you had nothing to do with Niles's death."

"I appreciate it. Give my love to Faye."

"I will. She'll be sorry she missed you." Melanie wedged a hand on her hip. "I'm not driving you two away, am I?"

"We were just leaving when you arrived." Connor pointed at the door. "But you ladies can have a few more minutes. I'm going to get that bag from the car, Savannah, and pack up a few of those files you wanted from Niles's office."

"Okay." Savannah watched Connor leave with a furrow between her eyebrows. Files? Maybe he meant that bottle of scotch. Melanie wouldn't miss that, as she was a recovering alcoholic. Niles was the only Wedgewood sibling who had escaped that scourge.

She and Melanie chatted for a few more minutes until Connor returned with an empty gym bag hitched over his shoulder.

"I'll be done in a minute."

By the time he emerged from the office, Savannah and Melanie had said their goodbyes and Savannah joined Connor at the front door.

"Keep me posted on the funeral plans, Melanie."

"I will. I know I'll have to wait until they release Niles's body." Melanie closed her eyes and clutched her hands in front of her.

Savannah asked, "You sure you'll be okay here by yourself?"

"Killer's not coming back, is he?"

As they stepped down the front porch, Connor whispered in Savannah's ear, "I wish he would so we could wrap this up."

"What's in the bag?" Savannah pinged the side of the black canvas with her fingernail.

"That scotch, the pieces of the broken pen and the rest of that stuff from the false-bottom drawer." He hugged the bag to his chest. "You never know."

As they wound down the hill, Savannah glanced at Connor. "Someone was following me or listening to me with that pen."

"Or both. I'm not sure what kind of device it is. I just know it's not a pen, or at least it's more than a pen."

"If someone was listening to me, they could've heard my conversation with Letty. Could've shown up early to kill her and take that button."

"The person listening in also knows exactly our train of thought, knows we went to see Tiffany, knows we were at the house. I can't even think of what else."

"B-but it definitely looks like someone is trying to set me up, right? That pen must've been planted in my purse the night of Niles's murder. I've never seen it before." She pressed a hand to her forehead. "I haven't been imagining this, and that same person put the knife in my car and tried to steer the detectives toward it."

She slid one hand from the steering wheel and pressed it against her fluttering belly. "That means he knows where I live, somehow broke into my car and stashed that knife in my trunk."

"Or he broke into your house, got your car keys and used them to get into your car. Did you have your keys with you that night, even though you'd left your car at home?"

"I didn't."

"How'd you get into your house when you got home?"

"Used the code on my garage door to get in that way. I always leave the door from my laundry room to the garage open."

"Bad idea."

She rolled her eyes. "That's a moot point now. Someone set me up for Niles's murder, but why? Why take out both of us by killing him and framing me?"

"Who stands to gain with both of you out of the picture? Who gets the company?"

"My mom is beneficiary for almost everything I have. As...unconventional as my mother is, I don't think she'd be killing Niles and framing me for his murder."

"And Niles's share?"

"His sister."

"Melanie?"

She poked his thigh. "No way. Melanie doesn't even care that much about money."

"Her boyfriend? Spouse?"

"Wife. Faye has a great career as an attorney with a big firm in San Francisco. They're set, happy. They're not interested in what Niles has, especially since Melanie saw how much wealth changed her brother—and not for the better."

"Maybe money isn't the motive. Is there someone at the company who hates the two of you? Disgruntled employee?"

Savannah sucked in her bottom lip and squinted at the road. "There was a guy, Brian Donahue. We had to let him go. He was in charge of quality-assurance testing and couldn't get along with anyone. He threatened to destroy code and we had him escorted out of the building and off the premises."

"How long ago was this?"

"Three or four months."

"Did he threaten either of you?"

"On his way out of the building? Hell, yes."

"You need to mention his name to the detectives tomorrow."

"There's a lot I could tell them tomorrow, but half of

it would implicate me, so I'd better keep my mouth shut." She flipped down her visor. "I wonder if anyone has discovered Letty's body yet."

"I'm sure you'll find out tomorrow when you go in for questioning." Connor rubbed the back of his neck. "Don't you ever eat? I'm starving."

"I suppose I could force down some food. Should we stop on the way back to your place or wait until we get to San Juan?"

"If you can hold out for another twenty minutes, let's wait. I think you should show your face around town a little more, get people used to seeing you there. I also want to find out if there's any news about the fire. Now that we found that pen, there's a very real possibility someone followed you out to my place and set fire to that shed for some reason."

"To smoke out the knife. Someone could've been watching you when you went outside to hide it."

"I wasn't waving it around when I went to the storage shed."

"The person could've just made the assumption, or even verified the assumption when we left for lunch."

"I'm not dismissing the idea. That's why I want to keep my ear to the ground in San Juan for any news."

By the time they rolled into San Juan, Savannah's stomach was rumbling with hunger. This time Connor did direct her to one of their old haunts—a funky beach hut with plastic tables and chairs spilling onto the sand.

When Savannah stepped out of the car, she stretched her arms over her head, interlocking her fingers as the ocean breeze toyed with the ends of her hair. She took a deep breath of the salty air and forgot about Niles, Letty, the blackout…all of it. At least it had all led back to this town and this man—at least for a few weeks. Months?

The beach spell must've cast itself over Connor, too. He laced his fingers through hers and tugged her toward the café.

The morning surfers had long cleared out and the restaurant wasn't open for dinner, so a straggling late-lunch crowd greeted them as they walked through the door.

The waitress waved her hand around the small room. "Sit anywhere you like."

"We're going to head out to the sand."

Keeping hold of Savannah's hand, Connor led her past the tables inside to the ones nestled in the dry sand beyond.

Savannah plopped down in the plastic chair while Connor adjusted the umbrella to ward off the afternoon sun. She kicked off her sandals and dug her toes into the sand. "What a morning. Do you think it was productive?"

"I do." Connor leaned back in his chair and rested one ankle on his other knee. "We know that Tiffany had her ex on the side while she was engaged to Niles, and that her ex is an imposing guy with a gun."

"Niles was stabbed."

"I remember, but Denny could've used the gun to intimidate Niles. He also has his motorcycle gang connections."

"Can I get you something to drink?" the young waitress called from the edge of the patio, not willing to make the trek across the sand.

Savannah called back, "Iced tea."

"Make it two." Connor held up two fingers in the air. "We also got that scotch from Niles's wet bar that one or both of you had probably been drinking that night. If you think you were drugged, we can get a test run on that."

"Now we have the knife and the scotch." Savannah wedged an elbow on the table and sank her chin into her palm. "How are we going to get those tested?"

"I have a friend who's a PI and he has friends and they

have friends. I know he'll do this for me. I worked with him on a few cases when I was a cop. He's a good buddy. I can count on him."

"Without asking questions?"

"He trusts me, and I've done a few favors for him in the past—not that I have to bring those up."

"Like I did." Savannah stirred the sand with her toe.

"You were just using some insurance. I don't hold that against you." Connor brushed his thumb across her inner wrist. "I don't hold anything against you, Savannah."

She blinked behind her sunglasses. He had lots to blame her for—if he knew the truth.

The waitress had sent a busboy out to their table with the drinks, and he plodded across the sand, holding one in each hand.

Savannah broke away from Connor and smiled at the busboy. "Can you tell the waitress that we're ready to order?"

Before he could answer, a woman shrieked behind him and traipsed across the patio. "I heard you were back in town."

Savannah jumped up from her chair and hugged her friend Jamie. "In the flesh."

Jamie squeezed her in return and then punched Connor in the shoulder. "You could've told us you two were back together."

Connor smirked. "I didn't want to jinx anything."

Jamie waved her hands at the busboy. "I'll take their order, and you can tell that lazy Annie she can stick to the tables inside."

She turned back to Savannah. "I was so glad to hear you were back in SJB, but I'm sorry about your ex." Jamie curled a hand around her throat. "That's terrible."

"Awful. I still can't quite believe it happened." Savannah grabbed her drink and plunged a straw into the liquid. "I hope the police catch the guy who did it."

"I know. So creepy." Jamie reached into her rear pocket and whipped out a notebook. "I'm sorry it's taken so long to get your order. I figure if you don't want to walk in dry sand, you shouldn't work at a beach café."

"I'll have the grilled chicken sandwich with fries."

"And I'll have the cheeseburger with fries." Connor tucked the small plastic menus into the menu holder on the table. "Jamie, have you heard anything about Jimmy Takata setting that fire at my place yesterday?"

"I did hear some rumors, but I don't know if the cops have talked to him yet. I wouldn't put that past Jimmy or any of the Cove Boys. They're out of control. Think they own this town." She aimed her pencil at Connor. "It's not the same without your dad and the San Juan PD."

"Thanks, Jamie."

As she walked away, Connor pulled out his phone.

"Who are you calling?"

"I forgot to call the sheriff's department to give them the tip about Jimmy."

While Connor was on the phone, Savannah looked through her text messages and a few emails. Her battery was already down to 30 percent and she'd barely used the phone all day, but she had no intention of replacing it now. If the police asked her about her cell tomorrow, she wanted to be able to show them the broken one.

"That's done." Connor snapped the phone on the table. "They'd already heard a few things about Jimmy, and when I told them what happened yesterday morning at the beach, they thought it was important enough to question him."

"Maybe Jimmy did set fire to that storage shed, but it doesn't change the fact that someone planted a pen in my purse to track my movements or conversations or both."

Connor raised an eyebrow. "Anything else unusual in your purse?"

"No, I checked."

Several minutes later, Jamie delivered their food, and they both ate as if it were their first meal in several days.

Investigating had definitely improved her appetite, Savannah thought. It beat sitting around waiting for stuff to happen—like an arrest.

On their way out of the restaurant, they chatted with Jamie and her husband, and then walked to the car for the drive to Connor's place.

Savannah dangled the keys. "You mind driving?"

Snatching the key chain from her hand, Connor opened the passenger door for her.

Savannah tipped her head back against the headrest, closing her eyes. "I can't take any more today and it's not even dinnertime."

"You have another big day tomorrow."

"I know—that police interview."

"And your appointment with Thomas."

"Yeah, and that." She opened one eye. "You know you can't sit in with me, right?"

He snorted, "I don't want that. I'm just hoping he can help you with the blackout. Help you with some memories."

I don't want to remember.

Savannah closed her eye again and settled her shoulders against the car seat.

When Connor pulled onto the road leading to his property, a sigh escaped Savannah's lips. Her second day here and it already felt like coming home. What would it be like to stay here forever? She could run the company from here, go into the office once a week.

By the time Connor parked, her foolish dreams had seeped away. The more time she spent with Connor, the more uncomfortable it was keeping the truth from him. She'd either have to spill the beans or she'd have to leave him...again.

She struggled to get out of the car on her heavy limbs. She wanted to lie down, curl up and sleep for a thousand hours, or at least until she could put all this mess behind her.

"Are you okay?" Connor had come around to the passenger side after retrieving his gym bag from the back seat and slinging it over his shoulder. He ran his hands down her arms. "Your eyes look heavy."

"The food and the sun made me sleepy."

"Take a nap. We have nothing to do, unless you have Snap App business. I'm going to make a few calls."

"The only business going on at Snap App right now is gossip. I do want to call a meeting for later this week, though, and give the troops a pep talk."

"Then go to sleep. You need it." He took her arm and they walked up the two steps to the porch together.

Connor shoved the key in the dead bolt and cocked his head. "I thought I locked this before we left."

He removed the key from the top lock and inserted it into the one on the door handle. "At least this one's locked."

He pushed open the door and held his hand behind him. "Wait a minute."

Savannah's heart rate picked up. "What's wrong?"

"Give me a minute to look around."

She balled up the sweater in her hands and hugged it to her chest as she watched Connor walk into the hallway.

He disappeared for several minutes and then called out to her, "It's all right. Everything looks fine."

Savannah's shoulders sagged and she tripped over the threshold, slamming the front door behind her. "Don't scare me like that. What was the problem?"

"Thought I locked that dead bolt. I always do."

"I'm throwing you off your routine." She tossed her purse onto the nearest chair. "Are you going to call your PI buddy to get the blood on that knife tested and have him look at the scotch?"

"I sure am. Are you going to take that nap?"

"I feel like I could sleep forever right now." She shuffled into the kitchen. "I'm going to get some water and lie down."

She reached into the cupboard above the dishwasher and grabbed a glass. "You want some?"

"I'm good." Connor sat on the couch and kicked his feet onto the coffee table, his phone in one hand.

Savannah dispensed some water from the refrigerator and wedged one hip against the counter. As she took a sip from the glass, her gaze scanned the countertop where her phone charger cord lay coiled in a circle.

She frowned. Connor must've unplugged it. She always left it in the outlet, as she needed to constantly charge her stupid phone—like now.

She shoved off the counter and then gasped. Spinning back around, she gripped the edge of the counter and gulped. She swept her hands across the smooth granite, pushing Connor's bills and mail to the floor.

"What are you doing over there?"

She flattened her hands on the cool surface and hunched forward. "My file is gone. Someone broke in here and stole that file folder."

Chapter Eleven

"I knew it." Connor sprang from the couch like a jack-in-the-box and ate up the distance between them in two steps. "Where was it?"

Savannah slapped the counter with her palm. "Here. I left it right here. When I charged my phone, I was putting it on top of the file folder."

"You're sure?" Even as the words left his mouth, he realized their stupidity. The look on Savannah's face told him she was sure.

She plucked at the phone charger and wrapped it around her finger. "I noticed this first. I always leave my charger plugged in. You didn't unplug it, did you?"

"No." Connor swiveled his head, his gaze darting about the room. "He or she was careful. When the lock tipped me off, I looked around carefully and didn't see anything out of place."

"The knife." Savannah's violet eyes darkened, or maybe they just looked dark set against her white face. "Where's the knife?"

"Why would he take the knife? If he is trying to set you up, he'd want to leave that with you."

"But if he located it, he might call those detectives again and give them a hot tip—just like he did about the trunk of my car. We both know that's why they looked in my trunk."

"Stay here." Connor ran outside, letting the screen door bang behind him. He circled around to the back of the house and charged toward one of two oak trees where a hammock usually hung. He plunged his hand into the hole in the trunk, his fingers twisting around the plastic bag. He dragged it out and carried it back to the house.

"This is becoming a game of hide the bloody knife." He dropped it on his fireplace mantel. "Anything else missing? Your laptop?"

Savannah flew out of the kitchen and down the hallway. Several seconds later she popped her head around the corner of the hallway. "It's there. Too bad he didn't take it. That, at least, I could've tracked. That file is gone forever."

"Why was that set of data in hard copy instead of online?"

"I couldn't tell you. I originally tried to look it up and when I couldn't find it online, I asked Niles, and that's when he told me he'd printed it out and had a hard copy of it."

"Why did you want to see it?"

"I was surprised by our quarterly earnings and had been going through the different departments to double-check the figures. I couldn't find this one department's. Niles didn't explain why he had it separate."

"Could Niles have been cooking the books?"

"Niles?" Savannah drove two fingers into her temple. "I doubt it. Why would he? It's not like the company wasn't doing well—isn't doing well."

Connor walked into the living room and snagged the strap of the gym bag. He swung it onto a kitchen stool and unzipped the side pocket. He gathered the pieces of the broken pen and dumped them on the counter.

"I now know this pen was a listening device. How else would the intruder have known you had this file? He heard you talking about it and wanted it."

"Oh, my God. Why?" Savannah placed her hand on her forehead. "My head's spinning. I don't understand why anyone would want that file."

"Whoever took it just tipped his hand. Once you figure out why the file is so important, it'll lead you to Niles's killer."

"By then, the killer will have destroyed the file and any evidence it contains."

"You can't get that data online? It must've existed online at some point. You're the computer genius, not me, but there has to be a way to recover it."

"I'll get on that when I go into the office for this meeting. In fact, I'm going to schedule that meeting right now by sending out a company-wide email."

"After your nap?" He raised one eyebrow.

"I'm wide-awake now."

"And it looks like I have another call to make before asking my friend to run a few tests for me."

"What call would that be?"

"Security system. I'm getting cameras installed—arson, burglary. What next?"

Clenching her teeth, Savannah raised her shoulders to her ears. "I don't want to think about what's next."

"What's next for you is setting up that meeting and then taking a nap. You look run-down."

"Do I?" She ran her hands over her face, still beautiful even with dark circles beneath her eyes and tension in every muscle.

"Tired." He touched the end of her nose with his fingertip, even though he wanted to do much more than that.

She blushed and coughed. "I'm going to grab my laptop, compose and send out that email and then curl up like a cat."

She slid from the kitchen stool, and he grabbed his phone and parked himself on one end of the couch. He had someone in mind already to set up the security system. He'd been planning to have one installed for the winery anyway. It just got fast-tracked.

His head jerked to the side when Savannah sat next to him and took his hand.

"You believe me now, don't you, Connor?" She squeezed his fingers. "You believe that I didn't kill Niles—in self-defense or otherwise? You believe that someone is trying to set me up?"

Curling his other hand around the back of her neck, he drew her close and touched his forehead to hers. "I do— the knife, the pen, the break-in."

"I—I mean it's clear that someone's trying to set me up, right?"

"It looks that way." Her lips were so close to his he could feel their warmth.

She broke away from him on a sigh. "You don't know how much I needed to hear that."

He raised a finger. "That doesn't mean I don't want you to still see Thomas tomorrow. If you can remember what happened at Niles's, it might help to ID his killer."

"I'm fine with seeing Thomas." She pushed up from the couch. "Looking forward to it, actually."

Through narrowed eyes, he watched her disappear down the hallway to get her laptop.

That was a lie. She was looking forward to seeing Thomas about as much as he'd be looking forward to a root canal. What other lies did she have on the tip of her tongue?

There was definitely something she wasn't telling him. This smelled like a setup all right, but who was setting up whom?

EARLY THAT EVENING, after Savannah had scheduled her meeting and taken a nap, she joined Connor on the floor in front of the TV and a pizza box.

She crossed her legs beneath her and grabbed a paper plate. "You got all your stuff done?"

Connor held up a hand and ticked off one finger at a time. "Set up an appointment to get a security system installed. Contacted A.J. about testing the blood on the knife and the bottle of scotch. Hid the knife in a different spot and did some winery work. Just a typical day."

Savannah nudged his foot with her toes and held up a slice with cheese hanging off the edge. "Vinny's is still the best pizza in town."

"It is, and I didn't even need to consult you to know you'd want the pepperoni and Italian sausage—despite your vow to cut red meat from your diet. Now is not the time to stick to diets...or any other resolutions." He held up the bottle of red wine. "Another glass?"

"Just a half for me." She raised her index finger and thumb to give him the measurement and he dumped in a little more.

So much for those other resolutions.

"A.J. told me he knows a guy who can test that scotch for any added substances."

"And the knife?"

"He's working on it. That one's a little harder."

"No kidding." She swirled the ruby liquid in her glass.

"You look better already after that nap." He cocked his head and his blue eyes did a quick inventory of her features.

She didn't tell him that his admission that he believed she wasn't responsible for Niles's death went a long way to lifting the burden she carried on her shoulders. One burden down, one to go.

"I needed the rest. Now I need this pizza." She bit into the corner of the slice, the spiciness of the pepperoni exploding on her tongue.

"Any blowback from the meeting you called?"

"No, several members of upper management responded

with their support. I can count on Nick Fresco and Lucy
Shepherd and Hector Villalobos to have my back—Dee
Dee, too. She was Niles's right hand…and his left, come
to think of it."

"Would Dee Dee know about that file?"

"Maybe." Savannah dropped some crust on her plate
and wiped her greasy fingers on a napkin. "I think I can
ask her about it discreetly."

"Be careful while you're there, Savannah. This could
all be work-related. Maybe you were supposed to die along
with Niles."

"Thanks." She dusted the pizza crumbs from her fingertips and took a swig of wine. "That's just what I needed to
hear. Someone's either trying to set me up for a murder I
did not commit, or they're gonna kill me."

He pinched her knee. "Not while I'm around."

"Do you want to come to the office with me day after
tomorrow?"

"I'll be there if you want."

"I want." She tore off another piece of pizza. "You can
even accompany me to Thomas's office tomorrow, if you
promise to wait outside."

"Savannah, Thomas is a professional. What goes on between the two of you is strictly confidential." Connor put
the wineglass to his lips and then pulled it away. "Makes
me wonder, though."

"Wonder what?"

"Why you're so nervous."

"Oh, I don't know." She dropped the pizza slice. "We're
both lying about where I was the night my ex-husband was
murdered. I think I have a little to worry about."

"We'll get through this."

"Sometimes I feel like I can get through anything as
long as I have you by my side." She cupped his strong jaw

with her palm, the bristle from his five o'clock shadow tickling her skin.

"You only feel like that *sometimes*?" He twisted his head to the side and pressed a kiss against her palm. "I know having you here can make anything better, but you're not here, are you? Even when you're here, you're a million miles away. Be here. With me now."

Her eyes blurred with tears and Connor's face swam before her eyes. She couldn't love this man any more than she already did, but she could show him how much even if she couldn't tell him.

Curling her arms around his neck, she pressed her cheek against his and inhaled his masculine scent—mixed with pepperoni and red wine.

He plowed one hand into her hair and tugged back her head. He slanted his mouth across hers and caressed her lips in a soft, spicy kiss.

She answered with a sigh. She'd been waiting for that kiss ever since she'd thrown herself at him in his driveway, her hopes and her anxiety level high. And he'd helped her in every way, despite breaking the law, putting himself in jeopardy and not quite believing in her.

He pulled her against him in an awkward embrace, but really, nothing was ever awkward between them. They were made for each other.

She settled into his lap, hanging on with an arm wrapped around his waist, and he finished that kiss, pressing his lips against hers, invading her mouth with his tongue.

She toyed with his tongue as she slid her hands beneath his T-shirt and smoothed her fingertips across the muscles of his defined chest. "Your body is as perfect as I remember."

"And yours—" he ran a hand up her belly and tucked

his hand inside her bra, cupping one of her breasts "—I never forgot."

She slid from his lap and his warm touch. "I don't want to do this on the floor with a pizza box as my pillow."

"We've done it in a lot of crazy places."

"Oh, I remember, Wells." Using his shoulder as a prop, she struggled to her feet and held out her hand. "But it's been over four years and I want to take my time with you."

And it could be another four years.

He grasped her hand and stood up beside her. "Then I want to brush my teeth and wash this pizza from my hands."

"You first." She bumped his hip with hers.

As he ran the water in the bathroom, Savannah grabbed a candle from the living room, lit it and placed it on the nightstand in Connor's bedroom, then turned down the covers on his bed.

When he emerged from the bathroom, she was perched on the edge of it in the darkened room in her underwear.

His eyes burned with a heat as hot as that candle flame. "Nice—and I don't mean the candlelit room, although that's a nice touch, too."

She patted the bed. "Make yourself comfortable. I'm going to brush my teeth, too."

Connor strode to the bed, braced his hands on the mattress on either side of her and kissed her flat against the bed. "I don't mind pizza breath."

"Not fair." She pressed her hands against his chest and he relented.

As she got up from the bed, he smoothed a hand across her bottom. "Hurry back."

When she got to the bathroom, she washed her hands and brushed her teeth. She combed her fingers through her hair and whispered to her reflection, "Just this once."

She practically skipped back into the bedroom and stopped short when confronted with the image of Connor stretched out on his bed, in the buff, the candlelight flickering across his sculpted form.

"Ooh, you didn't even give me the chance to take your clothes off, piece by piece."

He sat up, folding his arms behind his head. "I can get dressed again if you want."

"Don't you dare." She rushed toward the bed and jumped on the edge on her knees. She then straddled him and rained kisses across his shoulders and chest.

Connor reached up and unhooked her bra. He caressed her breasts, running his thumbs across her peaked nipples. "Mmm, talk about perfection. Your body is as lithe and beautiful as ever."

She fell against him, and he rolled over, pinning her beneath him. He trailed his hands down her sides, hooking his fingers in the waistband of her panties and sliding them off.

He left a path of scorching kisses from between her breasts to her stomach, twirling his tongue in her navel until she giggled.

She slapped his shoulder. "Don't make me laugh. This is serious business."

"I like to make you laugh, and you haven't done much of it in a while." He slid his hands beneath her derriere, and she raised her pelvis.

"You can make me laugh later. Right now, make me sigh, groan, moan."

He buried his head between her legs and made her do all those things and more. When her orgasm claimed her and she reached her peak, she even screamed out his name.

He kissed the echoes of that scream from her lips as his erection skimmed her belly.

She brushed her fingers along his tight flesh, and his

frame shuddered. As he stretched out beside her on the bed, she continued to caress him and he took over the moaning and groaning and sighing.

He stifled a gasp and cinched her wrist with his fingers. "Ahh, I want to be inside you."

"I'm yours for the taking—always was, always will be."

He reached for the drawer on the nightstand and yanked it open. He withdrew a blue foil square and held it up between two fingers. "You wanna help me with this?"

She swallowed and pasted a smile on her face. They hadn't been together for years, but she'd been willing to make love to him without a condom. But he wasn't.

"Any excuse to touch you there." She snatched the condom from his fingers and ripped the foil open with her teeth.

Seconds later, Connor eased into her and she closed around him. She wound her legs around his torso as he drove into her over and over, and the only thing pounding into her brain along with the rhythm of his thrusts was *he doesn't trust you, he doesn't trust you*.

Panting, he balanced on his elbows above her and peppered her face with feverish kisses. "Are you going to come? I can wait."

She dribbled her fingertips across his flushed face, damp with sweat. "Go ahead. I already experienced my paradise."

He kissed her again and moments later his body stiffened before he plowed into her hard and fast, gasping out his release.

He lay motionless on top of her for a few seconds before rolling off her body. He stroked the side of her breast. "Was I smothering you?"

"Only in the best of ways." Her fingers traced the outline of the muscles on his flat stomach.

He removed the condom and put it on a tissue on the

bedside table. Reclining on his back again, he took her hand and laced his fingers with hers. "Just like old times. Better."

"Except for the protection."

His fingers tightened on hers for a second. "It's been a while since we've been together, Savannah."

Her heart began pounding, and she placed a hand against her chest in a lame attempt to steady it. "I killed him."

Chapter Twelve

The warm glow encasing him turned to ice and he jerked, Savannah's words like a physical jolt to his body.

His fingers, still entwined with hers, froze. Blood pounded in his ears and his jaw locked.

"Did you hear me?" Her voice, soft as a whisper, tickled his ear.

It broke the spell and he snatched his hand away from hers and bolted upright, the sheen of sweat on his body from making love to Savannah now giving him a chill.

"I heard you." His own voice came out like gravel on the pavement. "You killed Niles."

Savannah shot up against the headboard. "God, no. I didn't kill Niles."

Connor jerked his head to the side. What kind of games was she playing? "What the hell are you talking about? You told me you killed him."

"Not Niles. I killed *Manny*. I killed my stepfather."

A second jolt zapped his body, but this one juiced him with adrenaline, and he scrambled from the bed. "What do you mean? My father killed Manny for your mother, and then you and Georgie lied for him, telling the cops it happened in a self-defense, life or death struggle between my father and Manny."

She raised those violet eyes to his, her fingers twisting

into knots over her naked body. "No. It didn't happen that way, Connor."

He shook his head. "You lied to me. *He* lied to me. My father paid with his life for killing Manny."

"I know that." She dropped her head, and her dark hair fanned out over her breasts.

He grabbed his boxers from the floor and stepped into them. "Tell me everything. I want the truth—if you're capable."

Her hair swung in front of her face as she flinched. "Of course. I wanted to for the longest time."

She slid from his bed and pulled on her underwear, her back toward him. Then she grabbed the T-shirt he'd been wearing that day from on top of his dresser and pulled it over her head. She sat on the edge of the bed, stuffing her hands beneath her thighs.

"Not here." He jerked his thumb over his shoulder. "In the living room."

He turned his back on Savannah and the awful truths flowing from her lips. How could she be responsible for Manny's death? Why? Had she been trying to protect her mother, as Connor's father had claimed he'd been trying to do?

His anger and sense of betrayal fogged his brain, but he had to get past it long enough to listen to her, to find out what had really happened.

He collapsed on the couch amid the wreckage of their night and kicked the half-empty pizza box out of his way.

Savannah, twisting the hem of his shirt in her hands, followed him, and sank into the chair across from the couch. "I wanted to tell you so many times, Connor, but I didn't know how."

"You figured the best time was while I was providing

an alibi for you for another murder and after we'd made love? That makes a lot of sense."

"The time seemed right—necessary."

He sliced a hand through the air. "Tell me how it happened."

"Manny had been harassing me." She licked her lips. "Coming on to me."

"Sexually?" He swallowed, the tightness in his throat almost unbearable.

"Yes."

"Since when? Not when he first married your mother? Not when you were fourteen?" His hands curled into fists on his knees. If Manny weren't already dead, he could kill him himself.

"No, at least he wasn't into young teens, but as soon as I turned eighteen he started making moves. It began the first time I came home from college, at Thanksgiving."

He remembered that time. He'd been so happy to have Savannah home, and any changes in her behavior he'd put down to college life.

"Did you tell Georgie?"

"Of course I did, and I told Manny off in no uncertain terms."

"What was your mother's response?" Connor clenched his jaw. He knew Georgie and could figure out how she'd react to her husband of five years, a husband showering her with cars, gifts and money, showing interest in her beautiful eighteen-year-old daughter.

Savannah twisted her lips. "Mom didn't like it and she even talked to Manny, but she told me to grow up and handle it. There was no way she was kicking Manny out."

"Didn't think so." Connor raised his eyes to the ceiling. "This started when you were eighteen and went on for three years before…before you killed him?"

"His interest in me would wax and wane. Sometimes he'd come on hard, putting his hands on my body, trying to kiss me, and other times he hardly noticed my presence."

Connor's stomach churned. "And Georgie was okay with all of this?"

"She wasn't okay with it, Connor, but she didn't want to make waves. She had a good setup with Manny."

"You didn't."

"No." She ran her pinkie finger across her bottom lip.

"What happened? What changed the night he was killed?"

"I'm not completely sure."

"What?" He hunched forward, digging his elbows into his knees. "You don't remember something like that?"

She finally raised her gaze to his and held it for a few beats. "I blacked out that night."

Connor fell back against the couch cushions, smacking the heel of his hand against his forehead. "Are you kidding me?"

"Would I kid about something like that? I can't remember what happened." Her knees started bouncing and she clamped her hands on them. "Mom told me Manny tried to rape me. He'd ripped off my clothes and cornered me in my room. I must've escaped, grabbed his gun where he kept it by the front door and shot him."

Connor dug his fingernails into his scalp, sympathy for Savannah and what she'd had to endure making inroads into his shock. "Where was Georgie when all this was going on? Why wasn't she there to protect you?"

"She had gone to a friend's house, but her friend wasn't feeling well so she turned around and came back." Savannah rolled her shoulders forward and hugged herself around the baggy T-shirt. "Mom said she came home, found me naked with a wide-eyed blank stare, crouching in the corner of the living room, with Manny's dead body across from me and the gun on the floor."

"Then she called my father."

"Of course. Who else?"

Just as Savannah had come running to Connor when she'd found herself with another dead body.

He took a deep breath. "And the two of them concocted the story of Manny physically attacking Georgie, who then called my father. And when he arrived, Manny pulled his gun on him, the two wrestled for control and the gun went off, killing Manny."

"Yes."

"Why didn't my father just leave it at that? Why did he tell my mother that he'd killed Manny outright instead of giving her the made-up story about Manny pointing the gun at him? Why heap further blame on himself?"

Savannah pressed her hands to her cheeks. "That was my mom's idea. She thought she'd come out looking better and it would keep your mother from talking if the chief owed something to Mom. I know. It's twisted."

"And your mother did all this to protect you? A little late. I can't imagine what you went through." He raised his hand and dropped it.

She noticed the gesture and swallowed. "Because I blacked out and I didn't have any injuries, she thought the police might not believe it was self-defense on my part. Hell, I don't even know if it was."

"Except for the fact that you had no clothes on and were in shock." Connor pounded a fist into the cushion next to him. "Why didn't you tell me? Why didn't my father?"

"It was all so messed up. Then your father lost his life because of me and my mother. If we'd told the truth, Manny's associates would've had no reason to go after your dad."

"Maybe they would've gone after you instead."

Her eyes widened. "A twenty-one-year-old college student who was warding off a rape? I don't think so."

Connor tilted his head back, resting it against the cushion, and stared at the ceiling. "Savannah, don't you think it's strange that you blacked out twice and both of those times you come to with a dead body?"

"Of course."

"And it never occurred to you that the same thing that happened with Manny happened with Niles?"

"Did I imply it never occurred to me? It did, but that's why I checked everything at the house. There was no evidence I stabbed Niles—no cuts on my dominant hand, no blood on my clothes or body, no sign that I showered off any blood. Nothing. I didn't do it, Connor. The police haven't found any evidence of my guilt."

He squeezed his eyes closed and pinched the bridge of his nose. "When did you regain consciousness, or whatever, the night Manny died? And what's the last thing you remember about that night?"

"I remember being home earlier and Mom going to her friend's." Savannah twisted a lock of hair around her finger. "I wasn't too worried about being home alone with Manny because he'd been preoccupied all summer, barely giving me a glance, which was a huge relief. Still, I remember changing into my pajamas, locking my bedroom door and watching some TV. That's it. I don't remember leaving the room. I don't remember Manny coming into the room. I sure as hell don't remember taking a gun and shooting at him."

He scratched his chin. "Where were you when you woke up, or came to? I don't even know what to call it."

"I was sitting on our couch, in my pajamas. Manny was dead on the floor and your dad and my mom were crouched over him." She trapped her hands between her knees. "I panicked. I screamed. I cried. I didn't know what was going on."

"Your mother told you what had happened?"

"She came to me and grabbed my hands. She told me she'd discovered me naked in the corner when she got home, Manny dead. I was numb, unresponsive, but she figured out what had happened. She dressed me and called your father, and they were going to fix everything between the two of them. She had me wash my hands—to get rid of the gun residue—and then she told me the story they were going with. That Manny had got abusive, belligerent, so she called Chief Wells, who was off duty. The chief arrived, Manny had a gun on us and then turned it on your father. He lunged for it, they struggled and the gun went off, killing Manny."

"I wish..." Connor grabbed a pillow and chucked it across the room. "I wish you'd told me—all of it. I wish you'd told me Manny was bothering you. Why didn't you?"

"I don't know." She lifted her shoulders. "I felt ashamed, like somehow I'd invited his attentions. Th-that's what my mom implied."

Heat thumped through his body and a pure hatred for Savannah's selfish, vain mother beat at his chest. How could his father have worshiped that woman? "That's ridiculous."

"I didn't want to tell you, Connor. You saw me through some kind of rose-colored glasses. I never knew why, but I didn't want that to end—ever. That's why I never told you any of it."

"Your secrecy destroyed our relationship anyway." He clasped his hands behind his neck. "That's why, isn't it? That's why you ran, that's why you married Niles."

"I killed someone and then put the blame on your father, who ended up paying for it with his life." She sniffled and rubbed her nose. "I didn't think that was something you could ever get past... Could you? Can you?"

Folding his body in half, Connor leaned forward, almost touching his head to his knees. "I don't know, Savannah. I can't believe you've lived with this burden these past years. When you woke up with Niles, you must've relived everything."

"I'm sorry, Connor. For everything. I never should've come here. I'm just like my mother and I tried so hard not to be her."

His head shot up. "You're nothing like Georgie."

Several seconds of heavy silence hung between them.

"What now?" She folded her hands in her lap, her knuckles white.

"We carry on as before. We get to the bottom of what happened the night Niles died...and that's going to start when you see Thomas tomorrow. No holding back." He leveled a finger at her. "Promise."

"I promise. I'll tell Thomas everything." She rose to her feet in a jerky movement and stooped to pick up the pizza box on the floor.

"Leave it. Go back to bed. You have a busy day tomorrow."

She hesitated, dropped the box and took a step back. She threw him a glance from beneath her lashes.

Folding his arms, he closed his eyes. "Go to bed, Savannah."

"Yours?"

"I'll be in later."

She shuffled down the hallway, his T-shirt floating around her body.

His muscles coiled as he fought the urge to go after her, take her in his arms, comfort her for what she'd endured as a frightened young woman. Then he sank back against the

couch, placing his fingertips against the throbbing drum-
beat in his temples.

If Savannah had blacked out and killed once, she
could've blacked out and killed again.

Chapter Thirteen

The following morning, Savannah rolled over and buried her face in the pillow, the scent of Connor engulfing her and permeating all her senses. Connor, the man she'd loved...and betrayed.

The look in his blue eyes last night had told her everything she needed to know—justified her silence all those years. He hated her. Didn't trust her.

And she didn't blame him.

She ran her hands over the covers, which she'd straightened out last night, and knew Connor hadn't been back to bed—at least not this one.

A tap at the door had her sitting up and clutching the sheets to her chest. "Yes?"

"I have some breakfast for you, if you're interested."

She stared at the door handle, but Connor wasn't coming in. His footsteps faded down the hallway.

She scooted out of the bed and shed his T-shirt. Before she bunched it up and put it back where she'd found it, she hugged it against her stomach. She'd lost him.

She took a quick shower and pulled a pair of shorts and a blouse from her bag, then dressed in record speed. She scooped her hair into a ponytail, took a deep breath and went to meet her accuser.

As she turned the corner toward the kitchen, he held up

a plate. "Eggs and toast okay again? I can get some grocery shopping done while you're seeing Thomas."

On her way into the room, she stubbed her toe on the smooth wood floor. Had Connor had his own blackout and forgotten what she'd told him last night?

He placed the plate of food on the counter and turned away. "I already ate. I'm going to shower before A.J. gets here. He's gonna pick up the knife and the scotch. It's time we got some answers—finally."

He hadn't forgotten a thing.

He exited the kitchen and called over his shoulder, "The security company is coming this morning, too."

Even though he'd already discussed setting up a security system at the house, his words carried an ominous tone— like he was warning her not to try anything.

She stabbed a clump of scrambled egg. Now she was just getting paranoid.

She held her fork suspended over her plate as she listened to the water run in the shower. If she could've kept her mouth shut last night, she might be enjoying that shower with Connor right now. Nothing had changed between them physically. The passion burned between them hotter than ever. Their bodies fitted together seamlessly. She hadn't been able to tell where hers ended and his began. But after he'd pulled out the condoms, it had all seemed like a lie. Hot sex was one thing, but true love required trust.

Someone knocked on the front door and Savannah dropped her fork. She spun around on the stool and hopped off. When she reached the door, she peered through the peephole at a buff guy with a shaved head, a gym bag over his shoulder.

Resting her hands against the door, she asked, "Who is it?"

"Ah, A.J. I'm here to see Connor Wells."

She cranked the dead bolt to the right and opened the door. "Hi, I'm Savannah."

A.J. inclined his head. "Hi, Savannah. Wasn't expecting anyone out here with Connor."

"C'mon in." Connor hadn't revealed all her dirty little secrets to A.J.? What did he think he was doing here?

Connor swooped into the living room, hand outstretched. "Hey, bro. Thanks for coming. You met Savannah?"

"I did." A.J.'s eyes narrowed. "Savannah Wedgewood, right?"

"I prefer Martell, but yeah, that's me. The merry widow." Savannah clenched her teeth behind her smile.

A splash of red stained A.J.'s bald pate. "Sorry. I just put two and two together."

"You still in?" Connor cocked his head at his friend.

"Are you kidding? Of course. Maybe I can crack the biggest murder case of the year." A.J. rubbed his hands together. "Give me the details."

"We're not giving you any details, A.J. Not yet anyway." Connor strode across the room to the fireplace and unzipped the black canvas bag. He dipped his hand inside and pulled out the crystal decanter. "We need this analyzed for any added substances, drugs."

A.J. took the decanter and swirled it so that the liquid sloshed up the sides. "Easy enough."

"And then there's this." Connor spread open the plastic bag and held it in front of him.

Even though A.J. must've known what to expect, his eyes widened. "This will be harder, but I think I can get a guy. Whose blood am I looking for?"

"Wait." Savannah held up her hand and pounced on her purse. She plunged her hand inside and pulled out a stiff piece of carpet. She cupped it in her palm and held it out to A.J. "This is Niles Wedgewood's blood."

Connor hunched over her hand and poked at the material with his fingertip. "Where did you get this?"

"From the house yesterday afternoon. It's part of the carpet that was underneath Niles's body."

"You cut off a piece? When?" Connor drew back, his eyebrows slamming over his nose.

"Of course not," she snapped. "The rug must've been sliced during the attack and this piece was hanging by a thread. I ripped it off. It's a lot better than A.J.'s friend raising red flags by trying to get the report on Niles's blood, isn't it?"

"It sure is." A.J. dipped his hand in the gym bag still hitched over his shoulder and shook out a plastic bag. "Drop it in here. Anything else?"

Savannah pinched the rug between two fingers and slipped it in. She rubbed her fingers together even though the blood on the rug was dried up. "You'll need to test it for my blood, too."

A.J. dropped the plastic bag and stooped over to retrieve it. When he straightened up, a light sheen of sweat had broken out across his forehead. "Is there something I should know?"

"Nothing." Savannah tossed back her hair. "It's just for ruling-out purposes, because *some people* need more proof than just someone's word."

Connor crossed his arms and clenched his jaw.

"All you have to do is poke your finger and squeeze out a few drops onto a card or something."

"I can do that." She rested a finger on her chin. "Or maybe Connor wants to do the honors. He'd like to make me bleed right now."

Connor threw up his hands. "Do not ascribe acts of violence to me. I do not want to see you bleed."

A.J. cranked his head back and forth between the two

of them. "If you wanna give me your blood, Savannah, I'll get out of here."

"You're scaring him off." Connor marched to the kitchen and yanked open a drawer. "Here's a safety pin. I'll hold it under a flame for a few seconds to sterilize it and then you can poke the hell out of yourself."

Savannah put a hand on her hip. "Told you."

Connor snorted, cranked on the flame beneath a burner and held the tip of the safety pin in the fire with a set of tongs. Then he swiped a piece of paper towel across the tip. "Don't want that black carbon in your skin."

As she took the pin from him, she skewered him with her gaze and tilted her head to the side. His joking manner indicated he'd loosened up a bit, but they still weren't back on solid ground. Would they ever be? Had they ever been since the night she'd shot Manny and blamed his father?

She pressed her thumb against the tip of her index finger and squeezed the skin tight. Then she jabbed her flesh with the tip of the pin. A bubble of blood formed immediately, so she held her finger over a note card and let the blood drip onto the surface.

She looked up at A.J. "Is that enough?"

"Plenty. You'd be surprised how little blood is needed for a good read these days."

A shiver ran up her spine as she plucked a wet paper towel from Connor and wrapped it around her finger. Had the crime scene investigators found a spot of her blood in Niles's bedroom?

A.J. waved the card in the air. "I'll just let this dry for a few minutes before sealing it in a plastic bag, and then I'll be out of your hair."

"I really appreciate this, A.J." Connor clapped his friend on the shoulder. "Let us know the results as soon as you get them."

"Do you want anything to drink before you leave?" Savannah opened the fridge door to pull out the orange juice.

"No, thanks." He shook out another plastic baggie. "I'm waitin' on the wine to start flowing out of this place. How much longer, Connor?"

"I'll harvest the grapes from next year's crop, and that'll start the process."

"Good thing you're independently wealthy." A.J. slid a glance toward Savannah.

Connor did have money and property, but that look at her meant A.J. probably knew about her wealth, which was about to explode. Every article about Niles's death so far had mentioned her and what she stood to gain from the murder.

A.J. left, promising to get back to them as soon as he had the results.

Savannah glanced at her phone. "Just over an hour until I see Thomas. When is the security company getting here?"

"Should be here any minute." Connor jerked a finger toward his laptop. "I'm going to do some work, and then we can drive over together once the security company gets here—if that's still okay."

"It's still okay with me." She rinsed her glass out in the sink, her head hanging, her hair creating a curtain around her face. "I'm sorry, Connor."

"I know. I… I can't imagine what you've lived with these past years. You should've seen someone, a therapist like Thomas to help you cope."

Tears flooded her eyes and she swiped a hand across her stinging nose. "My mom told me not to go. She was afraid I could still get in trouble."

"Yeah, right." Connor huffed out a breath and strode toward his laptop.

While he met with the security company, Savannah

spent the time on Snap App business and replying to emails. She sent one to Dee Dee, asking about archived files. She didn't know what the person who'd stolen that folder from her hoped to discover or hide. Niles had already reviewed that file. In fact, the folder was dog-eared. If it was something someone was trying to hide, it was too late for that.

Shortly after she sent an email to Nick Fresco, Snap App's CFO, he called her on her cell.

"Sorry I haven't called before now, Savannah. I didn't know what to say. The three of us were a team at the beginning...before the trouble between you two."

"I know, Nick. It's terrible. How's the vibe at the company?"

"Hard to judge. It's quiet here. You *did* tell people to take some time off, didn't you, boss?"

Savannah's gut tightened. Was that some kind of dig at her? "You don't think that was a good idea?"

"Great idea. Looking forward to having you back here full-time, if..."

"If what?" Savannah gripped the phone. Nick always was the king of implication.

"Just wondering if those detectives are investigating you, Savannah. Do you think you need an attorney? I know Niles's guy, Neelon, isn't a criminal attorney, but he could recommend someone."

"Whoa, slow down. The cops aren't looking at me for this. I had an alibi that night. I wasn't even in San Diego at the time of the murder."

Nick clicked his tongue—another annoying habit he had. "I'm sorry. Didn't mean to hit a nerve there. I just thought...you know, the spouse is always the number one suspect, especially the ex-spouse."

"You should know, Nick. You have two of them."

"Okay, okay. Don't need to get snippy." He chuckled, which sounded totally fake to her.

"What about Brian Donahue?" She waved at Connor, who'd stepped through the front door and was jerking his finger over his shoulder.

Nick sucked in a breath. "What about Donahue?"

"You're the one who fired him. Do you think he did it?"

"No way. Going postal in an office shooting, maybe, but not a planned murder like this." He cleared his throat. "Do you need any help with the meeting tomorrow? I know you've been out of the loop for a while and Niles probably wasn't all that forthcoming with you."

"Thanks for the offer, but this is going to be more of a pep talk and a 'rah-rah, the fight will go on' kind of meeting."

"A few people are filtering back into the office today. Of course, they're upset about Niles, but they're also worried about their jobs."

"Their jobs aren't going anywhere. Despite some losses, the company's in good shape."

"Losses?"

"I need to talk to you about a few things, Nick. Can we have a meeting after the meeting?"

"Of course, but I don't know about any losses. Are you telling me Niles has been hiding a few facts and figures?"

"Not sure yet. We'll discuss." She waved at Connor, who was practically hopping from foot to foot by the door. "Have the homicide detectives interviewed you yet?"

"You mean good cop Krieger and bad cop Paulson?"

She slid from the kitchen stool and hung her purse over her shoulder, which sagged in relief. "Oh, you found them that way, too?"

"I guess it's standard procedure, but yeah. Paulson's the

one who grilled me about my alibi and my position in the company. Real jerk."

Connor had walked outside, leaving the front door open, and Savannah scrambled to follow him out, Probably thought she was stalling.

"We'll talk more tomorrow, Nick. Thanks for phoning, and I'm sorry I snapped at you." She ended the call and got into the passenger seat beside Connor. "Nick Fresco, our...my CFO."

"Maybe he knows what's in that missing file, if it covered financials."

"We're having a meeting after my pep talk tomorrow." She put on her sunglasses and cracked the window. "Are you coming with me to the police station after my session with Thomas?"

"Do you want me to?"

"I do—even though you don't owe me anything now. Hell, you could turn me in if you wanted to."

He ran his hands up and down the steering wheel. "I never did any of this because I felt I owed you something, Savannah. You don't know that by now? You don't know how I feel about you? How I've always felt about you?"

She gave him a quick side glance from beneath her lashes. "How you used to feel about me before I spilled my guts and told you about Manny?"

He closed his eyes, and his nostrils flared. "I still love you, Savannah—no matter what you've done."

She let the words hang in the car, savoring their sweetness, ignoring the bitter undertone. He might love her and she sure as hell loved him, but that didn't mean they could ever overcome their baggage and be together. Heck, Connor still wasn't entirely convinced she didn't kill Niles, and maybe Letty, too, for that matter.

She folded her hands in her lap and stared out the window. "I know that."

Fifteen minutes later, Connor swung his truck into a small parking lot behind a two-story office building. He shifted into Park but didn't turn off the engine.

"Give Thomas my best. I'm heading over to the police station. They called me this morning while you were still asleep and told me they had some evidence against Jimmy Takata."

"Well, that's one mystery solved." She opened the car door and slid out. Then she ducked her head back inside and said, "I love you, too, Connor."

She slammed the door and hustled toward the stairs on the outside of the building, running away from Connor and her feelings for him.

When she got to Thomas's office, she tried the doorknob. It was unlocked and she pushed through. He had a small anteroom with a rack of magazines and four chairs, two on each side of a healthy potted plant. The sign next to a button on the door invited his clients to press it.

She did, listening for the echo of it in the office. Must've been hooked up to a light, because Thomas opened the door to his inner sanctum seconds later.

She held out her hand to the thinly built African American man with the warmest smile she'd ever seen. "I'm Savannah Martell."

"Welcome, Savannah. Thomas Bell." After he shook her hand he waved his own toward his cozy office. "Have a seat anywhere."

Her gaze floated across the sofa and a deep leather armchair, a table with a box of tissues on it situated between the two. She opted for the other chair and sank into its embrace, already feeling at ease for some reason.

"Would you like some water, coffee, tea?" He cupped a mug of steaming brew in one hand.

"No, thanks."

Thomas settled into the chair across from hers and balanced his cup on his knee. His dark eyes met hers, one eyebrow slightly shifting, but otherwise he remained mute.

She tugged on a lock of her hair. "Umm, my ex-husband was murdered—and I blacked out. I was there, at the scene, but I swear I didn't kill him."

"You blacked out."

"Yes, but there was no evidence that I'd killed him. If there had been... I would've stayed and called the police."

"Do you typically have blackouts?"

"Only once before."

Thomas waited. He even took a sip of tea.

After a few stammering beginnings, Savannah poured out the entire story of Manny's death, her role in it, the cover-up.

She hadn't even finished the entire tale when Thomas glanced at his watch for the fifth time in five seconds. "We'll have to wrap it up here, Savannah."

She gawked at him, eyes wide, mouth open. "Is—is that it? What are you going to do?"

He steepled his fingertips. "Do you want me to do anything?"

She licked her lips. "I want to know what happened that night Manny was killed."

"You just told me what happened."

"I told you what I remembered and what my mother told me happened." She rubbed her upper lip. "I want to remember on my own, *my* memories."

"We can do that. Have you ever been hypnotized?"

"No, but I want to be if you think I can recover those memories."

"What about the other memories? The ones from a few nights ago—the other murder."

Savannah shot forward in her seat. "Those were different. I was drugged. I'm sure of that, and pretty soon I'm going to have the proof—to show Connor."

"It's important for you to show Connor."

"Of course."

Thomas hunched forward out of his seat. "Can you come back tomorrow for a hypnosis session?"

"Yes."

He slid his laptop from his desk and returned to his seat. "You can have my first appointment, at nine o'clock. Can you make that?"

"I'll be here." And she meant it. Now that she'd revealed the truth to Connor, she wanted to know the whole truth herself. She wanted to know if she was a cold-blooded killer or if Manny had given her no choice.

Could she have run from the house that night? Fought him off? Called Connor? She'd chosen to shoot Manny through the heart instead and she wanted to know why.

When she reached the parking lot, she spotted Connor talking to a cop, both of them standing next to his truck.

She got a hitch in her step and swiped her damp palms on the back of her shorts, but she forced a smile and approached them. "Parking ticket?"

Connor turned toward her. "Good news."

Savannah eked out a sigh. "What?"

"Jimmy Takata just confessed to firebombing my shed. The police traced the jar used for the Molotov cocktail back to Jimmy's grandmother, and they even matched the print from his size nine flip-flops."

"Crack detective work." Savannah smiled at the cop.

"Hope to do the same for your ex-husband's murder case, ma'am."

Savannah's smile froze on her face. Was that a dig at her? A fishing expedition?

She rolled back her shoulders. "Thanks. I hope so, too."

When the fresh-faced cop left and they got into the truck, Connor turned toward her. "Everything okay?"

"Everything is fine. I'm going back tomorrow morning, first thing."

"Really?" He put the truck in gear and pulled out of the parking lot.

"Thomas is going to put me under. I'm going to try to find out what happened the night Manny died."

Connor paused and tensed his hands on the steering wheel. "And the night Niles died?"

She smacked her knee. "I'm telling you. That was different. I was drugged that night."

"I'm glad, and that's all I'm going to say." He brushed his knuckles against her thigh. "Do you want lunch before heading to San Diego and your interview with the detectives?"

"Of course." She squared her shoulders against the seat. "Fortification."

Over a lunch of fish tacos, their talk in the restaurant revolved around Jimmy Takata's arrest for setting the fire at Connor's place. A few side glances were thrown her way, but most of the people in San Juan didn't know Niles Wedgewood and didn't care about his death…even if they did know her connection to him.

Lunch ended all too soon and she and Connor hit the road to San Diego and her second interview with the police.

"Have you looked at the other files I took from Niles's desk or that flash drive?" he asked.

"No."

"I'm just wondering if the flash drive might contain the file that was stolen—you know, like a backup."

"Maybe." She drummed her fingers on the dash. "I didn't even check the file I took from Niles's desk."

"How do you know it was the one you wanted?"

"It was labeled. Niles was always very careful about labeling and marking everything properly. Even his computer files are organized."

"Sounds like he'd be the type to back up stuff, even beyond the normal archiving. You should take a look."

"Will do." At least Connor had stopped growling at her and flaring his nostrils, but now they'd reached a level of civil, businesslike discourse. Except for when he told her he loved her.

She pressed a hand against her belly. She'd keep those words safe and hold them close for when she was back on her own, back in San Diego running Snap App. She'd take them out and cup them in her hands now and then, just to remember what it felt like to be loved by a man like Connor Wells.

"We're here." He pulled around the back. "Do you want me to wait? Come with you?"

"That would probably look weird—like I need support or something." Her phone buzzed. "I hope that's not them canceling on me."

She pulled out the phone, swept her finger across the text message and gasped.

"What is it?" Connor leaned over, bumping her shoulder.

She held her phone higher so he could see the picture of her hunching over Letty's dead body.

Chapter Fourteen

"Damn." Connor smacked his fist against the center console. "Same sender as before? Unknown?"

"Yes." Savannah's hand trembled and she curled her fingers around the phone. "Can you read the words?"

"Words?" Connor squinted at the display, but it was too unsteady for him to make out the text.

"It says 'in case they ask you.'" She dropped the phone in her lap. "He knows I'm here, Connor. How?"

"You talked about this appointment before, when he was still listening to you."

Savannah dumped the contents of her purse in her lap and scrabbled through the items, sending some to the floor of the truck.

"What are you doing?"

"Looking for another pen. What do you think?" She grabbed a perfectly innocent-looking ballpoint from Thomas's office and chucked it out the window.

Connor circled her wrist with his fingers. "Stop. When you still had the pen in my house, you talked to the police about coming in today."

"But now?" She crushed the empty purse against her chest. "Right now, while I'm about to go in for an interview... And what does it mean? How did he get that picture?"

"He may have set up a camera in the warehouse."

"What does he plan to do with this picture? The button? The knife? If he's trying to set me up, why doesn't he just do it already?" She let out a scream. "I'd rather have him turn over everything to the police so I can see his endgame, start defending myself."

Connor reached over and squeezed the back of her neck. "If he wanted to turn you in to the police, he would've done it already."

"That must've been his intention when he made the anonymous call about the knife in my trunk—because you know he's responsible for that." She tipped her head back as Connor kneaded her tight neck. "What changed?"

"I don't know. The alibi I gave you? The fact that you cleaned up and got the hell out of Niles's house that morning without a backward glance? Maybe he expected you to fall apart."

"Then he's obviously someone who doesn't know me well." She yanked open her purse and started shoveling her belongings back inside. "He can keep sending pictures and stupid texts—and I'm going to keep doing what I'm doing."

Connor's hand slid down and rubbed a circle on her back. "You always do, Savannah. You're a survivor."

She leaned back and trapped his hand between her body and the car seat. "I learned from the best—my mother."

He rescued his hand and cranked on the ignition. He didn't like her comparing herself to Georgie. Savannah lacked the grasping desperation of her mother.

"Get in there and survive." He tapped the phone in his pocket. "Text me when you're done."

She dropped a key chain in the cup holder. "Do me a favor?"

He'd offered her an alibi. How could he possibly refuse her anything? "Sure."

"Go to the La Jolla house and snoop around a bit more.

If anyone discovers you there, you can claim to be checking on the cleaning crew you set up for Melanie. That's a legitimate reason."

"I wasn't done looking around anyway. I'll check it out. And, Savannah?" He smoothed a hand against her tousled hair. "It's gonna be okay."

She leaned forward in a burst and planted a hard kiss on his mouth. "Damn right it is."

He watched her walk toward the doors of the sheriff's department through narrowed eyes. The last time he'd dropped her off, she told him she loved him. This time she'd kissed him. How could he still believe she was a killer?

Because she was—she'd killed Manny.

As Connor pulled the truck into the driveway of Niles's house, the scene of the crime, he released a breath. Niles's sister had left, or at least had gone out. Had she stayed overnight in the house where her brother had been murdered?

He jingled the keys in his hand as he walked up to the front door. The crime scene tape had been removed, most likely courtesy of the cleanup crew.

When he stepped across the threshold into the large foyer, he held his breath. He didn't know what he expected, but he raised his nose in the air and sniffed, the smell of bleach making his eyes water.

He took the stairs two at a time and entered the master bedroom. The drapes billowed into the room from the open French doors. The cleaning crew must've left the windows open to air out the place—not that a burglar could make his way up to the house this way…or a killer.

The reports mentioned no signs of a break-in that night, so Niles must've let his killer in—or he was already here.

As he walked toward the balcony, Connor skimmed his fingertips along the bed, stripped of its covers. No blood stained the mattress, and he'd noticed before, on his first trip, that the walls were free of blood splatter.

The stabbing had been controlled. That could've happened if Niles had been killed in his sleep...or in a drugged state. The killer could've rolled him out of bed or carried him upstairs, placed him on the floor and proceeded to rip up his flesh with the blade of a knife.

Connor had been a cop, not a crime scene investigator or even a detective. If he could figure this out, Homicide must've already come to that conclusion. The number of stab wounds Niles had should've resulted in blood droplets all over this room.

If Niles had been drugged, why not Savannah, too? Someone could've spiked the scotch; they both conked out downstairs and were carried up here and undressed. The killer placed Savannah in the bed, slicing her hand—the wrong one—and dumped Niles on the floor and stabbed him to death, leaving Savannah to wake up with a dead body. Probably figured she'd panic, thinking she'd never get away with this, not remembering what happened, and that she'd call the police.

The killer obviously didn't know Savannah. Tiffany? That woman never could've pulled this off herself. Maybe Denny, with or without Tiffany's help.

Why set up Savannah? Connor twitched back the drapes and stepped onto the balcony, inhaling the salty sea breeze. The knife, the button, the incriminating picture with Letty—that could all be for blackmail purposes, especially once they realized Savannah had no intention of caving and copping to a murder she didn't commit—or at least one she couldn't remember committing.

She didn't remember killing Manny, either.

Bracing his hands on the stucco wall that separated him from the waves crashing on the rocks below, he leaned forward, feeling the breeze lift the ends of his hair from the back of his neck.

Why had his father continued to lie to him about that night? And to Mom? Hadn't he realized it had wrecked Connor's faith in him? Knocked him off that pedestal his son had been constructing since the time he was a small boy and dreamed of being just like his dad?

Georgie had done that to his family. Georgie had sacrificed her own daughter, as well. Sacrificed her to a low-life drug dealer in exchange for a fancy car, diamonds and trips to Vegas to fuel her gambling habit. She'd forced Savannah into the position she'd found herself in that night—facing a rapist in her own home.

Connor shook his head and pulled back from the drop-off. He turned to face the room and inspected every corner of it.

No more buttons. No more blood. No more evidence linking Savannah to the murder. The cleanup crew had done a bang-up job.

Connor closed his eyes, trying to imagine Savannah waking up in this room with her ex-husband dead on the floor. Most women would've panicked and run, without a thought to any evidence left behind, or maybe most women would've called 911. Savannah wasn't most women.

His eyelids flew open as a frisson of fear tickled the back of his neck. Murder changed a room—a house. All the bleach in the world couldn't erase the bad vibes that hung over this space like a dark curtain.

As Connor walked out of the room, he said aloud to no one, "Poor sap."

Had Niles's fate been sealed the day he fell in love with Savannah? Had his?

Connor jogged down the stairs and crossed the great room to the office. He searched through Niles's desk again, rapping his knuckles against the space on the desk where a computer should be. Too bad they couldn't get their hands on that computer.

The cyberforensics team at the sheriff's department would give it the once-over, but Savannah would be the one to know if the computer held any clues to Niles's murder.

Crouching, Connor pulled open the desk drawer with the false bottom. Maybe that missing file held the key to everything.

A slight whisper behind him made the hair on the back of his neck quiver. But before he could turn around something landed on the back of his head with a thump that echoed through his brain, and he slumped forward.

As his eyes drifted closed, he thought about Savannah blacked out in this house…and then everything went dark.

Chapter Fifteen

Savannah ordered a car from the ride app and then cupped her phone in her hand to track the driver's progress.

She planned to replace her phone as soon as possible now that she had proved to the police that the thing was on the fritz. They'd had plenty of questions about why she didn't have her phone the night of Niles's murder. The device had performed like a champ in the interview room with the detectives, losing 50 percent of its charge in the hour she'd been in there.

They hadn't asked her anything about Letty. She hunched her shoulders against the chill wending its way up her spine, which even the warm San Diego sun couldn't melt away. She hated the thought of Letty's body in that warehouse. Had her family reported her missing yet? Had anyone made the connection between Letty and Niles? Maybe the cops knew and were waiting for some kind of slipup on her part. Paulson was a sneaky bastard.

She tapped the toe of her sandal. Where had Connor gone? She'd texted him twice and called him. If he'd gone to the beach at the foot of the house, he may have lost service, but why would he be down there?

Maybe he'd had enough of her and had taken off to go home. Telling him about Manny had been one of the hardest things she'd ever done in her life—but necessary. Maybe the truth never could repair what was broken between them, but the lies never gave them a chance.

And she wanted a chance with Connor. Being with him the past few days had made it clear to her that she belonged with that man and no other.

If she stuck out this therapy with Thomas, maybe she and Connor could start fresh. Of course, she'd have to get past her current dilemma.

Damn Niles for getting himself killed. Nobody deserved murder, but Niles had been playing with fire for too long, juggling women and their exes.

Her ride pulled up to the curb in front of the sheriff's department and she hopped in. Even though she'd indicated the La Jolla address when she ordered the car, she still gave the driver directions, impatient to get to the house and find out where Connor went.

When the driver dropped her off, she blew out a sigh, seeing Connor's white truck parked out front.

She went up to the door and, rattling the handle, discovered it was locked. She banged on the solid wood. "Connor, are you in there?"

Stepping back, she tipped her head to scan the windows of the second story. He had her keys.

She went around to the side of the house and tried the sliding door to the kitchen. No luck. She pressed her nose against the glass and peered inside. The gleaming kitchen stretched before her—empty. Not that she expected Connor to be in there eating a sandwich.

Her steps a little quicker, her knees a little shakier, she went back to the front of the house and clambered through the flower bed outside Niles's office. Cupping her hands around her face, she looked through the window.

She let out a scream when she saw Connor crumpled on the floor behind Niles's desk. Dear God, not again.

She beat her fists against the glass. "Connor! Connor!"

Spinning around in the dirt, she scanned the ground and picked up a sizable rock. It was her house now and she didn't give a damn.

She smashed the rock against the windowpane closest to the handle. It took her three tries to break the glass.

When the window sported a jagged hole, she reached through and flipped up the lock, swung it open and stepped through, into the room.

Connor's body lay less than two feet away, and Savannah dropped to her knees beside him.

She placed two fingers against his neck and let out a sob when his pulse beat strong against her fingertips. She ran her hands over his face and chest. No blood.

Then she readjusted his head, and her hand came away wet and sticky. She gasped at the red stain on her palm.

"Connor, Connor."

She staggered to her feet and rushed to the wet bar. She grabbed a towel from beneath the sink and soaked it with water.

When she returned to Connor, she swiped the wet cloth across his face. "Connor, wake up. You're not dead."

She cradled his head in her lap and pressed the damp towel against the wound on the back of his skull to staunch the flow of blood. Head wounds always looked worse than they were; Connor had taught her that.

"Connor, don't you dare leave me in this house with another dead body. Wake up, damn it." She patted his face—maybe a little harder than she intended.

His lips parted and he emitted some sound—not quite a word, but she'd take it.

"Connor!" She brushed her hand across his brow and tucked his hair behind his ear. "C'mon, baby. Come back to me. I need you."

His thick, stubby lashes fluttered and he muttered another incompressible word.

She slid his head from her lap and wedged the towel beneath his cut. She rose to her feet and returned to the wet bar, this time filling a glass with water. Her hand hovered over a decanter of whiskey. Maybe he needed something stronger. She poured the amber liquid into a second glass and returned to the patient carrying both drinks.

She sat cross-legged on the floor beside him and carefully lifted his head again. She put the glass of booze to his slightly parted lips and tipped a small amount of the liquid into his mouth.

Most of it ran down his jaw and neck, but he sputtered and blinked.

"Keep it going, baby. You can have the rest when you come to."

Connor groaned and her heart sang. He wasn't going to die on her.

He reached for his head and she swatted his hand away.

"You have a big gash on the back of your skull. I have that covered—literally." She curled an arm around his shoulders. "Does anything else hurt? I didn't see any other injuries. What happened, Connor?"

He struggled to sit upright, and she placed a hand on his shoulder. "Are you sure you should be moving around?"

He cleared his throat and winced. "I'm fine."

"Obviously not." She helped him sit up and lean against the desk. "You were out cold when I got here, and must've been in that condition for quite some time because I've been trying to reach you to pick me up from the sheriff's department and you didn't answer."

His limbs jerked and his eyelids flew open. "How do you know it's safe? Someone hit me."

"Whoever attacked you is gone now. The house was

locked up when I got here." She stirred the broken glass on the floor with her toe. "I had to break a window to bust my way in here."

His lip twitched. "Bust your way in?"

"Oh, you think that's an exaggeration?" She raised one eyebrow. "I peered in and saw you on the floor. I thought I had my third dead body on my hands in the space of a week."

He coughed. "Not dead."

"Here." She thrust the whiskey at him. "Down some of this. You still look a little white around the lips."

"Damn. He took me by surprise." He wrapped his long fingers around the glass and took a gulp.

"You didn't see him, I suppose."

"No."

"What were you doing? What does he want?" Savannah peeled the towel from Connor's head and parted his hair to inspect the small wound, which was still producing a steady stream of blood. She clamped the towel back on.

"This." Connor hit the desk drawer with his fist. "I was checking out Niles's secret hiding place again. That's when he hit me."

"How did he even get in? The house was locked up when I arrived." She tipped her head toward the gaping hole in the window. "You saw what I had to resort to."

"I have no clue, but I'm guessing he was here before I was. Hiding, maybe just like the night of Niles's murder. I didn't hear any noises in the house when I was upstairs, but I've been pretty clueless in general, allowing him to get the jump on me."

Savannah rolled her eyes. "Would you stop focusing on that? Why would he want any more of Niles's files? He stole the one he wanted from me, didn't he?"

"I don't know, but somebody wants these files and it

seems as if it's someone who has access to the house."
Connor switched the whiskey for the water and drained
the glass. "Do you think Tiffany has keys to this house?"

"I'm sure of it. You think Tiffany whacked you on the
back of the head hard enough to knock you out?"

"No, but her biker boyfriend could've done it."

"What do you think they want with information about
the company?"

"Who says it's info about the company? It could be anything."

"You're right." She took his free hand and held it against
the towel. "Hold this in place while I get another. I think
it's finally stopped bleeding. Does it hurt?"

"Throbs."

She jumped up and got another towel, a dry one this
time. "I have some ibuprofen in my purse."

When she returned to him, he struggled to his feet and
she grabbed his arm. "You gave me a scare, Connor."

"Thanks for rescuing me. Who knows how long I
would've been bleeding out on the floor?" He took the dry
towel from her and folded it up against his head. "How'd it
go with the detectives?"

"I think it went okay. They did have questions about
my phone, but I was able to show them that it was broken.
They didn't mention Letty at all, which is strange. Hasn't
her family reported her missing?"

"Maybe they have and the sheriff's department hasn't
made the connection yet." Connor sucked in a breath as
he twisted his head from side to side. "Did you get your
digs in about Tiffany and Denny? Tell them about Brian
Donahue?"

"I told them I thought Denny was staying with Tiffany,
and they already knew about Brian. People at the office
told them…and he's missing."

"Donahue is missing?"

Savannah dug into her purse and took out a little bottle of ibuprofen, shaking it in the air. "Maybe *missing* is too strong a word, but they haven't spoken to him yet because his mother said he went on a trip."

"He lives with his mother?"

"He does." She tapped out two gel caps and handed them to Connor.

"Did he take the trip before or after the murder?"

"They didn't tell me those details."

"Maybe Donahue's busy skulking around setting you up—two birds with one stone." Connor popped the pills into his mouth and washed them down with a shot of whiskey.

"That's what it feels like to me. Someone killed Niles, getting their revenge on him, and someone's setting me up and torturing me, getting their revenge on me. Two birds."

"You'd better make a call and get that window fixed while we're still here. You don't want anyone else breaking in. Might not be a bad idea to repair the security system when you get a chance." He crumpled up both towels, wrapping the wet one in the dry one. "Do you want these?"

"I think you should keep one in case your head starts bleeding again on the ride back to your place." She took out her almost-dead phone to find a glass repair place.

"Good idea." He shook out the towels and glanced at the wet one. "Do you want it?"

"Toss it in the trash." She held up her cell. "I just found a place with twenty-four-hour emergency repair."

"What are you going to do with this house, Savannah?"

"Sell it—at a reduced price."

"You'll always have to disclose the murder."

"Just like we did when we sold Mom's place."

Savannah placed a call to the glass repair company and

explained the break. When she hung up, she said, "Can you stand to be here another hour or so? They can get here in twenty minutes."

"Sure, but when we get back, I want you to start looking at the files you do have. It's a good thing you locked them up." Connor took the two glasses to the bar and washed them out. "You can ask Dee Dee about the other one tomorrow."

"I plan to. I'm getting together with her before the general meeting and Nick after."

"When are you seeing Thomas? Didn't you say the two of you had another session tomorrow?"

"First thing in the morning." She pointed to the office door. "Let's wait somewhere else—outside preferably. I've had enough of this place."

THEY ROLLED INTO San Juan Beach around dinnertime. Even though Connor's new security system was programmed to notify his cell phone of any activity, he went straight to his laptop and looked at the footage.

He glanced up from clicking. "Just the mail carrier so far."

"That's good. Doesn't mean someone's not watching us." Savannah broke off a piece of banana and stuffed it in her mouth. "I feel like someone is tracking my every move—and yours. How did someone know you'd be at the house?"

"That was the pen. That's how he knew about Letty—or he set up Letty himself and that's how he knew you were heading to the interview with the detectives." He snapped his laptop closed. "It's also how he knew about the desk drawer. We were talking about it right before I discovered the pen wasn't a pen. And this time? Maybe he's just watching the house. Speaking of the desk drawers, are you going to pull out those files now?"

"I can't." She waved the banana at him. "They're in your safe and you didn't give me the combination."

"Don't take offense. I don't give anyone that combination."

"None taken." She snapped her fingers twice. "But can you open it for me now? Nothing from A.J. yet?"

"Nope. You'll be the first to know." He disappeared into his bedroom, and she could hear him opening the closet door. He emerged moments later, clutching the files in one hand and dangling the flash drive from the fingers of his other. "Let's not forget this."

"Okay, I'm ready." She hopped onto a kitchen stool and patted the counter. "Let's see what Niles held near and dear."

"Not you, that's for sure."

When Connor dropped the file folders on the counter, Savannah grabbed his wrist. "I should've never married him."

"I could've told you that." He slipped from her grasp. "While you look at those, I'm going to do some work, and then we'll have dinner. Sound like a plan?"

"It does." She glanced at her charging phone. "As long as I don't get any more anonymous messages. I'm just waiting for the other shoe to drop. When is he going to turn that stuff he has on me over to the detectives?"

"He's not. He would've made a move by now. He wants something else."

"If it's not money, I don't know what he wants from me. Why doesn't he just ask?"

"He's trying to keep you unsettled."

"It's working."

"I'll pour you a glass of wine. You need it." Connor opened a cupboard and took down two wineglasses.

She flipped open the first folder and ran her finger

across the text. It contained information about offers for the company—they'd had several. She sucked in her bottom lip and closed the folder, smoothing her fingertips over the edge of the label in the upper-right corner.

"What's wrong?" Connor set the glass of wine in front of her.

"This label does not match the contents of this file. All the paperwork in here deals with offers we received from other entities to buy out Snap App, and the label is for human resources."

"Misfiled?" Connor cupped his wineglass in both hands and swirled the ruby liquid.

"Niles didn't misfile anything—he was organized to a fault."

"You think he mislabeled the folders on purpose?"

"Maybe." She sat up straight. "So perhaps the file I took from the drawer the night Niles was killed, expecting financials from last year, didn't contain financials at all."

Connor stabbed a finger at the stack of folders. "And that's why someone cracked me on the head today in Niles's office. He stole the file from you yesterday and it didn't contain what he expected."

Savannah's pulse picked up speed. "The HR papers that should be in this folder might be in another one. There could be something in Brian Donahue's personnel record he doesn't want anyone to see."

"We're back to Brian?"

"Those detectives are sure interested in him, since he's disappeared." Savannah shuffled through the remaining four folders, flipping through the papers inside. "No HR stuff at all, so the labels are totally random."

Connor touched his glass to hers. "I'll let you figure it out. Dinner in an hour?"

"Gotcha." She went back to the first folder and started

skimming the offers. None surprised her, but she could understand why Niles would want to keep this information confidential.

She moved on to the next folder and flipped through some data on acquisitions—again, nothing earth-shattering, but nothing you wanted in a public forum or even employees to know about.

When she studied the spreadsheets in the next folder, her heart skipped a beat. "Here's the stuff I wanted in the first place, the stuff our thief thought he was stealing."

"Good. I guess Niles outwitted him."

Savannah trailed her finger down a column of numbers. "This is exactly what I was looking for. Payments received for orders placed for the past two years for our service contracts."

Connor called across the room, "That reminds me. I need to get a new accountant for the winery. Mine retired and I'm not great with numbers."

"You're not the only one." Savannah lodged the tip of her tongue in the corner of her mouth as she grabbed her charging phone and brought up the calculator.

As Savannah got deeper and deeper into the figures, her fingers became unsteady as she tapped in the numbers. Finally, she slumped forward and dropped her phone.

Connor looked up. "Get what you wanted?"

"Yes and no. It looks like Snap App's books have been cooked. Payments for deals we made for service contracts lasting several months have been reported in lump sums for the year. It's called accelerating the revenues."

"Explain to the dummy, please."

"So a company places an order with us for four million dollars for a four-year contract, with an agreement to pay us a million a year."

"Sounds sweet."

"Yeah, but these figures show we weren't amortizing the payments over four years, but reporting them as a lump sum in the year the contract was signed." She scooped up the papers and waved them in the air. "It's been done with several contracts, amounting to recorded payments in the hundreds of millions—payments that aren't real."

Connor shoved his computer from his lap and jumped up. "That's it, Savannah. Whoever falsified that information is the one who killed Niles and doesn't want you to discover his misdeeds."

"I know. There's just one problem with that deduction."

"What?"

"It was Niles who did it."

Chapter Sixteen

Connor hit the side of his head with the heel of his hand, as if to knock out his confusion. "I thought I had a handle on this."

"You do. Your theory would make total sense, but the truth is here in black and white. Niles has been fudging these numbers for two years." She tapped the folder. "He'd been keeping the real numbers along with the fake numbers so he wouldn't get confused, but the fake numbers are in the computer system. The fake numbers are the ones our stockholders are seeing—the ones I saw."

Connor circled the counter and faced Savannah. "His death is related to this. It has to be, but how? If someone found out and threatened to blackmail Niles, that person wouldn't kill him."

"Unless he confronted Niles, they got into a fight and the blackmailer stabbed Niles to death."

"That doesn't make much sense. When he killed Niles, he killed any chance for a payout." Connor turned the folder around to face him. "Savannah, Niles had no intention of giving you these spreadsheets. He knew you'd take one look at them and figure out his scam—just like you did."

"What are you saying?" She grabbed her wineglass and took a swig.

"Why did he invite you back to his house if he knew he wasn't going to give you the figures you were asking for?"

"Stall tactic?" She shrugged, but her violet eyes had turned dark.

"When you went back to his place, he gave you that scotch, didn't he? You saw your lipstick on the glass, so you know you at least took a few sips."

"Yes." Her fingers curled around the stem of her wineglass. "You're saying Niles is the one who drugged me?"

"Who else? It was his house, his scotch, his misdeeds."

"No, no." She slid from the stool and paced to the window. "You think Niles was going to kill me?"

Connor slammed his fist on top of the folder. "He wasn't going to give up those numbers. He wasn't going to tell you he'd been cheating and lying. He knew you'd never go along with that...didn't he?"

"Of course he knew that." Her eyes flashed at him.

"Sorry." He held up his hand. "Then the only reason for him to invite you back to the house and drug you was to kill you. Keep you from ever finding out what he'd been doing."

She closed her eyes and her chest heaved. "Even if I believe that—and I'm not saying I do—what went wrong? How did he wind up dead and I wind up scrambling to avoid an arrest for his murder?"

Connor's shoulders slumped. "That I don't know. Why was Brian Donahue fired?"

"Poor social skills. He couldn't get along with anyone he worked with and actually threatened our CFO. We had him escorted off the property." Savannah wrinkled her nose. "The whole thing was uncomfortable."

"Could he have been involved with this? It's obvious someone else knew what Niles was doing, or found out."

"But why wouldn't that person want it to come to light? Because that's why he's after this folder. He thought he stole this info from me the first time, and then thought he could get it from Niles's office when he bashed you on the head." She touched the back of her own head. "How's your wound anyway?"

Connor's eyebrows shot up. "That's hardly important right now...and it's fine. Maybe he's working so hard to get Niles's secret folders because there's some evidence of his blackmail scheme and even his murder of Niles."

Savannah slid the incriminating file away and pulled another one in front of her with a finger. "Last one to go through."

She flipped it open and squinted at the single page inside. "Oh, God."

"What now?" Connor leaned over her shoulder, taking in a bunch of names and dollar amounts. "What's this?"

"Niles's private payouts. Apparently, he was using the company funds for personal payments."

"What a piece of work. I'm surprised the company didn't collapse under him." The names blurred under his gaze and he rubbed his eyes. "Anything big enough for a blackmail payment?"

"Could be, but it's the names that are giving me pause— and making me sick to my stomach." She placed a hand on her belly.

"Like who?"

She skimmed the tip of her finger down the page. "He has payments here to Tiffany, which doesn't surprise me, but Dee Dee is on here. I can't imagine what that's for, and I don't think I wanna know."

He snatched the paper from her and flapped it in the air. "Looks like a list of suspects to me. That meeting with Dee Dee is going to be more interesting than you originally thought. Now, can we take this to dinner with us and pore over it while we eat? I'm gonna drop dead of starvation."

THE FOLLOWING MORNING, Savannah woke up in the guest bedroom. Connor had come a long way since the moment she'd confessed to Manny's murder, but making love again didn't seem like the right move...for either of them.

She had her hypnotherapy session to get through with Thomas this morning before heading to the office, which she was now dreading.

Why had Niles made an undercover payment to Dee Dee? To his sister? Why was he using company funds? And had he really been plotting her murder?

Connor tapped on the door. "I made some breakfast."

"Thanks. How's your head this morning?"

He cracked the door and poked his head into the room. "Sore and I have a big lump—bigger than the one you had when you arrived on my doorstep."

She reached back and traced the bump on the back of her head, wondering if it had been delivered by the same person who'd attacked Connor. "That seems like a lifetime ago."

"I'm glad you turned to me." Connor's face reddened to the roots of his hair. "And I'm sorry."

"For what? You took me in, lied for me, are helping me find out what happened that night. You have nothing to be sorry for."

Connor walked into the room and sat on the edge of the bed. He took both her hands in his. "I'm sorry I had my suspicions about you and the night Niles died."

"Someone was trying to set me up. Why wouldn't you have your suspicions? The truly amazing takeaway is that despite your suspicions, you took me in." She raised his hands to her lips and kissed his knuckles.

"Don't you already know I'd see you through anything?"

"Even though I killed Manny and blamed your father?"

He disentangled his fingers from hers and smoothed the covers over her thigh. "You act like you did that on your own, like it was your idea. You were a young woman in shock." When Connor's phone buzzed, he held up his finger. "Hang on. A.J.?"

Savannah scooted forward in bed, clutching the sheets.

Connor nodded. "I see. Thanks, man. I appreciate it. I owe you a case of wine when the time comes."

He ended the call. "You were right. The scotch showed traces of Rohypnol. You were roofied—and maybe Niles was, too."

Savannah fell back against the headboard, her nose stinging. "I knew it."

"Savannah, maybe it's time we go to the police."

She threw off the covers. "Are you crazy? We lied. *You* lied. You interfered with a police investigation, obstructed justice or whatever. You're not going down for any of this, Connor. I'm not going to allow that."

"This information that A.J. has could go a long way toward clearing you."

"Those detectives may suspect all they want, but they still have no proof I was there that night. I'm not going to give it to them and neither are you." She pushed at his broad back. "Now, get out of here. I have to shower and dress for my big day."

An hour later, Connor dropped her off in front of Thomas's office and she made her way up the stairs, her stomach fluttering. She'd skipped breakfast this morning and she knew she'd made the right move, as she felt like throwing up.

She followed the same protocol as last time and settled into the chair across from Thomas's. "Should I lie down on the couch instead?"

"Wherever you're comfortable, Savannah."

She'd be comfortable in Connor's arms right now, but this chair would have to suffice. "I'm comfortable and ready."

Thomas opened his hand to reveal a silver pen. "Just something to focus on while I put you under."

"No watch swinging back and forth on a chain?" She giggled and put her hand over her mouth.

He smiled his patient smile. "We can do that, if you like."

"If the pen works, I'll do the pen." She clasped her hands between her knees.

"It works better if you're relaxed." He nodded toward her knees. "Put your hands at your sides or in your lap. Relax your muscles. Lean back in the chair. You look ready to blast off."

"I am." She let out a jagged breath and fell back against the chair.

Thomas began at once, his soothing voice acting like a salve on her nerves. When he told her that her eyelids were getting heavy, she blinked slowly and had a hard time lifting them. Her breathing deepened and her head bobbed once, twice.

They were arguing again.

"Who?" Thomas's voice had somehow found its way into the house she'd shared with her mother and Manny—a big house, bigger than anything they'd lived in before.

"Mom and Manny."

Arguing, always arguing. Why wouldn't Mom leave him? He bothered her—always found some excuse to touch her or stroke her hair. She hated him.

She covered her ears. She should go out. Call Connor. But Connor was a grown-up now. He'd graduated from the police academy with top honors. He'd be a cop, like his father, and always be there for her.

She'd go out there and tell them to knock it off, but she didn't want to get in the middle of one of their fights. If only the fight were about her. If only Mom was warning Manny to stay away from her.

But they were fighting about money. Mom wanted more.

She sat up and yanked the earbuds from her ears. Something had changed. Mom was threatening Manny. Threatening him with exposure. Mom was accusing Manny of dealing drugs.

She shimmied off her bed and pressed her ear against the bedroom door. *Stop, Mom.* She jumped back from the door when she heard a loud thump.

If Manny had hit Mom, she'd have to do something. Call the police.

Then she heard an even more terrifying sound.

"What did you hear, Savannah?"

"It's a gunshot."

She flung open her door and rushed into the living room. She screamed.

"What do you see, Savannah."

"Manny is on the floor, bleeding. Mom is standing there with a gun in her hand. I'm screaming. I can't stop screaming."

Was she really screaming?

Mom dropped the gun and shook her. Shook her into silence. She couldn't speak. Couldn't move. She felt frozen. Suspended in space and time.

Mom's voice came at her from a long way away, but she couldn't understand her. Couldn't respond.

Mom shook her again. Slapped her face. She didn't even care. She wanted to curl up in a ball. She slumped in her mother's arms.

Mom pushed her away and grabbed her camisole. Mom ripped her camisole from her body. She didn't care.

Mom tugged down her pajama bottoms and her underwear. She didn't care. She wanted to curl into a ball and go far away.

Mom's voice filtered into her brain. "It's okay, Savannah. You didn't mean to do it. Manny tried to rape you."

Did he?

Mom's hands, soothing and protective, stroked her arms. "Sit in the corner. I'll fix everything."

She sank in the corner, naked, confused, shocked. Mom would fix everything.

She blinked and met Thomas's steady gaze. Then she covered her eyes with one hand. "I remember. My mom shot Manny and blamed me."

Chapter Seventeen

Connor watched Savannah walk down the stairs, and his lips curled up on one side despite everything they were dealing with right now. He couldn't help himself.

As she got closer, the smile faded from his face and his gut twisted into knots. She had a tissue clutched in her hand and kept dabbing at her eyes and her nose. Her rounded shoulders made her look about two inches shorter and her hair hung on either side of her face, practically hiding it as she kept her gaze pinned to the ground.

Connor jumped from the Lexus and jogged toward her. "Savannah? Babe? What's wrong? What happened in there?"

Lifting her head, she raised her eyes, flooded with a fresh set of tears to join the ones rolling down her cheeks. "I learned the truth."

He swallowed and gritted his teeth, bracing for the worst. What could be more terrible than killing a man in self-defense? He dug his shoes into the asphalt. Killing a man in cold blood.

"What is the truth?"

"My own mother killed Manny—and she set me up and made me believe I'd done it." She emitted an animallike wail and dropped into a crouch at his feet.

A white-hot rage engulfed him like a wave and he staggered back. His hands clenched into fists.

Moaning, Savannah doubled over, wrapping her arms around her waist.

Connor's breath came out in gusts, and then he knelt beside Savannah and took her in his arms. He stroked the hair back from her hot face, damp with a million tears, and whispered in her ear, "It's all right. It's all right. You're free."

"F-free?" The word came out muffled against his shoulder. "My own mother. My own mother."

Connor's eyes locked with those of a woman heading into the office building, and her gait slowed.

"I'm going to get you in the car. Is that all right?"

Savannah nodded against his chest, and he tucked an arm around her waist and rose to his feet, half dragging her with him. He lowered her to the passenger seat and then lifted her legs inside.

When he was behind the wheel, he reached into the back of the car and plucked a handful of tissues from the box on the seat. "Here you go. You had me so scared."

She bunched up several and blew her nose. "Why would she do that, Connor?"

"To save her own skin. That shouldn't surprise you, Savannah. In fact, I don't know why I didn't think of it myself." He wedged a knuckle beneath her chin. "Georgie has always been about Georgie first…and you second. This doesn't mean your mother didn't love you. She did. That was clear to anyone who saw the two of you together. She just didn't know how to be the best mother. Her needs always came first. She was the same with my father. I know she loved Dad, too, but she loved herself more—always."

"I have to confront her." Savannah shredded the used tissues, creating a snowstorm in her lap. "I have to make sure she knows that I know the truth."

"Of course you do." He brushed the bits of paper from her lap. "But not now."

"Oh, my God. The meeting." She flipped down the visor and studied her puffy eyes and red nose in the mirror.

"Cancel it. Do it another day. You need time to process this."

"There's no way I'm going to cancel this meeting."

"Delay it a few hours. Get yourself together."

She aimed a grimace at the mirror. "Maybe I should go into the meeting looking like this. People will think I'm really broken up about Niles and figure I never could've killed him."

"Whatever you want, Savannah, but I think you need more time." He trailed his fingers down her arm. "It's still early. You can delay the meeting until later this afternoon. You want to go into Snap App looking like a million bucks. You're the CEO of the damned company now."

She sniffled and ran her fingers through her hair. Then she gasped, "Do you know what this means?"

"It means you didn't kill Manny...or anyone else."

She dug her fingernails into his thigh through the light wool of his slacks. "I didn't kill Manny, Connor. I mean, I still went along with Mom's story, which ended your father's life, but I didn't pull that trigger. I didn't black out because I'd murdered someone. I blacked out from the shock of knowing my mother had."

"My father was an adult, a police officer. He should've known better than you or your mother. He made the decision to take the blame and then paid the consequences."

"He would've done anything for Georgie."

Connor leaned over and kissed Savannah's damp cheek. "I can't blame him. That's the kind of love I can understand."

Her bottom lip trembled. "It's all so messed up."

"It's not messed up. It's all straightened out now." He started the engine. "And we're going to straighten out this other business, too."

"Not by going to the police." She put her hand on his arm. "I told you. I'm not putting you in that situation."

"We're getting close to the truth on our own. Maybe we can hand those homicide detectives a done deal, a solved case."

She gave him a watery smile. "If anyone can do it, you can. I have faith in you, Connor Wells."

"I wish I'd had faith in you, Savannah."

"I gave you no reason to and you still had my back." She squared her shoulders. "I'm going to delay the meeting for two hours, have lunch with you and fix my face."

"Don't do anything to that face." He touched her cheek. "It doesn't need fixing. Nothing about you needs fixing."

She snorted, "Now you're just getting carried away."

A phone rang in the car and Connor reached for his on the console. "It's yours."

"If it's my mother, you're going to have to restrain me." She glanced at the display and her jaw tightened. "Unknown."

"If it's your blackmailer, you're going to have to restrain *me*."

She tapped the display and answered. "Hello?"

"Savannah?"

She'd put her phone on speaker, and the man's voice filled the car.

"Yes. Who is this?"

"Brian Donahue."

She jerked her head toward Connor. "Did you kill Niles?"

"No! And neither did you."

"Damn straight. Who said I did and where are you?"

"I know what's going on, and I can fill you in if you meet me tonight."

"Tell me now, over the phone."

"Can you be sure your cell isn't bugged?"

Savannah held the phone in front of her face and studied it, as if seeing it for the first time. "No."

"Give me another number to use and I'll text the time and location."

"Not the same place where I met Letty."

Donahue made a strangled noise. "You met Letty?"

"You're trying to tell me you didn't know about that meeting?"

"Savannah, Letty's dead."

"I know that." Savannah jabbed Connor in the shoulder. "But how do you unless you were there?"

"Where have you been? It's on the news."

Savannah gasped, "What do you know about Letty?"

"Nothing. Give me the number and I'll text you the meeting info."

Connor held up his phone and tapped it.

Savannah reeled off Connor's cell number and ended the call. Seconds later a time and location for the meeting came through on Connor's phone.

Savannah put her hands together as if in prayer, holding her phone between them. "They found Letty."

"I'm glad they did, aren't you?"

"Yes, but it makes that photo of me with her body a stick of dynamite now."

"It always was, but I think it's just insurance to use in case you get too close to the truth." He pulled the car into a grocery store parking lot.

"I thought we were getting lunch before the meeting."

"We are." He parked the car. "Here. We'll pick up a few things and head to the beach, have lunch there and relax."

She plucked at her navy slacks. "Dressed in office clothes? Even you're dressed up."

"We'll be careful."

She took his hand. "Thanks for putting my mom's betrayal into perspective for me."

"You're not a killer, Savannah—self-defense or otherwise. But I'm not letting you off the hook."

Her cheeks flushed. "You're not?"

"You're going back to see Thomas. You need a professional to help you process this. I'm just a bandage."

She pressed a kiss against his palm and folded his hand over it. "Best damned bandage I've ever had in my life."

CONNOR WAS RIGHT—as usual. The lunch, the beach and just being together all helped to set her spinning world back on its axis. But Savannah still felt a hole in her stomach—a hole where her mother's love should've been. But she had work to do and that bandage had to do its job for now.

Later that afternoon, Connor pulled into an executive parking space beneath her building. "Are you sure you want me to go in with you?"

"I'd like to show you the office—what I helped build— even if it *is* all going to turn to ashes before my eyes."

"If anyone can repair the damage, you can."

"With the help of my CFO, Nick. He's the money guy." She slid from the car and shook out her jacket before putting it on.

Connor opened the glass door that led from the parking structure to the offices of Snap App.

Kelly, the receptionist, squealed and scooted around the desk. She threw her arms around Savannah. "Welcome back, Savannah. We're all so happy you're back in charge… but of course, devastated by Niles's murder."

"Of course. It's been horrible."

Kelly put a hand to her throat. "Do you think his house-keeper had anything to do with it? She committed suicide."

"I have no idea. I'll let the detectives figure things out." She patted Kelly on the back. "I'm here to figure things out for Snap App."

She and Connor took the elevator up to the seventh floor. When the doors opened, she said, "My office is up here, but the big conference room is on the first floor. We'll be having the meeting there, but first I'm going to have my chat with Dee Dee."

"Nice digs." Connor turned in a circle, taking in the glass-walled offices with their views of the marina and downtown.

"Savannah." Nick Fresco emerged from his office, straightening his impeccable tie, and took her hands in his long, bony fingers. "It's good to see you back. This company needs you."

"Needs something right now. I just hope I have the right words to say."

"You will." He squeezed her hands and then glanced at Connor, his dark eyes jumping to the curls at his hairline.

"This is Connor Wells. Connor, my trusty CFO, Nick Fresco."

"Nice to meet you, Connor." As he shook Connor's hand he stooped slightly, a habit he'd likely developed from being six foot six. "New employee?"

"No, I'm just her chauffeur."

Savannah poked Connor's arm.

Connor tilted back his head. "Basketball player?"

"I've shot some hoops in my day."

She tugged on Connor's sleeve. "Do you want to see my office? I haven't occupied it for a while, but I kept it intact."

Dee Dee peered out of another office. "Hey, Savannah. Are we still meeting before the meeting?"

Savannah swallowed and curved her stiff lips into a smile. "Yeah, I was just going to show Connor my office."

Dee Dee stepped into the corridor and flipped her dark hair over her shoulders. "Oh, this is the famous Connor Wells."

Savannah introduced them and then showed Connor her corner office.

"I'm impressed." He wandered to the window with his hands in his pockets and gazed at the view. "Are you going to be working here?"

She came up behind him and wrapped her arms around his waist. "I can do my work anywhere…even on a vineyard."

His back stiffened and she held her breath. Had she gone too far, too fast?

He turned and smoothed a lock of her hair from her forehead. "Can I look around while you're with Dee Dee? I'll show myself out when I'm done and do a little work at that coffeehouse down the block while you finish with your other meetings."

"Sounds good. I'll text you when I'm finished for the day…or night, and then we can eat if we have time before that meeting with Brian."

"We're still on for later?"

Nick's voice startled her and she spun around, jerking her hair out of Connor's fingers. "Yes, we have a lot to go over."

Nick rapped his knuckles on the door frame. "I'm going to go down to the conference room and make sure everything's set up for the meeting. Nice to meet you, Connor."

Connor held up his hand.

As soon as Nick left, Dee Dee took his place at the door. "Ready?"

"I am." Savannah flicked her fingers toward the door.

"Make yourself at home, Connor. I'll text you when I'm ready to leave, and then I'll meet you downstairs at my parking space."

"Good luck." He shut the door behind him.

Savannah took a deep breath and perched on the edge of a love seat against one wall. "Have a seat, Dee."

Dee Dee pulled a chair across from Savannah and sank into it. "What a crazy week. You heard about Letty, right?"

"I did."

"Do you think she killed Niles? Was blackmailing him or something and then took her own life?"

"I don't know. That doesn't sound like Letty, but then I guess you never know about people, do you?"

Dee Dee cocked her head. "I guess not."

"Dee—" Savannah pulled a folder from her briefcase "—can you tell me why Niles made a lump sum payment to you that he was trying to hide?"

Dee Dee's face dropped and she clutched the arms of the chair. "What do you mean?"

Savannah whipped out the sheet of paper. "It's here in black and white, Dee Dee. What happened?"

"Are you going to tell the cops?" She pressed her hand against her heart. "I swear I didn't have anything to do with Niles's murder."

"What's the payment for?"

"Sexual harassment."

Savannah's mouth dropped open. "Niles harassed you?"

"We had a brief affair, Savannah." Dee Dee dropped her head.

"While he was still married to me?"

"Yes. I'm sorry."

"It was consensual and mutual?"

"Aside from Niles being my boss, it was. I am sorry."

"And then you threatened to sue him?"

"He was so arrogant, Savannah. You know that."

"But he took money from the company to pay you. Did *you* know *that*?" Savannah smacked the file on her knee. "You should've just sued him for sexual harassment and settled with the insurance company."

"I—I didn't want my husband to find out. It would've killed Victor."

"Give me one good reason why I shouldn't tell those homicide detectives."

"I protected you, Savannah." Dee Dee pushed up from the chair. "We all did. You don't think you're their prime suspect? You are. We could all tell that, and we tried our best to steer them away from you."

"I didn't do it." Savannah shouted the words, with more confidence than ever. She hadn't killed Manny. Someone had drugged her the night of Niles's murder. She was no killer.

"Neither did I." Dee Dee leaned against the window. "I was home with Victor. The police already checked my alibi."

"Mine, too."

"Then neither of us has anything to worry about."

She wouldn't go that far.

Dee Dee turned, clutching her hands in front of her. "And you have no reason to tell the police about my agreement with Niles, right? It has nothing to do with anything."

"I wouldn't say that, Dee Dee. As I mentioned before, you never really know anyone, do you? You're fired."

"Savannah. Is it because of the affair? It didn't mean anything, and you were so over Niles by then." She tipped her head toward the window, where Connor had appeared. "Because of him, right?"

Connor raised a pen and pointed toward the exit.

Nodding, Savannah waved at him. Then she turned back to Dee Dee. "It's about trust, Dee. I'm sick of being betrayed by people I thought I could trust." Savannah stood up and brushed off her slacks. "The good news? You don't have to go to the meeting."

Savannah walked out of her office and looked around the empty floor. Everyone must be at the meeting…waiting for her. Time for her to start acting like a CEO, and she'd just taken her first step.

When she walked into the conference room, it erupted in applause and then everyone stood up. Savannah crossed her hands over her chest. Maybe you never really knew anyone, but this felt good.

Nick ushered her to the front of the room with a grin. "Snap App's founder and our new CEO, Savannah Martell."

The applause swelled again, and Savannah strode to the podium to take her place in front of her employees.

For the next hour, she stuck to her script. She praised Niles, although the words stuck in her throat, and she put forth a plan going forward. She didn't mention the funny business with the accounting, but she planned to address it with Nick.

The meeting seemed to fly by, but by the time she finished it was past quitting time for everyone, and then it got even later as half the company approached her to say hello, shake hands and even drop a few weird hints about Niles.

Finally, the room cleared, until she faced Nick, alone.

"Whew." She dropped into the nearest chair. "How'd I do?"

"Great. Didn't you see the reaction of the troops?" He crossed one long leg over the other.

Savannah patted her chest. "It warmed my heart. Should

we get down to business? I have the papers I want to discuss with you in my briefcase."

Nick pointed at the ceiling. "And I have mine upstairs. Let's have this discussion in my office. I have a surprise for you."

"I don't need any surprises, Nick." She tilted her head to one side. Nick was usually by the book. That was what she liked about him.

"Okay, no surprises." He held up his hands. "I bought a nice bottle of champagne to celebrate your homecoming. Just a sip or two."

"Actually, I could use a sip or two. I've had a rough day—rough week."

"I'll take this for you." He grabbed her briefcase and hitched it over his shoulder.

As they rode up the elevator together, she broke the news about Dee Dee.

Nick's eyes popped out of their sockets. "Dee and Niles? That fool. I'm sorry, Savannah, but the man had no discipline."

"Tell me about it."

When they reached the executive floor, Nick ushered her into his office. He reached into the minifridge on the floor beside his desk, withdrew a magnum of champagne and hoisted it in the air. "The good stuff."

He took a couple glasses from a credenza. "Do you mind if they're not crystal flutes?"

"You're mistaking me for Niles."

"Never." He popped the cork and splashed a quantity of the sparkling liquid in each glass, where it foamed and bubbled. He raised his glass to her. "To a new era at Snap App."

"A new era." She clinked her glass against his and took

a sip. Then she reached into her briefcase and pulled out the file with the misrepresentations. "And it's going to start right here."

Smoothing out the papers on the table in front of them, she launched into a description of what Niles had been doing with the orders.

She didn't have to explain much to Nick. He was their finance guy. He'd know all about the practice of accelerating revenues.

"There's more, Nick." She took another gulp of champagne, her long discourse making her thirsty. "I think Brian Donahue may have known something about this."

"Brian?" He rolled his glass between his hands. "He's missing."

"Not anymore. I—I'm meeting him tonight. He contacted me and told me he had info about Niles."

"That's not safe, Savannah." Nick tipped more of the shimmering liquid into her glass. "That guy's a loose cannon."

"I'll be taking Connor with me. He'll keep me safe." She yawned and tapped the file. "But what are we going to do about this mess, Nick?"

"I'll take care of it, Savannah." He scooped up the papers and shoved them back into the folder. Then he tossed it onto his desk.

She wrinkled her nose and yawned again. "What are you doing?"

"I'm gonna bury that information so deep it'll never surface."

Savannah's head buzzed and she tried to work up some outrage, but she was too tired. Her gaze tracked to the champagne still fizzing in her glass. As she reached for it again, she knocked it over with one flailing hand.

She struggled to hold on to consciousness, but felt it slipping away. She was going to black out again...but this time the dead body in the room would be hers.

Chapter Eighteen

Connor checked his phone again for what seemed like the hundredth time. The meetings must be going well. Maybe Fresco, Savannah's CFO, would be able to help right the Snap App ship.

He shoved back from his laptop and stretched. Even though they'd had that late lunch, he'd be ready for dinner before their meeting with Brian and the drive back to San Juan Beach.

He swirled the dregs of the coffee left in his cup and then set it down. He'd head over and wait for her in the parking lot. He didn't much trust this Brian character she was meeting later.

His cell phone buzzed and he checked the display. He read the text from Savannah with a groan, and then eyed the refrigerated display case next to the register.

Savannah had decided to go out with Dee Dee for a drink before the meeting with Brian, and had asked him to pick her up at the bar in another two hours. His stomach rumbled.

He didn't think it was a great idea for her to drink before seeing Brian, but she'd had a rough day—and he'd have her back. He responded to her text with a thumbs-up emoji and ordered himself a bagel and cream cheese.

As he sat down with the warm bagel, the woman at the

next table smiled at him. "Do you have a pen I can borrow? Mine just ran out of ink."

He felt in his front pocket for the pen he'd grabbed from Nick Fresco's desk on his way out of the Snap App offices and plucked it from his pocket. "Here you go."

"Thanks. I just need it for a minute." She took it from him and flipped open a notebook.

Connor scooped out some cream cheese and spread it on one half of his bagel. He crunched into the bagel and pulled his laptop close to finish reviewing the report from his chemist on the winery.

The woman stretched across the space between their tables and tapped the pen on the surface before dropping it. "Thank you."

The pen rolled off the table and fell to the floor, where a piece broke off.

"I'm so sorry. Was it an expensive pen?"

Connor leaned to the side to retrieve it. As he picked it up, a feather of fear brushed the back of his neck. Where had he seen this particular type of pen before?

His heart slammed against his chest and he almost tipped out of the chair. He dropped the pen to the floor himself and scrambled out of his seat. Under the woman's wide eyes, he brought the heel of his shoe down on the object, splintering it into pieces.

"Wh-what's wrong? I'll replace the pen if you like."

He pinched the pieces in a napkin and plopped back in his chair. Hunching over the table, he stirred through the bits of plastic, his chest slamming against his rib cage.

The pen he'd taken from Nick Fresco's desk was a spy pen. The same type Savannah had been carrying around in her purse for a few days. The type someone had slipped into her purse the night Savannah was drugged and Niles was murdered. The same kind that had broken in just this way that day in Niles's office.

And Savannah and Nick had a meeting tonight together, alone.

HIS HEART GALLOPING, Connor pulled into the empty parking structure. Everyone had left. The meeting was over.

Savannah had given him her location badge to get in and out of the building, and he used it now to gain access to the reception area. Some small voice in his ear kept him from charging up seven flights of stairs yelling Savannah's name.

He eased open the door to the stairwell and glided up the steps barely breaking a sweat, his pumping adrenaline giving him the strength of ten men. He'd need it—that and his gun. He patted the weapon in his waistband he'd brought for the meeting with Brian.

When he reached the seventh floor, he held his breath and pushed down the door handle. He gave the door a little shove and stopped, peering through the crack. The stairwell was down the hall from the main offices and he could see the only lunchroom from his vantage point.

He opened the door wide enough to slip through, and then closed it on a whisper. He crept toward the offices and paused when he heard voices, male and female. Shutting his eyes, he blew out a breath. He'd recognize Savannah's voice anywhere.

If she and Fresco were still meeting, Connor would get her out of here, and then they could compile the evidence against Fresco without the CFO even knowing they were onto him.

The voices became clearer, and still, Connor held back, inching his way toward a cubicle across from the offices. He flattened himself against one wall of the cubicle and waited until he could hear the voices again.

Savannah's voice, low and slightly slurred, came from the office—her office. "This is not going to work, Nick."

"Of course it is. You murdered your husband to get your hands on the company, his life insurance, the house—take your pick. Then you killed Letty because she was going to blackmail you with the button. I have proof of that."

"That's not proof. And I have the knife, remember?"

Nick laughed, "I should've realized you'd be a formidable foe, Savannah. Niles was easy. That button will be good enough. And when the cops find your dead body here at the office, they'll assume you were filled with remorse and hanged yourself."

His words hit Connor on the back of the head like a sledgehammer. His muscles coiled, ready to pounce. But pounce on what? He couldn't see into the office. He didn't want to push Fresco into doing anything yet.

"I have...whatever you drugged me with...in my body. The autopsy report will show that."

"So what? You needed to take something before the act to steady your nerves...just like you drugged Niles to make stabbing him easier."

"I don't understand why you're doing this, Nick. You were never even on my radar. I had no idea you and Niles were cooking the books together. The paperwork doesn't implicate you."

"It was my plan from the start—kill Niles and frame you. Your meeting with Brian tonight just accelerated the timeline."

"Brian knows, doesn't he? That's why you fired him. He was going to tell me everything tonight."

Fresco snorted, "I wouldn't count on that. He's all over the place, but I can handle Brian—I've done it before."

Savannah coughed. "Why didn't you just kill both of us that night?"

"And leave the cops searching for a suspect? No, thanks."

The sound of a dragging chair had Connor dropping to his hands and knees and making a move out of the cubicle. He had to see what was going on. Had to determine a way to stop this madness.

"Connor is coming back here to pick me up any minute. This is not going to work, Nick. We can make a deal. I'll work with you."

Savannah's speech had lost its drowsy edge and contained a hint of desperation.

Connor clenched his hands into fists, cursing the modern glass walls of these offices. The minute he popped up, Fresco would spot him.

"I took care of Connor, too."

"What?" Savannah choked.

"Oh, not like that, but if he doesn't stop snooping around, I will take extreme measures." Fresco clicked his tongue. "I meant I sent him a text from you toward the end of the all-hands meeting, letting him know you'd be going out for drinks with Dee Dee. He doesn't even know you're still here. He'll be waiting for you at some bar downtown in about an hour. And like you said—you two never suspected me. Did you really think that nitwit Tiffany could've pulled this off, or even her psychotic boyfriend? Letty? Come on."

"I won't tell anyone, Nick. You can resign from the company with a fat bonus and I'll fix everything."

Fresco laughed, "I don't believe that for a second. You were always the moral partner. Niles was the dirtbag. That's how I knew he'd be up for a little financial maneuvering."

"Stop this."

Was that a plea to him? Connor couldn't stand to listen to any more of this.

Clutching the gun in his hands, he rose slowly from the floor to face the windows of Savannah's office. Rage boiled his blood and seared his skin when he saw Fresco slipping a noose around Savannah's neck as she stood on a chair.

Fresco spun around, one hand on Savannah's back, the other on the rope encircling her throat.

Connor growled, "Let her go."

"Are you sure about that?" Fresco tapped the leg of the chair with the toe of his wingtip. "One solid kick and she swings."

"One shot and you're dead." Connor took aim at Fresco's head.

"I'm not going down alone, Wells. She'll come with me. And then you'll have quite a bit of explaining to do—maybe starting with how you impeded a murder investigation by lying about the prime suspect's whereabouts." Fresco moved closer to the chair. "I have to admit Savannah impressed me with her criminal know-how. I thought the cops would be arresting her right away once they pinged her cell phone, and found that knife. If I were you, I'd be a little worried about being with a woman who knows how to cover her tracks as effortlessly as Savannah does. Lots of practice there."

Connor's jaw hardened. He could take the head shot and maybe Fresco wouldn't have time to kick that chair out from under Savannah. Or maybe he would have time, but Connor could rush across the room and grab her before she hanged.

He stared hard into Fresco's eyes, his finger tightening on the trigger.

A split second later, Savannah hoisted her feet from the chair and slammed them into Fresco's ribs.

The man staggered to the side and then lunged for Savannah's legs, which were bicycling in the air.

That was his girl, and nobody was going to hurt his girl ever again.

Connor took the shot.

Epilogue

Savannah stretched out in the hammock and curled her toes. She held up her wineglass to the setting sun. "Yours is going to be better than this, isn't it?"

Connor, on the other side of the hammock, facing her, took a sip of wine and swirled it around in his mouth. "Damn right."

"You'll have to send some to the detectives when it's ready. Detective Paulson called me this morning and told me they were wrapping up the case against Nick Fresco."

"I'm not sure Paulson ever did believe you weren't at the house that night."

"Maybe not." She trailed a hand over the edge of the hammock through the tall, cool grass. "But when they found the murder weapon with both Niles's and Nick's blood on it, that sealed the deal for them, and Brian Donahue's statement helped."

"Told you A.J. was a pro."

She slid her sunglasses down to the tip of her nose. "I don't know why Nick would keep the murder weapon with his own blood on it."

"He didn't keep it. He planted it on you and figured you'd dispose of it. Probably didn't realize his blood was on the knife, but knew yours was because that's what he used to cut you. Didn't remember that you were left-handed, though." Connor grabbed her bare foot and ran his knuckle down her arch. "That was a stroke of luck when I grabbed that pen from Fresco's desk. I can't believe he'd leave something like that out in plain sight, but then he probably figured he could plant another one on you when you were in the office. Did he ever explain why he made his move that night, when you didn't even suspect him?"

"He always planned to stage my suicide." She shivered despite the warm sun beating down on her legs. "But when I stupidly told him I was meeting Brian, he snapped. He thought Brian might've decided to tell me that he discovered the anomalies in the finances and had been paid off to keep quiet."

"Who knows if that's what Brian was going to do?"

"I still don't know. He won't return my calls." She pinged the side of her glass with her fingernail. "But my mom finally did."

Connor sat up and the hammock swayed from side to side. "Georgie called you back? Did you confront her?"

"I did."

"I'm sure she had excuses for what she did."

"Of course. She told me in all seriousness that the cops would've gone easier on a young woman who'd been fighting off Manny's advances than an older woman who stood to get her hands on Manny's assets." Savannah swiped the back of her hand across her stinging nose. "But she told me she loved me."

"She ain't the only one." Connor chafed her foot between his hands.

She tossed the rest of her wine overboard and placed the glass on the ground. "You're too far away."

Connor held out his arms, and she scrambled across the swinging hammock and landed on his chest, tucking her head against his shoulder. "I thought of a good name for the winery."

"Really?" He stroked her hair and kissed the top of her head. "Let me guess… Savannah's?"

"Nope. Alibi Vineyards."

Connor wrapped his arms around her, and they laughed so hard the hammock flipped over and dumped them on the ground.

"Be careful. You're going to have Detective Paulson knocking on your door again."

"Let him come at me. Let 'em all come at me." Resting her head against his chest, she ran her fingers through his long hair. "If you believe in me, I can face anything."

"Oh, I believe in you, Savannah Martell…"

Her head jerked up and she met his blue eyes. Had he almost said *for now*?

Then he took her face in his hands and kissed her…and she didn't even care.

* * * * *

PERSONAL PROTECTION

JULIE MILLER

For Jana Boyll Thompson, my singing buddy.
I so enjoy hanging out with you at City Singers and
doing a show together every now and then. We'll try
not to get into too much trouble.

Prologue

May 1—Lukinburg Day in St. Feodor,
on the steps of the historic palace square

"In three months, St. Feodor will play host to a group of dignitaries from our sister city in the United States. We will introduce the Americans to the charm of our country and show them that they need us as much as we need them. They need our rugged mountains, our beautiful beaches, our vast supply of natural resources, the skills and grace of our people."

Cameras flashed in the crowd, and the low white noise of television and radio commentators from across Europe and the United States, speaking a dozen different languages, buzzed in the background beneath static from the old broadcasting system. The world was waiting for tiny, mountainous Lukinburg in Eastern Europe to blossom after decades of oppression to take its rightful place on the world stage once more.

A black-haired woman in a cream-colored suit moved in behind the prince at the podium and tapped him on the shoulder. "Do not forget to mention the city's name, Your Highness," she reminded him.

"Thank you, Galina," the prince whispered before

turning back to the microphone. "Kansas City, Missouri, our sister city, will become Lukinburg's partner in worldwide respect and future prosperity. We shall be great friends."

The crowd erupted in applause. He adjusted his glasses at his temple and scanned the throng of onlookers through the bulletproof glass surrounding the podium. He looked past the placards here to support the new regime to the handful of scowling doubters with their own less supportive signs, waiting for the opportune moment to voice a protest.

A public gathering of this size in the capital on one of the country's biggest holidays once would have been a prime target for dissidents. Change was hard for any citizen. Change was the enemy to those who'd once held positions of power, who were now either imprisoned or being asked to embrace what was good for the country over what was lucrative for themselves. But the prince had reached out to those dissidents, had listened to their complaints and fears, had formed alliances and reached compromises with many of them. Yet, some of the most die-hard rebels hadn't given up the fight, and they would always see the new monarchy as their enemy.

Lukinburg's army had some of the finest trained soldiers in the world, and the plainclothes security force that now surrounded the country's leaders at every venue were on constant guard against any threat that would topple the fragile new government. He looked at his friends and former military comrades flanking him on the podium. They were doing this. They were making Lukinburg great again. Their hard work and dedication had given the country reason to celebrate today.

Ivan Mostek, the crown prince of Lukinburg, was

nearing the end of his long fight to replace the corrupt government of this country. A hardworking regency government and brave voters had replaced the corrupt dictator and mafia-like power brokers who had made Lukinburg a haven for criminals and arms trafficking. Part of electing a new Parliament and reestablishing the democratic monarchy this picturesque country had enjoyed before World War II was locating a true heir to the Lukinburg throne. As a distant cousin of the last legitimate king's late grandnephew, that dubious honor fell to Ivan. Plucked from graduate school where he'd been earning his MBA, he'd accepted the position. Patriotism and DNA had left him with no other choice but to say yes, and accept that within the next year, he would be crowned king.

With the discovery of gold and mica deep beneath the mountains east of Lake Feodor, Lukinburg now had raw materials that countries in the West and Far East were clamoring to build their electronics and develop new computer technologies. The prince had implemented environmentally safe mining practices to sustain the new resources. From his newfound position of power, he was jump-starting the country's economy, feeding the poor, capitalizing on new industries and putting people to work—all while paying tribute to Lukinburg's traditional culture and storied history.

Public appearances were necessary to assure the citizens of the solidity of the new government. And public appearances meant crowds of people and noisy fanfare and making speeches. After the cheers had died down, he continued, "Kansas City's manufacturing, agricultural and business leaders will be in our beautiful country, in this fair city, in three weeks. A carefully chosen delegation of representatives from Lukinburg will negotiate trade agreements and cultural exchanges that will benefit both our countries."

He spied movement in the shadows of the pointed Gothic archways in the cathedral across from the palace steps where he stood. He looked across the podium to his friend Konrad Pavluk. They exchanged a nod of awareness. Konrad had spotted the movement, too. The other man drifted across the dais to stand beside Galina. Anyone less observant would have missed the hidden squeeze of hands, the subtle whisper of a warning. She nodded and moved up behind the prince again to relay a message.

The military marksmen stationed in decorative ramparts atop the stone buildings surrounding the public square didn't seem concerned by the hooded man in the long coat making his way through the crowd of bystanders. Maybe they didn't see him. Or perhaps, as the prince had confided to his best friend only days earlier, someone within his inner circle was still working with the extremists. Did the uniformed guards' lack of response mean they were unobservant? Traitors? Was he overly paranoid about the prince's safety because an attempt had already been made on his life?

Although that sniper had been captured and taken into custody, the threats against Ivan's life continued. It had been random gunfire that had wounded his driver and ignited the engine of the car they'd taken to an ore refinement facility being built outside the city. Were the extremists here today? Mingling with this crowd of innocent civilians? Would they strike again, regardless of the casualties a group this big might sustain? Was the man in the hooded coat one of them?

He glanced over to the security chief, Filip Milevski. Although the dark glasses he wore made the direction of his gaze unreadable, the stocky man with salt-and-pepper hair was on the radio pinned to his wrist, no doubt asking for a situation update from his men and hopefully sounding a potential alert to stop the man who was now circling the fountain in the middle of the square.

The prince's voice was slightly less composed, tinged with a bit of anger, when he continued. "I promise to make Lukinburg great again. We will move past the shame of our former leaders. We will return to the democratic monarchy of our ancestors. I will work closely with the new prime minister and your votes will count. All your votes," he added, perhaps emphasizing to the extremists in the audience that they were not excluded from the new government.

Another round of cheers from the crowd nearly drowned out a lone dissenter who booed him. "You're selling us out, Ivan!"

Security Chief Milevski sidled closer to the prince. "Wrap it up, Your Highness." He moved Konrad and another one of his men farther down the granite steps in front of the podium. "There are too many of us exposed here. We're all in danger."

His gaze zeroed in on the hooded man. He'd sat on the edge of the fountain and was unbuttoning his long coat. The prince kept talking into the microphone, keeping the crowd engaged while members of the security team made their way through the onlookers to reach the suspect. "We need free trade. Our people need food."

"Our people need a leader they can respect!" The protest came from another corner of the audience.

"I agree. For too long, we have been led by men our people fear. Fear doesn't put food in people's bellies. Our people are working again. They aren't afraid to leave their homes and share their opinions and vote however they please."

A tall man, with hair as black at the prince's himself, moved in beside him with a whispered warning. "Your Highness. We need to go."

The security team converged on the fountain as the hooded man stood. "End Ivan!"

"Bomb!"

There were too many screams to make out the words that followed. The crowd split and ran like a tidal surge away from the fountain.

"Stop him!"

"Save the prince!"

Armed men in suits ran forward.

A sniper guarding the gathering from a turret high above the street raised his rifle and took aim at the insurgent. But he was too late.

"Save yourselves!" Prince Ivan warned. His bodyguards swarmed around him and shoved him to the stone steps behind the podium. The square erupted with light and the deafening roar of an explosion.

The prince's cheek scraped against stone as the black-haired man covered his body with his. His ears were stopped up by the concussive blast. But he heard the screams of his people, the stampede of running feet, gunfire, as if the violence was all happening far in the distance instead of a mere few yards beyond the podium.

He spotted blood on the steps a split second before something sharp and hot seared his skin, cutting through the invisible target on his back.

The prince's public rallying speech in the heart of Lukinburg's capital left him wounded. Landmarks had been damaged. People were injured, dead.

The dignitaries from Kansas City wouldn't be coming.

Chapter One

After the explosion in the palace square, the business-people and government officials Ivan Mostek needed to talk to in Kansas City had refused to travel to Lukinburg. They were concerned for their safety, and rightly so. The shrapnel scars on his back were still pink and tender from that attack.

But he wouldn't give up on the new government's vision to reform his country.

So, the prince had come to Kansas City. These negotiations were going to happen, no matter what a few leftovers from the old regime thought of him. They'd lost their power and weren't above using an assassination to get it back. Perhaps the threats he faced were coming from loyalists who believed the modernization of their country would irrevocably change it, and they'd lose their cultural identity. What they'd lose was any kind of standing as a first world country. Their economy was dying, and the old ways didn't feed his people.

Ivan Mostek, Crown Prince of Lukinburg, the symbolic leader of his country and heir to the throne, had no intention of giving power back to the thugs that had nearly ruined their country, nor did he intend to destroy any of the things that made Lukinburg so uniquely special. The plan was a good one. But he had to survive first. Survive this trip to the States. Survive until his coronation and hopefully live a long and healthy life afterward as the leader of Lukinburg.

The first step in that plan meant leaving his country and traveling to Kansas City for a week. The second step meant surrounding himself with people he trusted. That was proving more of a challenge than he'd expected since it seemed that no matter what security measures his team put into place, the threats kept coming. So, he'd put in a call to KCPD to ask for help from strangers. The local police had no ties to Lukinburg. He was counting on them to provide a layer of protection that couldn't be influenced by politics, fear of change or revenge.

Striding up the steps from his limousine, Ivan followed his chief of security, Filip Milevski, into the lobby of Fourth Precinct headquarters. His trusted adviser and good friend, Aleksandr Petrovic, followed right behind him, while another bodyguard, Danya Pavluk, brought up the rear. His third bodyguard and new driver, Eduard Nagy, would park the car and wait for them to finish their respective meetings.

After lining up their visitor badges, Filip, a tall, beefy man with graying sideburns, punched the button to call the elevator. "I will escort you to your meeting with Captain Hendricks. Then Danya and I will meet with the SWAT captain and senior patrol officer to coordinate security at your public appearances."

Ivan smoothed the knot of his tie and nodded. "Do not forget to have them set up extra officers outside the

Lukinburg embassy on Saturday. Your team can work with embassy security inside, but the ball will dramatically increase traffic and bring many wealthy and important local and state people to that part of town."

"I forget nothing," Filip huffed, as though it was an insult to remind him. The elevator doors opened, and he waited for the car to empty before leading them inside. "I do not understand why you could not stay at the hotel and let me handle the police department. This Joe Hendricks you are meeting with is not on my list of contacts." No, but Chief of Police Taylor had recommended the precinct captain when Ivan had called to ask for the secret favor. "I cannot control your safety when you surprise me with meetings that are not on your agenda."

Ah, yes. Filip loved his routines. If he had any idea what Ivan was planning behind his back, he'd be livid.

"I told you, this is personal. You do not need to be involved."

"But it is my responsibility—"

"I am inside a police station. I will be fine without you hovering over me." He grinned at Aleks, who was people watching the comings and goings of officers, detectives, visitors and staff through the lobby checkpoint and service counters. He flicked his friend's arm to get his attention. "You should have brought a camera," he teased.

Aleks's grin formed a bright crescent of white in his long black beard. "Did you see that plaque on the wall? They have created a memorial to a little girl—"

"Aleks…" Ivan urged his friend to join them. "Business first. Sightseeing later. You know we must—"

"Hold that elevator!"

Ivan's sentence trailed off and he instinctively

grabbed the door as a woman with a dirty, soot-streaked blond ponytail darted onto the elevator. She pulled in an equally grimy, handcuffed man by his upper arm and guided him to the corner farthest away from Ivan and his staff, ordering her captive to face the wall. Filip cursed under his breath as he and Danya quickly positioned themselves between Ivan and their guests and allowed the doors to close.

"Thanks." He saw the woman wore fingerless gloves when she pushed some flyaway strands of hair off her face. He also saw the badge hanging from a chain around her neck. Ivan's senses tingled with an alertness he had to hide. "Sorry. I didn't relish dragging this dirtbag up the stairs or waiting for the next elevator."

She wore a long, dusty man's coat over jeans and worn leather boots that were nearly as big as his own feet. Gloves? Coat? Boots?

In August?

No wonder there was a sheen of perspiration on her pink cheeks.

As intrigued by her apparent toughness as he was curious about her ratty, overheated appearance, he offered her a succinct nod. "We are happy to oblige the local constabulary."

Her prisoner glanced over his shoulder at Ivan. "What's that mean?"

"Quiet." The officer nodded toward the keypad and asked Filip to push the button for her. "Third floor, please."

"We should not share an elevator, Your High—"

"This is fine," Ivan insisted, reaching around his security chief to press the number three button himself. It was probably best not to advertise his real identity just yet. Not until all his security was in place. "We are here to make friends with the people of Kansas City, not make their lives more difficult."

"You talk funny," the handcuffed man slurred, laughing at their accents.

And he smelled funny. Dreadful, actually, as Ivan crinkled his nose up against the odors of urine, body odor and smoke filling the confined space. At least, he hoped it was the criminal and not the female officer escorting him who reeked of the streets. Ivan had been trained to keep such negative observations to himself and be a polite gentleman at all times. "English is not my first language."

"Your English is better than mine, pal."

"Dougie. Sorry about that, sir." The woman jerked on the handcuffs, warning her prisoner to be quiet again. Apparently, standing still and keeping his mouth shut was an ongoing battle for the twitchy bum. "I am already in a mood. Don't push it."

Even though the woman wasn't terribly chatty, Ivan noted that she was extremely observant. She marked their number and position on the elevator as it began its ascent. She sized up the flak vest and guns Filip and Danya wore beneath their suit jackets and pulled back the front of her coat to keep her gun within easy reach. Although he wanted to reassure the woman that they meant her no harm, backing up that claim would mean that he'd have to identify himself and his entourage. And Ivan wasn't ready to reveal anything when he had this much of an audience surrounding him.

His training in the Lukin military had made him observant, too. The woman had an ordinary face. She was of average height and indeterminate shape, thanks to the bulky coat she wore. In addition to a stylist, she needed a comb and a shower and a much more cooperative prisoner. Ivan curled his fingers into his palms, fighting back the urge to push Filip and Danya aside and assist her with the recalcitrant man who muttered and fidgeted instead of obeying her authority. Maybe a good twenty years older and hundred pounds heavier than her, the man seemed familiar with handcuffs and causing trouble. No wonder she'd been anxious to get him into a jail cell or interview room and off her hands.

He also noticed she had green eyes.

And lips. Ivan averted his gaze as if he'd uttered that ridiculous observation out loud. Of course, she had lips. But they had drawn his attention to the middle of her flushed face. Despite her determined lack of femininity, her lips were pink and asymmetrical, sleekly defined on top and decadently full on the bottom. She had a mouth that reminded him just how delightful it was to kiss a willing woman, and just how long he'd denied himself that pleasure.

"Y'all ain't cops, are ya?" Her prisoner twisted around again, ignoring her order to face the wall. "With your fancy suits and fancy accents. Damn foreigners."

"Douglas Freeland," she warned. "You be nice to these people."

"I ain't been nothin' but nice this morning. I got a sickness and you know it. You set me up." He called her a crude name that fisted Ivan's hands with the need to shut him up and make him apologize. He was embarrassed to see his bodyguards ignoring the verbal abuse and staring fixedly at the elevator doors as they slowed to a stop. "I ain't goin' back in."

The moment the doors slid open, the prisoner twisted

out of her grasp. In the next second, he spun around and butted his fat, bald head against her more delicate skull.

The urge to intervene jolted through Ivan's legs as she tumbled to the floor. But Filip and Danya pushed him against the railing, blocking him from the scuffle. "Protect the prince!"

Not that the officer apparently needed his or anyone's help. Before the man got both feet off the elevator, her legs shot out and she tripped him. Then she was on top of the guy with a feral yell as she smushed her attacker's face to the floor. Several other officers from the third floor had rushed to help, but they stopped in their tracks, backing up a step as she hauled the prisoner to his feet. The big man wasn't muttering anymore. She pushed him against the seam between the wall and the elevator, using him to prop the door open while she checked his cuffs and evened out her breathing.

Filip took Ivan by the arm to lead him off the elevator. But Ivan didn't need to be sandwiched between his bodyguards. The woman, despite the blow to the head, seemed to have the situation under control.

Still, he knew the toll hand-to-hand combat like that could take on a person. There would be bruises, and her head would be throbbing. He shrugged free of Filip's grip. "Are you all right, miss?"

"Officer. Officer Valentine." Her green eyes widened with a message that could be understood in any language. *Get off the damn elevator already and let me do my job.*

"Very well. Gentlemen." They all exited the elevator and headed to the sergeant's desk for directions to the captain's office.

With a nod to the officers who'd come to her aid, Officer Valentine pushed a long tendril of caramel-colored hair off her face and walked her prisoner through the maze of desks on the main floor. Her dialogue trailed off as they went their separate ways. "That was your big plan? Escape onto a floor filled with cops? Now I get to add a second assault charge..."

Relief that Officer Valentine was all right, as well as admiration at how she'd handled the situation herself, eased the tension inside him. Ivan wondered at the rush of adrenaline he felt ebbing from his system and chalked it up to jet lag finally catching up with him.

"THIS IS EVERYTHING on my schedule while I am here in Kansas City." Ivan forwarded the text from his chief of staff, Galina Honchar, to Captain Hendricks's phone. In turn, Joe Hendricks, the captain of the Fourth Precinct, copied the list of events and locations to his administrative assistant in the adjoining office and asked her to make a printout. "Occasionally, a meeting runs long or something unexpected comes up..."

"Last-minute changes could be handled by the liaison officer you're asking for," the captain finished. "She'll be able to keep me in loop, so I can have whatever assistance is needed on standby."

That was part of his plan, Ivan conceded. "That would be a benefit to your department." But he was asking for something more than a communications liaison with the local police.

After sending Filip and Danya off to their respective meetings, the only person from Lukinburg here with Ivan on the third floor was Aleksandr Petrovic. Last he'd seen, Aleks was cooling his heels in Captain Hendricks's outer office, chatting up the captain's administrative assistant. Even though the woman wore a wedding ring and was obviously pregnant, flirting and having a good time seemed to be hardwired into Aleks's DNA. He had survived the mines and poverty of Moravska, relying on hard work and sheer determination to leave his past behind him. His friend had been a city kid, raised in a modest neighborhood in St. Feodor, and had used that innate charm to impress the right people and negotiate one successful business deal after another. To look at them now, with their tailored suits and limousines, Ivan and Aleks seemed to be cut from the same cloth, but their personalities and backgrounds couldn't be more different. Still, Aleks was the one confidant the prince had trusted with the real goal of this meeting, and, if he wasn't too distracted by the woman out there, was keeping an eye out for when Milevski and the rest of the security team returned.

Ivan was learning that secrecy was practically impossible for royalty. But that secrecy was necessary. The crumpled note sitting like a fishing weight in his pocket warned him that keeping his secrets was a matter of life-and-death. "I told my security chief that I have reconnected with an old flame in the US from my military days, when we did joint operations with other countries. That is why I am making this request privately. They believe I am being discreet for romance's sake, not because I suspect a breach among the members of my entourage."

The black man with the weathered face and receding hairline nodded. "I can help you with your request to place an undercover operative inside your delegation for the duration of your visit. I've lined up a couple of candidates of the appropriate age for you to meet."

Ivan reminded him why he sought him out for assistance. "Finding a woman who served in the military is the only plausible way I could think of for me to have met an American and have had the time to develop a relationship with her. I worked with several American soldiers when I was in the military police."

"I haven't told them why they've been summoned to my office yet. I have to admit, this feels a bit like I'm playing matchmaker."

"I assure you, that is not the case, Captain." A tinge of awkwardness heated his skin. "I do not like that I have been forced into this situation. But I must choose a woman today, before I leave this building. My people must get used to seeing her with me. Masquerading as my...paramour...is the only way I can guarantee that we will have time alone to discuss who wants to kill me and devise strategy to unmask the traitor or traitors before they do me or anyone else harm. If I simply take on an American bodyguard, my security team will expect to be working together with that person. Since I do not know who I can trust, I require an ally who reports only to me, one who can convincingly play the role of consort to a prince, and whose qualities meet the needs of this very delicate investigation. I do not care what she looks like or if she fits some profile I would put on a dating site. She only needs to be good at her job."

"That's what I needed to hear." Hendricks pressed a sturdy index finger into the blotter on his desk, the gesture making Ivan think that warning finger would be pressed against his chest—royalty or not—if he dared to misuse one of Hendricks's officers. "If I hear that anything freaky happens to my officer while she's working with you, I promise I will bring the full force of this department down on your head."

"Understood. A good officer protects his troops. I respect that. And I will respect her."

Hendricks nodded. "Then let's do this, Your Highness."

Ignoring the urge to rub at the tension cording the back of his neck, Ivan nodded his appreciation. He was still getting used to answering to *prince* and *Your Highness*, although the proud posture and cautious, controlled movements that had been drilled into him during his stint in the military and on a UN coalition team in Bosnia served him well in conveying the air of authority he needed to project. The suit and tie he wore were better fitted and more expensive than the clothes he'd worn when he'd been a happy, anonymous commoner. He'd put on the hand-me-downs he'd worn growing up in the poor mountain village where his aunt and uncle had raised him if it meant he could go back to being an ordinary guy without the death threats and suspicions about the people closest to him churning inside his brain. He'd trade his penthouse suite for his old studio apartment in Moravska if it meant he'd no longer have the future of an entire country resting on his shoulders.

But those shoulders were broad and strong from the years he'd worked in the mines. The military had disciplined him, and a technology degree had given him a better life. He would do whatever was necessary to save the fledgling monarchy and put the discontents who would bring their country to its knees again out of business forever. Saving his own skin would be an added bonus.

He adjusted the glasses that pinched his nose and

looked across the desk into Joe Hendricks's golden-brown eyes. "You understand my need for secrecy?"

"I do." The man with the salt-and-pepper hair that receded into twin points atop his coffee-colored skin leaned back in his chair. "The fewer people who know about this charade, the better. Only you, me and the officer you select will know exactly what's going on. I'll serve as her undercover handler on this assignment." He rose from his chair and crossed to a set of blinds and opened them, revealing a bank of windows that overlooked a hallway and a beehive of desks and cubicle walls beyond that where uniformed officers, detectives, administrative staff and even a couple of criminals handcuffed to their chairs—including the lowlife who had attacked Officer Valentine—worked or waited. "If there's any chance the threat is legit, and one of those people—what did you call them?"

"They call themselves Lukin Loyalists. I call them the remnants of the mafia thugs who used to control our government. Lukin is a nickname we gave the citizens who were part of the underground resistance during World War II. These people are nothing like those brave souls."

"I thought I heard on the news a while back that the Loyalist situation had been resolved."

"So we thought." Ivan inhaled a deep breath and slowly released his frustration with the entire situation. "There are still some philosophical disagreements, but we've given them a voice in the new government. The minority whip in our Parliament is a Loyalist. He denounced the assassination attempt in the capital."

"There could be some fringe members of the party who feel their leadership has sold them out."

"Seven people died in that blast in St. Feodor, including a friend of mine. Whoever these people are, I take their threats seriously."

Hendricks agreed. "If one or more of these Loyalists are in Kansas City, planning an assassination attempt, then I want to know about it. I want to prevent any attack if possible and minimalize casualties—including you and my officer."

He pointed through the blinds to two female officers, one wearing a crisp blue uniform. She was engaged in an animated conversation with Aleks. Ivan grinned. Leave it to his friend to find someone new to practice his charms on. It was hard to remember a time when he'd been that carefree and able to stay squarely in a happy moment to enjoy it to the fullest.

The two of them looked very much alike, both with jet-black hair and blue eyes behind the glasses they each wore. Although Ivan stood half an inch taller, Aleks packed more muscle onto his frame. As the prince, he wore his hair cropped military short and kept his beard trimmed close to the angles of his jawline while his friend took his curly facial hair to a shaggy professor look. They'd done their requisite two-year stint in the army after university, where they'd met and become friends. After that, their paths had diverged—one remaining in the military, and the other going back to graduate school—until they'd come together again in service to the new government. They shared looks, history, pride in their country. And yet, the prince's world was vastly different from that of Aleksandr Petrovic. The orphan and the prince. The charmer and the disciplined soldier. Ivan's jaw clenched as his smile faded. Had he sentenced himself to a life of loneliness by answering the call of duty and giving himself over to the needs of his country and its people?

Ivan studied the female officer as she laughed at something Aleks said, and he felt a stab of envy at the normalcy of their interaction. But he reminded himself of the reason why he was here—to find a bodyguard he could trust without question, and an investigator who could help him identify the traitor in his inner circle. Knowing Filip Milevski and the rest of his security detail would be returning in the next fifteen to twenty minutes, Ivan rose, buttoned his jacket and joined Captain Hendricks at the window. He needed to evaluate the officers' suitability for the assignment before selecting his undercover partner.

The uniformed officer sat in one of the chairs lining the hallway, while Aleks stood beside her holding a paper cup of coffee. She touched her hair and ate up Aleks's attention. She was light, fun, perhaps not a strong enough presence to portray a convincing royal consort.

Meanwhile, the other woman, probably a detective, judging by her gray slacks and jacket, was plugged into her earbuds, and was scrolling through information on her phone as she paced the hallway outside the office's glass windows. Her expression remained stern as the uniformed officer caught her attention and tried to share the joke with her. The detective shook her head and continued her pacing. The woman's gravitas would certainly come through as they made their public appearances. She'd be a beauty if she smiled. But the tight lock of her mouth indicated a rigidity that might make it hard for her to adapt to the spontaneous opportunities for secret conversations he expected to arise as the investigation unfolded. And thus far, not much about being a prince was going according to any organized plan.

Captain Hendricks buried his hands in his pockets. "Either one of those women would make a fine liaison officer between you and KCPD."

They were both no doubt competent law enforcement officers, although neither type initially appealed to him. Not the way Officer Valentine's earthy vitality and tempting mouth had switched on his male radar. However, he wasn't here to meet the love of his life. If the woman could act her part as half of a convincing couple, then so could he. His life and the future of his country might depend on making the right choice here. A lightweight or a hard case. "They both have undercover experience?"

"Yes. Detective Wardyn is a few years past her last UC assignment, but she's a seasoned investigator. Officer Rangel is fairly new, but she has a higher marksmanship score."

Brains or brawn? He needed both.

"Then I suppose we should bring them in for a conversation. I don't want to reveal too much to either of them. The fewer people who know the specific details…"

And then a dusty ponytail and long black coat came into view as Officer Valentine shot up from her chair and circled her desk to point her finger in the face of the fat man who was mouthing off at her.

"Tell me more about her." Ivan nodded toward the argument that was not ending well for the handcuffed man. The grungy woman slapped a photograph on the desk in front of the man and forced him to look at it.

"Officer Valentine?" The captain chuckled at something Ivan failed to understand. "Looks like she's brought in a perp for processing."

Perp. Perpetrator. Ivan quickly translated the American slang and determined that Officer Valentine was a brave woman. The man she'd handcuffed made two of her, even with the heavy coat she wore. And yet she…

Ivan felt the hint of a smile relaxing the tight lines beside his mouth. "What about her? Does she have a military background? Earlier, she used a move on her prisoner that I learned during hand-to-hand combat training. Skills like that might be more useful than marksmanship when it comes to a protection detail."

"Carly Valentine? You think *she* can be your princess? Or, you know, personal bodyguard?" Hendricks didn't seem to be a man who was used to stuttering over his words, and he quickly shook off his surprise at Ivan's interest in the woman. "Valentine does a lot of UC work for us. She's a natural on the streets but—"

"Can she look professional when she is not in that costume?" Ivan paused for a moment, wondering if he should trust logic over what his instincts were telling him. "That *is* a costume, yes?"

"Let's hope so. You want to meet her?"

"Yes. There is something about her that seems like we could have worked together before. Under different circumstances. It might make our cover story more believable."

"It's your call." The captain crossed to his desk and picked up the phone to call his assistant. "Brooke? I need to see Carly Valentine in my office ASAP. And pull up her personnel file for me, please. Thanks."

Ivan was still at the window, watching as Carly Valentine answered the phone at her desk. Her shoulders sagged before she glanced back toward the captain's office. She spoke to the man sitting at the desk across from hers. After he nodded, she unlocked the perp from his chair and handed him off to the other officer, who led the prisoner out of sight down a long hallway.

Officer Valentine brushed off the sleeves of the oversize coat she wore, sending up a puff of gray dust in a cloud around her. The shake of her head told Ivan she was nervous about being summoned to the captain's office. She tried to tuck the loose waves back into her ponytail but stopped to inspect her hands. Another officer pointed to her face and Ivan could read the curse on her lips at the streak of soot her fingers had left there. She peeled off her fingerless gloves, quickly wiped her hands and face on a wad of tissues, and then steeled her shoulders before crossing to the captain's outer office. Her coat billowed out around her like the dusters cowboys wore in the American Western movies he loved to watch.

Joe Hendricks stood at his desk, reading information off the computer screen. "I've got Valentine's file here. She did have MP training in the National Guard. Looks like her stint with them ended earlier this year about the same time she earned her associate degree in criminal justice studies. She's been with the department four years. That's not as much experience as either of those officers in the hallway."

Didn't matter. "What does she do for you?"

"Right now, she's working an undercover assignment. She's attached to our human trafficking task force."

"Human trafficking? As in prostitution? Sex slavery?"

Hendricks nodded. "She's on the streets, identifying runaways and at-risk individuals."

Ivan turned back to the window. "And the man she brought in?"

"I'm not sure. But with Valentine, I'm guessing she caught him with his hands on the wrong person. She's a natural-born protector. Can't imagine what kind of fierce mama bear she'd make if she ever decides to have kids."

"Fierce mama bear?" She was in the hallway right outside the office now. Her gaze met and held his through the window. Her eyes were green like the mountain meadows of his homeland—and narrowed with suspicion.

"That's our Valentine."

She blinked, breaking the momentary connection between them. Oblivious to Aleks's curious interest as she walked past him and the other two female officers, she tossed her long ponytail down the center of her back and strode into the assistant's office.

Grimy. Plain. Fierce. Intriguing. Very good at playing her part.

A woman he just might have something in common with.

Chapter Two

"Hey, Brooke." Carly Valentine closed the door behind her and crossed the small office over to her friend's desk. Her pulse thrummed in her ears with more nerves than the adrenaline charge that had raised her heart rate when Dougie Freeland had whacked her in the temple with his big, bulbous head. "Can you give me a clue? What did I do?" She thumbed over her shoulder to the bull pen where the detectives and uniforms worked when they were in the office. "Did those guys in the elevator complain about me or my gruesome twin out there? I swear I didn't let Dougie touch them."

"You didn't do anything wrong." Brooke Kincaid looked up from her computer and smiled. The gesture was meant to reassure her, but that smile shifted into an apologetic frown, leaving Carly feeling anything but. "I'm still not sure what's going on, other than I've pulled service records and promised that anything I see or hear can't leave this office. By the way, are you okay?"

"Nothing that an ibuprofen won't cure. I've been hurt worse wrestling with Frank and Jesse." Although, unlike the man she'd brought in for booking, her older brothers hadn't meant her any real harm. They'd simply been picking on her for getting in their space or being the annoying little sister who'd done her best to keep them fed and dressed in clean clothes after their mother had died. Carly nodded toward the hallway where she'd passed the other two female officers and the geeky-looking guy who'd been flirting with Emily Rangel. "Does it have something to do with them? Am I getting transferred? A reprimand in my file?"

"I don't think it's anything bad." Brooke stood, resting a hand on her pregnant belly as she circled the desk to get close enough to whisper. "The guy in there with Joe is an honest to gosh prince from a little European country called Lukinburg."

"Lukinburg?"

"I looked it up. There's a delegation here from his country negotiating trade agreements. They're even hosting a ball, a fund-raiser for scientific research, while they're here in the US."

"A ball? Like dancing and sparkly gowns? Men in tuxedos?"

"The same."

"What's he doing here at the precinct?"

Brooke crinkled up her nose and sat back on the edge of her desk before answering. "Everything's all hush-hush. The prince called early this morning and asked to see Captain Hendricks as soon as I could fit him into the schedule. You should have seen it when he arrived—he has bodyguards."

"I met them in the elevator. That explains why they said, 'Save the prince' when Dougie went wacko on me."

"He called me *madam* and he bowed when he introduced himself—Ivan Mostek. He's no Atticus..." Brooke smiled, referring to her husband, the detective who oversaw the task force Carly was assigned to. "But he's hot. He's not soft underneath that suit and those manners. I think he could take care of himself if he had to."

Hearing Brooke refer to anyone besides her husband as hot was something new. Bowing and madam-ing certainly didn't sound like the visitors they usually got around here, either. Carly's heart rate wasn't slowing down. "He runs his own country? And he wants to see me?"

She glanced down at her dirty clothes and ruined steel-toed boots that she'd borrowed from her older brother Frank, who ran a construction business. It was already ninety degrees at lunchtime, and she'd been out most of the morning working her contacts. Dougie had taken exception to her interfering with his gross habit of flashing and had peed on her. The fact that there had been so much traffic through the old burned-out Morton & Sons Tile Works warehouse near the Missouri River had been reason enough to follow Freeland inside. But when she found him strutting his wares with a young prostitute she was certain was underage, Carly had broken her cover and placed him under arrest. Tackling him in a pile of charred debris from the fire and rolling in dust and ash that had been there for four years had turned her disguise from homeless to filthy.

She held up her hands, admitting the obvious. "I'm hardly looking my best."

"Or smelling it." The phone buzzed on Brooke's desk and she pushed to her feet. "That's Joe. He said there's a time crunch on whatever Prince Ivan needs. You'd better get in there." Brooke's nose crinkled up again and she clapped her fingers over her mouth, looking as if she might be sick. "You're a little ripe."

Carly instinctively retreated a step. "Sorry about that. Dougie didn't come quietly when I arrested him."

"The baby seems to make me really sensitive to smells right now." She turned her head to the side to inhale a deep breath, then reached out to Carly. "Better let me take your coat, at least."

Nodding her thanks, Carly quickly shed her brother Jesse's old duster coat from his cowboy days. That phase had lasted about two months, once he realized that a real working cowboy got a lot dirtier and smelled a lot worse than the ones he'd seen in the movies. Not all that different than what she was smelling like right now. She didn't have to be pregnant to know how Dougie's crude attempt to scare her off had left its mark on her.

She plucked the white T-shirt she wore away from skin that was damp with perspiration and tucked it beneath the belt and holster on her jeans with the holes in the knees. Then she adjusted the chain that held her badge around her neck as if it was a piece of jewelry that could dress up her poor girl from the streets look and gave Brooke a hopeful smile. "I don't look too scary?"

"It'll have to do."

Brooke turned her toward the captain's office just as Joe Hendricks opened the connecting door with an impatient whoosh of air. "Valentine. Good. You're here." He shifted his attention to Brooke while Carly sidled past him into his office. "We're not to be disturbed. Not even if his men call."

"Yes, sir."

The door closed behind her and Carly stopped in her tracks as the man with coal-black hair that she'd seen through the windows rose to greet her. The tailoring of his suit emphasized the width of his shoulders and tapered waist, making him appear taller, though she guessed he was about six feet in height. He practically clicked his heels together and offered her a curt nod. *Bowing.* Wow. Had any man ever been so formal about meeting her before? "Officer Valentine. I am pleased to meet you."

"Hey." Was she supposed to say something more? Shake his hand? No. Not in the shape she was currently in. "Nice to meet you."

The captain gestured to one of the two guest chairs while he circled around to his side of the desk. "Take a seat, Valentine."

With a nod, Carly tore her gaze from their guest and perched on the edge of her chair. Partly because it helped her sit up straight and gave her a stronger posture, and partly because she was painfully self-conscious about her soiled clothes leaving a stain on the beige fabric. "Will this take long, sir? I promised Gina Cutler that I'd cover her citizen self-defense training class after work, so she and Mike can go to birthing class." It seemed that several of her friends were well beyond her in the get-married-and-start-a-family department. "I'd like to grab a shower before then. I think the class would like me to, as well."

Her attempt at humor fell on deaf ears. "This will take as long as it needs to." The captain loosened the tie that cinched his collar and gestured to the man seated beside her. "I'd like to introduce you to His Royal Highness, Prince Ivan Mostek of Lukinburg."

Carly pushed to her feet. "Wait. Should I have curtsied?" She skimmed her hands over the hips of her frayed jeans and frowned at the stains on her boots. "I'm so sorry. I would have changed into my uniform if I'd known I was meeting a dignitary. I just came in off an undercover assignment. I had to blend in with the homeless community in No-Man's Land. I…" She threw her hands up, helpless to deny the truth. "I'm dirty and I stink."

The prince stood when she had risen from her chair. With a perfectly straight face, he said, "All I smell is the smoke from a fire. I trust you were not hurt."

"Aren't you a gentleman?" A nervous laugh snorted through her nose, and embarrassment warmed her face. "Of course, you're a gentleman. You're a prince. I'll be okay. I mean, my pride is shot to…" Carly bit down on that word and the heat in her skin intensified. She was pretty sure that one didn't curse in front of royalty. "I'll have a few bruises, but nothing serious. Thanks for asking." She turned to the captain, silently begging for backup. "Sir, tell me to shut up."

Now the captain chuckled. Great. Way to impress the boss and visiting royalty.

"At ease, Valentine," Hendricks ordered. As he had before, the prince waited for her to sit before he took his seat. She didn't deserve that kind of chivalry with the impression she was making, but his patience with her had a surprisingly calming effect on her nerves, enabling her to concentrate more on what the captain was saying rather than the humiliation she was feeling. "Lukinburg's capital city, St. Feodor, is the sister city of Kansas City. Prince Ivan and his delegation are here for a week to negotiate trade agreements, do a cultural exchange with the Nelson-Atkins Art Museum, meet with local and state officials, host a charity ball at their embassy—you get the idea."

"Uh-huh. What does that have to do with me?"

"The prince has a proposition for you."

Carly turned her attention to the man beside her. Good grief, his eyes were as blue as she'd imagined when she glimpsed them through the office window a few minutes earlier. The lenses in his glasses didn't dim their intensity one bit. Whatever this guy had in mind, it wouldn't be the worst offer she'd ever gotten from a man. Brooke was right, Ivan Mostek was attractive in a polished, faintly arrogant sort of way. In fact, if she met him in a bar, she'd be…lusting after him from afar because she had no clue how to come on to a guy, especially one who looked like he'd stepped out of the self-made CEO section of *Forbes* magazine and was way out of her league. But she'd definitely enjoy her beer and appreciate the scenery from a distance. Still, she knew Captain Hendricks wasn't setting her up on a date. She broke the connection with those penetrating blue eyes and looked to her captain. "What sort of proposition?"

"Captain, if I may?" The prince leaned onto the arm of his chair, close enough to catch a whiff of a scent that was much more pleasant than her own. Something clean, all business, masculine. "Due to instability in my country, as we transfer from a corrupt dictatorship to a democratic society, I am required to step up security. Not every Lukinburger is eager to support the new government."

Ivan articulated every word and avoided contractions. He'd practiced that delivery, so his English would be clearly understood. His tone was less guttural than German, more articulate than Russian, deep in pitch and seductive like fancy poetry. She wondered what that voice sounded like in his native language, whatever language a Lukinburger spoke. Lukinburger? The urge to laugh tickled her thoughts. That made her think of a hamburger. And this guy was nothing but prime steak.

"You find something amusing, Miss Valentine?"

That tone was a little less mesmerizing and a little more *His Imperial Majesty*, and she shook off the inappropriate detour of her thoughts. "Uh, no. No, sir. But I saw your geeky science guy and bodyguards on the elevator. That's not security enough?"

"Geeky science guy?" He repeated the phrase, a question in his eyes. Right. Language barrier.

"You know, nerdy? Thick glasses? Needs a haircut? I bet if he trimmed that mountain man beard and got the bangs out of his eyes, he'd clean up as good as you."

"I assure you he has showered."

He hadn't understood the slang she'd used. "Clean up as in he'd be attractive if he, you know, took care of himself a little more. Like you." The blue eyes narrowed. Great. She'd just admitted she thought the prince was attractive. Or had she just insulted his friend? "No offense. Clearly, the guy's a charmer. Making a woman laugh is a good thing." Heat crept into her cheeks again. "I'm rambling again. I'm a little self-conscious right now. I don't know the etiquette…am I allowed to have a regular conversation with you?"

"No matter the etiquette, it has not stopped you yet."

Her blush intensified. "Sorry."

"Do not apologize. You are very observant, Officer Valentine. A good soldier should be. I understand that you served in the military before joining the police force?"

"That's right. Army National Guard. That's how I paid my way through school."

"I, too, served in the army of my country. I admire that sense of duty." His compliment altered the heat she felt into a bud of self-confidence. As he went on, steering the conversation toward work further distracted her from her embarrassment. "The man in the hallway is my friend, Aleksandr Petrovic. He is a trusted adviser to me. He has, as you Americans say, a nose for business."

"You mean a head for business? It's a nose for news, a head for business," she pointed out. When his eyes narrowed, she pressed her fingers against her lips and apologized, "I'm sorry. I shouldn't interrupt."

"No. I must use your language correctly." His fingers spanned her wrist, pulling her hand away from her mouth. The light touch sent tendrils of warmth skittering beneath her skin before he released her. She was just as sensitive to the calluses on his manicured fingers, and surprising strength of his hand that she'd associate more with a working man like her father and brothers than a fairy-tale prince. But the charm was certainly there as he bowed his head to her again. "Thank you for the correction."

"You're welcome. You were saying?" Man, was she blowing it in the public relations department. "Your Highness?"

"Ivan will do fine when we are in private like this."

She was supposed to call a prince by his first name? In what universe? Had she taken a harder hit to the head from Dougie than she realized?

"Just as with our embassies in Washington and now Kansas City, we are coordinating with the Department of State and local law enforcement to ensure that our visit here is a safe one—both for ourselves and for your people. Your captain is indulging a personal request while my chief of royal security and his team are meeting with others in your department."

"That makes sense." Carly turned to Captain Hendricks again. "Are you looking for volunteers to work extra duty shifts?"

"Not exactly."

"Then what? Why the private meeting?"

Prince Ivan touched the arm of her chair to recapture her attention. "I need a personal bodyguard. An American who can assist with my understanding of local idioms, someone who knows the city and can provide security specifically for me while I am here."

"You mean a liaison officer between your men and KCPD?"

The men exchanged a look. This time she bit down on the urge to keep talking and waited for one of them to explain why she was here.

Captain Hendricks steepled his fingers together on top of his desk. "The prince believes there is someone inside his delegation who is feeding intel to the dissidents who tried to kill him in Lukinburg. He doesn't know who it is. He's not sure who he can trust."

Carly nodded as understanding dawned. "You're looking for an outsider. Someone who isn't a part of your inner circle." The captain and the prince were looking for a cop who could convincingly portray a member of his security team. Maybe a reporter covering his visit. Or even waitstaff or a maid at their hotel. "You want me to sniff around, see if I can find out anything. I can probably get in and out of your functions without drawing any attention to myself. I'm pretty good at blending in."

"You misunderstand. I want you to be my escort at those functions."

Carly realized her jaw was hanging open, and quickly snapped it shut. "What?"

"His girlfriend," the captain clarified. "He's looking for a female police officer who can be his date at public events. The cover story is that he has an old friend who works at KCPD, someone he met during a military training exercise, and a romance blossomed. His trip to the States has reunited you. She'll provide a level of security no one will question. Someone who can be seen with him, or even stay the night in his hotel room without anyone questioning why you're there."

"Undercover girlfriend? Stay the night?" She snorted a laugh when she heard what the captain was proposing. Then she saw the look in his dark eyes and stopped abruptly. "You're serious? No. No, sir. Do you see what I'm wearing? Do you see how I look?" She pointed to the bull pen. "I'm in the middle of another case. Emily or Detective Wardyn or any other number of female officers would be a better candidate for that kind of assignment than I would."

"Valentine—there were two attempts on the prince's life in Lukinburg."

"The last one was three months ago," the prince added. "I have fresh scars from that explosion. Seven people, including a member of the Royal Guard and the bomber himself were killed that day. I felt that coming to Kansas City would ensure the safety of my delegation, and of your people. By distancing myself from the threat."

Scars? Seven dead? Her panic ebbed at the sobering news. "They tried to kill you?"

"Twice. The bullet missed. The bomb did not."

"And the threat followed you here to the US."

"I believe so." He pulled a note from his pocket and handed it to her.

"You dusted this for prints?"

"There are none," Ivan answered. "At least, not according to my chief of security, Filip Milevski."

"One of the guys you're not sure you can trust?"

"It appeared in my attaché case on the plane during the flight. I do not recall seeing it there when I left St. Feodor."

With a nod from both the prince and Captain Hendricks, Carly unfolded the typewritten note.

Prince Ivan. The false prince.

We won't let you sell our country to the Americans.

We will stop you. Dead.

Lukin Loyalists will rule.

Carly let out a low whistle. "Does Homeland Security know about this? The terrorists may be yours, but they're on our soil." She folded the note and handed it back to the prince. "No offense, pal, but you need to go home."

"Valentine—" the captain chided.

The prince waved off his defense and leaned toward her again. "It is all right, Joe. I appreciate her frankness. Miss Valentine—I cannot tell you for certain that the threats are politically motivated. Perhaps they come from criminals seeking revenge for what the new government has taken from them. It could even be something personal I do not yet understand."

"Personal?"

"Perhaps. This is why I need your help. Whoever is behind this will try again. I want to stop him before any of your people get hurt."

"Prevent collateral damage."

"These trade negotiations must happen to ensure the economic success of my country. I need a strong Kansas City police officer, one who knows undercover work. I need a woman to fulfill this role, one who can handle herself as I saw you handle that criminal out there. I need someone I can trust, who is not influenced by the crown, someone who is there to watch *me* and help *me*. Lukinburg's security contingent are trained Special Forces soldiers. If one of them is against me…" He sat back, lifting his shoulders in a weary sigh. "I would like to have an ally in my corner. I would like it to be you."

She paused a moment to consider what these men were asking of her. "I won't fit in with royalty. I'm working class right down to my dad's plumber's truck. I don't even own a dress."

"We'll get you the right clothes, the right hairstyle, to play the role we need you to. You'd be working straight through the week he's here in Missouri. We'll comp you the time, give you a vacation once the assignment is done."

Prince Ivan nodded. "I will pay for all of these expenses. You will keep anything I purchase for you as a thank-you gift."

"Dressing me up won't make me a lady."

Hendricks rolled his chair back, looking as if this meeting was over and the decision had been made. "You'd be protecting Kansas City by preventing anything from happening to him. You can do this."

"Are you ordering me to?"

"Do I need to make it an order?"

"No, sir. I took an oath to serve and protect my city. That includes its visitors." She stood when the captain did. She was okay with the cop part, investigating and protecting, and with keeping a secret. But the rest of this assignment? She only hoped these men understood what kind of magic it would take to turn her into a woman who would date a prince. "When do I start?"

His Royal Blue Eyes rose and buttoned his jacket. "I need you to start the job now. Right here. Before my people return to the captain's office. I worked as military police when I was in the army, so it is plausible that we are acquainted."

"How long ago did we allegedly meet?" She'd better start prepping for this part if she was to have any chance of pulling it off.

"Two? Three years ago?"

Carly nodded. "I was deployed to Bosnia two years ago. Guarded the base near Tuzla."

"I took part in a training exercise in Sarajevo."

She recognized the city southwest of the base where she'd been stationed. "Then it's believable that we could have met. If the dates coincide."

Captain Hendricks circled his desk. "I'll prep your cover file to make sure they do, in case anyone runs a background check."

Carly inhaled a deep breath. "Then I guess we're doing this."

The prince crossed to the door leading into Brooke's office. "My first public appearance is tomorrow. I am in meetings throughout the day, but I will have lunch with you to go over the information I have on these threats in more detail, and to discuss the protocols my countrymen would expect from a woman I am with. That will give you until tomorrow morning to get whatever you need to look the part. Aleks will set up an account you may use to buy anything you need."

At least she didn't snort this time when she laughed. "I'm gonna need more than a day to make that kind of transformation."

"Make it work, Valentine." Captain Hendricks was done with any more excuses. "You'll be reporting directly to me."

"I hope you don't live to regret this, sir."

"I hope I don't, either."

When she opened the door, Brooke was pouring coffee for the armed men from the elevator. A glimpse of a wire curling beneath their collars reminded her that this was Ivan's security contingent.

"Your Highness." The man with slicked-back dark hair striped by silver sideburns stepped forward. "Coordination with the local police, providing traffic clearance and venue security is in place. They have your schedule and have assured me they have the manpower to provide the backup my team and embassy security will need. I will coordinate the joint agency security team, of course."

"Of course." Ivan laced his fingers through hers, and Carly startled at the unexpected touch. He pulled her up beside him, ashes, grime, stink and all. He hadn't been kidding. The charade was starting right now. "I want to introduce you to my good friend. Miss Carly Valentine. My valued chief of security, Filip Milevski."

Um, uh… *Think, Carly!* Not homeless, not hooker, not task force cop. *Girlfriend.* She summoned a smile. "Hi."

Brilliant. Convincing. Not.

The security chief's dark eyes bored through her with a different sort of intensity than the electricity that charged Ivan's blue eyes. Yep. That was less of a *nice to meet you* and more of a *what the hell?* expression on his clean-shaven face. "This is the woman from the elevator. Why did you not acknowledge her at that time if she is your friend?"

"She was working," Ivan explained, spewing out lies as if they were second nature to him. "Besides, it has been so long since I last saw her—her hair is much longer now and we are both older—I was not sure it was her."

Carly could play the lying game, too. "And I wasn't— I'm not—exactly looking my best. I was a little embarrassed for him to see me like this."

"Nonsense, *дорогой*. You know I love to see a woman in action." What did he say? Huh? Was she going to have to learn a new language for this assignment? Learning to be a proper lady would be hard enough.

Filip Milevski didn't bother to mask his disapproval of her—although whether it was the idea of his boss having a girlfriend or her, in particular, he disliked— and he acknowledged her with a nod and dismissed her at the same time. "I contacted Eduard. Our car is waiting for us out front to take us to the embassy to meet Ambassador Poveda. The rest of the delegation has gone on to the hotel. Galina is discussing protocol with the hotel staff. She will meet us at the embassy."

Ivan's grip tightened around hers, and she got the idea that Milevski's reaction hadn't pleased him. "I will finish introductions first, as you will be seeing more of Miss Valentine throughout the week." He gestured to the sour-faced man with the reddish-brown buzz cut and blotchy skin. "Danya Pavluk. He has worked palace security for years. The Eduard whom Filip mentioned is Eduard Nagy, another bodyguard, specifically, my driver. You will meet him later."

"I look forward to it."

Danya Pavluk looked like making polite conversation pained him. All he said was, "Madam."

"How do you do?"

Danya drank his coffee. Apparently, that conversation was over.

Ivan squeezed her hand again, and she was reminded of the strength and heat of even that casual, deceptively possessive touch. He called to his friend in the hallway. "Aleks, are you ready to leave?"

The nerdy numbers guy said his goodbye to Officer Rangel and came to the doorway. Without waiting for an introduction, he crossed the room to take Carly's free hand. He kissed her knuckles before stepping back and straightening his glasses on the bridge of his nose. "I am Aleksandr Petrovic. It is my pleasure to meet you."

She couldn't help but smile at the way his natural geekiness softened his effusive charm. "Carly Valentine." He looked like a shaggier, softer version of Ivan. His nose was straighter, his shoulders slightly less imposing. And so far, he seemed to be the friendliest Lukinburger she'd met. "The pleasure is mine."

So these were some of the suspects Ivan thought might betray him to the Lukin Loyalists who wanted to kill him. She'd need to run background checks and spend some time observing and conversing with all the delegation members to get a better read on who was trustworthy and who hated the prince enough to send a death threat.

She made a mental note to make sure she carried a gun or Taser with her at all times. The security men were armed. Pavluk was built like a tank, and though Milevski was older and had more paunch, she suspected he would be equally hard to take down if she had to protect the prince from one of them. And geek didn't necessarily mean defenseless, so she couldn't count Aleks out as a threat, either.

But investigating would have to wait. Sizing up her odds in a physical altercation slipped to the back of her mind, too, when Ivan moved to stand in front of her. With his back to the others, his blue eyes locked on to hers, sending a silent message of gratitude for her alone. Or no, that was a warning. Warning her about what?

Her eyes widened as he dipped his face toward hers and kissed her. Not some fake air-kiss or polite European cheek-to-cheek greeting, either. His firm mouth pressed against the seam of her lips, warmed the spot with moist heat, lingered. His beard and mustache tickled, and she was curious enough about the texture of the dark spiky silk teasing the skin around her mouth that she lifted her free hand to stroke her fingertips across his jaw. The lines of his face were strong, unyielding. She discovered the firm ridge of a scar hidden near his ear when she stroked against the grain of his beard. From his time in the army? A previous attempt on his life?

A blush of feminine interest in his controlled, masculine touch heated her skin as much as self-conscious embarrassment had warmed it earlier. Every instinct inside her wanted to push her mouth more fully against his. She wanted to part her lips and feel that ticklish heat on the tender skin inside. The kiss was easily the most potent she'd ever received, certainly the most unexpected. Ivan's touch was mesmerizing, magical... *Fake, Valentine! The kiss is fake.*

A pair of invisible fingers snapped beside her ear, waking her from the momentary spell she'd been under. She quickly curled her inquisitive fingers into the palm of her hand and stepped back. She needed a shower and some nice clothes and a seriously intense lesson in royal etiquette before anyone would believe the prince's interest in her was real.

"I will see you tomorrow," he promised.

"Right. Oh." Before he turned, she pulled a card from the wallet behind her badge and tucked it into his jacket pocket. "That has all my numbers on it. If you need to call."

He laid his hand over his heart as if she'd given him a treasure. He looked to Brooke, who stood with one hand curved around her belly, the other clutching the back of her chair, as if she was too shocked by what she'd just seen to stand on her own. Ivan bowed his head. "Mrs. Kincaid. Thank you for your hospitality—and your discretion."

Brooke cleared her throat before she spoke. "Of course, sir. My pleasure."

"Captain Hendricks," he acknowledged. Then Ivan bowed to Carly. "I look forward to our next meeting, *дорогой.*"

There it was again. The foreign word rhymed with *the frog boy.* Only it sounded secretive, sensual, anything but insulting, in his deep, accented voice. She wished she had anything half as clever to say. "Me, too."

Ivan and his entourage left, closing the door behind them and heading past a dozen curious glances from the main room to the elevators before Carly released the breath she'd been holding and turned to Brooke. "*Dorogoy*. What's that?"

Brooke typed the word into her computer and pulled up a translation program. "Darling. Sweetheart. It's an endearment."

An endearment. She should have guessed as much simply from the tone of his voice. Oh, he was good at this. Carly seriously needed to step up her game if they had any chance of making this undercover mission work. She also had to remember that the charm and kisses would be fake. She was no fairy-tale princess, and he wasn't really her prince. But he was just shy enough of handsome to make him really interesting to look at. He treated her like a lady, even when she reeked of the streets. And he needed her. It was a potent combination guaranteed to turn her head.

Right then and there she sent her heart a warning that she couldn't have real feelings for Prince Ivan Mostek of Lukinburg. This was a job.

Joe Hendricks's gruff voice sent the same message. "Valentine, you're done for the day. Process your perp and get out of here. Brooke? We need to arrange a leave of absence for Carly. Dismiss Rangel and Wardyn and meet me in my office."

"Yes, sir."

He went back into his office and Brooke grabbed a notepad and pen from her desk. She handed Carly her coat and stood there, searching for the right thing to say. "You're going to explain this to me?"

Of course, she was. Just as soon as she figured out

what to say. "Ivan and I go way back. To my army days. I didn't put it all together when you said Lukinburg earlier. I had no idea he was in town. In the country, even." Rambling was never a convincing way to establish a solid cover story. She was supposed to be a better liar than this. "Meeting him…again…was definitely a surprise."

Brooke nodded, still looking confused. "For all of us."

She hated lying to her friend. Not that she didn't trust Brooke completely. But orders were orders. The truth couldn't leave Hendricks's office. Still, she needed a friend who had some relationship experience right about now. "Do you have a place you go to get manis and pedis?"

"Sure. I can get you the number."

"And where exactly does one purchase a ball gown?"

Brooke frowned as if she'd spoken gibberish. "Why?"

"Apparently, for the next week… I'm dating a prince."

Chapter Three

Carly folded her cotton socks down over the tops of the worn leather boots she'd just tied off. She was happy to be in shoes that fit again, happy to be in a tank top and cutoffs instead of a coat that was way too hot for August, happy to be showered and clean and back in the comfort of the home she shared with her father.

Her room, bathroom and the laundry room were down in the basement, while her dad lived on the second floor where her two older brothers had stayed before leaving home to get their own places. Carly didn't mind the low ceilings and cold concrete beneath the carpeted floor. She had enough windows to bring in the summer sunlight, and walls thick enough to give her privacy and quiet from when her brothers and their friends stopped by for a visit. Plus, the freedom to decorate everything down here as she wanted—from the antique oak furniture to the turquoise paint on the walls to the bookshelves crammed with cookbooks, travelogues, romances and fantasy novels that had entertained her for countless hours and were too dear to part with— allowed her to create her own haven from the dangers and stress of her job and the loneliness of her misfit life.

She crossed to the oval mirror above the dresser

and pulled a comb through her hair, plaiting the damp waves into a loose braid and securing it with a band. She dabbed some lip balm on her mouth and hurried up the stairs, anxious to get to the kitchen to start dinner before her dad discovered the cherry pie she'd put in the oven. Carly and her father, whom she'd been named after, shared a love of sports, books and sweet things. But while Carly included regular exercise in her daily routine to counteract those sugar indulgences, Carl Valentine was more of an armchair athlete as the back issues he'd struggled with since a work accident some time ago affected him more and more with each passing year. If he got to the pie first, he'd fill up on that and skip dinner. It was a nice compliment to her baking abilities, but hardly the healthy diet she wanted for a man who needed to watch his weight.

Besides, she deserved a piece of that pie and a scoop of ice cream herself after a very long, very weird, very unsettling day.

"Dad? Did you get the grill started?" She hurried through the living room into the kitchen, stopping to pull a pair of hot mitts from a drawer as the timer went off on the oven. "Dad?"

She heard a high-pitched whir of machinery coming from the backyard and paused, cradling the hot plate in her hands. Was that a power saw? That meant company. The odds of getting a slice of cherry pie after dinner just diminished.

The back door leading onto the deck smacked shut as she set the pie on the cooling rack. "Hey, Carly Barley."

With a mock groan, she tilted her face to the muscular man with the wheat-colored crew cut. Her big brother. "Frank. What are you doing here?"

"I had some free time. Thought I'd come over and make those repairs on the deck that Dad's been whining about all summer. He's out back watching the charcoal, making sure we don't burn down the house."

Carly eyed the sawdust sprinkled across his forearms, sticking to the perspiration there. When he reached for the piping hot dish, she nudged him back onto the rug in front of the door, ordering him to brush himself off and wash his hands before he touched any of her food. "Invited yourself to dinner, did you?" She opened the refrigerator to pull out a five-pound package of thawed hamburger and an armload of veggies and condiments.

"Invited myself to find out what's going on with you." When she set everything on the counter beside the stove, Frank was leaning his hip against the lower cabinets, drying his hands. He tucked the towel around the handle of the oven door before crossing his thick arms in front of the Valentine Construction T-shirt he wore. "Are you still available to play on our coed softball team this Saturday? We need you at second base."

Was she free this weekend? She hadn't been informed of Prince Ivan's schedule yet. Was she supposed to forgo her normal life, as well as her regular work hours, to be available for his protection detail 24/7? She was guessing a community league softball game wasn't on his itinerary. She opened the pantry to pull out the spices she needed. "I don't know. I'll have to get back to you."

"I knew it. There *is* a guy." Frank pounded his fist on the counter. "Damn it, I just lost a bet."

"What are you talking about? What bet?"

"Jesse texted that some fancy dude came by the precinct offices to see you." Jesse would be her other big brother, a jack-of-all-trades with an ear for secrets and a mouth that often got him into trouble. His current job as a bartender at the Shamrock Bar, an establishment frequented by several of her colleagues, put him in the perfect place to fine-tune those gossiping skills. "Some officers were in the bar after their shift, talking about this guy. They say he kissed you in front of everybody. I bet ten bucks Jesse was makin' up a story."

"You bet against me?" Embarrassed that her own brother didn't believe in her feminine appeal, she channeled her frustrated anger into the onion she was chopping. "You don't think a 'fancy dude' would want to kiss me?"

"I didn't think any guy would…" He seemed to suddenly realize that the woman glaring at him held a sharp knife in her hand. He wisely backed off a step. "You know how Jesse's always… I mean, the fact that some guy is hittin' on you at all…" His cheeks flushed brick red above the golden scruff on his square jaw. "Jesse also said you were cooking dinner tonight. That you called him to bring beer for the sauce. I've never eaten anyone's food better than yours. That's why I'm here. To eat."

"Pretty weak save, Frank." She split the onion between a saucepan and a sheet tray before pushing him aside to wash her hands. "Now tell me again why you can't keep a girlfriend?"

"I'm sorry." He followed her to the bag of potatoes and back to her cutting board, still trying to make amends for his jab at her ego. She came by her questionable social skills honestly. Although, whether a lack of tact was imprinted in the Valentine DNA, or a by-product of being raised in a motherless household, it was a mystery for the ages. "Do you need me to check this guy out? He's not messin' with you, is he? Those cops said they could tell he had money. He had guys opening doors for him. Drove off in a limo. Guys like that think they can throw around some cash, and girls will—"

"Stop before you stick that big foot of yours any farther into your mouth." Carly didn't consider herself a diminutive woman, but next to Frank, she was downright delicate. That had never stopped her from standing up to him, though. "One, I am a woman, not a girl. I can kiss whoever I damn well please. And two, why is it so far-fetched that a man might like me?"

Despite the square jaw and workingman's build, Frank could still pull off that sweet little boy expression that had gotten her to do more than her fair share of chores growing up and made her forgive him just about anything. "I love you, sis."

Carly shooed him out the back door. "Get out of my kitchen. Make sure there are no power tools on the picnic table and the deck doesn't collapse by the time dinner is ready. And try to have a little more faith in me, okay?"

Then maybe she'd have a little more faith in herself that she could pull off this assignment.

IVAN STEPPED OUT of the limousine onto the sidewalk. He buttoned his jacket and straightened his tie before sliding his hand into the pocket of his slacks, burning his fingers against the latest gift that had been left for him in his hotel suite. Unlike the flowers, gift baskets and bottles of wine, this one had no color, no wrapping, no welcoming message. It had no words at all on it. Just a set of numbers scrawled across an old black-and-white photograph.

Another death threat.

Carly needed to see it. Someone he trusted needed to know the danger he was facing—the danger a lot of innocent people might be facing if he couldn't unmask who was behind this terror campaign. Who wanted the Prince of Lukinburg dead?

A startled gasp tore him from his thoughts. He took a deep breath that expanded his chest. He nodded to an elderly woman with hair that was as curly and white as the small dog she held by its leash. "Madam."

With her eyes wide and the poodle dancing back and forth across the sidewalk, she eyed him and the black car behind him. "Are you a movie star?" With a squeak of excitement that made the dog yip at her feet, she pressed her hand to her chest. "Did Carl win one of those lottery giveaways?"

He arched an eyebrow at the question he did not understand and smiled. "I am here for Miss Valentine."

Other car doors opened and shut as advisers and security gathered around him. "For Carly? All of you?" The woman scooped the dog up into her arms and stepped closer, dropping her voice to a whisper. "Is this one of those television shows where you pull a prank on somebody? Am I on TV?"

"Why? Have you seen any cameras?" Aleks teased, climbing out of the limousine behind him. Like Ivan, his gaze swept the neighboring houses. Just a normal evening in American suburbia, it seemed. But while Ivan's gaze continued to study their surroundings, Aleks straightened his tie and grinned at the older woman. "How do I look?"

Ivan allowed them their laughter before he made proper introductions. "I am Prince Ivan of Lukinburg."

Her eyes widened with recognition. "I saw you on the news, getting off your plane at KCI."

"We are visiting your beautiful city." He extended his hand. "And you are…?"

"Gretchen Pischnotte. You're really a prince?" He nodded. "What are you doing in this part of town? I've known the Valentines for years. Carl moved in with Carly and the boys right after their mama died."

Carly's mother was deceased? Yet another unfortunate detail they had in common.

Schooling his curiosity to ask for more information about the woman who would be his secret weapon against the traitors who wanted him dead, Ivan fixed a smile on his face. He lightly clasped the older woman's fingers as she gave him a little curtsy. But before she released him, her dog nuzzled against Ivan's hand and licked him. His smile turned genuine. When was the last time he'd been able to run with a dog, or simply pet one? He scratched his fingers over the dog's head. "Who is this little guy?"

A shadow loomed up beside him. "Madam, I need you to move away from the vehicles. Now." Filip Milevski's stern tone made Ivan's stilted conversation sound suave and charming, by comparison. With Filip's right arm blocking Ivan across the chest, pushing him back toward the car, the chief of security pointed up the street. His jacket gaped open, revealing the gun holstered beneath his left arm.

The older woman's skin blanched. "Did I do something wrong?"

"No—"

Filip inched his bulk in front of Ivan. "He is not signing autographs or taking pictures this evening. Move along."

"It was nice to meet you, Mrs. Pischnotte." Ivan bristled at the curt dismissal. With a fearful glance up at Filip, the woman dropped her dog to the ground, and they hurried along the sidewalk that circled the end of the street. She stopped to chat with a man wearing some sort of workman's uniform. He was digging holes in his front lawn. Perhaps not his lawn, since there was a white van in the driveway with a company logo on the side panel. But he seemed to know Mrs. Pischnotte. With a tired sigh he leaned against his shovel as she took his arm in a fearful grasp, pointing at them in an animated conversation. Ivan pushed Filip's arm away, his glare conveying his displeasure at the needless bullying. "Was that necessary? The idea of this visit is to build a good rapport with our sister city, not show them we are a bunch of thugs like the previous regime. I hardly think an elderly woman is a threat to the throne."

"Is it necessary to be here at all, Your Highness? What about the man she's talking to now? The family next door? I haven't vetted any of these people to see if they're on any kind of watch list. We do not know if the Loyalists' threats have followed us from home." The photograph burned a hole in Ivan's pocket. Perhaps he'd been wrong to keep his security team out of the loop. But a member of that team was as good a suspect as any other passenger who'd been on the plane with him. At least the note confirmed his suspicion that there was a traitor among the royal delegation, someone feeding inside information to the dissidents. No one else would have access to his briefcase. No one else could have taped the photo on the mirror in his penthouse bathroom. "You are not the first leader I have served. I am responsible for your protection. Deviating from your schedule and leaving the hotel to visit your mistress on a whim—"

"You will not refer to Miss Valentine as my mistress, and certainly not in that condescending tone." He waited for Filip to lower his gaze and bow his head slightly. The big man needed the reminder of the hierarchy and just who worked for whom. The fact that Ivan didn't know exactly how this relationship between him and Carly was going to work made him hesitate. All he knew was that she was doing him a favor, and he would not tolerate the snide subtext in Milevski's words. "She is to be treated as an honored guest to the throne."

"As you wish, sir." Filip snapped his fingers for the other bodyguards to split up to do a reconnaissance of the tree-lined street. He made a show of buttoning his jacket, his shoulders bristling with irritation at not being in control of the situation or location. "This is an uncharted part of the city. There are no police officers patrolling the area."

"There is a police officer inside that house." Ivan pointed to the white columns and soft yellow siding on the porch in front of the Valentine home before gesturing to the other houses. "It is a fine neighborhood. The homes and yards are well taken care of." He nodded to the couple in the driveway next door, who'd paused in the middle of loading two boys and bags of baseball equipment into the back of their minivan to watch the interchange between the delegation and their neighbor. "It is hardly the mean streets of the inner city."

"Springing surprises like this on me makes it difficult to plan safe travel routes and make sure my men have time to scout ahead for potential security breaches." Filip waved his hand toward the curve of houses at the top of the street. "This is a dead end. Hardly a street I would have chosen in case we have to make a quick getaway."

It was no surprise that Aleks made a joke to diffuse the tension in the air. "Yes, because that killer poodle was an assassin in disguise. It's a veritable hotbed of terrorist activity here on—" he craned his neck to read the road sign at the corner "—Maple Street."

"Aleks..." Ivan chided, even as he welcomed the levity. Filip didn't share his friend's sense of humor. He wondered if he'd heard Milevski laugh even once since being put in charge of the royal security detail. Still, a growly chief of security with an obsessive need to control Ivan's every movement meant negotiating time alone with Carly would be practically impossible. He desperately needed the normalcy of an informal conversation with someone he knew didn't want him dead just as much as he needed private time to discuss suspects and expand the cover story between them so that no one in the prince's inner circle would suspect the ruse. He smoothed things over with Filip as best he could without surrendering the opportunity at hand. "I will endeavor to give you more warning in the future. But understand that I wish to see Miss Valentine as frequently as possible while I am here in the United States. We have a lot of catching up to do. And my schedule, as you well know, is incredibly busy. Since I have this evening free, I thought it would be fun to surprise her at home."

"Fun?" the security chief growled.

"Honestly, Filip." A woman's cultured, melodic voice chided the man as Galina Honchar stepped out of the opposite side of the limo. The scent of her expensive perfume reached Ivan a few seconds before she did. "Has it been so long since you've been with a woman that you've forgotten all the juicy bits about being in love?"

Filip glared daggers at the raven-haired beauty, but Galina deflected the silent accusation as though flicking away a raindrop. Filip stepped aside as she approached, avoiding a verbal sparring match he had no hope of winning.

She reported on the phone call she'd been finishing up in the car. "I cleared two hours on your schedule for lunch and sightseeing Wednesday, Your Highness. But you will need to be ready for cocktails with the Mayweathers at five thirty. They'll be cohosting the fundraiser ball at the embassy on Saturday. I've noted which suits are to be worn at each event on your phone."

Still in mourning over the death of her fiancé, Konrad, black was her color of choice. Galina had lost a little weight since that fateful day in St. Feodor. But something about losing the man she loved in that bombing had galvanized her into becoming more than Ivan's administrative chief of staff. She would not allow for Konrad's death to be without meaning. Now, Galina guarded the prince's interests as well as his time, serving as an extension of his royal hand. She'd become his emotional protector as well as his personal planner, as they neared his coronation at the first of the new year. She had been efficient before, but now Ivan suspected she could run the palace and even Parliament without him.

Her black suit remained wrinkle-free, despite the

long hours of traveling they'd been through today. "Filip does make a point. Why haven't we heard of Miss Valentine before now? An 'old friend' from your army days?" Galina, a mix of efficiency and deportment, would have made an ideal consort for a prince.

Yet despite her classic beauty and flair for social networking, she did absolutely nothing for Ivan. Even if she didn't still wear her late fiancé's engagement ring, she didn't stir his hormones. Didn't stimulate his curiosity to get to know her on a more personal level. Didn't engender trust with the calculating sharpness of her dark brown eyes and knack for getting things done behind the scenes, handling details he never knew about. He wasn't chauvinistic enough to eliminate her as the traitor in his inner circle simply because she was a woman. He watched everything he said or did around her. Galina, perhaps more than anyone else in this delegation, would be able to spot a charade. Whether or not she was the mole leaking information to his enemies, she would be a hard one to fool. Even if she was innocent, her suspicions would most likely put the real traitor on alert about his relationship with Carly.

Ivan had carefully considered the lies he needed to tell. Ones based on a truth would be the easiest to remember. "I do not say much about my military service and the people I worked with or missions I took part in. And I certainly do not discuss my love life. With anyone," he added for emphasis.

A bright grin appeared in the middle of Aleks's curly black beard. "You never thought you were going to see her again, did you? Now you cannot stand to be this close—in the same country, the same city—and be away from her for a moment longer." He flashed that smile at Galina. "It's called passion, darling. Perhaps yours died with poor Konrad."

"Aleks," Ivan scolded. "You take your teasing too far."

"I am fine, Your Highness." Galina arched one perfectly sculpted eyebrow upward at Aleks, silently informing them both that she was perfectly capable of taking care of herself. "I have not forgotten what love is like. Nor have I forgotten the cause that Kon died for. As long as the indulgence of this affair doesn't distract the prince from the goals at hand, I will support it."

Eduard and Danya returned from their reconnaissance of the nearby homes in the cul-de-sac. Eduard Nagy, Ivan's personal driver, the more sedate of the two, peeled off the sunglasses he no longer needed on the shady street. "Everything looks secure. Almost every house has eyes on us, though. I talked to the man digging up that yard, a Bill Furness. He's the caretaker. The retired couple who lives there is away on a mission trip to Central America for several months. He said the only new residents in the neighborhood are the moles destroying his lawn. He hasn't seen anything unusual." He turned his gaze, scanning the entire neighborhood. "I'll need to pull up the city map on my laptop and mark the through streets and potential bottlenecks in this area if we're going to be frequent visitors."

"We will be," Ivan insisted.

Filip grunted his acceptance before firing off another command to his staff. "Run that watch list of names Homeland Security gave us, too. Make sure there are no potential enemies nearby."

Danya seemed irritated that they hadn't found anyone who seemed an obvious threat. "Your lady friend is cooking on a grill in the backyard, and a man is doing construction work there."

"A man?" Ivan asked. Surely, Carly would have mentioned if she had a boyfriend or fiancé who'd throw a wrench into their pretend relationship.

Danya muttered a word of frustration in their native language. "I didn't take names. I was looking for weapons, not checking out your competition."

Ivan wondered at the anticipation quickening his pulse. It was probably just relief that he'd get to share his suspicions with Carly sooner rather than later. "Just do the job you are paid to do, Danya. And do not use language like that in front of Miss Valentine."

"She speaks Lukin?"

"She understands the tone, if not the words."

Aleks rubbed his hands together in a different sort of anticipation. "You said grilling? I have read that Kansas City is famous for this cuisine. We will be staying for dinner, yes?" He climbed back inside the limo to retrieve the basket of fruit and one of the bouquets that had been delivered to Ivan's hotel room to welcome him. "Perhaps we will bargain for a bite to eat?"

Ivan hated the idea of regifting the items, but he hated to show up empty-handed as well as unannounced even more. He patted the chest pocket where Carly's card rested against his heart. He'd considered calling first, to see if they could meet. But he worried she'd make up an excuse to say no. Plus, upsetting the schedule with this impromptu detour might just put the traitor off his or her game long enough for him to pick up on a clue that might reveal their identity.

Appreciating Aleks's ability to defuse a tense situation, Ivan moved up the sloped driveway to the concrete steps. "We can ask."

Filip lengthened his stride to move ahead of Ivan. "Eduard, stay with the vehicles. Find out what you can online. Danya, you're with me. I'll lead the way. I want to do a sweep inside the house, as well."

Ivan jogged up the second tier of steps onto the raised porch. "I remind you, we are knocking on the front door, not invading a neighboring country."

He bit back the same Lukin curse Danya had used as Filip pressed the doorbell before Ivan could reach it. "Indulge me, sir. I don't have my full team with me in the States. That means I must be more vigilant than ever."

And yet someone had managed to get around that vigilance and send him a death threat. Twice.

Ignoring the urge to point out the failure, Ivan smoothed his fingers over the angle of his beard. "Fine." Flanked by Aleks and Galina, with Danya watching the street from the steps behind them, Ivan motioned Filip to stand aside. "I speak first. I do not want you frightening anyone else."

The inner door swung open, revealing a stocky man with a royal blue and white ball cap pushed back past the receding points of his graying blond crew cut. Although the face was older and male, the green eyes were the same as Carly's. "Mr. Valentine?"

The older man looked at the entourage on his front porch and frowned. "Yeah?"

"I am Ivan Mostek of Lukinburg."

"I'm Carl Valentine of Kansas City," he echoed with sarcasm, raising his voice to be heard over the whir of an electric saw from somewhere in the back of the house. "I ain't interested in anything you're sellin'."

"I am not selling anything."

"Then what do you want?"

"To see your daughter."

Carl Valentine laughed.

Chapter Four

Ivan didn't get the joke.

Apparently, Carly hadn't mentioned him to her father. While it was not allowable for her to share the details of her new assignment, she might have at least prepared her family for the new man who would temporarily be a part of her life. "Is she at home?"

"Is this KCPD business?"

The lies came more easily as he grew impatient. "This is a social call."

His thin eyebrows arched toward the brim of his ball cap. The grinding noise of the saw stopped abruptly, leaving the shock of Carl Valentine's incredulous words filling the room. "Like a date?"

Carl's obvious surprise at meeting the man who'd come to call on his daughter was hardly the kind of reaction that lent believability to this relationship. "Sir, Carly and I—"

"Dad, if that's Jesse, tell him I need one of those beers right away." He was relieved to hear Carly's voice shouting from the kitchen. "Then he can be a lazy butt and watch the game."

"You got company, Carls." Her father stepped back from the door and invited Ivan and the others onto the landing that opened into the living room and split into stairs going up and down to his left. "Better get in here, girl."

"What are you talking about?" Carly strolled into the main room, drying her hands on a towel. "I still have to finish the potato salad... Ivan?"

She stopped in her tracks when she saw the prince and his entourage. It took a split second for her startled expression to soften into a smile, and in that moment, he breathed a sigh of relief. Yes, she'd be able to play this undercover role. Even on the fly like this.

But relief wasn't the only thing he was feeling. She had on no makeup, but that only revealed that her skin was tanned and smooth, glowing with a sheen of perspiration. Her hair was a rich mix of caramel and wheat, and it hung in a loose braid over her shoulder. Even the black leather boots with the thick soles and scuffed, gray toes looked sexy on her, their heft balancing the athletic curve of her legs and making them look impossibly long in those raggedy denim shorts. His body hummed with an awareness that was as invigorating as it was foreign, since he'd purposefully shut down any male needs months ago when he'd agreed to take this position. Carly was no conventional beauty. But she was unique. Intriguing. He suddenly wished he knew her as well as he pretended to.

Their gazes locked for several moments before he realized she was struggling with the protocol of the unexpected meeting. "Should I have said, Your Highness?"

He put up a hand, urging her, and reminding himself, to relax. "Ivan will do fine."

When he took a step toward her, her father put out his hand to stop him. "Wait a minute. You're a prince?

Like, you're going to be a king one day? In my house? For my girl?"

The moment Carl's hand touched Ivan's shoulder, Filip was there. With a sweep of his hand, he sent Danya up the stairs and poked his finger in the middle of Carl's chest, knocking him back a step. "No touching."

Carl swatted the offending finger away. "What are you doing? Where is he going? This is my house."

"Filip!" Ivan grabbed the security chief himself and dragged him back to his side. "We are guests."

He needn't have bothered. Carly moved in front of her father, her eyes locked on to Filip like a lioness siting her prey. "It's okay, Dad. This is Prince Ivan's security team. They're checking the house. Your man will find my father's hunting rifle locked in a gun cabinet in his bedroom closet. My badge and service weapon are in a lockbox downstairs beside my bed. My brother is out back using power tools. Otherwise, we're unarmed." Although her demeanor remained calm, there was no mistaking the warning in her tone. "If you ever touch my father like that again, I will break that finger."

Ivan swallowed a grin as she faced off against the man who was twice her size. Either deciding a confrontation wasn't good for international relations, or perhaps wondering if she could make good on that threat, Filip offered the Valentines a curt nod and hurried down the stairs. "My apologies."

After tucking the towel into the back pocket of her shorts, she tilted her eyes up to Ivan, sending a silent look that was filled with frantic questions. *Why are you here? Did something happen?*

When we're alone, he wanted to answer.

Her words came out in a surprisingly casual tone. "I thought we were meeting tomorrow. For lunch."

"I could not wait that long to see you again. Is it rude if I invite myself to dinner?" He sniffed the sweet, spicy smells coming from the kitchen and wafting around her. "It smells delicious."

He was as aware of everyone in the room watching them as he was of her transformed appearance. If they were alone, this meeting might go very differently. But with an audience, he took her hand and played the attentive suitor. He leaned in to press a kiss to her cheek, lingering longer than he intended because he couldn't resist inhaling the essence of something tasty on her warm skin. Although he still detected a faint wisp of smoke clinging to her, her scent was cinnamon-y, with a hint of onion and something warm, like molasses or brown sugar, just like the food he smelled from the kitchen. Carly's homey, natural scent was much more appealing than the stain of body odors that had wafted about her at their meeting earlier in the day. He pulled away, stroking his fingertip across her cheek to remind her to blink instead of looking so stunned by his attention.

Her voice was a breathless whisper, for his ears alone. "Are you going to kiss me every time we meet?"

He answered just as quietly. "Are you going to blush every time I kiss you?"

If anything, the rosy tone on her cheeks intensified and she pulled away. She cleared her throat before addressing him in a normal voice. "I swear I don't always smell like ashes. I've been wrestling with the grill out back." She smiled up at her father. "Somebody left the bag of charcoal out in the rain."

"I said I was sorry." Blushing much like his daughter, Carl quickly changed the conversation. "You might as well stay. Carly's been fussin' over a big dinner. Plenty of food. You folks like baseball?" he asked, gesturing into the living room where the television was broadcasting a sporting event. "The game's about to start."

Ivan gave him an honest answer. "It is not a sport we play often in Lukinburg. I follow football, er, soccer. But I wish to learn more about your country."

Aleks stepped up beside Ivan, hugging the flowers and fruit basket against his chest. "I understand your team is called the Royals? That seems to be a fortuitous sign with the prince here. I would like to watch."

Carl nodded. "They're actually named after the American Royal livestock show that's been around since we had stockyards and cattle drives in KC. But it sounds like good luck to me. Come on in and sit."

"Thank you." Needing no other invitation, Aleks pushed the flowers and basket into Carly's arms and followed her father to the sectional sofa.

Galina took his place at Ivan's side, extending her hand. "We have not had the pleasure to meet. I am Galina Honchar, His Royal Highness's chief of staff. I coordinate his appearances and manage his schedule."

Juggling the gifts she held into one arm, Carly reached out to shake the other woman's hand. "Carly Valentine. Nice to meet you. I…date him."

"Whatever you are cooking smells amazing." Ever an icon for etiquette, Galina asked the question Ivan should have. "Are you sure we are not imposing?"

"It's not fine dining, but you're welcome to stay." The basket and flowers teetered over the edge of Carly's arm, and Ivan reached out to grab the cellophane-wrapped basket of apples and oranges before they hit the floor, forgetting for a moment that the future leader of Lukinburg did not haul anything, especially when there was staff there to do it for him. "Thanks. I'm grilling burgers." She grinned. "For Lukinburgers." As quickly as she'd smiled, she frowned. "Wait. That's not an insult, is it?"

Galina laughed politely as Ivan hastened to reassure Carly. "Not if the food tastes as good as it smells."

Or as good as Carly smelled.

Her smile reappeared, and Ivan suddenly felt as successful as he would once the Kansas City agriculture and trade officials signed the new business contracts with his government.

But any feeling of victory was short-lived when the front door burst open behind him. A young man with shaggy brown hair, wearing a T-shirt and a leather vest entered with a bellow. "What the hell are those cars doing out front? I had to park way... Whoa."

The security team returned in a blur and shoved the young man up against the wall. He lifted the six-pack of bottled beer he carried out of Danya's way when the bodyguard felt beneath his leather vest and patted down the sides of his jeans. "Hey, pal, you ought to buy me dinner first."

"Danya." Ivan ground the order between clenched teeth. "Retreat."

The bodyguard pushed to his feet. "He is not armed."

Green eyes. Square jaw. Another Valentine. Great. He was scoring zero points in the public relations department with this family. But the young man didn't seem to mind the rude greeting once his gaze landed on Galina. Instead of complaining about the welcome, he smiled. "Nice. Wish you'd have frisked me."

"Jesse!" Carly chided. Including the young man and Danya in her glare, she slid between the two of them, motioning for Danya to back away. "This is my brother Jesse. If you try to frisk my brother Frank, he'll punch you."

She linked her arm with her brother's in protective solidarity. Her smile tightened into a grim line as she went through the introductions. "His Royal Highness, Prince Ivan. The prince's friend, Aleksandr Petrovic. His chief of staff, Galina Honchar. Chief of security Filip Milevski. And Danya... I'm sorry, I didn't catch your last name."

"Pavluk."

"Have the Russians invaded?" Jesse asked.

Danya stepped forward, taking the joking remark as an insult. "We are not Russian. We are proud citizens of Lukinburg."

"Oh, hell. It's true. Hey, Frankie! You here? You owe me ten bucks." The rhythmic pop of a nail gun that had underscored the entire conversation stopped as the young man extended his hand. "Nice to meet you, Ivan. What's your business with my sister?"

Before he could answer the question, another Valentine entered through the kitchen. This one was bigger, blonder, but the family resemblance was the same. "What are you on about now, Jess?" He pulled a ball cap off his head to mop at the sweat on his brow and pointed the cap at Danya. "You're that guy I saw lurking around the Fitzes' yard. What are you doin' in our house? With guns? The kids don't need to see those."

"It's okay, Frank. My older brother." Carly made the

round of introductions again, and Ivan shook his hand. He didn't like admitting the relief he felt to learn this was her brother, and not a potential rival for her time and attention.

Frank Valentine appeared to be about the same age as Ivan, in his early to midthirties. He crossed his brawny arms over his chest. "You really a prince?"

"Are you really her brother?"

Jesse, clearly the more outgoing of the two, laughed. "A wiseass, huh?"

Carly pinched his arm. "You don't say things like that in front of—"

"It is fine." Apparently, plain speaking was a Valentine family trait. Ivan could appreciate that. In fact, he envied their openness. He didn't have to second-guess what they were thinking and if they were plotting against him. "Before I had to bow to royal protocol, I, too, had a penchant for sarcasm. It still slips out every now and then."

"I'll take this off your hands." Galina plucked the fruit basket from Ivan's grip and moved forward to take Frank Valentine's arm. "It is time for us to leave the prince to the reason for his visit. Spending time with Miss Valentine. Filip, Danya—perhaps you should check with Eduard to see what information he has discovered?" After the security team exited onto the porch, Galina's smile included an invitation for Jesse to join her and Frank. Both men seemed eager to oblige. "Teach me about this baseball."

While the others settled in front of the television, Ivan followed Carly into the kitchen. "Does no one help you prepare the meals?"

"I like to cook. This is my therapy when I need to

think." After setting the flowers on the counter, Carly stirred beer into the pot bubbling on the stove. Then she opened the refrigerator and took out a tray of hamburger patties. She peeked into the living room, confirming that everyone was busy with the game or engrossed in conversation, then dropped her voice to a whisper and hurried to the back door. "Does that jacket come off?" she asked when he moved in beside her to hold the door open. "You might want to roll up your sleeves and loosen your tie. It's hot out here."

Sensing the urgency in this sudden shift in behavior, Ivan shrugged out of his jacket and draped it over the back of one of the kitchen chairs before following her down the steps into the backyard. He joined her at the grill. "I need to speak with you privately."

"I didn't think you were here for a booty call."

He folded the crisp white cuffs of his sleeves. "I do not understand."

"You know, when a guy calls or drops by to…" Her cheeks blushed bright pink and she shoved the tray into his hands, asking him to hold it while she added the extra burgers to the grill and slipped ones that were already cooked to a warming bin.

"Carly, I need you to speak always so I understand you. What is *booty call*?"

"A quickie. Sex." She patted her backside. "It's slang for this. That guys want to… Women, too…" Her cheeks heated with another blush that he doubted could be attributed to the hot coals or humid summer weather, and she went back to flipping burgers. "That's why your friends think you're here, isn't it? Why you want to see me? Only you and I know the truth."

Ivan's gaze had settled on the curve of her denim

shorts the moment she'd touched herself there. What was wrong with him? Why did this earthy woman make him forget every bit of protocol that had been trained into him? Why did he care if she blushed adorably when he paid attention to her or feel a knife-hot urge to defend her when anyone said something demeaning or took advantage of her? But he remembered the photo, he remembered his duty to his country, he remembered the promise he'd made to her police captain, and politely raised his focus to her eyes. "I will remember this slang. Because you have a memorable booty."

"Um... Thank you?" She took the empty tray and set it on the shelf beside the grill. "Tell me why you're here. We weren't supposed to meet until tomorrow, so something must have happened."

Ivan nodded. His shoulder brushed against hers as he turned, keeping his back to the living room windows, in case there were curious eyes on them, and pulled out the mutilated photograph. "I did not know who else to trust with this."

She closed the grill and took the photo from him. "It looks old."

"I am afraid its meaning is new." He pointed to the rectangular image, in shades of gray and black, centered in the picture. "It is the flag of Lukinburg, draped over a coffin. It is an historic picture. The last rightful king was assassinated shortly after the Second World War. A bomb went off at his summer house on Lake Feodor. He lay in state in the palace. A few months later, while the government was in transitional chaos, there was a coup. Our democratic government as we knew it was over."

"Until you stepped in?" Carly tilted worried eyes up to his, keeping her arm flush against his so she could return the photograph without being seen. "It's dated this upcoming Saturday."

"It is the night of the embassy ball." The message might be symbolic, but the meaning was clear. If he didn't step down, *he'd* be the next head of state lying in a coffin. And his death would happen on Saturday. "It was left in my hotel suite. Anyone in my delegation could have put it there. We held a meeting there this afternoon."

"Someone on the hotel staff, or pretending to be, could have left it."

He shook his head as he folded the photo and stuffed it back into his pocket. "Filip has limited the staff who has access to my suite. He personally ran background checks on each of them and cleared them."

"He could have cleared someone with ties to the Lukin Loyalist movement. You think he's your mole?"

"I do not know." The heat and humidity of the summer evening burned through Ivan's skin, reminding him of the pressure building inside him since he'd agreed to take this job. If he had a clear enemy, he'd know how to handle this. But the mind games, the threats, the collateral damage that could result if he made a mistake—how was he supposed to fight that?

Carly bumped her shoulder against his, drawing him from the dark turn of his thoughts. "The obvious question is—can you cancel the ball?"

"No."

"Right. Too important to you and your country." She glanced behind her, then laced her fingers with his down between them. "How many messages like this have you gotten?"

Was her touch for comfort? Or for show? Was someone watching them? Ivan decided he didn't care. He liked the sure grip of her hand in his as much as he liked everything else about her. He tightened his fingers around hers, absorbing some of that strength. "Two since I've touched down here in the US. Several more back in Lukinburg. I believe they are trying to scare the prince into abdicating the throne, letting someone more malleable lead the new government."

"The prince?" She laughed softly. "You just referred to yourself in the third person."

"Did I?" Perhaps jet lag was getting the better of him. Or stress. No wonder he couldn't keep his thoughts straight. He needed to be on point every waking moment if he was going to accomplish all he'd set out to do. Who was he kidding? He couldn't even afford to sleep without being on guard for his life.

"It's probably easier to think the threats and attempts on your life are happening to someone else."

"Perhaps." The marks of the injuries peppering his neck and back burned with the enormity of the challenge he faced. "Yet I am the one with the scars. If they cannot frighten me from my duty, then they will kill me."

"No pressure, hmm?" She released his hand to reach up and trace her fingertip against the scar that cut through his beard. Although it was meant to be a comforting gesture, every nerve ending seemed to rush to the spot, pulsing beneath her touch. The moment he thought the contact might mean something more to her, too, she pulled away and went back to work, opening the grill and flipping the hamburgers. The hiss and pop of the moisture hitting the coals masked her words as much as the steam and smoke hid their expressions from any curious onlookers. "All right. I'll talk to Captain Hendricks, and we'll try to get as many people undercover next Saturday to beef up security as we can. We can put SWAT teams on alert and lock the embassy down as tightly as possible without alerting your traitor. You and I will have an emergency evac plan in place that Milevski doesn't know about. In case it's him."

"I will make sure you have an opportunity to tour the embassy this week."

"In the meantime, I'll do everything I can to identify whoever is behind the threats and get him out of the way before Saturday night."

"*We* will do this. We will work together."

"We're a team. The prince and the commoner. The European and the American. The uptown leader of his own country and the downtown nobody." She closed the grill before pulling the towel from her back pocket and wiping her hands. "Are you sure your people are buying this between you and me? A few kisses and holding hands are one thing, but somebody's still going to have to teach me how to dance."

"I would be honored to do this." She thought of herself as a nobody? How could any man miss her vibrant energy and brave spirit? There were beautiful green eyes in that ordinary face. And, judging by the awareness still fizzing through his blood, he was extremely glad that he'd added the word *booty* to his English vocabulary. "It would not be a lie to say I find you attractive. Perhaps you are not the typical royal consort, but that part, I do not have to pretend. Thank you for helping me."

"Nobody's blowing up anyone in Kansas City on my

watch." She tilted a smile up to him. "And nobody's blowing up our most honored guest."

Answering that smile with one of his own, he turned her into his arms. "First lesson." Her forearms flattened against his chest and she was suddenly stiff, as if bracing herself for something unpleasant. He placed her left hand on his shoulder and folded her right fingers into his palm before settling his hand at her waist. "A simple waltz is three steps. Right, left, right. Left, right, left. Your feet move the same direction as mine, like a reflection in a mirror."

One boot came down on the toe of his polished oxford. "Sorry. Clearly, these aren't the right shoes for this."

"Again. Right, left, right. Left, right, left. Feel my hands pull you with me when we turn."

"There's a turn?" She froze. Stomp. Ivan gritted his teeth at the pain stabbing through his little toe. "Sorry."

When she tried to push away, he tightened his hold on her waist. "Carly, do you practice any kind of martial arts or fight training?"

"Of course, I do. It's required to maintain my badge. I run, kickbox, do yoga once a week to take a break from working out."

"This is no different than learning an attack sequence or exercise routine. Memorize the pattern. Then feel your way through it." He shifted her in his arms, pulling her hips against his. "Do you feel the rhythm when I move?" She nodded, still trying to peek over his arm down at the patio. "Look in my eyes, not at our feet. My arms and thighs will lead you in the direction you need to go."

Those pretty green eyes fixed on to his. Ivan

hummed a strain from Strauss, emphasizing each down-beat. Gradually, she relaxed against his arm at her waist and she eased the death grip on his shoulder. This time, she spun with him in a dramatic turn. "I'm doing this."

There were only a few more stumbles of her boots knocking against his shoes before he swept her into a turn. She laughed until a snort made her pull up with embarrassment. He pressed a kiss to the bridge of her nose, enjoying the genuine sound of delight before pull-ing her into step again and waltzing across the patio with her.

She was humming *The Tales of the Vienna Woods* with him when the back door burst open and her brother Jesse ran out onto the deck. "Carly! Get in here. Some-thing's wrong with Frank."

Her smile vanished. The music stopped. The grill was forgotten. She charged up the stairs. "Frank?" Ivan ran into the living room behind her. He paused in the archway, taking in the convulsions of the big man writh-ing on the floor. "Frank!" Carly dropped to her knees beside her brother, grabbing at his stiff arm. "He's hav-ing a seizure. What happened?"

"Is he epileptic?" Ivan asked.

"No."

He spotted the cellophane ripped off the fruit bas-ket. Galina was picking up fruit that had spilled out and rolled across the carpet. Frank crushed the remains of an apple core in his fist. This was familiar somehow. But how did he help?

Carl Valentine was on the phone to 9-1-1. "My son—"

"Tell dispatch I'm with KCPD," Carly shouted, giv-ing her badge number. "Get a bus here now." Carly turned Frank onto his side as her father continued the call. Ivan knelt beside her, helping her position the big man as his back arched and he became harder to control. "Don't let him hit the fireplace."

Jesse knelt opposite her, the three of them fighting to keep Frank in a position where he could still breathe and not knock into any furniture. "He said he couldn't wait until dinner. First, I thought he was choking. I tried to give him the Heimlich. Then he started doing this."

Carly slipped a pillow beneath her brother's head and held it in place. "He's burning up."

Ivan had never witnessed a fit like this himself, but he'd seen pictures, training films when his unit had been briefed on nerve gases and other toxins that had been hidden and forgotten in eroding bunkers and old army bases from World War II. One of his earliest assignments had been with a team sent in to destroy any weapons that could leech into the environment or be accidentally triggered by an innocent explorer who happened upon them.

Aleks tiptoed past him and squeezed his shoulder. "We need to get you out of here. This is not the kind of publicity—"

"No!" Ivan shrugged off his touch. "I know this. It was a torture from the old days. Strychnine." He pried the smushed apple from Frank's hand and sniffed the bitter chemical smell of the pulp. Galina was reaching for an orange that had rolled over by the brick hearth. "Do not touch that!" The startled woman snatched her hand back. "He has been poisoned. We must get him to a hospital right away."

"Ambulance is on its way," Carl reported, kneeling

beside Jesse. "They said he only has a couple of hours before the internal damage becomes irreversible. Son?"

But Frank couldn't respond.

Ivan didn't bother stating the obvious, not when another man's life hung in the balance. Not when Carly could lose her brother.

That fruit had been a gift to him.

He was the one who should be dying.

Chapter Five

Ivan stood the moment the door to Frank Valentine's room opened. Saint Luke's Hospital was quiet, yet surprisingly busy for this time of night. His eyes burned with fatigue after being up for over twenty-four hours, but he didn't intend to sleep until he knew for certain that he hadn't gotten Carly's brother killed, and that there wouldn't be lasting effects from the poison.

So many lives were impacted by every choice he made. But he didn't intend for his desperation, his utter isolation from people he could trust, to ruin the life of the woman he was foolishly learning to care for in a very short time. Carly Valentine felt like salvation to him, like something real despite the charade of their relationship. She was the touch of humanity he'd been missing from the pomp and circumstance of his life as the crown prince.

The doctor came out first, chatting with Joe Hendricks, who'd been called in to take the official report for the police department. Carly followed next, with her father and Jesse right behind her.

Still in her tank top, cutoffs and boots, Carly now wore her gun holstered on her belt and her badge hanging around her neck. Despite the tough facade, there was something vulnerable about the way she ran her hands up and down her bare arms and hugged herself. There were small divots of shadow beneath her eyes now, indicating fatigue and stress, even as she hung on to every word exchanged between the doctor, the captain and her father.

"Give me a few minutes with Miss Valentine." He paused when Filip shot to his feet, preparing to follow. Ivan put up his hand, warning him that he didn't need any help walking across the room. "Send the others back to the hotel. A few of us, at least, should get some sleep before the meetings tomorrow morning. I plan to stay until I get a full report on Frank Valentine, and I know Carly is all right."

"As you wish. I will also be staying."

Ivan tipped his head to the sterile ceiling, his nostrils flaring with a measured breath. He admired Filip's dedication to his job even as he found his need to hover irritating. Or was his attentiveness something more purposeful? Like keeping his prey in sight? An instinctive male need to call him on his behavior had to be squelched. "You have been up longer than I have. Leave Danya or Eduard and get some rest. I will have Captain Hendricks with me. I am perfectly safe."

Filip adjusted the flak vest he wore beneath his shirt and jacket, as if the protective armor didn't quite fit his muscular bulk. Maybe he didn't feel comfortable wearing it, if his next words were any indication. "I failed to protect you this evening. I should have checked every delivery myself. I will not fail again. I am staying."

Ivan nodded. He wished he could trust this longtime servant to the crown without hesitation. Right now, he could only act as if he did. "Very well. But, privacy? Please?"

Filip gestured to the end of the hallway. "I have secured a room for you, just around the corner. I anticipated you would wish to speak to Miss Valentine. You will not be disturbed. I will dismiss the nonessential personnel and wait for you here."

"Thank you."

With a sharp nod, Filip crossed the waiting area to speak to his team, plus Aleks and Galina and a pair of uniformed officers who had accompanied Captain Hendricks to stand watch and keep a trio of local reporters away from the family and the royal entourage. Ivan shrugged off his suit jacket and went to join Carly the moment the doctor excused himself.

Up close, Ivan could see the goose bumps dotting Carly's skin. He hadn't imagined the chill she felt. He draped his jacket around her and squeezed her shoulders in a subtle show of support before moving in beside her to join the circle of hushed conversation. "Is Frank all right?"

She clutched the jacket together at her neck, offering him a weak smile of thanks. "Dr. McBride said Frank probably feels like he's been hit by a train with the severity of those muscle spasms and pumping his stomach. He's on pain meds. Stimuli might trigger new seizures until it's completely out of his system, so they're keeping him mildly sedated in a quiet, dark room."

"Barring any complications, the doc says he's going to pull through." Carly's father looked as if he'd aged since they'd first met earlier that evening.

Even her smart-mouthed brother seemed subdued by the close call. "I've always looked up to Frank. He's the strong one. Seeing him hooked up to all those IVs and beeping machines freaks me out as much as seeing him writhing on the floor did."

Carly linked her arm through Jesse's and rested her head on his shoulder. "Dr. McBride said everyone's quick actions, including yours, saved him. Frank *is* strong. He's too stubborn to die. Focus on that."

Jesse leaned over to press a kiss to her temple. "Nice pep talk, Carls. But we all know this was no accident. Are you gonna get this guy for us?"

"Of course, she will." Carl winked at his daughter. "That's her job."

Not for the first time, Ivan wondered at the balance in this family. Was Carly a strong woman by nature? Or was she forced to be that way because her brothers and father needed her to take care of them? "Mr. Valentine, I am sorry that your son was hurt, when clearly, I was the target. I wish to pay for any medical expenses—"

"Did you poison Frankie?"

"Of course not."

"I didn't think so. So don't apologize. And don't think you gotta throw your money around to make up for what happened to my boy. You've got enemies, Your Royalness. And if you're going to be dating my daughter, that means we have enemies, too. But you're not one of them. Of course, you hurt my little girl and all that changes."

How was he supposed to respond to that? He would never intentionally hurt Carly. And yet, he feared he already had. "Sir—"

"Dad..." Carly began.

Carl removed his ball cap and waved off both of their protests. He rubbed the top of his head down to his nape, sighing as if that burst of anger had drained whatever stores of energy he had left. He clapped Captain Hendricks on the shoulder. "Joe, you get the bastards who did this."

The police captain nodded. "I will."

The other man's promise seemed good enough for Carl. "I'd better sort through that insurance mess."

There was nothing subtle about Carly widening her eyes at Jesse and pointing toward their father as he walked away. It took a split second for him to catch on before he snapped his fingers. "Wait up, Dad. I'll come with you."

He hurried to catch up to Carl and squeezed a hand around his shoulder, offering his support so that none of them would be alone.

Captain Hendricks waited for Carl and Jesse to move out of earshot before he leaned in. "We need to talk. Your Highness?"

Ivan inclined his head toward the bodyguard pacing the waiting area. "There are ears here." Placing his hand at the small of Carly's back, he led them into the private room around the corner. "I wish to hear anything you have to say."

It was no secret that Carly was a cop and that Joe was her precinct commander, so no one questioned why an officer of his authority was on the scene when a crime like attempted murder occurred in the company of a visiting dignitary. But the real gist of their conversation needed to remain between the three of them.

As soon as the door closed behind him, Joe pulled a notepad from the pocket of his jacket. "Since this is such a high-profile case, I expedited the tox results on that fruit basket through the crime lab. Every apple was injected with strychnine."

"Just the apples?" Carly ran her hands up and down the silk-lined jacket that hung around her, as if Ivan's coat alone wasn't enough to chase away the chill she felt. "Why not the oranges?"

Ivan had the answer to that. "The prince does not like oranges."

Her eyes darted up to his, and a tiny frown mark dimpled her forehead. Great. He'd just referred to himself in the third person again. But when Joe didn't mention the odd phrasing, Carly didn't ask the question stamped on her face. She crossed to the minibar that held a steaming pot of coffee but didn't pour herself a cup. "That would narrow down the possibility of the wrong person eating the poison. If it's common knowledge."

"Most of Lukinburg knows this. There was an embarrassing news report during the last orange harvest about how difficult it is to peel an orange. I did not take the time on camera to eat one presented to me. The reporter suggested I hire someone to peel oranges for me. It became a jab at increasing government spending on what some consider to be frivolous programs." That attempt at humor had given the Loyalists some unnecessary ammunition against the new government.

"Are they?" Carly asked, facing him again. "Frivolous? It could be motive for the threats."

"I do not consider bringing in agricultural consultants to reclaim our overtaxed land and increase crop production to feed my people to be a frivolous expense." Ivan bristled at how the old guard resented change, even if it was to their own benefit. "We spend a fortune importing grain and meat. One of our goals during this visit is to negotiate more equal trade with your farmers, as well as meet potential consultants. In the long run, we will save money by doing this."

Joe tucked his notepad back into his jacket. "Save the political speeches for your official appearances. Right now, I'm looking to narrow down our list of suspects. The forensics report wasn't much help." He included both Ivan and Carly in his dark gaze. "The lab dusted the basket and remaining fruit for fingerprints. Somebody wiped it clean."

Carly pushed away from the counter and paced to the door. "I didn't think to secure it right away. I was worried about Frank."

"Actually, it narrows down our suspect list," Joe said. "By the time the lab got a hold of it, the plastic wrap was completely missing. Whoever did it had to be someone at your house, covering his or her tracks."

Carly stopped in front of Ivan, tilting her face to his. "Could he or she have wiped the prints to protect you from being a suspect? You handled the basket."

"So did you. And Galina and Aleks."

"Dad and Frank, too." She shook her head and continued to pace. "There should be a ton of prints."

The rest of Joe's report wasn't much more enlightening. "The lab also matched that first note you showed me to the printer on your airplane. I think we can safely confirm that this is an inside job."

"But is it one person? Or is that inside man the representative of an entire rebel faction? Could there be others from the Lukin Loyalist movement here in Kansas City?"

"If there are, we'll find them. Hopefully, before they

make their move." The captain buttoned his collar and straightened the knot of his tie. "In the meantime, I'll have a lab team go through everything in your suite with a fine-tooth comb to see if there are any other threats there."

"You will have to go through Filip for security clearance."

Grinning, Joe buttoned his jacket and headed for the door. "It's a Kansas City hotel, not embassy property. All I need is to wake up a judge and get a search warrant." He turned his dark eyes to Carly. "Sorry about your brother. You okay, Valentine?"

She nodded. "Yes, sir."

"Good. You're going to need sharp eyes and a clear head. I need you with the prince as much as possible until we figure out who the mole is and what his ultimate plan might be. You're our first line of defense and our main source of intel. I want to get ahead of this guy."

"So do I."

Ivan extended his hand. "Thank you, Joe."

They shook hands. "This may have started out as a courtesy to a visiting dignitary. But now they've threatened my town. They've hurt one of my citizens. It's personal."

After Hendricks left, Carly resumed her pacing from the untouched coffee to the door and back again. "Do you recognize the handwriting on that photograph with Saturday's date?"

Ivan propped his hands at his waist, anchoring the center of the small room as she moved past him. "There is not enough to tell, no."

"And the fruit? Who gave you the fruit?"

"There was no card. I assumed it had come with

something else. The welcome gifts were all from local officials, companies I am meeting with, the embassy."

"Someone either snuck them in or doctored them after delivery." Her gaze flickered up to his as she walked by again. "Is there a log of every single person who enters your suite at the hotel?"

"Filip would have that."

"And we don't know if he would tell us the truth. If *any* of your people would tell us the truth." She caught the edges of his jacket and hugged herself more tightly inside it. "Have you at least run a background check on everyone in your entourage? Would any of them have a connection to these Loyalists? A family member? A lover?"

He regretted that he couldn't guarantee the answer to that question, either. "Filip—"

"Filip is in charge of that, too." She exhaled on a stuttering breath, and for a split second, he thought she was crying. But there were no tears, only a white-knuckle grip on his jacket and shoulders that were visibly shaking. "It's so damn cold in this hospital."

He caught her by the arm when she walked past and drew her up against his chest. Ignoring the token protest of her hands bracing between them, he wound his arms around her, rubbing large circles against her back. He wrapped her up, jacket and all, absorbing every shiver, warming her with the heat of his hands and body, standing strong for her when she was ready to crumble. He rested his cheek against her temple, tangling strands of her hair in his beard as he whispered into her ear. "Take a deep breath, *dorogoy*. It is the adrenaline crash after so much stress and worry. You have had a long day and are very tired. You will get through this."

Seconds, maybe minutes, passed before she moved. Then her arms snaked around his waist. He felt the imprint of ten fingers fisting into his shirt and pressing into the skin underneath as she burrowed into him, snugging the crown of her head beneath his chin. Ivan widened his stance, letting her move as close as she wanted to be. Comforting this woman—warming her, calming her—seemed like the most useful thing he'd done in the past few months. Feeling capable again, like he was the right man for this particular job, soothed some of the tension he carried inside. He treasured Carly's faith in him and prayed that her trust wouldn't be misplaced. "I am sorry that your brother—"

"Shh. Dad's right. No apologies. It's ninety degrees outside tonight, and I can't get warm. Just hold me a little longer."

He smiled against her hair, liking that she told him what to do, completely ignoring royal decorum and the fact he was about to lead an entire country into the twenty-first century. She didn't need him for who he was supposed to be—she just needed him. "If you insist."

Ivan held Carly until the shivering stopped and comfort changed into a subtle awareness of her sleek, athletic body relaxing against his. Her small breasts pebbled beneath the nubby friction of his jacket catching between them. The scent of her hair reminded him of the laughter they'd shared beside the grill, dancing on her patio. The clutch of her fingers in the back of his shirt eased their grip and flattened against his spine, mimicking the stroke of his hands on her.

A warm sensation pooled around his heart that had nothing to do with the exchange of body heat. He was falling for this woman. He wished he could simply be a man and not a prince, that, like at this moment, her needs were more important than his responsibilities. They were both creatures of duty, both accustomed to hiding any weakness, both isolated by the need to keep their true mission a secret. She had beautiful green eyes, those crazy, sexy legs and a penchant for speaking her mind that made him want to discuss all kinds of topics with her, from politics to what she liked to cook best to how she'd react if he kissed her. A real kiss. Not for show, not for anybody but the two of them. Would she blush again? Would she take charge, or would he have the pleasure of training her how to do that, too?

Carly took a deep breath and pushed away from him, cutting off his errant thoughts. "Where does strychnine come from? Who'd have access to it?"

It took a second for him to switch topics with her. The woman wanted to work.

Ivan retreated a step, tamping down the nerve endings that were prickling with disappointment at not being in contact with her anymore. "There are remote stashes of chemical weapons in my country that contain this poison. We are in the process of disassembling them. If one has the proper clearance, you could access them."

"How would you get it into the United States?"

"On a jet with diplomatic clearance," he was embarrassed to say. "In small quantities, it could pass for powder in a toiletry bag."

Her eyes narrowed as she considered another option. "Strychnine is the deadly ingredient in rat poison. That'd be easy enough to purchase stateside. You could liquefy it and turn it into an injectable liquid."

Rat poison? Those sensitized nerves went on alert again, but this time for a different reason. "Would it be used for killing moles, as well?"

"They're similar critters. I imagine the poisons would have the same ingredients. I'd have to do some research. Why?"

Ivan replayed a conversation from the evening before. "One of your neighbors, an older gentleman—my bodyguard Eduard talked to him—said he was baiting traps to kill moles when we arrived."

"Mr. Furness?" She shrugged. "I don't know him all that well. He couldn't have poisoned my brother, though. That fruit went straight from you to me to Frank. It never left the house."

"You do not know Mr. Furness as well as say, Mrs. Pischnotte?"

"Mrs. Pischnotte has lived across the street for years. I've known her since I was a little girl, back when her husband was still alive. Mr. Furness isn't really our neighbor. He works for a company that's house-sitting for the Abshers. Sometimes, he shows up. Sometimes it's another guy. I've met a couple of them when I go running."

A full-blown alarm raised the hairs at the nape of his neck. "Then Furness lied. He told Eduard that everyone on your street has lived there for years. Including him." He shook his head, searching for a more hopeful answer. "Maybe it was a language problem and Eduard misunderstood."

"Or your bodyguard lied."

"Why would he...?" Of course. What did he truly know about anyone in his inner circle? Before that bomb had gone off in St. Feodor, he'd trusted every one of them. Now he trusted no one. He was glad to have a fresh set of eyes to look at them as suspects instead of employees or friends. "Eduard is new to my security team. Filip thought we needed some younger blood. I confess I do not know him as well as Filip or Danya."

Carly snorted through her nose. "You mean Mr. Personality?"

He frowned at the nickname. "Sarcasm?"

"Oh, yeah." She paced the room again, but this time he could see the thoughts running through her head, energizing her, instead of the stress leaking through her pores and sapping her resilience. "What Danya Pavluk lacks in charm, he makes up for in grouchy negativity. He has a big chip on his shoulder. He's not friendly. He's really unhappy about something for him to be so grumpy."

"Unhappy about the changes happening in Lukinburg?"

"Or it's personal. Somebody really hates your guts. Enough to kill you in a dozen different ways. Poison. You said someone shot at you. Bombs." She stopped in front of him again, her hand finding his where it rested at his waist. She squeezed his fingers, emphasizing the dire turn of her suspicions. "Maybe there's a team of would-be assassins, each with his or her own specialty. Different members of these Lukin Loyalists." She closed her eyes and shook her head as if the possibilities were overwhelming. "Or one person wants us to think it's a group of individuals who are after you by varying the means of their attacks." Her eyes popped open. "Since there are a lot of suspects with motive, maybe we should focus on the means—how these crimes are being committed. We should look at anyone who has experience with explosives, as well as anyone with access to poison, syringes, that kind of medical or chemical expertise."

"More than one assassin?" He muttered Danya's favorite curse. "Every able-bodied citizen in Lukinburg is required to serve at least two years in our military. Not everyone sees combat, but theoretically, any of my people could have knowledge of explosives. Or poison."

"We should check their service records, then. Maybe someone worked as a medic? Nurse? An exterminator? Can you do that? Do you know how to do research? Or does someone always do that for you?" She released his hand, frowning as if the idea of him using a computer or analyzing data was foreign to him. "If you give me access to that information, I could look it up for you."

"Not easily. All but the most basic personnel information is encrypted for security reasons. Filip changes the codes regularly."

"So, that's a dead end. How are we ever supposed to get an upper hand on this predator?"

He caught her hand before she pulled away. This time he was instilling some clarity into her. "I have not always been the prince. Once upon a time, I worked in my uncle's business. Growing up, I worked in a mine. I was a soldier for six years. I know how to get information. I know how to get a job done." He paused when he realized he was defending his manhood, at least a little bit. He released her hand to rake his fingers through his short hair. "Filip would be suspicious if you make inquiries. I will do this. I do not want the threats against me to become threats against you."

"Just tell me where to look and I can—"

"This job is more impossible than I could have imagined." He wasn't going to argue about this. As much as he needed an ally, he didn't want to see her hurt. Or crashing into an emotional catharsis again. "I never meant for anyone in your family to get hurt. I will speak to Captain Hendricks to remove you from the investigation and find another way to deal with the threats."

"I'm not going anywhere."

"I have asked too much of you. Too much of anyone who is not a part of the Lukin—"

"I agree with the captain. It's personal now." She crossed her arms beneath his jacket, looking up at him with the same grit he'd seen when she'd taken down that pervert at the police station. "Even if this Loyalist group didn't intend to hurt my family, they did. I made a deal with you. You didn't ask me to help because I look pretty in a party dress and can dance in high heels—which, incidentally, I don't know that I can. You needed a cop. You needed someone who could find answers without it looking like an official investigation. If I quit, who's going to have your back?"

A smile spread slowly across his face.

That faint pink blush crept into her cheeks as she pulled back a step. "Why are you smiling? What did I say?"

He reached out to capture a lock of caramel-blond hair that had fallen over one eye and tucked it into place behind her ear. "Usually, people are not allowed to lecture the crown prince. You may advise me, but I make the decisions."

"What are you deciding?"

"I like how you talk to me, like you are talking to the man—not the crown. Although, you should not do this in public. It undermines royal authority."

"My badge is the authority I answer to. If I think you're doing something wrong, something that might endanger you or anyone else, I have to speak up."

He pulled his fingers from her silky hair and curled them into his palm. "Very well. I can see you are a stubborn woman. But I am a stubborn man. You may have my backside if you wish." He knew his English phrasing wasn't quite right. He'd find a translator if she didn't understand. "But you will also allow me to have yours."

"You can't risk your life for me. I won't—"

"Those are my terms. I cannot carry a gun, but there are things I can do to protect you and your family. I will not have you fighting this assassin, maybe an entire rebel faction, on your own."

"I can call KCPD for backup."

"Your booty is mine."

Ivan felt the heat creeping up his own neck when a giggle snorted through her nose.

"Is that not the right word for your backside? I have yours as you have mine."

"It's okay, Ivan. I like keeping an eye on your booty, too."

He didn't need a translator to understand that. She'd just admitted that the attraction he felt wasn't one-sided. Good to know. The timing and situation stank, but the possibility of something impossible between them smoothed the raw edges off his embarrassment and protective anger. "Then, despite my reservations, we shall continue working together. You are not alone."

"You aren't, either." There was neither flirtation nor argument in her tone when she spoke again. The police officer was back. "Is there anyone in your delegation you trust without hesitation?"

His choices were limited. His bunk mate from basic training was the only one he'd reveal a secret to. "Aleksandr."

"Then we need to enlist his help."

Ivan scrubbed at the tension cording the back of his neck. "I would rather not."

"You need every ally you can get."

If he'd believed teaming up with Aleks had been a real option for this covert mission, he wouldn't have needed to go to KCPD for help. "Aleks…is smart and has great vision for the future of our country. But he is also…how do you say it? His mind is absent."

"Absentminded? He gets distracted?"

"Yes." She should understand how preoccupied Aleks could get when he focused on his work—or on whatever pretty face or passing scenery caught his eye. "I do not know if he could handle himself in a dangerous situation. I would not want to put him in that position."

"Then you have to let me investigate. You have to let me talk to your people, search through your records. I need answers, Ivan. Someone nearly killed my brother. They keep trying to kill you, and the more I get to know you, the more I don't like that." She fingered the badge that hung around her neck, perhaps reminding him of her oath to protect and serve, perhaps reminding herself. "They're threatening to kill a lot of innocent people next Saturday. I need to stop them."

He'd taken a similar vow when he'd agreed to become the crown prince. "*We* need to stop them. I will do what I can to get the information you require."

"Don't get caught, okay?"

He smiled at her persistence. "I will do my best."

"I imagine your best is pretty good." He followed her to the exit, reaching around her to open the door. She paused in the open doorway and tilted her face up to his. "Thank you."

"I believe I am the one who should be thanking you, Carly." He caught the end of her braid and rolled its dark golden weight in the palm of his hand. "Does your name mean lioness, by any chance?"

She glanced down at the strands he held, then back into his eyes. "No."

"Surely you are named for your bravery and determination."

She tugged the braid from his hand. One of those endearing blushes heated the apples of her cheeks. "It's the feminine version of Carl."

"It is not short for something else? Carlotta?"

She shook her head. "Carly Rae Valentine. What you see is what you get."

"I like what I see."

She leaned back against the door frame, keeping her gaze locked on to his. She might not be used to intimacy with a prince, but she wasn't afraid of it. "Are you trying to charm me, Your Highness?"

He braced his hand on the metal frame above her head, drifting in to maintain the closeness between them. "Is it working?"

She captured the end of his tie and examined it the same way he had studied her hair. "Thank you for caring about my family, about me. I know you have a lot on your mind."

"At this moment, you are the only thing on my mind." His voice had dropped to a husky whisper.

When she tilted her gaze back up to his, she tugged

on his tie and stretched onto her toes. She kept coming until her mouth pressed against his. Her lips were tentative, perhaps unsure of their welcome, but the fingers curling into the front of his shirt and sliding against his jaw to hold his mouth against hers told a different story. Ivan was powerless to resist the sweet thank-you and eager invitation. Leaving one hand above her head, he slipped the other beneath the jacket, curving his fingers around her waist. His knuckles brushed against the gun she carried, but all he could feel was soft cotton and cool skin and the sinewy flex of the muscles running from her flank over the flare of her hip. Her kiss seemed to be an exploration, and Ivan seized the opportunity to learn the taste of her mouth, as well. Running his tongue against the seam of her lips, he coaxed her to open for him and swept his tongue into the soft heat of her mouth.

Her throaty squeak of surprise muted into a hum of pleasure as she welcomed and returned the need in his kiss. Her fingertips clung to the skin beneath his beard as her tongue darted into his mouth. They danced together in a new way, advancing, retreating. A gentle stroke here, firmer pressure there. A nip, a suckle. His body caught fire with the electricity surging between them. The slow build of heat burst into flame and he longed to back her into the door and sandwich her body against his. He wanted to learn her curves, match her strength to his. He wanted to get drunk on the scents of smoke and spice that clung to her skin and hair. When her hand slid around the collar of his shirt to dig into the tension he carried there, he was the one growling a hungry approval in his throat.

"Carly…" He tried to retreat. He wanted too much,

too soon. "We are tired." He kissed her. "I want you." He kissed her again. "The hour is late." He couldn't seem to stop.

She dragged her teeth across his bottom lip and desire arced straight down to his groin, erasing any of the restraint he'd tried to grab onto. "Please tell me this isn't part of the charade. It feels convincing to me."

"Are you pretending?" he whispered against her lips. "No."

"Neither am I." Claiming her mouth in a kiss that was anything but pretend, he drifted closer, sliding his hand down over the curve of her rump and squeezing its beautiful shape as he pulled her thighs into the arousal straining behind his zipper. His brain burned with the fever to have all of her. His heart pounded against his ribs. His pulse thundered in his ears.

A bright light flashed in the corner of his vision, shocking him back to common sense.

"The prince and his local Cinderella," a man's voice said. Ivan swore as a second flash went off from the hallway, capturing them in the open door. "Readers are going to eat this up."

Ivan lifted his gaze to drill the reporter taking pictures of the embrace, even as he moved to stand between Carly and the unwelcome interruption. "I ask you to leave, sir. This is a private moment."

"Obviously. Could I get a name, miss?" the reporter asked.

Ivan's hand fisted at his side. A smaller, surprisingly strong hand curved around his, and Carly moved up beside him. "It's all right." She pulled back the front of the jacket to reveal the gun and badge she wore. She glanced at the man's press credentials hanging around his neck. "Listen, Mr. Decker. I'm armed and danger-ous. If I see that picture in the paper with any kind of crude story or suggestive headline, my boss at KCPD will be calling your boss."

If her voice hadn't started in that breathless tone, he might have thought she was unaffected by that mini make-out session. Still, Ivan wasn't sure if he should ad-mire her self-possession or feel offended that she could get over his kiss so easily. He shouldn't have let things get out of hand. Losing focus like that was all on him. It was up to him to make this right.

He turned and called down to the waiting room. What the hell was security for if they didn't do their job? "Filip!" He eyed the name badge and credentials hanging around the reporter's neck. Ralph Decker. *Kansas City Journal*. Ivan didn't recognize the man's name from the press packet he'd reviewed on the plane. "I trust you will be as diligent about reporting on the fund-raising efforts my people are working on for your city this week, Mr. Decker?"

"You give me an invitation to that embassy ball, and you're damn straight I'll cover it. Unless you've got something a little meatier you'd like me to write about?" Decker had been fishing for an inside scoop all along. But he winked at Carly. "You never gave me your name, Miss…?"

"*Officer* Valentine."

Decker nodded and reached for his phone to type in the name. "Gettin' a little personal protection, eh, Princie?"

Filip Milevski's bulk rushed past them in a blur. "I am sorry, Your Highness." He clamped his hand around the reporter's arm and dragged him down the hallway. "You lied to me. You said you were going to—"

"Hey, if I'm getting stuck with this lousy story, then I'm going to make sure I have something to write about."

"You go. Now."

Decker raised his free hand in surrender, and Filip released him, staying right by the reporter's shoulder as he walked to the elevator under his own power. The rest of their conversation became inconsequential.

Carly shrugged out of Ivan's jacket and pushed it into his arms. "I need to check with Dad and Jesse. Find out what you can. I'll call the crime lab later to see if they can tell me anything else."

He caught her by the arm before she sprinted away. "That kiss was not a charade," he articulated as clearly as he could. "Not for me."

"It makes our cover look authentic, though, doesn't it?" Her brusque dismissal left him thinking she might not believe him. "Good night, Ivan." She twisted away before he could stop her, nearly plowing into Aleks as he turned the corner. "Mr. Petrovic."

"Miss Valentine." And then she was gone. Beyond Ivan's reach, beyond his line of sight. Beyond any chance to talk about that kiss and the potential fallout she might endure from the press. Aleks's dark brows arched above the rim of his glasses as he ambled up. "That should have been 'Good night, Your Highness.'"

Ivan shook his head, torn between duty and doing the right thing by Carly. "Don't start with me, Aleks," he muttered in their native language.

"A late-night rendezvous?" Aleks glanced toward the elevators where Filip waited with the photographer to escort him out of the hospital. He spoke purposeful English, as they'd agreed to while they were in the States. "I cannot wait for that headline."

"It was one kiss." One hell of a kiss. A kiss that could have led to something more if the world would just leave him the hell alone. He pulled on his jacket, unable to ignore the faint essence of grill smoke and cooking spices clinging to the wool from Carly's skin and hair. "I thought you left with Galina."

"Temper, temper, my friend. You are forgetting yourself. And the promise you made to me, to our entire country." Aleks's amusement faded as he circled around Ivan into the private room. "May I talk to you for a moment? As your friend?"

Ivan exhaled a deep sigh of frustration before closing the door behind him. Weariness dogged at his heels, so he dropped onto the room's love seat, crossed his right foot over his left knee and leaned back into the stiff cushions. "Go ahead."

"I know you have not been the prince for that long." Aleks poured himself a cup of coffee. Ivan refused the offer for a cup of his own. He was already exhausted and didn't need caffeine to disrupt the two or three hours of sleep he'd be getting. "You cannot be seen in an embrace like that with someone like—"

"Like what? Be very careful what you say next, Aleks." His friend wisely chose not to complete that sentence. "You are the one who seems to be treating this trip as if it was some grand adventure. Am I not allowed to have a few moments where I do not have to be *on* for meetings or the public or press? Carly means something to me."

"Does she?" Aleks challenged. "You and I both know she is not your old friend from the army."

"That does not mean the feelings are not real." Ivan pulled off his glasses and rubbed at the bridge of his nose.

Aleks sipped his coffee, made a face at the taste and dumped it down the sink before tossing the paper cup into the trash. All a stall for time, and the opportunity to come up with the right words, Ivan suspected. "I do not begrudge you this relationship. But there are expectations. We need our trade partners to know we are serious, and not think we are in Kansas City for you to fool around..." He took a seat across from Ivan and leaned in. "She is delightful to converse with, but she seems...coarse. Tell her to wear a dress. Tell her to at least hide that gun. It looks as though you are consorting with a gangster. Like someone from the old regime."

Ivan shot to his feet, towering over his friend. "She is an honored police officer. A military veteran."

"Even if she was in uniform, it would be an improvement." They'd known each other for too long for Aleks to be truly intimidated by him. He slowly rose to his feet to face him. "Put body armor on her and she could be one of the Lukin rebels. Please, if you must have this affair..." He put up his hands when Ivan started to protest. "I remember a prince's speech saying that we must earn the respect of the world again to save our people. I am only telling you this because I know you want the best for our country. I know you have been lonely since taking on the responsibilities you have, that you have not had time to pursue any kind of personal life. But fraternizing with Miss Valentine in public is not the image that will earn that respect."

Only his best friend could talk to him like this—could insult Carly like that—and not find himself flat on the floor. "You want me to dress her up in public and keep my feelings for her private?"

"Yes. If you must have her with you."

"I must." Ivan's hand went to the tension at the back of his neck, which Carly's grasping fingers had temporarily dispelled. "Aleks, she reminds me of where I came from. Where *we* came from and what we have overcome. She reminds me of the strength that lies within me, which I will need to complete this job. I need her. Plus, I will not abandon her when she is dealing with this attack on her family."

"That attack was meant for you."

"That mistake does not lessen the impact of nearly losing her brother."

"So, this is guilt?"

"This is the way I say it will be." Ivan buttoned his collar and straightened his tie, putting on his princely facade once more. "Now, we have bigger concerns than my love life." He headed out of the room, waiting for Aleks to fall into step beside him. "Tell Filip to bring the car around. Have Galina prepare a short statement to release to the press regarding this unfortunate incident. And Aleks? Find me a laptop."

He'd made a promise to Carly. There was work to be done.

Chapter Six

"Brooke? Help me."

Carly got the zipper of the sleeveless polka-dot dress partway down. But no matter how she twisted and stretched, there was no way to reach the little tab to pull it down the rest of the way unless she dislocated her shoulder to do it.

Yesterday's luncheon and shopping on her own had been an absolute disaster. Carly had picked out a little black dress that apparently wasn't the universally chichi thing the magazine she'd read through had indicated. Her father had asked what funeral she was going to. Galina Honchar had tsk-tsked at her before ushering her to her seat. Ivan had been a compelling speaker, and if she was a farmer, she'd certainly be willing to talk more about selling her beef and soybeans to Lukinburg. But during the mingling with the guests afterward, someone had mistaken her for one of the servers and asked her for a refill of coffee.

About the only thing useful that had happened was the chance to stand back from the group and observe Ivan's staff. Aleks was a natural-born salesman, probably Ivan's greatest asset when it came to discussing facts and figures, as well as entertaining guests around the conference room. Galina carried her computer tablet with her everywhere, and seemed to either be whispering into Ivan's ear, making introductions, or steering someone away from Ivan if their conversation ran on too long. Danya stood inside one set of conference room doors, avoiding all conversation, keeping his eyes on Ivan as he moved about the room. Eduard stood at the other set of doors and acknowledged her with a friendly salute. Although his earpiece and concealed gun indicated he was security, he interacted with guests who came and went, even laughing with some of them. Filip moved through the crowd with Ivan, never two or three feet away from the prince.

Ivan had been kind enough to pull her to his side and introduce her to the Lukin ambassador and the president of the American agri-business group. Both men made her feel welcome enough, but she'd been more interested in why Filip had put more distance between himself and Ivan when she was at his side, and who he was talking to on his cell phone when he did slip away. And what had Galina and Eduard been arguing about before she sent the young bodyguard out of the room to do her bidding.

Afterward, Carly had been dropped off with no time for debriefing or goodbyes beyond a quick kiss. And though he said that he'd rather spend the rest of the day with her watching a ball game and eating the barbecue he'd missed out on the night before, Galina had tapped him on his shoulder and reminded him that they needed to get to the TV station to tape an interview for the evening news. Ivan had brushed his finger across Carly's cheek, whispered something in Lukin that sounded like a promise and climbed inside his limo to drive away with the rest of his delegation.

She was beginning to understand time alone, time away from being the prince and representing his country was a rare, precious thing for him. Carly vowed then and there to make the most of the time they'd have alone—to go over answers together and give him a break from the heavy responsibilities he carried on those broad shoulders.

But so far, today hadn't been much of a success. She hadn't been able to find more than basic public info about the suspects who might be threatening Ivan, and she was stuck in this stupid dress.

Carly flexed all ten fingers out straight, eyeing the strange spots of pale pink polish where her plain, stubby nails used to be. Then she took a deep breath and contorted herself in the dressing room's three-way mirror in an effort to reach the back of the dress. "My toes and fingernails feel claustrophobic. Can nail polish numb them?"

"Really?" Her friend's pregnant belly appeared in the mirror a split second before her gentle smile did. "You're a tomboy, not a shut-in. You said you enjoyed the foot scrub. They're beautiful. Tastefully done without looking flashy." Brooke reached in and unzipped the back of the dress. "You're just not used to seeing yourself all spiffed up."

"How do you girlie-girls put up with this stuff? I wouldn't have been able to use my hands at all if the manicurist had put those tips on the way she wanted to. I don't remember the last time I wore pink." Carly pushed the dress off her shoulders and let it fall to the floor before stepping out of it. "I'd say this one's a no. If I can't even undress myself..."

"You can't wear the navy pantsuit all week." She held out her hand for Carly to pick up the dress and returned it to its hanger. "Ms. Honchar's note said you'd specifically need a dress for the university reception tomorrow. I think we've determined that black is not your color. It's either this or that cream floral with the short sleeves."

"I think Ms. Honchar would prefer that I dress in something that makes me invisible." She eyed the floral dress. "You're sure it's proper for a university reception?"

"It's flattering and has a little color without being over the top. Besides, you can get in and out of it all by yourself. That's a plus."

"Ha ha," Carly deadpanned. She eyed the open boxes of shoes on the dressing room floor. "What do I wear with it? The sandals?"

"I'd go with the beige heels with the bows on them."

"The ones that pinch my toes?"

Brooke laughed. "You've survived on the streets working undercover in No-Man's Land. You can survive dressing up and going to a party."

With a mock groan, Carly reached for her friend's hand and squeezed it. "Thank you for doing this. I wasn't sure who to call for this wannabe princess makeover."

"I'm a regular fairy godmother." A bit on the shy side of things, Brooke Kincaid was quite possibly the kindest soul Carly had ever met. She didn't know if their friendship stemmed from their opposite personalities drawing them together, or from being the two awkward outcasts at the Fourth Precinct offices who'd found themselves on the sidelines at more than one social event. Brooke hung the dress behind the vintage-looking floral with the easy-to-reach buttons. "I think you should get this one. After this week, you could wear it to church or out on a date."

Carly snorted. "I've never worn anything but jeans on a date."

"When was the last time you went out with a man? And I don't mean out with the guys to a bar after your shift." Brooke dropped her voice to a conspiratorial whisper. "You know, the kind of evening that ends with intimate conversation and a good-night kiss?"

A brush of electricity skittered across Carly's lips at the memory of the kiss she'd shared with Ivan at the hospital. Even though she'd initiated the kiss, he'd quickly made himself an equal partner, inviting her to do whatever she liked with his handsome mouth, so long as he got to have his way with hers, as well. She thought he'd given her a glimpse of the man behind the crown. He'd called her a lioness, like she was brave and golden, a woman to be admired. If he'd called her sexy or beautiful, she'd have been less turned on, less likely to believe the connection growing between them.

Yesterday's goodbye kiss had been a perfunctory farewell, kept necessarily short because of too little time and too much of an audience. But even that simple touch had crackled with electricity, reminding Carly of those private moments they'd shared in the hospital.

That kiss had been heady and decadent, the most grown-up, intense kiss she'd ever shared with a man. Despite his genteel facade, Ivan was all sharp angles and hard edges. His beard tickled her fingers, lips and palms. His jaw was warm, unbending, saved from perfection by the ridge of scar tissue that bisected it near his ear. But even more than the draw of his lips, she'd loved it when he'd held her in his arms before that kiss. She'd been on the verge of breaking down with fatigue and stress and self-doubts about being the right woman to pull off this job. She hadn't been able to protect her brother, much less a visiting prince and the whole of Kansas City. Ivan had been rock-solid, more so than she'd expect from a man who filled his days with business meetings and press conferences, and she'd treasured the unfamiliar sensations of warmth and strength surrounding her. She was always the strong one in her family—on the emotional front, at any rate. She'd never dropped her guard and melted into a man's chest before, trusting, for a few moments, at least, that someone could protect her for a change.

But Monday night hadn't been a date. She wasn't even sure it counted as a real kiss, despite yesterday's picture in the society pages of the *Kansas City Journal*. Local Connection to Visiting Prince? hardly described whatever stars had aligned between them that night. Somewhere along the way, she'd lost track of everything except Ivan and the way his hand and mouth and heat had made her feel. He could have deepened that kiss for the reporter's benefit, or to seal the believability of their cover story as reunited lovers for the curious eyes of Aleks Petrovic and suspicious glares from Filip Milevski. She didn't have enough experience to read real passion versus a guy who was pretending he was into her. She only knew what she herself had felt. She was probably lucky they'd been interrupted before she followed the urge to climb right up the prince's body and wrap herself around him.

"You're thinking about *him*, aren't you?" Brooke smiled, politely ignoring Carly's deer-in-the-headlights expression in the mirror. "Who'd have thought my best friend would be dating a prince?"

"For a week, Brooke. And it's not dating so much as…" She almost ended the sentence with *work*. But remembering the need for secrecy, knowing that even a well-meaning friend could accidentally let it slip that she'd only known Ivan for a couple of days, that she was more bodyguard than girlfriend, Carly blinked her eyes and looked away. "Ivan wasn't a prince when I knew him…before. I'm hardly going to get serious with a man who's about to go off and run his own country in a week."

"But that kiss…" Brooke had the good grace to blush at the photograph that might as well have been on the front page from all the teasing and comments she'd gotten from her brothers and coworkers. "It looked so romantic."

Romantic wasn't the half of it. Carly shrugged off the visceral memory, reminding herself not to make too much of the bond she felt to Ivan. This was a job. A responsibility. Not a happily-ever-after in the making. "I'd never fit into that world. My life is here. My job? Dad and the bros? They need me."

Brooke seemed disappointed by her answer. "What about what you need?" Then she smiled again, as if she thought Carly needed cheering up. "That doesn't mean you won't find someone else after Ivan's gone back to Europe."

Carly silently thanked her for the unknowing save.

"Point taken. Maybe the wardrobe upgrade will help in the romance department. Maybe there's an Atticus out there for me, too." The fact that Brooke's husband, a protective, by-the-book detective, doted on her gave Carly hope that one day she, too, would find a guy who'd either look past her lack of feminine charms or who'd embrace her awkward, kick-ass self for who she was. Princes with stellar kissing abilities need not apply. Time to change the conversation. "I'm lucky Captain Hendricks gave you today off to help with my make-over. Clearly, I wasn't making the magic happen yesterday on my own."

"I was already scheduled off this morning for my OB appointment." Brooke dug through her purse and pulled out a bag of crackers and nibbled on one. Carly frowned, wondering if she'd been pushing her friend too hard today. Those crackers had been Brooke's constant companion for the past eight months. "It gave me the opportunity for some last-minute pampering before the baby arrives."

Carly hugged the discarded dresses to her chest and urged Brooke back out to the waiting area to hand them off to the clerk who'd been waiting on her. "You are not having that baby on my watch. I've got enough on my plate right now."

Brooke laughed, rubbing her belly as she sat. "Relax. She's not due for another three weeks." She waved Carly back behind the curtain, reminding her that, even though this was the women's department, she'd come out in her bra and a half-slip.

"You found out she's a girl?" Carly tugged off the slip and added it to the pile of clothes she wanted to purchase.

"We didn't want to know." Brooke raised her voice to be heard through the curtain. "That's what Atticus is hoping for, though. I guess with all his brothers, he's tired of having so much testosterone in the family."

Carly smiled at her friend's humility. "He's probably looking forward to a daughter who's as sweet and pretty as her mama."

"As long as she or he is healthy, that's all I care about."

"Are you sure you're holding up okay? We've been at this for hours. I'm exhausted, and I'm not pregnant." She poked her head out around the curtain. "Do you need to take a break?"

"Are you kidding? I wouldn't miss seeing Carly Valentine in a dress and high heels for anything. I plan to take a picture, by the way. No one will believe me, otherwise." She swallowed the last of her cracker. "You'd better start on the gowns. It's after twelve thirty. Isn't Prince Ivan meeting you at one?"

"I guess I can't put it off any longer." Carly groaned at the thought of all the lace, sequins and spiky heels waiting for her.

Twenty minutes later, with five of them spent trying to get a pair of strappy silver sandals cinched around her ankles before giving up on shoes altogether, she'd modeled lavender, champagne and blue gowns. Any one of them would do, as far as Carly was concerned, although Brooke had pointed out faults in too much skirt, showing too much skin, or looking like one of her spinster aunts.

Carly opened the curtain and stepped out in a pale turquoise gown with a beaded bodice and a simple, flowing skirt. "This is the last of them," she announced. "Which one should I get?"

"That one," a deep, accented voice answered.

Carly curled her toes into the carpet, lamenting the heat that crept into her cheeks the moment she realized Brooke wasn't alone. Ivan was perched on the back of the couch, chatting with her friend. But he stood when Carly appeared, tucking his handkerchief into his pocket and sliding the glasses he'd been cleaning back over his gorgeous blue eyes. Hungry eyes, she thought, as he raked his gaze up and down her body. Happy to see her. Liking what he saw—if she could read a man correctly, and if this man's expression actually conveyed the truth. Not everything was as it should be in royalty land, though, judging by the lines of fatigue framing those piercing blue eyes. Carly's heart squeezed in concern over whatever stress was worrying him now. Had there been another threat? Another attempt on his life? A long, difficult meeting that hadn't gone his way? Ivan revealed nothing but a smile.

"That color is stunning on you." He pointed to her bare toes. "Although I do recommend shoes. There will be a lot of dancing at the ball."

Carly backtracked from her initial worry. She was the bodyguard here, not his girlfriend. She looked beyond his shoulders, quickly scanning the store out to the double front doors, spotting Milevski waiting just outside. Reminding herself that she shouldn't let her feelings get real for this man, she distanced herself with a joke. "I didn't think my boots went with the look." There was no one else in the shop save the clerk at the counter who'd paused in the middle of hanging up the dresses Carly had discarded to gawk at the handsome, raven-haired man who'd strolled into her department. "Where's your security team?"

"Filip and the police are outside keeping anyone else

from coming in. Danya and Eduard are clearing the floor of any other customers and staff."

"Can you do that? Close down a store?" Carly asked, perhaps understanding for the first time the level of security necessary to allow a prince to be out in public. She saw Danya herding a group of employees into the break room. She traded scowls with the surly bodyguard before he closed the door and raised his arm to report into the radio he wore on his wrist. Then she saw Eduard chatting with a trio of young women as he opened the glass doors and walked them outside. "Of course, you can. You've already done it." She dragged her gaze back to Ivan, hiking up her skirt and retreating to the dressing rooms. "I don't want to hold you up. I'll get changed and be ready ASAP."

"ASAP?" Ivan asked.

"As soon as possible," Carly and Brooke echoed together.

"I see. No rush," he assured them, signaling Eduard stay by the front doors. "I am yours for the next two hours." He bent to kiss Brooke's hand. "Mrs. Kincaid. You are looking radiant today. Will you be joining us for lunch?"

"No, thank you. I wouldn't dream of intruding. Besides, I'm meeting my husband." Flustered by the prince's attention, Brooke quickly excused herself. She looped her purse over her shoulder and picked up the large Doc Martens shoebox on the seat beside her. "I've worked all the miracles I can. She's coiffed, painted and dressed for success. Don't let her buy the boots." She placed the box in Ivan's hands. "They're the only thing she picked out on her own."

"Traitor." Carly watched Ivan peek at the thick-soled boots that had caught her eye.

He laughed. "They would certainly make a fashion statement with that dress."

Carly grabbed the box from him, finding it impossible not to smile as the tension around his eyes eased. "At least they're in better shape than the ones I usually wear. I was going to pay for them myself."

Brooke reclaimed the burgundy boots. "Ms. Honchar said princess, not goth chick or biker babe. I'm putting them back for your own good. You know I love ya, Carly."

"Love you, too." Carly hugged her from the side, carefully avoiding her pregnant belly. "Thanks for everything. Tell Atticus hi."

"I will. Good luck. With everything," she whispered the last bit into Carly's ear, reminding her that Brooke thought this relationship was real. Brooke carried the boots over to the clerk before pulling out her phone. Carly could hear how her friend's tone softened as she called her husband to let him know she was ready to be picked up. Eduard pushed the door open for her and exchanged a nod as she left the store.

Carly touched the stack of clothing and unmentionables that Brooke had deemed were necessary for this week's public appearances. "Are you sure this isn't too much? I got something for every event on Galina's list. Brooke made sure they were appropriate."

Ivan gathered up the items from the couch and snapped his fingers for Eduard to handle the purchase. "She can be a stickler for details."

"That's why Brooke gets to run the captain's office.

Captain Hendricks thinks he's in charge, but we all know who keeps the precinct running."

"I meant Galina. She's planned my days down to the minute. She's asked that any changes go through her." Right. Different taskmaster. "I am sure your friend is very good at what she does. I apologize for being late, but my meeting with the mayor ran longer than planned."

Carly headed back into the dressing room to change into the blue pantsuit. "Did everything go okay?"

"I spent longer than I wanted talking about Ralph Decker's photograph of us in the paper. It was not my intention to make you the center of local gossip."

"No one will question whether you and I are the real deal or not now. That's one good thing about being caught off guard like that." A mortifying thought made her stick her head back out through the curtain. "It didn't cause trouble at the meeting, did it?"

Ivan shook his head and touched his watch to remind her of the time before waving her back inside to finish changing. "Actually, everyone seemed to think it was positive publicity for my visit. They likened it to a royal wedding. Although I am not sure I like my new nickname—Prince Charming. How will anyone take me seriously?"

"Prince Charming?" Carly groaned on Ivan's behalf. "Have any of them actually talked to you?" she teased.

"Very funny, Officer Cinderella," he teased right back.

Her groan was legit this time. "Is that *my* nickname?"

Ivan laughed. "When we got down to business, the new mayor was very welcoming, and amenable to moving forward with our proposed research and agri-business deals."

"That's good, right?"

"That is very good."

Carly pulled the jacket on over her new pink blouse and slipped her feet into the ballet flats Brooke had chosen for her. She tucked her gun into the holster at the back of her belt. Then she picked up the package of baby blankets in shades of green, yellow and peach and draped the evening gown over her arm before rejoining Ivan. "Is this okay? It feels a little like I'm in uniform—without the sturdy footwear."

"To be honest…" He leaned in to kiss her cheek and whisper beyond curious ears and prying eyes. "I like the shorts better." He brushed the tip of his finger across the cheek he'd kissed, seeming amused by the heat she could feel coloring her skin before he pulled away. "But this is more flattering than the black dress. Perfect for a luncheon with a prince."

Idly, Carly wondered if any man's attention would make her blush like a girlie-girl, or if it was Ivan Mostek's superpower to make her react to every intimate word or touch they shared. And since she had no words to ask him if he meant half the compliments he gave her, she headed to the checkout counter. "I want to buy these baby blankets Brooke was admiring. To thank her for helping me out. I'll be just a few minutes."

Ivan plucked the package from the baby department out of her hands and gave it to the clerk with a smile that made the other woman press her hand to her heart. "We will take these, as well. Put them on my account and have them delivered to Miss Valentine's home with everything else."

"Yes, sir," the clerk answered, looking equally flustered when Eduard joined them.

"Shall I bring the car from the parking garage, Your Highness?" Eduard asked. His wink to the clerk left her scurrying to do her work.

"I thought we could do something different," Carly suggested. "We're only a couple of city blocks from a really good, yet casual, authentic Kansas City barbecue restaurant. Since you didn't get to try any of mine Monday night."

Ivan looked pleased by the suggestion. "It is a warm, sunny day. I believe we will walk. The fresh air will do me good." He scanned the store before fixing his gaze on Eduard again. "Notify Filip of the change in plans. And tell Danya to release those people to do their jobs. We are not holding prisoners."

"Very good, sir."

While Eduard radioed the security team to do the prince's bidding, Ivan settled his hand at the small of Carly's back to walk her to the door. They were barely out of earshot before his fingers tightened around the bulge of her Glock beneath her jacket. "Is that necessary?"

Carly kept her voice equally low. "Have you figured out who's sending those death threats yet?"

He shook his head.

"Then yes, it's necessary. Still not sure where it's going Saturday night, though."

His tired smile didn't reach his eyes. "I have no doubt you will figure out an interesting solution."

Once he'd opened the break room door and dismissed the staff, Danya strode through the store, his eyes drilling holes through Carly. Did he blame her for the change in security protocol? Or was the man simply incapable of smiling? Maybe he had a thing against cops. Or women. Or Americans. Maybe he resented how closely Ivan wanted to tie their country to the United States. Wasn't that the reason the rebel Lukins had protested the new government? The surly bodyguard was definitely on Carly's suspect list.

Ignoring every cautionary instinct that warned her she shouldn't care what Ivan was feeling, she faced him. "Are you going to tell me what's wrong now?" She touched one of the lines creasing his temple. "You didn't have these yesterday."

He covered her hand with his for a moment before pulling it down and lacing their fingers together. "Not here."

Something *had* happened. But before she could press him for details, she realized Ivan was slipping a small rectangular object into her palm. A flash drive. Carly tightened her grip around the tiny device and slipped it into the pocket of her jacket. "I assume there's something you want me to read on here?"

"Personnel histories and notes from Filip's investigation into the threats and bombing in St. Feodor," he whispered. "I finally had a chance to download them last night."

"You said Filip encrypted his files. How did you get past his security codes?"

"I am good with a computer." He glanced beyond her, no doubt making sure their exchange remained private. "May I stop by tonight after the cocktail party I am attending to discuss anything you find on it?"

"Of course."

"I accessed Filip's files using Aleks's laptop but had

time to do little more than make a copy. I translated as much as I had time to do so into English. But some of it is still in Lukin. We can go over that together. I am not sure what is on there. It is hard to be alone. I deleted the browser history afterward. Hopefully, Filip will not know you have these."

"Or that someone's been snooping in his records." She reached for Ivan's hand again and squeezed it with a promise. "I'll keep them safe, use my computer at home so that no one knows what we're doing."

The chatter of the employees coming back out onto the floor ended the hushed conversation. Still, she startled at the grumble of Danya's voice behind her. "Are you ready to depart, Your Highness? I will follow you and Miss Valentine since you insist on walking. The police and Filip will make sure your path is clear." Carly hadn't realized how icy the bodyguard's pale gray eyes were until they zeroed in on her. "If you would be so good as to give me the name of your destination?"

Carly had seen the same distrust in the gazes of homeless and trafficking victims she worked with on the streets. But there was a mean streak rather than fear lurking behind that distrust. Still, she wasn't going to give him the satisfaction of thinking he could intimidate her with either his bearing or his disapproval. "The barbecue restaurant on Wyandotte Street." She tugged on Ivan's hand and started for the front doors. "I thought you might enjoy a sampler of authentic Kansas City burnt ends."

Danya's hand clamped over her arm, stopping her, forcing her to face him again. "You're taking the prince to eat burnt food? That is beneath him. *You* are beneath him." His fingers dug painfully into her arm as he shook her. "This whole affair distracts him from what needs to be done. You are not royal. You are not Lukin. I should not have to put up with you."

Chapter Seven

"Danya!" Just as Carly was twisting away from the bodyguard's rough grip, with her free hand poised to strike his bulbous nose, Ivan palmed the center of the bodyguard's chest and shoved him back. With a precise turn of his wrist, Ivan had the bodyguard's arm pinned behind his back and his face planted on a display table. "You overstep your duties, Danya. You are not to touch Miss Valentine again."

His warning was as crisp and concise as an officer commanding his troops.

"Are we clear on this?" Ivan prompted when he got no response beyond Danya's heavy breathing.

Carly stayed back, mindlessly massaging the five future bruises on her upper arm. She had nothing against chivalry, but what the hell? Where did a prince learn a move like that?

Allowing time for his anger to ebb, Danya finally nodded. "Yes, sir. We are clear."

Only then did Ivan release the stocky man and back away. His glance across the store to Eduard and the wide-eyed clerk dared either one of them to utter a word about what they'd just seen. Eduard nodded and turned his attention back to the clerk to reassure her that everything would be okay. Ivan straightened his cuffs and the front of his jacket, keeping his body positioned between her and Danya. "You will apologize to Miss Valentine."

"My apologies." Danya straightened his own clothes and made a token effort to stack the piles of scattered T-shirts back into place. "I am too loyal a patriot who has had too little sleep. I was not...thinking clearly... when I touched you."

"A change in plans messes with your routine. I get it. No harm, no foul." Both men looked at her with a quizzical expression. "Basketball? The phrase comes from when referees call too many fouls for little infractions..." She was the one who needed answers about what had just happened. "You didn't do any serious damage, so there's no penalty. Apology accepted."

Ivan's eyes narrowed. "I will have to learn more about this sport. It sounds violent."

As good as their English might be, apparently, they didn't teach American idioms in Lukinburg schools. She was guessing they didn't teach that hand-to-hand combat suppression trick, either. "How long ago were you in the army?"

Ivan smoothed his hands over his short hair and adjusted his glasses instead of answering.

"I could have handled Danya myself," she insisted, stating a fact, not bragging. "You shouldn't put yourself at risk like that."

"I saw you do something very similar at the precinct office to the last man who assaulted you."

Carly shook her head at his faulty reasoning. "I'm not about to be crowned leader of my own country.

You have responsibilities. There are precautions you need to take."

Danya cleared his throat. "That is the point I was trying to make. I am only concerned for your safety and your reputation, Your Highness. I feared you were being reckless."

"And you thought insulting my companion was the way to express yourself?" Ivan challenged. "I will not allow this."

"Of course not." Danya's head remained bowed. "I was merely concerned about you taking a stroll through Kansas City on this woman's invitation. It deviates from the plan Filip and Galina agreed to for the day. You are to be in the car at all times and dine at specific locations we have already scouted out. Walking through a public neighborhood such as this without barricades and proper crowd management creates security variables that we cannot control. At least, let Eduard drive you."

"Make it work," Ivan ordered, dismissing Danya's plea. "I have two hours of time free of diplomatic obligations. I wish to see and sample more of this city firsthand. I wish to meet the people. Miss Valentine will be my guide. You are the one who will adapt to *my* wishes. Not the other way around."

"Yes, sir." Danya took a step back.

"What exactly are burnt ends?" Ivan asked, perhaps trying to relieve the sting of Danya's attack, or perhaps genuinely curious.

"Smoked and glazed little nuggets of barbecue heaven." Carly smiled up at Danya, making more of an effort to make him feel welcome than he had done for her. "Would you like to join us?"

"He would not," Ivan answered for his underling,

nudging the store's front door open. "It is hard to be romantic with that face glaring at us."

Danya grunted at the teasing and led the way outside. "I will make sure your path is clear. Eduard will follow in the car."

"Not in this traffic, he won't." Once they reached the sidewalk, Carly tilted her face to Ivan's, squinting against the hot August sunshine. "The Plaza is full of tourists in the summer. He won't get anywhere very fast if there's an emergency." She dropped her gaze to their surroundings, assessing the crowds gathered at crosswalks and popular stores, gauging the flow of traffic and determining the most direct route to the restaurant. "We should talk to KCPD, ask them to block off the streets."

"And draw even more attention to my movements?" He studied their surroundings over the top of her head. "Having a rigid schedule makes it too easy to find me and plan an attack. An impromptu walk and smaller security presence should make me harder to find."

"But if there's an inside man—"

He clasped her hand, silencing that argument. "Then he will not have time to readjust to the changes. His plan will be scraped."

"You mean scrapped?"

"Thank goodness you and I can communicate in other ways." He dipped his head toward hers, and for a moment, she thought he would kiss her again. She shocked herself with just how much she wanted him to put his lips against hers. Instead, perhaps because of the audience of bodyguards and bystanders, he brushed his fingertip across the apple of her cheek. Who was she kidding? She didn't need Ivan's kiss, not when she reacted to even that simple caress with an instant, answering heat.

"Thank goodness," she whispered, her voice dropping to a husky pitch. Had she been foolish to think, for any moment, that this connection between them had been pretend? The history between them might be a fiction, but everything she felt for Ivan Mostek was real.

She inhaled deeply and pulled away as another thought struck her. She was going to get her heart broken, wasn't she? In a matter of days, she was already halfway in love with Ivan. But days were all they had, all they could ever have. There was no commitment to this relationship, not when it was built on lies and danger and political intrigue. Was this her life? That she would give her heart to the one man she could never have?

Sealing up her heart against caring too much, Carly relayed the route she planned to take through the Plaza to Filip. She was here to be a cop, to be a secret protector. Ivan wasn't really her Prince Charming, she wasn't any stinkin' Cinderella and she had no business falling in love with him.

While the security team moved out, Carly stayed by Ivan's side and pulled out her phone. "I'm going to call the captain and let him know our location. He can put some officers on standby. Just in case."

"Already done," Filip declared, tucking his phone into his jacket pocket. He jogged up to join them. "Maybe you're right, and you can blend in with the tourists."

After Filip headed out, Carly reluctantly put her phone away. "How far do you think someone like Danya would go to maintain his standards of honor and Lukin tradition? Clearly, he doesn't think I'm worthy. Would he go after a prince who is modernizing and maybe even Americanizing his country?"

"Everyone around me is suspect," Ivan confessed. "Danya might feel he is putting country before king by sending those threats."

"No more gallant moves to defend me, okay?"

"I make no guarantees." Despite the distance she tried to keep, Ivan gripped her hand and they set out side by side. Although his team cleared the area immediately surrounding them, there were a few pointing fingers and whispers about a TV appearance that morning from the people they passed. One brave soul asked if she could take a picture with Ivan, and he obliged. Carly was aware of a few more phones capturing a snapshot or video, of bodyguards warning onlookers to keep their distance and of friendly questions from pedestrians they passed.

Ivan answered each request with a wave and a smile and something complimentary to say about Kansas City. No one spoke to Carly directly, although she was certain she was included in some of those informal photographs.

Lunch was a yummy mix of brisket, scalloped potatoes and conversation with a man who was both funny and endearing. Who was she kidding with the whole this-is-a-charade-don't-let-your-heart-get-involved vow? Carly was already involved.

She didn't think she'd ever tire of looking into that polished, angular face that was more interesting than handsome. And she didn't think she'd tire of listening to Ivan's sexy accent—whether he was discussing food, the Lukin economy or the dribble of barbecue sauce he dabbed from the corner of her mouth. The more time she spent with Ivan, the less she thought of him as a prince and the more she thought of him as a man. An attractive man. An attractive man who made her feel feminine, and yet who respected, or perhaps was even fascinated by her independent spirit.

The more time she spent with Ivan, the more the lines blurred between charade and reality. She might not fully trust that his kisses and flirtations were real, that he was falling for her the same way she was falling for him, but she could think of him as a friend. And she liked that. She liked that a lot.

They polished off the crème brûlée he'd insisted they share for dessert while Ivan told her about his childhood in the poor mining town of Moravska, nestled in the mountains near the Lukinburg border. Including their military service and working-class upbringing, they had more in common than two people raised on different continents with such different futures might expect.

"What happened to your parents?" Carly asked since he'd only mentioned the aunt and uncle who'd raised him. "Sorry. That was a little abrupt." She cushioned the blow of the forward question by revealing her own loss. "My mom died in a freak accident. She was carrying laundry down to the basement, fell on the stairs and hit her head on the concrete floor. Dad was at work. Frank and Jesse were at school. I had half day kindergarten. I called 9-1-1 when I heard the crash. We'd just learned that at school—what to do if there's an emergency."

His eyes narrowed behind his glasses, and it was becoming less and less of a surprise when he reached across the table to take her hand. "You found your mother?"

Carly was touched by his concern, but then shrugged it away with a smile. Her mother's death was a tragedy that had impacted her entire life. But she'd also come to terms with the loss. "The ME said she died almost immediately. Not that I would have known how to help her. I just held her hand until the paramedics came."

Ivan's thumb rubbed against the pulse point of her wrist. "You have always been a brave woman."

She wondered if he could feel the blood hammering through her veins at the subtle caress that was as arousing as it was comforting. "I was five years old. Hardly a woman."

"You took action. You did what needed to be done at a very difficult time. Even so young. I am sorry for your loss."

"Losing her so young also explains why I'm better at taking down bad guys than I am at dressing up and playing princess. As you might imagine, Dad and my brothers were never very good at that girlie-girl stuff."

He smiled at the joke for a moment before the laugh lines disappeared and he leaned into the table. "My parents were murdered by Vasily Gordeeva. He was head of a crime family who had great influence on the previous leaders of Lukinburg. Mother and Father took exception to having their wages garnished at the munitions factory where they worked to pad his bank account. They protested working conditions in general. When they led the movement to unionize laborers, there was a car bomb. My uncle whisked me away right after the funeral."

"Oh, my God. How awful. I'm so sorry." She switched their grip to capture his hand with both of hers. Then she leaned in as a frightening possibility turned her compassion to suspicion. "Ivan. A car bomb? The bombing at St. Feodor? The king who was blown up? Couldn't the incidents be related? Could what's happening now be a part of the protests your parents were involved with?"

"Of course not. Mother and Father were never…" He released her and sat back in the booth, pulling off his glasses and rubbing at the dimples on either side of his nose left by the frames as if he was plagued by a sudden headache. He set his glasses on top of the table and focused those blue eyes at her. "Gordeeva died in 2012, after serving time in prison. His influence on the former government's regime died when he did. The king's assassination happened when my parents were children. They are not related."

But Carly couldn't ignore the obvious similarities between the crimes. "Ivan, we can't dismiss any possibility right now. Even something that happened years ago. When you're investigating a case, you look at all the facts and then come up with a theory. You don't force the facts to fit into whatever theory you might have."

"Their murders are not related to any of the threats against the crown." On that royal dictate, he slid out of the booth and buttoned his jacket, preparing to leave.

But she was neither a Lukinburg citizen, subject to his will, nor ready to give up on the potential source for the threats against him. "Crime families are known for exacting their revenge. If your parents' murders are the reason he went to prison—"

"My parents' deaths have nothing to do with the threats now," he snapped in a hushed tone. End of discussion.

For him, maybe. "You forgot these, Bossy Boots. Excuse me, Your *Royal* Bossy Boots." She scooped up his glasses from the table as she stood, refusing to ignore what he'd told her. "Did Gordeeva have family? People who feel they've been wronged have long memories."

"Bossy Boots? The words make no sense to me. But I understand by your attitude that I was rude. No better than Danya." He inclined his head in a brief bow. "I apologize for my tone. We should go." He slipped his glasses on and headed for the front door.

Once they reached the lobby, Filip stepped in to handle the bill and tip. Carly pulled Ivan into a relatively private corner of the foyer. "What's wrong? What aren't you telling me?"

His chest expanded with a deep breath before he captured her face between his hands and touched his forehead to hers. "I have been as honest with you as the dictates of this position allow me to be." His fingers slipped into her hair and tightened around her skull as he pressed a hard kiss to her lips. She felt the stamp of his mouth like a brand against her skin. Her blood quickened in her veins and pooled in places that made her feverish with desire. But he ended the kiss before she could fully respond. "Please do not hold this against me. I cannot tell you how important your trust is to me."

Carly wound her fingers around his wrists to keep him from pulling away. "Do you really think keeping secrets right now is the smartest way to go? How can I protect you if I don't know everything I need to?"

"I have said too much already. You…" He smoothed her hair into place as his mouth twisted with a wry smile. "You distract me. You are a breath of fresh air in a life that has not been my own for these long past months. But I cannot forget my duty to my country."

He pulled away, capturing the braid that hung in front of her shoulder before releasing that, too. "I am sorry, *dorogoy.*"

She studied him intently, on the verge of understanding something she couldn't quite put her finger on. Maybe after all these years, her feminine intuition was finally kicking in, and she was recognizing the genuineness of his interest in her, along with the regret he felt at starting something that couldn't last. She stretched up on tiptoe to capture his mouth in a quick kiss that didn't convey half of what she was thinking or feeling, only that she was thinking about and feeling more for this troubled prince and this impossible relationship than a street-smart survivor like her should.

"We're still partners in this. Even if you can't tell me everything. Right now." She hinted that maybe he would before this week was over, although he gave no indication that he might. With her undercover work, she understood about keeping secrets better than most. Still, when it came to her personal life, she wasn't a big fan of holding back the truth. With a mental slap to the back of the head, she reminded herself that her relationship with Ivan *was* an undercover assignment, not the real deal, no matter what her blossoming feminine intuition might say. "We'd better get going. I won't have Danya accusing me of making you late for your next appointment in addition to forcing you to eat burnt American food."

He laughed at that, his expression relaxing into a more natural smile. "Do you know how many people are afraid to stand up for what they honestly think if it differs from my opinion? Other than the threats, they kowtow to the crown and tell me what they think I want to hear. Never be that person."

"Mouthy? Pushy?"

"Honest."

The irony that he wasn't being completely honest with her wasn't lost on either of them. She could read the regret in his eyes. Maybe that was a hazard of politics. There were always secrets to keep.

Filip nudged Ivan from behind before she could decide how to respond to that compliment. "We are ready, Your Highness."

Ivan linked his hand with hers and they walked out the door together. This time, in addition to the suffocating envelope of humid air pressing around them, a group of pedestrians had gathered on the sidewalk outside the restaurant, blocking their path.

"He was on TV."

"I saw him in the paper."

"I thought he was single."

"He's cute."

"Prince Ivan!"

Cars stopped on the street beyond them, too, the drivers curious about why people were congregating there. And although a few pedestrians walked on by, most of them stopped, growing the size of the crowd in either direction. Almost all of them raised their phones to snap pictures and videos, and call or text their friends to share this brush with fame. Others held out pens and various items like notebooks and coffee cups for an autograph.

Ivan pulled up, smiling and waving for a few pictures. A school-age girl handed Carly a flower and asked if she was a princess.

But there was no place for them to go without walking into the crowd.

Danya grumbled behind them. "I believe the tourists are now aware that there is royalty among them. We should go back inside and wait for the car to pick you up."

Filip stepped toward the crowd, pushing them back as he gave Danya an order. "Get them moving toward the parking garage." He turned to their audience. "Ladies and gentlemen, please. Prince Ivan is grateful for your interest and support, but he must get to his next engagement."

Carly wondered how anyone could possibly get used to this kind of attention when she saw a white van pulling up on the other side of the median. A man scrambled out from behind the wheel and hefted a camera onto his shoulder. She recognized the dark-haired woman from a local news station scurrying after him with a microphone. "A TV crew is here, too." Someone in the crowd called her Blondie, told her to smile and snapped a picture. She was certain she'd looked more startled than photogenic. "Is this normal?"

Ivan managed to speak under his breath without losing his smile. "Not spur-of-the-moment like this. There are other public appearances planned, with larger venues to accommodate this many people. This is unexpected. Someone must have posted to social media that I was at the restaurant."

Not anyone who wished him well. "This could turn

ugly fast." She tugged on Ivan's hand, pulling him with her a few steps. "Someone could get hurt."

But it seemed that for every square foot of pavement Filip cleared in their forward route, the curious onlookers who'd spotted the visiting celebrity pushed in that much closer behind them. Soon, Carly's and Ivan's backs were against the stucco walls and storefront windows, and their path to the next cross street was blocked. Traffic was quickly backing up beyond that. It didn't help that Ivan was being his cordial, diplomatic self and answering questions on everything from "What did you have to eat?" and "Do you have a crown?" to "How much gold is in Lukinburg?"

"We have plenty of gold now that we have developed new mining practices," he explained. But either she tugged, or he nudged with each answer to keep them moving toward the street. "Our real treasure is quartz, which is used in high-tech applications, such as circuit boards and computer components here in your country." He planted his feet and stared into the crowd as people jostled for position to see and hear him. Carly understood now that he was trying to control the crowd, to keep them from stampeding or stumbling off a curb or getting pushed in front of a moving vehicle. The crowd pulsed like a living, breathing thing. And while Carly searched for a clear path, Ivan raised his voice to be heard. "Please. I am happy to answer your questions. Perhaps if we all take a deep breath."

Carly turned her face to his shoulder. "I'm sorry I got you into this mess. But we need to get out of here."

The click of cameras and phones and whispered conversations sounded like the buzzing of bees. "Any ideas?"

"I'm thinking." She scanned up and down the street, looked past the crowd, glimpsed everyone's reflection in the display window behind them. Something wasn't right. She turned, trying to make eye contact with every face in the crowd.

Ivan answered a question about the upcoming ball. Maybe if he kept talking, they would stand still and listen. "We are hosting a joint fund-raiser with one of your local universities to develop clean technology that will use our natural resources. I will be meeting with Dr. Ian Lombard and his team tomorrow to discuss this exciting new research."

"Is it true that someone tried to kill you?" someone shouted.

Ivan's smooth facade slipped for a moment. His grip tightened on Carly's hand and the crowd fell silent. Like Carly, he skimmed the faces in the crowd to see who had asked that. "I am sorry. Who…?"

The chatter started up as suddenly as it had stopped, growing louder as people shouted questions and turned to each other to voice curiosity about Ivan's well-being and concern about the threat of danger to themselves.

"Have those threats followed you to Kansas City?" The television camera caught them in a spotlight as the female reporter thrust her microphone toward Ivan. "I heard that someone tried to poison you."

Ivan shielded his eyes and muttered under his breath to Carly. "I did not publicize—"

"That reporter at the hospital," Carly seethed beneath her breath. "He wasn't after a scandal. He wanted to know what happened to Frank. He must know about the threats."

"If I get my hands on Ralph Decker—"

"Please. Ladies and gentlemen." Filip moved in front of them, his sheer bulk forcing the crowd back a couple of feet. "Prince Ivan's security and that of your people is our top priority. As you can see, he is perfectly fine." The camera's bright light swung toward him. "We are working very closely with the local police to ensure everyone's safety throughout our visit to your lovely city."

Danya cursed ahead of them. "Where are all your police friends now?"

Good question. Lunch had lasted over an hour. Hendricks should have had officers on the scene long before now. "Did you call for backup?"

Filip bought them two more steps. "Of course I did."

Did he? Did he really?

"Where are they?" Carly glared at him. There should be bicycle cops, patrol cars. She should have followed her instincts and called Hendricks herself.

But this wasn't the time for placing blame. Maybe the traitor had countermanded Milevski's order. Maybe Milevski had seen an opportunity to create chaos to mask an attempt on Ivan's life, and had never called for local reinforcements at all.

Danya shouted to them from the corner. "This way!" But the path he'd made to the crosswalk filled in before they could reach it. "Eduard! Get the car. Now!"

"Yes, sir!" The younger bodyguard pushed his way through the mass of people. When he reached the relative opening of the boulevard, Eduard put up his hand to stop traffic, running across to the median and onto the next block.

"Go." Filip looked over his shoulder and used his head to point them toward Danya. "I will handle this." He turned back to the reporter. "If you want specific details about the poisoning incident, you should contact Galina Honchar at—"

"Your Highness!" Danya moved a pair of teenagers aside and waved Ivan closer.

They weren't going to make it. Ivan bumped into Carly's back when she stopped abruptly.

Ivan's hands clamped around her shoulders. "Carly?"

Something wasn't right here. This was no ordinary gathering of fans and curiosity-seekers. "Do you feel like you're being herded to a particular place? In a particular direction?"

Ivan considered her assessment. His fingers tightened in a silent yes. "We have no other way to go."

The crowd had become a living, pulsing entity, pushing forward, nearly encircling them, as if someone was egging them on in pursuit of the prince. All it needed was a spark of panic to flash over into a mob. Carly glanced up at the second-story windows and rooftops. They had no advantage here if things went south. Everyone's eyes were on Ivan. Who knew how many more people she couldn't see might be watching them right now? Maybe if she removed the star attraction, the crowd would disband. Carly looked back at Filip. "Where's the car?"

"Parking garage across from the bookstore. Lower level." Filip had one hand on Ivan's shoulder and his other arm extended to keep anyone from coming any closer.

And then she saw a reflection in the display window. A man who didn't fit with the rest of the fans. He wore a hooded coat, masking most of his face. He wasn't asking questions, wasn't taking pictures. And the shadowy maw inside that hood was focused squarely on them.

Chapter Eight

"Why is he wearing a coat?" Carly murmured, feeling the threat rising like the heat on her skin.

Ivan had seen him, too. "That is him."

"Him who?"

"End Ivan!" someone shouted. The hooded man?

To Carly's surprise, Ivan lunged toward the threat. She caught his arm and pulled him back. "Are you crazy?"

"That is the same threat the bomber yelled before the explosion in St. Feodor. These people are not safe."

When she scanned the crowd again, the hooded man was nowhere to be seen. "The best thing you can do for these innocent bystanders is leave. You're the target. If he loses his target, he'll move on." She pushed Ivan back the way they'd come, knocking Filip out of the way. "Cover us. Get these people out of here."

"What? It is my responsibility to—"

"I've got an idea." Carly grabbed Ivan's hand and opened the door of the nearest shop, pushing her way through the staff gathered at the windows. She pulled her badge from her pocket and thrust it into the face of a startled clerk. "You got a back door?"

The woman nodded and pointed to the back of the shop as two other people snapped pictures.

"Don't follow us," Carly warned. They ran through the store into the storage room, distance dulling the noise of the crowd outside.

"This way." Ivan spotted the rear exit. Understanding the gist of her plan, he pushed open the door that opened onto a loading dock in the alley behind the store.

Carly slipped in front of him, ensuring the alley was clear before leading him down the ramp and past the trash cans and power poles to the sidewalk that ran perpendicular to the one in front of the store. The blare of honking horns and sound of an approaching siren raised the decibel level again.

"Which way?" Ivan asked, scanning the parked cars and bumper-to-bumper traffic ahead of them.

She pulled him into the street, flashing her badge again to stop approaching vehicles as they jogged across to the center median and onto the opposite side of the street. Carly shrugged out of her jacket and tied the sleeves around her waist to keep her gun masked. "Lose the tie and roll up your sleeves." Ivan had already fallen into step beside her as he shed his jacket and transformed his look into something more casual, so they blended in with the businesspeople hurrying back to work after lunch meetings and shoppers who hadn't yet picked up on the mob scene just a couple of blocks away. Carly lengthened her stride to match Ivan's. They turned the corner and spotted the bookstore. "The parking garage is this way."

Ivan dipped his head close to her ear, never taking his eyes off the people around them, never breaking stride. "What if there is a bomb back there? Those people could be in danger."

"Those people are safer now that you're not there. You're safer."

"I do not want to be responsible for any more deaths."

"If we figure this out, you won't be." She caught his arm to stop him as a delivery van pulled out of the driveway in front of them. "Did you notice that the guy in the coat disappeared?"

"I was momentarily blinded by the television camera. I thought I had lost him in the crowd."

Carly glanced over her shoulder to see if the man was following them. But there were too many people, too many buildings and streets and cars to focus in on just one of them. "It might be a coincidence. A lot of the homeless people wear all their clothes, coats included. It could be nothing."

"It is not. He was there for a reason." Ivan sounded certain. "Perhaps you were right, and he set a trap for us. He was using the crowd to move us toward it."

"Moving toward what, though? And where is he now?" She had her gaze on continuous scan now. "And where are Filip and Danya? Shouldn't we be running into your security team?"

"Perhaps they stayed back to help with the crowd." He tilted his head toward the man running down the entrance ramp into the parking garage just half a block ahead of them. "There's Eduard." He urged her into a jog. "Come on. When we get to the car, we will be safe. We can compare notes of what we saw back there."

Carly spotted two bicycle officers maneuvering through the gridlock of vehicles. A black-and-white was coming down the hill from downtown. Good. Backup was arriving. Hopefully, soon enough to keep all those people safe. She could focus solely on Ivan now.

They hit the gated entrance into the parking garage. She saw Eduard Nagy racing down the ramp to the lower level.

The clerk in the booth waved to them. "Hey, you're that prince on TV."

"Prince Ivan?" a voice from the sidewalk called to them. "Get his picture."

"He's not as handsome as those British princes."

"I can't believe I'm this close to a real prince."

It was starting again. People milling together at the entrance to the garage. They couldn't get trapped by another mob. "Ivan?" Carly prompted.

"Eduard!" Ivan pointed out their escape and pulled her into a run beside him. "Start the car!"

Because of its length, the limousine was parked off by itself across two spaces against the far wall.

Carly's nostrils flared to draw in more oxygen as they raced toward the safety of the polished black car. They were thirty yards away. Twenty. Eduard climbed in behind the wheel. The headlights came on as he inserted the key and started the engine.

A bright light flashed beneath the car's black hood and Carly skidded to a stop. It was too late to retreat.

"Get down!" she yelled, shoving Ivan toward a concrete pillar.

Strong arms snapped around her, pulling her with him as the limo exploded with a deafening roar. A concussive wave of heat swept over them, carrying them several feet through the air before they hit the concrete and rolled to a stop against the wheel of a truck. Every point of her body was bruised or numb from the crashing fall. Knuckles, elbows, knees, heels. Ivan's full weight on top of her made it hard to breathe. But even as her lungs protested and her vision spun in circles, Carly clamped her hands around his biceps, trying to reverse their positions and drag him behind the shelter of the pillar.

But in the next second, Ivan shifted, bracing his elbows on either side of her and palming her head, tucking her face against his chest and shielding her body with his as flying metal and burning car parts rained down around them.

A heavy chunk of twisted fender clanged down beside them. Carly shoved at his chest, hating the vulnerability of his position. Instead of budging, his hold on her tightened. "Damn it, Ivan. *I* protect *you*!"

He jerked once, and she knew he'd been hit.

"Ivan!"

"Shh. Shh." He brushed his lips against her ear, calming her fears and anger, stilling the fists drumming against his chest, shielding her until the flying pieces of car parts grew smaller and ended with a staccato of tiny fragments of metal and plastic landing on the concrete around them.

The mini crashes of settling debris gave way to people screaming and the crackling whoosh of the fire burning through the remnants of the car. The telltale warning of a car horn followed by the crunch of metal on metal told her there'd been an accident on the street at the top of the ramp. At least one of those drivers had been paying more attention to the crowds and explosion than to traffic. She wasn't sure what else could go wrong.

And then she knew. "Eduard?"

When Ivan inhaled a deep breath, Carly released the death grip she had on the front of his shirt and rolled him off her. They sat up and Carly pushed to her feet. But orange-and-gold flames swirled through her vision and she stumbled against the pillar. She felt the icy cold concrete warming beneath her hand from the heat of the fire fifteen yards away as she circled around to the other side to see if there was any chance of saving the driver.

But there was no saving the bodyguard, no chance of pulling him from the flames that engulfed the car. Carly's eyes stung with tears. He'd died in the line of duty. "Poor man."

What a waste of a good, loyal man. That could have been them. It was supposed to be them.

"He is gone!" Ivan shouted in her ear.

She startled and spun around to see him on his feet, leaning against the pillar behind her. The force of the blast must have impacted Ivan's hearing. She reached up to cup his jaw, turning his face from one side to the other, checking for pupil dilation and head injuries. She didn't see anything beyond the charred bits of debris in his hair, which she brushed away.

"The blast must have hurt your ears. You're shouting."

"What? I can't hear you."

Carly smiled at the unintended humor of that tragic moment so that she wouldn't burst into tears. She'd like to blame the fumes from burning oil and gasoline on this uncharacteristic urge to cry, but she knew the emotional letdown had more to do with the shock wearing off than it did the sting of chemicals in the air. Shutting off her emotions and relying on her training, she ran her hands over Ivan's shoulders and down his arms, gently pulling away the shredded material at his elbow to see the oozing skin that had been scraped away in their tumble across the concrete.

But it was hard to check for anything more serious because Ivan's hands were on her, too, framing her face, feeling up and down her arms. "Are you hurt?"

"I need to call this in." Was her phone even working? She pulled it from her pocket. Thank goodness. Everything lit up as she swiped her thumb across the screen. She'd lost a shoe in that tumble. She needed to find it and get moving. "And make sure there are no other casualties."

The man at the gate booth was on his phone already, calling 9-1-1. She gave him a thumbs-up when he asked if they were okay, and he returned to his call, alternately yelling at bystanders to stay back and reporting the situation to the dispatcher. A second man in a maintenance uniform had run up to the blaze with a fire extinguisher, but he was fighting a hopeless battle and had to back away from the heat.

"Carly, are you hurt?" Ivan's tone had returned to its normal volume. He captured her hand to inspect her scraped knuckles, then caught her chin between his thumb and fingers. "Are you dizzy? Nauseous?"

"I was dizzy at first. It passed. I'm okay." Her gaze landed on the smear of blood on the pillar and her heart dropped to her stomach. "You're not." She moved behind him to inspect the blood-soaked tear in his shirt. There was a one-inch spike of metal protruding from the back of his shoulder. "That shrapnel needs to come out."

"I've been hurt worse."

That was supposed to reassure her? "Do you have

a handkerchief? Something I can stanch the bleeding with?"

He picked up his soiled jacket from the floor and pulled out a handkerchief. He muttered a curse when she pulled the shard from the wound and pressed the cloth against his skin. "You need a doctor."

"One travels with my entourage. He is at the hotel."

"Then that's where we need to go."

Ivan braced his fist against the pillar and watched the car burn while she fashioned a makeshift bandage with the handkerchief and her belt around his neck and beneath his arm to keep it in place. Although his breathing was measured and deep, there were no more curses as she doctored his injury. His entire focus was on the burning limo, the people on the other side of the flames and the man he'd lost. "Poor Eduard. I do not even know if he has family. Those files. We need to read them."

"The flash drive!" Carly fumbled with the jacket still tied at her waist. The material was dusty and splotched with a smear of oil from the concrete, but the flash drive was still there. It was intact. "It's okay. I don't see any damage."

Despite the sirens she could hear in the distance, more people were gathering in the sunlight outside the parking garage entrance. "The man from the ticket gate needs our help to keep everyone away from the fire. I need to find Filip. Where is he?"

After spotting a uniformed officer jogging down the ramp to help secure the scene, Carly punched in Joe Hendricks's number on her phone. Then she pulled Ivan deeper into the garage. She'd already spotted the basement level entrance to one of the shops above them.

"I'm sorry, *dorogoy*, but we can't wait for Filip. And KCPD doesn't need our help. We have to go."

He tugged her to a stop. "What did you call me?"

"Didn't I use the nickname right?"

"Your Lukin was perfect." He leaned down and pressed a quick, hard kiss to her mouth. They traded several emotions in that one brief kiss—caring, relief, worry, a sense of urgency, desire that time and circumstances allowed for nothing more to pass between them. "I might like it if you call me that." Pulling away, he shrugged into his suit jacket to hide his wounds, wincing at the pain. He took her arm and followed her through the empty part of the garage. "Lead the way. Talk to Joe, and then I will call Filip. If I may borrow your phone."

"You don't have a phone?"

He reached into his pocket and showed her his. The cover had fractured like a spiderweb and the screen was dark. "Not anymore."

"I thought maybe you couldn't. Because you're a prince."

"My country is not so backward that we do not have cells."

"But security? Couldn't someone call in a threat or track you? I know some countries don't allow royalty—"

Her call picked up and Joe Hendricks's voice boomed over the line. "Valentine? I've got 9-1-1 calls overloading dispatch at your location. What's going on?"

"Bomb in the Forty-Seventh Street garage. Somebody blew up Ivan's limo. Killed the driver." Ivan tore the remnants of his phone apart and tossed it in a trash can as they hurried past, perhaps taking her tracking concern to heart. "Looks like traffic is bottlenecking. You'll need a tow truck to clear a fender bender at the Forty-Seventh Street entrance before KCPD can get a truck in here. About the only good thing is the limo was parked away from other vehicles, so I don't think the fire will spread."

She pulled her badge from her pocket and looped it around her neck as they entered the store. She paused a moment to ask the staff and customers watching from the door if they'd seen anything or anyone suspicious in the garage. The general response was no help. They'd heard the blast and had come to look after the fact.

Warning everyone to stay back and let the first responders work the scene, she and Ivan headed for the escalator that would take them up to street level. "I have the prince with me," she reported to Captain Hendricks. "Ivan is okay. We're separated from his team."

"Securing Ivan is priority one. Get him someplace safe."

"Will do." She eyed the stalled line of traffic outside the front doors and crossed the street to the opposite side where the cars were at least crawling along. A patrol officer was diverting traffic off onto a side street to help get a fire engine through the intersection. Ivan stayed right at her side. He flipped up his collar and kept his head down to avoid recognition, but she was aware that his eyes were studying every face they passed as thoroughly as she did. She wasn't sure where she was leading him, other than as far away from the Plaza as they could get. Did she take him into the nearby residential neighborhood, where there was no hope of finding transportation? Head for Saint Luke's Hospital that was only a few blocks to the north? He wouldn't want the kind of attention that came with a wounded celebrity walking through their doors would bring. Maybe, they could at least catch a bus to get them out of the congested area. But why exactly *was* it so congested? This wasn't rush hour. And yes, there were tourist attractions and stores and offices in this historic area, but the chaos had gotten crazy fast, *before* that bomb had gone off. "Sir? We had a mob scene about five blocks from here. Did Milevski call in for backup down at the Plaza?"

"Backup is on its way."

"I mean about eighty minutes ago, before the explosion."

She heard the suspicion creeping into the captain's tone. "I'll have to check with his department contact. SWAT Team Two just left the building and are en route. But there was no tactical team dispatched before that. I'll see what patrol officers were sent in."

"Check social media, too. That crowd got big and rowdy awfully fast. Without enough security on the scene, we had no choice but to hit some back alleys and make a run for Ivan's limo. We're lucky more people weren't hurt."

"You think this was a setup?"

"That bomb was no accident." They reached the next intersection where another officer was directing traffic and hurried on across. As more police reached the area, pedestrians were being funneled away from the parking garage to the same side of the street they were on, packing the sidewalk with the crowds she'd been trying to avoid. "We had no other place to escape to besides the limo."

"Is the prince safe?" Joe Hendricks asked.

Carly looked up at Ivan, who was doing his best to

avoid bumping into anyone and aggravating his wound. She knew he needed medical attention. Still, he was moving like a soldier advancing through enemy territory, his hand on her back moving her forward as much as she was leading him. "He's hurt."

"A minor injury, Joe," Ivan insisted, dipping his head close to her phone. "I am fine."

"He will be as soon as I can get him out of here."

"My hotel," Ivan suggested while Captain Hendricks ended the call with a demand to keep him posted. He steered her around the next clump of pedestrians. "It is downtown. Do you have your car?"

She shook her head. "It's at the precinct. Brooke's husband dropped us off. I'd planned to be riding with you."

He punched in Filip Milevski's number and gave his security chief a sit-rep about losing Eduard, the name of the cross streets where they were now and that he was with her. She didn't need the phone on speaker to hear Filip's tirade about running off and getting so close to the bomb—or to hear the warning about staying put and letting Filip and Danya come to them. "Do you have a car?" Ivan challenged, cutting him off when she heard her name among the angry words. "Then you are not driving me anywhere. You deal with the police, and I want someone to stay with Eduard's body."

A glimpse of stillness among the rush of activity filling the streets and sidewalks drew her attention and slowed her pace. A chill skittered down her back, despite the heat and humidity and man standing so close beside her. "Ivan?"

"You do not think a man shouting, 'End Ivan!' is threat enough? Call the hotel and make sure that Aleks,

Galina and the others are safe." He ended the call and slipped the phone back into Carly's pocket. "What is it?"

"Ten o'clock. On the other side of those parked cars."

When she stepped toward the curb, Ivan's arm folded around her waist and pulled her back against his chest. She was certain the curse he muttered in his native language was something blue and damning.

The man in the hood had reappeared. Despite the material shading his face, there was no mistaking the "I'm watching you" signal he sent, gesturing with two fingers to where his eyes would be before pointing at them. Carly reached behind her back, nudging Ivan aside to pull her gun. But when she blinked, he'd disappeared. Moving west, she thought. But she didn't have eyes on him anymore. "Damn it. I can't leave you to pursue him."

She felt Ivan's fingers on her wrist, keeping her gun in its holster. "There are too many people here to draw your weapon."

True. She'd probably cause more panic if she did pull her gun and race after the suspect. Plus, going after him meant leaving Ivan completely unprotected. Or worse, he'd insist on coming with her, putting himself in the line of fire. "Did you see where he went?"

He pointed to the west. "That way. But I lost him behind the cars. He had a backpack. He probably stuffed his coat inside and blended into the crowd."

Being out of uniform with no radio, she turned back to the officer directing traffic and identified herself. She gave the officer a general description of height and build, plus the hooded coat and backpack, and asked him to put out an APB on the suspect. Although she guessed that Ivan was right about the man changing his outfit and clearing the area.

"Let's keep moving." She reached back to lace her fingers together with Ivan's. "How are you doing? You're not bleeding out on me, are you?"

"If you will not complain about the scratches on your hands and face, then I will not complain about my injuries."

She halted again, lifting her hands to see the black-and-violet bruising and raw skin on her knuckles. "I hadn't even noticed."

"I notice everything about you." He touched the tip of his finger to a tender spot on her jawline. "My doctor will be treating you as well, when we reach the hotel."

Suddenly, she realized how much her body ached after flying across the concrete, and just how much worse her injuries might be if Ivan hadn't shielded her with his body when the bomb had gone off. "Thank you for protecting me." She sensed she was due for a physical and emotional crash once the adrenaline of these past several minutes wore off. But that time wasn't now. And Prince Blue Eyes needed a stern reminder about the rules of this charade. "I'm the bodyguard, remember? The relationship is for show, but the gun and the badge and my job are real. If you ever do anything like that again, I will—"

A car spun around the corner and screeched to a halt in front of them. The passenger side window went down and Ralph Decker, the reporter who'd photographed them at the hospital leaned across the front seat. "Need a ride?"

"What do you want?" Carly asked, suspicious of his timely arrival.

"To do you a favor." Decker pulled his hands from the steering wheel and shrugged. "Unless you want to fight your way through this crowd and get stuck in traffic for another hour."

Carly spotted Filip on the far side of the street, doing just that, fighting to get through the crowd. Ivan had seen him, too. He opened the back door for Carly and nudged her to get in. "We accept your offer, Mr. Decker."

Carly braced her hands against the door frame. "We don't really know this guy."

"Please, Carly. We need to see the doctor." She shivered at the whisper of Ivan's lips against her hair and responded to the plea in that accented tone. Although she suspected this was more about getting her away from the danger than getting himself to his physician, Carly relented, climbing in and sliding across the back seat. If she was far from any threat, then he would be, too. Ivan slid in beside her. Clearly, he believed now, more than ever, that the person behind the threats was getting help from someone inside his delegation. Perhaps it was easier to trust this relative stranger than someone he knew had the means to betray him to his enemies. "This does not mean I am giving you an exclusive, Mr. Decker. Nor do I give you permission to take any photos of Carly and me today."

"Understood. But you can't tell me there's not a real news story here. Something a lot bigger than this affair you're having. An explosion and an attempted assassination? I can't help but ask a few questions."

"This was a mistake." Ivan reached for the door handle.

Carly stopped him. This time he had no argument

when she unholstered her gun and held it up for Decker to see in the rearview mirror. "He'll behave himself."

Decker grinned and shifted his car into gear. "You make a convincing argument, Officer."

She gave him the name of Ivan's hotel. "Go."

As they drove up the hill toward downtown, she saw Filip break free from the mass of pedestrians and run across the street to the spot they'd just vacated. He was joined by Danya now. Both men were breathing hard from exertion, both watching the car as it sped away. Filip dabbed at the perspiration on his forehead with a bright white handkerchief. When he pulled the cloth from his face, he looked pissed. Danya's hands were fisted at his sides. She didn't have to read lips to know he was cursing.

But were they angry that she'd taken over their job to keep the prince safe? That a coworker had been murdered?

Or that Ivan had survived the blast?

Chapter Nine

Carly thanked the doctor who had bandaged her left hand and cleaned the scrapes on her jaw and elbows. While Ivan washed up in the adjoining bathroom of his hotel suite, the doctor packed his bag and exited the bedroom where she'd peeled off her ruined blouse for him to check her injuries.

With the door propped open, the white noise of heated conversation she'd heard from the main room sharpened into words she could understand. Most of them, anyway, since some of the arguing seemed to be in Lukin. Seizing the opportunity to eavesdrop on potential suspects, she clutched the torn blouse to her chest, ducked behind the door to keep it from fully closing and listened.

Galina's shrill voice reprimanded someone. "We should be thanking God or fate or whatever you believe in that the prince was not in that car."

Filip didn't like to be lectured. "He should have stayed with me!"

"And been trampled? Shot?" Galina countered. "It's unfortunate enough we lost Eduard. But if Ivan had been killed, this entire trade mission would have been ruined—maybe even our alliance with the United

States, our sister city status with Kansas City. It could have thrown Lukinburg into chaos."

Aleks couldn't resist diving into the thick of the argument. "Our relationships with any foreign nation would be at risk. They'd all be saying, 'Keep your political troubles and unhappy citizens at home in Lukinburg.'"

"This is not my fault," Filip argued. "*She* altered the prince's schedule."

"And if she hadn't, the prince would have been in that car when it blew up, too."

"You don't know that," Danya Pavluk grumbled. "Maybe the bomber wouldn't have had the chance to plant the device if we'd stuck to our plan."

"What plan would that be?" an American voice asked. Ralph Decker had hung around to eavesdrop, too. The reporter had a knack for showing up when least expected. Was that luck on his part? Good reporting? A source inside Ivan's delegation feeding him intel? Could he have any agenda beyond covering a story?

"Mr. Decker," Galina snapped, then softened her tone to polite decorum. "Once again, I will ask you to leave. We thank you for your assistance today."

"The prince said he wanted to thank me personally. I'm curious to find out what he meant by that."

Danya muttered a curse, as if Decker had just made a point for him. "See? There are too many loose ends. Filip, you need to run a tighter ship."

Filip didn't bother to mutter. "Are you questioning my authority?"

Carly smelled a hint of icy fresh soap a split second before Ivan reached around her to close the door. "Learn anything new?"

More than not sensing his approach, Carly was startled to turn and discover a shirtless prince. Was that allowed? Showing off broad shoulders? Drawing her attention to a muscled chest dusted with a V of crisp, dark hair that trailed in a line over his flat stomach down to the button of the black dress slacks he wore?

A split second of heated admiration passed before she realized that he'd asked her a question. She blinked, wishing it were that easy to cool the spark that seemed to ignite deep inside whenever he got close like this. "Only that no one out there is taking any blame for what happened."

"I doubt anyone would admit that their assassination attempt was thwarted by you." He handed her a clean white T-shirt. "Are you sure this is sufficient? I can order you a new blouse from the gift shop downstairs."

"That isn't necessary. Unlike you, I'm not going any-place fancy this evening." He took her blouse and tossed it in the trash before crossing to the closet to pull a white dress shirt off the hanger. She gasped when she saw the crosshatched ridges of pink scar tissue peppering his back beside and below the square white bandage that covered the gash he'd gotten from the explosion this afternoon. *I have been hurt worse than this*, he'd said when she'd pulled the shrapnel from his wound. If the view from the front had been stunning, the view from the back squeezed at her heart and made her hurry across the room before he could don his shirt. "Ivan. What happened to you?"

She touched her fingertips to the scars. He shivered as she traced the marks. The scar hidden by his beard was a scratch compared to these injuries. His mus-cles tensed beneath her hand before he released a deep breath. "Souvenirs from the bombing in St. Feodor. I threw myself over the body of...a friend...to protect him from the shrapnel."

"Just like you did with me today." She splayed her fingers over the longest and most jagged of the scars, indicating he'd suffered burns in addition to the deep wounds. "You are not to do that for me again. Is that understood? You were seriously hurt. How could anyone want to...? I'm so sorry."

With a deep, stuttering breath, he turned to face her. He dipped his face close to hers, his blue eyes focused on her mouth. "Perhaps you had better stop petting me unless you intend to make me late for tonight's festivities."

"How would I...? Oh." Her gaze darted to the bed. "You mean..."

He touched her cheek, smiling as he followed the heat creeping into her face. "If our timing was better and my responsibilities were not so great, I would let you touch me in whatever way you wish. Does it shock you that I want you that way?"

She hugged the T-shirt close to her chest, fighting to assuage the inevitable response that stung the tips of her breasts and tightened the muscles between her thighs. "It shocks me how much I want you, too," she admitted. "I've never had such intense feelings with any man."

He feathered his fingers into her hair and cupped her warm cheek and neck. "Brave, honest, tempting Carly. Do you know how that makes me feel?"

"Not exactly. Most of my experience with men comes from annoying big brothers and taking down bad guys. You're a prince compared to the guys who usually hit on me." Her blush deepened when she heard the double entendre. The heat building inside almost made her light-headed. She needed more than the cooling caress of his hand to right the emotions tumbling inside her. "Thank you for taking the brunt of that explosion and collision with the concrete this afternoon. Those marks on your back should be on me." She leaned into him, winding her arms around his waist in a ferocious hug.

His arms closed around her, securing her against him. "Never. You are becoming important to me." He pressed a kiss to her hair before he leaned back against her arms and framed her head between his hands to study her. "This feels real to me. Perhaps, like two soldiers in the thick of battle together, our bond has formed quickly. Deeply."

She braced her hands against his bare chest, delighting at the discovery of how the crisp, curly hair tickled her palms, and his nipples sprang to attention beneath her curious exploration. "There were never any soldiers like you when I was deployed."

"Like what?" His voice thickened with a husky timbre that danced against her eardrums and quickened her pulse.

"Like I can't keep my eyes and hands off you. Like I already know everything important about you. Like I can tell you anything, ask anything, do…" Her hands stilled on his warm, muscled chest. "Am I foolish for thinking like that?"

"If so, then we are both fools." He leaned in and she stretched up to meet his kiss.

But a sharp knock at the door interrupted the moment. Galina was summoning Ivan to return to his princely duties. "Your Highness? We need you out here to make some decisions."

With a regretful sigh that caressed her skin like a

warm breeze, he rested his forehead against hers. "What was I saying about timing?"

As they pulled apart, Carly rested her hand along his bearded jaw and whispered her regret. "I know you're only in my life for a week, but I don't want this—us— to be a charade."

He sealed his lips over hers, completing the interrupted kiss with a firm stamp that left her feeling wanted and wanting more. "Neither do I."

Ivan stepped back, pulling the T-shirt on over her head. He freed her messy braid from beneath the collar and draped it over her shoulder. How could putting clothes on feel like he was *un*dressing her? The heat that flared between them whenever they dropped their guard and got close felt intimate, she supposed— whether clothes were going on or coming off, whether they kissed, or he simply brushed his calloused fingertip across her cheek as he did now, pulling away. He shrugged into his shirt, looped a tie around his neck, grabbed his suit jacket, then took her hand, opened the door and led her back out to the main room with the others.

Carly pulled her jacket on over the oversize T-shirt. It might be irrational, but she wanted to hide the soft cotton clinging to her skin, as if it were something sensual, protective, private between her and Ivan. Wearing his undershirt instilled her with a symbolic sense of caring that she'd never felt when she'd borrowed clothing from her brothers.

Taking in each of the senior staff gathered around, Ivan buttoned his shirt and tucked it in, running the impromptu meeting even as he prepared for his next command performance. "What needs to be done?"

Aleks handed him a bottle of water and asked, "How are you feeling? The doctor said you required stitches."

Ivan took a long drink before resealing the bottle and handing it to Carly. No one had offered her anything. "My back is a little tender, but I assure you I will make a full recovery."

"Will it leave a scar?"

"A small one." Did Aleks know about the other scars Ivan bore? Marks of survival. Marks of strength and toughness she wondered if Aleks, or anyone else in this room, completely understood. "Miss Valentine's injuries are minor, as well. Thank you for asking." Was it possible she'd just heard a snarky reprimand in Ivan's autocratic tone?

Aleks apparently had. He turned to Carly and gave her a deferential nod. "My apologies. I am pleased to hear that. We owe you greatly for helping our Ivan today."

"I'd hate to lose him." Ivan glanced over the jut of his shoulder at her, giving her a questioning look. *Yes, there was a personal meaning to that statement.* "It definitely helped to have the home field advantage today."

Aleks snapped his fingers. "That is a baseball phrase. I have learned a great deal from your father about American sports. I only wish we had enough time to see a Royals ball game in person."

"Perhaps on another visit, we will make the time," Ivan said.

Another visit? Was it possible she'd have the chance to see Ivan again after this week and her protection assignment was done? As quickly as hope rushed through her veins, it faded. He'd probably be king the next time he came to the US. There would be even more demands on his time, more people surrounding him. She'd still be a commoner who couldn't dance or pick out a proper dress on her own. Suddenly, her entire future shrank down to this week with this man. Ivan Mostek was everything she hadn't even known she wanted in a man. Strong of character. Caring. Brave. Undeniably sexy. Even if they did find the mole and she kept him alive, their time together was destined to end. The finality of that, the ticking clock counting down to the time he would leave her, made every moment together more intense—and too precious to waste on niceties like dating and decorum. If she truly loved this man, as she suspected she did, then she had only a few days to be with him—to love him—before she lost him forever.

Ivan buttoned his cuffs and pulled on his jacket before turning his attention to Galina and the computer tablet she held. "What decisions need to be made?"

Since Galina seemed to be a perpetually put-together woman, Carly guessed that the huff that lifted the other woman's dark bangs indicated annoyance. She gestured to the man sitting on the couch, drinking a bottle of water. "Mr. Decker, for one thing. He refuses to accept any payment for his services. What are we to do with him? He has been most…inquisitive."

Ignoring the dark-eyed daggers she shot his way, Ralph Decker rose and crossed the sitting area to join them. "It's an ingrained habit. I can't help but ask questions." He crushed the empty bottle in his hands and tucked it into the front pocket of his jeans. "Mr. Petrovic and your chief of staff have been regaling me with everything you hope to accomplish for your country while you're here in the US. Sounds admirable and ambitious. Go big or go home, eh?"

Ivan turned to Carly with that frustrated frown that meant he hadn't understood the slang. "You've got big plans for Lukinburg," she explained, "and you won't settle for anything less than what you came here for."

"That is true." He gave his answer to the reporter.

"And you're willing to risk your life to do that?" Decker asked.

"I am." Ivan didn't bat an eye when Decker pressed him for a more informative answer. "Galina, issue this man a press pass for the ball on Saturday. Clear his credentials, of course. The ball is black-tie, Mr. Decker."

"I can find a tux."

"Would you like to cover our visit to the research facility at the university tomorrow? You can see how our raw materials are being put to use in building American technology."

"I'd like to sit down for a one-on-one interview with you. But I'll settle for the invitations." Decker seemed to understand that helping Ivan escape the Plaza and get to the hotel didn't mean he'd earned full access to Lukin politics and conspiracies. "I thought royalty were all figureheads. But you've got a real agenda. You've got some stones, Your Highness."

Ivan looked to Carly again. The lewd colloquialism was something she'd rather explain in private. Or not at all. "It's a compliment. He respects you."

Decker's green eyes smiled as they met hers. "That's the polite translation." He turned his gaze to Galina and winked. "You saving me a dance at the embassy ball, pretty lady?"

Galina arched a regal eyebrow. "I will not be dancing. Certainly not with you. Allow me to show you to the door, Mr. Decker. I will get your contact information to send you the press passes."

Decker laughed. "I like her. She's all business. Kind of makes me want to see what's under that starched collar."

"I beg your pardon?"

"Figuratively, of course." Decker shook Ivan's hand and nodded to Carly before following Galina to the door. "Thanks, Your Highness. Good luck with everything. Officer Valentine. Hey, if a copy of the bomb squad's report on today's incident happens to fall into my hands…"

Not until she read it first. "I'll see what I can do."

Aleks laughed as Galina and Decker disappeared into the foyer. "I think she likes him. At least, she likes being flirted with. I haven't seen her flustered like that since losing Konrad."

After Aleks's matchmaking amusement had been dismissed, and the reporter had been ushered out, Ivan checked his watch. "We have twenty minutes before we are set to leave for the Mayweathers' cocktail reception." He spoke to Filip, who was adding milk to his coffee at the bar. "I assume you have made new arrangements for our transportation? And inspected each vehicle personally?"

Filip set the cup down without ever taking a drink. "There was nothing wrong with that limousine when we left the hotel this morning. I rode with you everywhere today. If I thought there was a bomb on it, would I have done this?"

Carly wanted a better explanation, a better alibi, than the security chief's excuses. "We don't know the details about the bomb yet. It could have been on a timer or remotely detonated."

"A remote detonation would mean someone was watching us to know when we would be in the limousine," Milevski argued.

"Someone *was* watching us today," she pointed out. The hooded man among hundreds of other less obviously suspicious bystanders at the Plaza was her prime suspect. If only she had a name, or even a face, to help identify him. And if she could prove the hooded man was working with any one of these people, she'd close the case and know Ivan was safe.

Ivan buttoned his collar and knotted his tie. "If it was triggered by turning the ignition as it appeared to be, then the bomb was put there sometime after we arrived at the store and went to dinner. That's only a two-hour window."

"One of our people stays with the car always," Filip insisted. "It was Eduard's assignment until we called him for backup to help manage the crowd."

"Eduard was in the store with us," Carly reminded them. "I remember him joking with the clerk who checked us out. Was the limo unattended during that time, too? A skilled bomber wouldn't need more than a few minutes."

Filip stormed across the carpet, his cheeks turning ruddy with temper. "What are you accusing me of? Not doing my job? An attempt on the prince's life? That is treason, Miss Valentine." He thumped his chest, leaning in close enough for her to smell the oily tonic he used in his hair. "*I* am a proud Lukin. If you had not interfered—"

"Are you angry because I got the prince out of a dangerous situation you couldn't control or because Eduard is dead?" Carly wasn't intimidated by Filip's bluster. She had two big brothers she was used to standing up to. She propped her hands on her hips and stood her ground. "Or are you upset because this latest attempt to kill Ivan failed?"

Her challenge left a long silence in the room. Ivan had moved in beside her, no doubt thinking she needed his protection. Now he stood shoulder to shoulder with Carly, awaiting Milevski's answer. Galina returned in time to hear the accusation, hanging back at the edge of the seating area. Aleks cleaned his glasses, either oblivious to or purposely ignoring the tension in the room.

From across the room, Carly heard a grumbling noise that sounded a little bit like laughter. Danya had avoided the whole conversation, but now he moved to the bar to pour himself a cup of coffee. "She knows, Filip. She knows about the threats. This isn't how we ran security in the old days. We should have canceled any royal appearances until we shored up the holes in our security network. Even that day we lost Konrad and the others in St. Feodor, we'd heard chatter about one last hurrah from the Loyalist movement. But you ignored it. Lives were lost that didn't have to be."

"The prince insisted on making that appearance. To show solidarity in the new government."

"The prince relies on us to keep him safe. When there's a threat, what needs to be done shouldn't be up for debate."

"Wait a minute," Ivan calmly interrupted. "What do you mean by holes in security? What is it, Danya? What do you know of today's events?"

Danya turned to his boss, giving him a mocking salute with his coffee cup. "You tell him, or I will."

Filip rubbed his fist in the palm of his other hand before the anger fell away and his face aged with remorse. "There was a security breach sometime last night. A hacker got into my computer files. He has our personal contact information, so it's possible he could be pinging our phones and tracking our movements. He would have known today's schedule, our security assignments." He shrugged his beefy shoulders. "With that information, he or she would have known where the limousine would be parked, and the time frame for your luncheon. He could even have called Eduard's phone to trigger the explosion. I know there were threats made against you in Lukinburg. I fear the Loyalists haven't honored their alliance. They followed you here to the States."

Ivan reflected on the revelation for a moment. Surely, he wasn't about to tell these people that he was the one who'd gotten into Filip's files. Carly reached into the pocket of her jacket and curled her fingers around the flash drive. Still there. Still safe. Still their best lead. Anyone else who had access to those files could have used the information as Filip had suggested—to follow Ivan, to set off the bomb. Ivan wouldn't admit he was conducting his own investigation of these so-called friends and colleagues, would he?

But the prince had a different confession to make. "I have received two threats since we arrived in the US."

Carly's sigh of relief was drowned out by the flurry of concern and protest from the circle of people closing in around Ivan.

Danya cursed. "This is what I mean. It's shabby—"

"Why did you not tell me?" Filip accused. "How can

you expect me to do my job when I do not have all the information I need?"

"Someone has that information," Galina chided. "On all of us. Now we are all in danger. How could you let this happen?"

Filip scoffed at the accusation. "Eduard was our tech man. We'd need an expert in technology to find out where the incursion came from."

From the corner of her eye, Carly glimpsed Ivan adjusting his glasses on his nose and studying Aleks, sending a silent message to the nerdy numbers guy. "This is your area of expertise, my friend."

Aleks blinked once, twice, not understanding any better than she did. "Are you accusing me of—?"

"I am not. But perhaps you could help?"

His adviser's confusion suddenly cleared. "Oh…yes. I am good with a computer. I will look at Filip's program this evening after the party to see what I can find out."

What was that all about? Carly wondered. Ivan had said Aleks was the only member of his delegation he trusted. Was this a regular exchange between the two men? Was he using his friend to cover up his foray into late-night hacking? Had he used his friend to help him keep other secrets before this one?

At first glance, the two men could be brothers, although she'd been spending enough time with Ivan that she noticed the subtle differences in their build and height. She was guessing Aleks didn't carry the scars Ivan did. Both men had blue eyes; both wore glasses, although Aleks had a slightly thicker lens in his. Both men had that rich, raven-black hair, but Ivan kept his hair and beard neatly trimmed while Aleks had embraced his curly locks and grown them out to the point he looked like a turn-of-the-century scientist pictured in one of her schoolbooks.

They couldn't be related, could they? No, their last names were different. Cousins? There were enough lies and secrets in this room that it wasn't completely out of the question. A man would trust his family, wouldn't he? Did the two men share a link beyond friendship? Even as Aleks scrolled through icons on the screen, she wondered if Ivan and Aleks cut their hair the same length and wore the same glasses frame, could they could switch places like twins sometimes did?

But what did their looks or relationship even matter? A man was dead. Multiple attempts had been made on Ivan's life. The threats were real, and as far as Carly could tell, Lukin security sucked. "We have computer specialists at the crime lab if you want me to call them," she offered.

"No," Filip snapped before she finished making the offer. "I want no foreigners looking through my records."

Was that embarrassment? Or did the man truly have something to hide?

Ivan was insistent. He sent her the same silent message he'd given Aleks. *Follow my lead.* "Thank you for the offer, but Aleks can spend some time working on this after our appearance at the Mayweathers' this evening." He dropped a hand onto Aleks's shoulder. "I will expect a report in the morning."

"Roger that, Your Highness."

"Roger that?" Ivan chuckled. "You are picking up many Americanisms." He tapped his watch. "Now go pick out a tie that does not have evidence of your lunch on it so that we may be ready to depart." He turned to

Filip, who was still stewing over the security breach. "Bring the car around, please."

Danya stepped forward. "I will be driving now, sir. Since we are not canceling any appearances, despite the threats. You are giving our enemy an unfair advantage."

Ivan nodded. "Your complaint is noted. Lukinburg is depending on us. On all of us. We shall simply be more careful." He addressed everyone in the room before they all went their separate ways. "We will move forward without Eduard. We will remember him as a brave young man, a Lukin patriot who gave his life for his country. We will not dishonor his memory by failing on our mission to the States. Any questions?"

With a flurry of *thank you*s and *yes, sir*s, Filip, Danya, Galina and Aleks all went in different directions, putting down coffee cups and checking their respective gear before heading out the door to their respective rooms to finish getting ready to depart.

Once the penthouse door had clicked shut behind them, Ivan hurried over to Aleks's computer and sat down at the desk. "Apparently, I need to do a better job of covering my tracks." He pulled down a command from the toolbar, clicked in a few places and typed in a couple of passwords before going back to the home screen and shutting everything down. "There. Filip should not be able to trace the incursion back to this computer now. If he somehow manages to get through these firewalls, and understands IP addresses, all he will find is a dummy account."

Impressive. Ivan seemed to have some skills she wouldn't expect to find in royalty. His penchant for protecting her from threats both physical and emotional? Encryption-breaking hacker skills? What exactly had his job been before being named the crown prince? Would he be on that flash drive, too? Now she really wanted to get to her own computer and dig into the files that were burning a hole in her pocket.

Carly picked up a towel from the wet bar and wiped Ivan's prints off the keyboard and mouse before using the towel to close the laptop. "Now we've really erased your trail."

"Well-done, my lioness." He tipped his face up to hers and smiled. "I sensed you would be a true ally. You have done much for me. You truly have my back. I do not know how I will ever be able to thank you."

Forget Prince Charming. This mysterious puzzle of a man, who made tough guy in a tailored suit and geek with glasses equally hot made her feel soft and feminine and important without having to sacrifice one iota of the tough, working-class cop she was.

"You're welcome." Feeling a connection to him as though they were tethered together at the heart, Carly leaned in and kissed him. She slid her palms against the tickle of his beard and cupped either side of his jaw. Swiveling his chair to face her, Ivan's hands settled at her waist. Then, with a deep-pitched sigh, he skimmed his hands over her hips and cupped her bottom, tugging her between the V of his legs until her knees butted against the edge of the chair and she tumbled into his chest.

Surrendering to the demands of his kiss, Carly parted her lips and sank into his hard, warm body. She made several demands of her own, running her fingers across his short hair and bemoaning the cinched-up layers of clothing between them. Her lips scudded across his. She pulled his firm lower lip between hers, found the point of his chin through his beard and lightly nipped him there, unleashing a feral groan from his chest that spoke to something primitive and needy inside her.

Ivan shifted position again, pushing to his feet and forcing her head back to plunder her mouth with his. He gently touched his lips to the strawberry on her jaw, then nuzzled his way to her earlobe and the sensitive bundle of nerves he discovered underneath that made her jolt with each stroke of his tongue or rasp of his beard against the tender skin there. His sexy, accented voice was a deep purr against her ear. "I will say 'thank you' many more times if this is how you say, 'you are welcome.'" Carly wound her arms around his neck and recaptured his lips. "Thank you," he growled against her mouth. "Thank—"

A sharp rap at the door washed over her like a splash of icy water. Galina's prim, succinct voice intruded. "Your Highness? We are ready. It is time."

Easing her grip around Ivan's neck, Carly dropped onto her heels. "That's…my cue to…to leave." Her lips and fingertips and breasts and blood were still tingling with the electricity that had arced between them, making it difficult to think, much less speak. "You have a party to get to."

"Carly…" His eyes were drowsy pools of deep blue behind his glasses, and she had a hard time looking away. "I wish with everything in me that you and I… that none of this stood in our way." There was another sharp knock. His expression hardened, and he whipped his gaze to the door. "I will be there shortly."

When he turned away, she glimpsed a spike of black hair sticking up from the top of his head and felt a stab of embarrassment. His trim hair spiked up in several places, mussed by her hands. She reached up and smoothed them back into place. "Sorry about that. You have to go out in public. You can't look like you just had sex. Like we... Of course, there wasn't time to... Oh, hell."

While her skin heated with embarrassment, Ivan laughed. He cupped her warm cheek in his cool hand. "My sweet, honest Carly. You are good for me in so many ways. I am filled with regret that I cannot make that wish come true for you."

Right. This relationship couldn't go anywhere. No matter how right it felt, it simply couldn't be. She dredged up a smile. "You are good for me in many ways, too, Your Highness."

She was surprised to see the humor fade from his eyes at her response. A sternness crept into his tone, as if their language difference had created a misunderstanding. "I mean, I regret that I cannot make that wish come true for you *at this time.*"

At this time. Meaning, they were going to finish that kiss at some other time? A light of understanding dawned. She didn't need any translation for what he'd just promised her. He wanted her as much as she wanted him. She pushed onto her toes and traded one sweet, perfunctory kiss. "I hope so."

"I do not suppose we can simply not answer the door and she will go away."

Carly laughed. "You have responsibilities." She pulled the flash drive from her pocket and held it up. "So do I."

He clasped her hand and walked her to the door. "Will you allow one of my men to drive you home?"

Um, bombs? Unknown traitor? Knowing his delegation wasn't especially fond of her involvement with the prince? "Under the circumstances, I believe I'll find my own ride. My brother Jesse won't be at work yet. I'll give him a call."

"Was I right to admit the new threats to my entourage?"

"I think the bomb this afternoon kind of gave it away." They stopped at the door, lowering their voices to a whisper, in case Galina or anyone else was eavesdropping from the other side. "It will certainly stir the pot. Your people will be working even harder to prove their loyalty to you and the crown. Either out of pride or because they want to cover up anything suspicious. That was clever, too, to divert suspicion from you about the stolen files. Aleks won't tell anyone that it was you, will he?"

"He will not. That is why I wanted him to be the one investigating the security breach. He will keep my secret."

"I'm sorry about Eduard. And for his family. He seemed like a nice man."

"Let us hope he is not a martyr for a cause."

She reached up to straighten his tie, but only seemed to be making it worse. Ivan stilled her hands against his chest, "What is it, *dorogoy*?"

"I feel like I'm leaving you alone with the enemy. I can go to the party if you want me to."

He lifted each hand to his mouth and kissed her fingers before releasing them. "I need you to start going over those files. I am tired of people dying and not having any answers to explain who is responsible."

Carly nodded. "I'll get you your own cell phone, too. A disposable one the others don't know about. You can use that one to call or text me. And no one can track you."

"I think that would be a good idea. Thank you for looking out for me."

She ignored the urge to answer his thanks the way she had over in the chair. Instead, she patted his arm. "That's why I'm here, isn't it?"

"It is not the only reason, *dorogoy*." He drew his fingertip across her uninjured cheek in a familiar caress. "I will see you later?"

A firmer knock rattled the door and Filip's harsh voice called to them. "Your Highness, we will be late. Miss Valentine? You must let him go."

That was prophetic.

Carly ignored the big rock of reality that weighted her down again and reached for the doorknob. "I'll be waiting for you. Be safe."

Chapter Ten

Ivan saluted the trio of men in the Valentines' living room with a forkful of cherry pie before stuffing the sweet, tart bite into his mouth and heading downstairs to Carly's bedroom.

It was strange to see Aleks so enamored with American baseball, and making friends with Carly's father and brother Frank, who was home from the hospital and staying with them for a few days while he recuperated from being poisoned. But then Aleks had always had a knack for socializing. He'd been an asset at the Mayweathers' cocktail party tonight, showing the most charming side of Lukinburg, as well as being a knowledgeable representative to help Ivan discuss their new government policies and trade ambitions with the US. Aleks had covered for him earlier this evening at the hotel, too, allowing him to keep his secrets from Filip and the others. Aleks deserved a break. The three men were spread out across the sectional couch, fixated on the televised game. Filip was in the kitchen, eating a late dinner after trading places with Danya, who sat in the car parked out front and made routine checks around the exterior of the house. The two bodyguards would swap out four-hour shifts, sleeping in Jesse Valentine's old room while the other kept watch. Galina was staying the night at the Lukinburg embassy, handling last-minute details for the ball.

They were all safe for now, the game was an exciting one, judging by their cheers and chatter, and they were all full of Carly's delicious food. Ivan was looking forward to several hours of uninterrupted time with Carly. Maybe to finish that kiss she'd started in his hotel suite, possibly to tell her the truth about how quickly she'd come to mean something to him, certainly to discuss the background records she'd been poring over since dinner, and just to have a few hours where he didn't have to be the prince. For a few hours tonight, he could just be the man who wanted to be with Carly Valentine.

Ivan turned on the lower landing to quietly open and close the door that led down to the finished basement that had been converted into Carly's private space. She had a bedroom area, an office space with a big antique desk and bookshelves, her own bathroom and closet. The ceiling had been soundproofed to give her privacy from her father's loud television and keep whatever noise she made down here from traveling to the upper levels of the house. The windows had been given the proper egress in case of an emergency, yet they were covered with shutters her brother Frank had made.

He turned the lock in the knob before heading down the last few steps. If Carly wasn't already a brave, sexy woman who spoke to everything he truly was, he'd want to be a part of her life just for her cooking. The fancy hors d'oeuvres and champagne cocktails at the Mayweather reception had been tasty, but not filling. Even reheated, the leftover grilled burgers, potato salad and coleslaw Carly had pulled from the fridge had been delicious.

He spotted her over a partition of shoulder-high bookshelves, sitting cross-legged on her bed with the computer in her lap, a pen jammed between her lips, and a yellow legal pad on the quilt beside her. Pausing for a few precious seconds before she looked up from her work, he drank in the sight of her cutoff shorts and long bare legs. Her hair, damp from an earlier shower, hung loose and tumbled around her shoulders. She still wore his T-shirt from earlier, and tremors of a now familiar desire scuttled though him. The decadence of her cherry pie was forgotten as he savored the even sweeter knowledge that that was his shirt on her, and that he didn't have to share himself with anybody but her right now.

The frown of concentration on her face vanished as she reacted to some sound he'd made. She pulled the pen from her mouth and started to shut the laptop.

"Don't worry. I locked the door." He strode around the bookshelves and resumed his place in the blue-striped chair near the foot of her bed where he'd draped his jacket and tie and kicked off his shoes earlier. "Your father, Frank and Aleks are watching the baseball game, Filip is in the kitchen, polishing off the last of your potato salad and Danya is patrolling outside. I warned my staff that unless the house came under attack, we were not to be disturbed. We are safe. We are alone." But she was still frowning. "Is something wrong?"

She hesitated a moment too long before answering. "Maybe. I don't know." She clicked on a file and turned the laptop around to show him the screen. "This is Aleks's file. It's still in Lukin. Except for his name, I can't read any of it. But I think it's been mislabeled."

The dessert suddenly sat like a rock in his gut. "Like I said, I was interrupted before I had the chance to translate all of them. Let me look at it. Trade?" He handed her the pie before pulling the computer onto his lap. "This was the last piece. I noticed you did not eat any at dinner. Sorry, I could not resist taking one more bite. Your cooking reminds me of growing up at my aunt's. Nothing was wasted, and everything was delicious."

"That's a nice compliment. Thanks." She ate a bite of the pie, and he watched her lips close around the fork and slide off. His body reacted with a jolt of need. It felt intimate to do something so simple as sharing food. But Carly quickly reminded him of the job at hand. "Is there a translation program you use? You don't have to read through it word for word and rewrite it in English yourself, do you?"

Mislabeled. A careless mistake for someone with his skills. He should tell her just what she'd find in the file. But she set the pie aside and picked up her legal pad and started going through the suspicious things she'd already found in Filip's records.

"I was surprised to see that Galina served in the army. She seems more like the I-don't-want-to-get-my-hands-dirty type."

Ivan grinned at the surprisingly accurate assessment of the chief of staff and ruler of all things royal protocol. "Every able-bodied Lukin, man or woman, serves two years after schooling. Then they can continue in the army, as I did, or go to university or into the workforce."

"I just don't see her going through basic training. Unless the Lukin version of that isn't as dirty or physical as our army?"

"I will put my training up against yours any day."

"Okay, tough guy. That must explain why you're in such good shape for a guy with a throne job." This time, they laughed together. "I couldn't find in there what she did, though. Medic? That could explain the poisoned apples. Admin?" Ivan pulled up her internet provider and logged into a Lukin public records site. "Please don't tell me she worked with explosives."

Ivan typed in his own access code, following a hunch. "Her fiancé did."

"Her fiancé? I didn't know Galina was engaged."

The familiar weight of guilt settled around Ivan's heart. "Late fiancé. He died in the bombing at St. Feodor."

"Oh. I had no idea." Carly exhaled a sigh. "Now I feel bad for not liking her. She's always so perfect. And feminine. Perfume and high heels all the time? Makes me feel like a slacker. I guess that explains the black she wears." She scooted closer to the foot of the bed. "Did you find what her job was?"

Nothing suspicious here. "Quartermaster's office."

"Supplies. Desk work. Hardly a red flag of suspicion. Manufacturing explosive devices isn't standard training in your army, is it?"

"No."

Carly put a check mark by Galina's name and went on to the next item on her list. "It looks like Filip's most recent search was on Ralph Decker, after he took that picture of us at the hospital. Decker grew up in Kansas City, but he's been gone for years, working mostly with overseas press junkets, reporting for the wire services. He's been embedded with military units all over the world, led a pretty exciting life. He's only been back in KC for a couple of months. He has a job with the *Journal*, but it looks as though he's only been doing fluff pieces."

"Fluff?" Ivan looked up from the screen.

"Human interest stories. Social stuff. Nothing that's hard news."

He pulled up the *Journal*'s website and scrolled through some of Ralph Decker's recent credits. An Honor Flight for veterans, a science fair winner, popular summer day trips around Kansas City, gave him a better understanding of the term Carly had used. "Maybe he is looking to be part of the action again, to break a big story."

"Like who's behind the assassination attempts on a European prince?" Carly wrote a question mark beside the reporter's name. "You don't think he'd create the problem, just so he'd have a story to cover, do you?"

"How would Decker have sent me the threat on the airplane?"

"For the right price, your inside man could have done it for him." Carly dropped her feet off the end of the bed, sliding close enough that her knee brushed his. He really should feel guilty about all the nerve endings that jumped to life at even that casual touch. But he knew the only thing he'd ever regret with Carly was if she got hurt. He blinked away the distracting thoughts, set his glasses on the desk and leaned in to focus on the note she pointed out to him. "Filip's records show Decker's been to Lukinburg. And if he's covered the military, he could have met one of your people then, just like you and I supposedly did."

"Put a star next to his name on your paper. He wants a one-on-one interview. Perhaps he lost someone important in the St. Feodor bombing. I will have this conversation with him at the ball."

"Only if I'm there with you. Saturday is when all hell is supposed to break loose, according to that picture and the date scrawled across it. The last thing you need is to be alone with anyone."

"I am alone with you." She blushed when he lifted his gaze to hers. She wasn't immune to the distractions of working closely together, either. He'd never known a woman so responsive to his voice or touch. He'd never responded to a woman like this, either. It made him want to share many long conversations and put his hands all over her body to discover every place he could touch her and elicit that same rosy heat on her skin. That most male part of him stiffened at the possibilities. But they needed to use this private time wisely. He picked up the legal pad and flipped through the rest of the notes she had written. "What else have you found in Filip's files?"

"A record of threats you've received, minus the two here in the US. Looks like Filip interviewed some of the Loyalist dissidents but didn't reach any conclusions. I called Captain Hendricks and asked him to see if any of the dissident names were in the country now." She wasn't making any effort to put space between them, and neither was he. Ivan liked working with her like this, bouncing their thoughts off each other, sharing her vibrant energy, breathing in her unique scent. "Your appearance schedule is there, right down to parking in the Forty-Seventh Street garage. Changes that were made to coordinate with KCPD, running late, et cetera. Can you tell if anyone else accessed these files before you did?"

Ivan pulled up the data. "Filip, of course. Galina. Eduard."

"Not Danya?"

"He is more of a blunt instrument when it comes to security. He has little faith in technology. But Filip would have shared everything with his team."

"Unless he's hiding something." Carly shot to her feet and hurried around the bed to pick up two cell phones from the bedside table. "I forgot." She opened a text on one phone and handed him the other. "Here's the phone I got for you. I went ahead and programmed in my number and Captain Hendricks's. It's nothing fancy, but it works."

"Thank you."

Ivan set the laptop and new phone on the desk when Carly perched on the arm of the chair and showed him the text. "The captain sent me a copy of the preliminary report on the bomb that killed Eduard. Nothing official yet—it'll take weeks to go through the crime lab. But it doesn't match Filip's report on the St. Feodor bombing. The hooded man, the crowd and the shouted threats are similar, but—"

"It's not the same kind of bomb." Ivan sat back in the chair, recalling what he could from Filip's briefing on the St. Feodor attack. "The St. Feodor bomber used a handheld trigger."

"Today's bomb was detonated by a cell phone. All the bomber had to do was call the number. Either he was watching and knew when you'd be close by, or he called when he thought you'd be riding in the car—according to Filip's schedule. We were late going to lunch and trying to get through the crowd made us even later," she pointed out. "If we were on time, you'd be dead."

"So would you."

"So would a lot of people."

His jaw clenched with the possibility of so many senseless deaths. What if Carly and his team had been with him in the limo? If they'd been in traffic? Or stopped at an intersection with people in the crosswalk? Losing Eduard today wasn't the first time he'd lost a friend. It appeared that whoever wanted to "End Ivan" was intent on destroying many lives before he got around to finally killing him.

"Danya Pavluk's younger brother, Konrad, used to be part of the royal security team. He was killed that day." She'd put a star by Danya's name. He picked up Carly's pen and, with a reluctant sigh, drew a star beside Galina's name.

"What's that for?" Carly asked.

"Galina was engaged to Konrad. Konrad died in her arms in St. Feodor Square."

Carly was silent for a moment, perhaps contemplating Danya's and Galina's grief. "You think one of them wants revenge for Konrad Pavluk's death?"

He'd considered the idea earlier but had dismissed it. The logic didn't make sense. "Why come after me? The Loyalists set off that bomb."

"You're uniting the country. Welcoming the Loyalists into your new regime." Her mouth twisted with an apologetic frown. "Maybe Danya feels like you're rewarding them—instead of punishing them for killing his brother."

"Possibly. Danya would have explosives experience.

He has advanced weapons training. And he came from the same mining region that I did."

"You know how to make a bomb?"

Ivan nodded. "A rudimentary one. It was part of working in the mines."

An uncharacteristic hesitation shadowed her features before she spoke again. "The mines in Moravska? You mentioned it once before—the town where you lived with your aunt and uncle."

"That is correct."

This time she didn't just look away, she got up and walked her phone back to the bedside table. Hesitation wasn't a side of Carly he was used to seeing. Since being forthcoming had never been an issue for her before, he didn't push for an explanation. But it worried him. Surely, there was nothing in these files that made her think that *he* had built and detonated those bombs.

Ivan turned to the last page of her notes. "I see one more entry. Vasily Gordeeva. Mob boss who used to run illegal arms through Lukinburg. Significant influence on the previously corrupt government. His people were the ones responsible for my parents' deaths. He spent his last years in prison and died of cancer." The hate he'd once felt as a younger man had mellowed to a melancholia that hit him when he thought of all that had been taken from him. As a grown man, he replaced the anger and sadness with a good memory from his childhood and then refocused on the tasks at hand—eliminating suspects who wanted him dead and finding out what was bothering Carly. He scratched through Gordeeva's name. "It is rumored that one of Vasily's last acts before his death was to kill the business rival who murdered his daughter. I do not believe there is anyone left with any significant power in either one of those criminal families."

"Unless this terroristic campaign against you is their bid to regain power."

Ivan shook his head. "The new government is too strong for that. They do not have the financial backing they once enjoyed."

"I hope you're right." Carly returned to her perch on the foot of the bed and leaned forward to rest her hand atop his knee. The same nerve impulses that had skittered with delight a few minutes ago now went on alert, bracing him for whatever she was about to tell him. "Speaking of criminals and Vasily Gordeeva... I couldn't find any record of your parents being murdered in your file. No mention of your aunt and uncle raising you in Moravska. That's why I thought the files might be mislabeled. You said they were victims of a mob hit, that the Gordeevas had influence with the government back then. Was the crime not investigated?"

That information was in Aleks's file. The one she couldn't read. The one he couldn't tell her about. He'd given his word to hide the truth.

Even from her.

"Why do you think he was in prison?" Ivan pushed to his feet. He tossed the legal pad onto the bed and paced to the far side of the room before an idea hit him that chased away all the sorrow and guilt. "Enough work." He crossed back to the laptop, found the site he was looking for and clicked on the file he downloaded. He turned up the volume as the melodic strains of a waltz began to play. "You wait on your family, do your job as a police officer, take care of me... It is enough. The rest of the night is about you." He took her hands and pulled her to her feet. "May I have this dance?"

"Touched a sore spot, huh? Okay. I'll stop asking questions." She tossed her hair behind her back and rested one hand on his shoulder as he'd taught her. "You're willing to put your toes through another lesson with me?"

She didn't fight him when he slid his hand to the small of her back and pulled her hips against his. If their knees touching had raised his temperature, feeling her sleek curves nestled against his harder frame nearly made him combust. He rested his forehead against hers, looking down into her upturned eyes. "I am willing to hold you. Always."

Her feet didn't move as he took the first step. Ivan let the music play without dancing until she shared what was keeping her from joining him in the waltz. "We don't have always."

Ivan tightened his hold around her waist and pressed his cheek to hers, wishing he didn't share the same hopelessness about their relationship. "Then I want to make the most of any time I do have with you," he whispered against her ear. "I care about you, my sexy lioness."

"I care about you, too. I want…" Her toes curled into the rug beside his stockinged feet. But her upper body began to sway in time with his.

"What do you want, *dorogoy*?"

"I know it's only been a few days, but I want you." She glanced at the bed and blushed. "There."

"Carly—"

"I know you're attracted to me, too. I mean…" Her thigh slipped between his, brushing against his arousal.

He groaned in helpless pleasure. Her astute powers of observation did indeed make that difficult to hide. "I've had sex. Ages ago, so I know the nuts and bolts."

"Nuts and bolts?"

"But it wasn't great," she hurried on without explanation. "I haven't had a lot of experience, and…" Her cheeks deepened to a rosy hue and she pushed against his chest, ending the dance, though not completely pulling away. "I don't know how to seduce a man."

Her honest confession made him embarrassingly, wonderfully hard. She wasn't the only one who reacted to a suggestive word or familiar touch. Knowing she felt as strongly as he did about how good the two of them could be together triggered an equally strong response in his heart. With all the lies swirling around him these past few weeks, Carly Valentine was one truth he couldn't deny. "Do you want to seduce me?"

"Yes." She broke away to dash into her bathroom and come back with a handful of condoms. That meant she'd been wanting this, hoping for this as much as he had. "I stole these from Jesse's nightstand. I don't know how long they've been there. I don't want to assume anything. But we have all night. And the enemy's at bay right now. No one can get in here." She paused for a moment to catch her breath. "We only have until you leave. Maybe it's crazy, but I don't want to miss out on my chance to be with you. Because I think it might— we might—be really great. Will you please say something, so I stop rambling?"

Ivan took the wrappers from her grip and tossed them onto the bed. He pulled her back into his arms and pressed a kiss to her warm cheek. "It is not crazy. I want you, too." He felt her trembling beneath his touch, but then she wound her arms around his neck and resumed their sensuous dance. They cared about neither the style nor the rhythm, only that they were close enough to feel the heat and shape of each other's bodies. "Tell me what you want."

"I want you to kiss me."

He dipped his mouth to capture hers. He tunneled his fingers into her hair to hold her lips against his as he took his fill of every delicious inch of her beautiful mouth. Her feet stopped moving and she hummed in her throat. Her fingers cupped the back of his head and neck, demanding the same freedom to explore his mouth. The music was drowned out by the pulse throbbing in his ears before he found the strength to end the kiss. Her breathing was as quick and uneven as his own. "What else?"

"I want to put my hands on your skin again."

He'd never truly understood how wickedly seductive true honesty could be. With a nod he stood back to unbutton his shirt, but Carly's hands were there, butting against his as she untucked it from his waistband and pushed the shirt off his shoulders. Her fingers trailed along every inch of skin she uncovered. A sea of goose bumps chased after every caress. His muscles quivered beneath every bold touch. Shoulders, arms, neck, chest, stomach—every part of him craved her touch. He wasn't going to be able to play the patient gentleman for much longer.

Her eager fingers dipped beneath the button of his slacks, yet she hesitated at his belt buckle to lift her gaze to his. "Shouldn't you be telling me what you want, too?"

He curved his fingers over hers, guiding her to undo

the belt and gently unzip his pants. "Trust me, I am enjoying every moment of this seduction."

"I'm doing it right?"

"Yes, my love." The desire that flushed her skin when she freed him nearly undid him. "Yes."

"Will you...undress me?"

Classical music swelled in the background as he peeled the T-shirt over her head and dropped her cutoffs and panties to the floor. As she stepped out of them, he pressed a kiss to her inner thigh. When he felt her shiver, he pressed another kiss to her weepy center, testing her readiness for him. Carly braced her hands against his shoulders, moaning with pleasure. "Your beard...tick...tickles there." He palmed her bottom and kissed her again, loving the grasp of her fingers digging into his shoulders as she came against his mouth. "Ivan. Please. I want..."

Ivan smiled and stood, shucking the rest of his own clothes before unhooking her bra and covering her small, responsive breasts with his hands. He angled one up to his mouth and laved the rigid tip with his tongue. "Tell me what you want, *dorogoy.*"

He was amused that she struggled to speak, but then found himself robbed of words when she tugged him toward the bed. They tumbled onto the quilt, the music long forgotten as this new dance consumed them.

Her hand boldly gripped his arousal and he growled his desire against the curve of her breast.

"Ivan? I don't understand."

Lukin. He'd used Lukin. He paraphrased his need in English. "You have a beautiful body. I want to be inside you. Do you understand what I am saying?" He grabbed the nearest foil packet and tore it open to sheathe himself. "Out loud. Say it. Say you want this, too."

"I want this. I want you. Now."

She swept her arms across the bed, clearing a place for them, tossing aside the legal pad with her notes. A moment of clarity and conscience pierced the haze of wanting Carly that filled his brain. He swung his legs off the bed and sat up. "There is something I need to tell you... You are so honest with me. I must..."

She pressed her fingers to his lips, shushing him. "No more words."

"I am not who you think I am."

"I feel everything I need to know about you. I don't want to waste another moment on anything but this." She climbed into his lap and slid herself over him. The pleasure of their connection robbed him of breath. Her body was magnificent. Tight. Warm. Perfect. "This feels so right, I want to scream. You're sure you locked that door?"

I feel everything I need to know.

"I am sure." Ivan moved inside her. He anchored her with one hand on her sweet, sweet bottom and the other fisted in her hair. He claimed her mouth in a kiss that muffled her scream as she climaxed around him. And while the aftershocks of her release still caressed him, he buried his face in the juncture of her neck and shoulder and squeezed her lithe body tightly to his, hiding the noise of his own completion before collapsing onto the quilt with Carly still snugged in his arms.

He'd never been this satisfied before. He wanted more. He wanted forever to feel like this.

But he was spent, and Carly had fallen, limp, on top of him. They lay there like that for several minutes, his fingers gently stroking up and down her spine until her skin cooled and she rolled onto the quilt beside him. "That was…" Her gaze locked on to his and her lips curved in a drowsy smile. "I knew we'd be great."

He nodded, understanding that there were no words to adequately express the connection they shared. He leaned over to give her swollen lips a quick kiss. "Never doubt your powers of seduction. I will treasure this night always."

"Me, too." She yawned, and her eyes drifted shut, breaking the connection between them.

Ivan slipped out of bed and went into the bathroom to clean up. When he returned, the only light left on was a dim lamp beside the bed. Carly had crawled under the covers and curled up with her pillow. Ivan took a mental snapshot of this serenely tender moment before slipping beneath the covers beside her. He spooned against her back, sliding one arm beneath her cheek and wrapping the other around her waist. He pulled that luscious fall of hair away from her bruised jaw and gently kissed her cheek before settling onto the pillow.

He couldn't remember a time when he hadn't been intrigued by this woman, when he hadn't trusted her to have his back, when he hadn't wanted to be with her like this. He knew Carly Valentine, deep in his soul. He would never know another woman like her. He pressed his lips into her hair and whispered, *"Obicham te, dorogoy."*

There. He'd said it. He'd admitted it to himself. To all the world. To Carly.

Only she was already fast asleep, snoring softly against his biceps, content in the perfection of this moment together.

I love you.

Chapter Eleven

Tonight, Prince Ivan was supposed to die.

The thought of losing the man who could never really be hers made Carly almost physically sick. She'd never really thought about what falling in love would be like for her, or what kind of man would capture her heart. But the moment she'd seen those piercing blue eyes sizing her up at KCPD headquarters, she'd felt a magnetic attraction to Ivan Mostek. From that evening at the house when he'd given her her first dance lesson and then anchored her in the storm of emotions that had buffeted her after Frank had been poisoned, she'd opened her heart to him. Every moment since then, through the danger and the kisses, the laughter and the long conversations, she'd been falling in love. It had happened too fast for her to realize it until last night when she finally understood that whatever was happening between them was completely mutual. She wasn't a convenient fling or a fake girlfriend. Ivan loved her, too. She was as certain of that as her sketchy knowledge of this whole man-woman thing allowed her to be.

She'd fallen in love with a prince. A relationship that could never work.

But even more heartbreaking than knowing he'd be

leaving the country tomorrow was the idea that someone wanted him to leave in a coffin.

That wasn't going to happen. She wouldn't allow that to happen. They might have to go their separate ways because of politics and distance. But nobody was going to *take* him from her.

So Carly smiled and played her part. She'd love Ivan as hard as she could for the short time they had left before she put him on that plane home to Lukinburg tomorrow.

The music had stopped for now, and Carly stood on the steps at the edge of the dais, scanning the guests in sleek black suits and colorful gowns for anything suspicious.

Waiters moved discreetly through the tables at either end of the massive ballroom carrying trays with flutes of champagne. Couples and groups of friends had stopped dancing and chatting to look to the podium in front of the orchestra. A wall of glass doors framed in handcrafted wrought iron led onto a wide veranda of gray marble. Uniformed security guards patrolled out there, while several more embassy security staff in black tuxedos and utility shoes stood at each interior entryway. She recognized two of the waiters as KCPD officers in disguise, and knew Joe Hendricks, a SWAT team and more patrol officers watched the gate, parking area and streets beyond the Lukinburg embassy.

The crystal chandeliers had been dimmed to spotlight the handsome man speaking there, thanking their hosts, the guests and donors, sharing his excitement over the prosperous future Lukinburg and Kansas City would share. He looked a little more robust than usual this evening, since he wore a flak vest underneath his tuxedo. But only she and the security team who had fitted him with the extra protection would know that. She spotted the Lukin ambassador, the mayor, Chief of Police Mitch Taylor, the university president and numerous other political and society dignitaries around the room.

Their known suspects were there, too. Filip Milevski, standing in front of the podium, his hands folded in front of his bulky chest, his eyes skimming the audience. Galina Honchar stood on the steps on the opposite side of the stage, looking stunning in her glittery black gown, holding her omnipresent computer tablet down in the folds of her skirt. Danya paced at the back of the room, moving from the archway of one wing to the other and back. His barrel chest indicated he was wearing body armor beneath his tux, and his expression indicated he'd rather be anyplace but at this party tonight. It took a bit more searching to locate Aleks in the middle of the crowd, grinning from ear to ear as the blonde on his arm whispered something in his ear that amused him. Ralph Decker had left the gathering of reporters filming and jotting notes about the prince's speech and waited at the base of the far steps near the railing where Galina stood. She could see his lips moving as he whispered something to the dark-haired woman, then he muttered something else when Galina waved him away, no doubt warning him to be quiet and leave her alone while she worked the party and listened to the speech. Interesting. Was Decker hitting on Galina? Probing her for answers to his questions? Or relaying some other bit of information about the danger waiting to strike tonight?

If only she could read lips, Carly thought. No, if only she could read minds. Then she'd be able to tell exactly who wanted Ivan dead. Surely, his enemy was plotting even now—counting down to the grand gesture that could kill countless innocent people, or savoring an intricate plan that was already playing out behind the scenes.

The full, flowy skirt of Carly's turquoise gown had been fun to dance in when Ivan had twirled her across the inlaid walnut floor for the opening waltz. But the fitted body girdle she wore underneath was squeezing the air from her lungs, and the holster strapped to her thigh was chafing. The sparkly heels she wore were beautiful to look at, but the three-inch heels were wreaking havoc on her calf muscles and pinching all sensation out of her little toes.

She pulled her cell phone out of her matching sparkly purse and texted Captain Hendricks.

Nothing suspicious.

He texted back, vibrating her silent phone.

Yet. Keep your eyes open and stay close to Ivan.
At the first sign of trouble, get him to the safety of the SWAT van.
We'll take it from there.

Carly texted back a Yes, sir, and tucked her phone back into the tiny purse she carried.

The ballroom erupted with applause at the end of Ivan's speech.

When she raised her hands to clap, she stopped. Ivan smiled and waved to the guests, but when he looked at her, those piercing blue eyes were sending her a silent message. Oh, hell. This was happening. Right now.

A slight shake of his head kept her from going to him. Instead, he swiped the notes he'd used off the podium and strode across the stage. He took her by the arm and led her down the stairs, pushing the crumpled paper into her hand as he turned his back to the audience to keep anyone from seeing what she was looking at. "It was on the podium when I got there."

"But the ambassador—"

"His notes were sitting on top of mine. Clearly, he did not see it. When I pulled my cards out, it was there."

Carly unfolded what she now realized was a crumpled photograph. It was the same picture of the late king's draped coffin, with a very precise message scrawled across the image. *Ticktock, Ivan. You've failed. Time to pay for your mistakes.*

Carly peeked around Ivan's shoulder, scoping out the room to locate their suspects again. Dr. Lombard from the university was at the podium, sharing a few words about how excited they were to have Lukinburg's support for their research. The ambassador who'd introduced both speakers shook his hand and thanked their guests before inviting everyone to enjoy the rest of the evening, including the special wines and dishes shipped in from Lukinburg for tonight's event.

Ivan stuffed the message in his pocket and faced the crowd, too. "Anyone could have put it there. Aleks helped me write my remarks. Galina put my notes on the podium. Filip and Danya checked the entire stage before the evening began."

The audience was applauding and the orchestra playing again as business was concluded and the festivities resumed. "He's here. He knows you have this. He's probably watching you right now to gauge your reaction."

"I had hoped our killer would lose his nerve."

"Not likely. He's probably getting off on the spectacle an attack would cause tonight."

"And there are too many places where he could hide, even among all these people."

"You've made your speech." Carly squeezed his hand and tugged him toward the nearest archway. "Will you let me take you home now? Or back to the hotel?"

He planted his feet, turning her into his arms and whirling her onto the dance floor instead. Carly put her hands where she was supposed to and kept her eyes peeled for anyone more interested in them than they should be while Ivan whispered into her ear. "I cannot leave. I may be the only one who can prevent everyone from panicking if this goes wrong."

"Goes wrong? Of course, it's going to go wrong." She stumbled over his shoe, silently cursing her strappy sandals. "We should be moving you to a safe location, clearing this building and looking for a bomb."

He tightened his grip at her waist and spun her into the heart of the dance floor. "You are right. We will look for the bomb."

Once they reached the other side of the dance floor, Ivan released her waist and grabbed her hand to lead her through the glass doors onto the veranda. The night air was still sticky with the summer heat, so there were few people outside—only a pair of men smoking near the far end of the surrounding stone wall, and a guard walking through the yard between the veranda and the iron bars that marked the edge of embassy property.

Thinking he'd brought her outside for the relative quiet and privacy, she was surprised when he kept moving across the granite paving stones toward the stairs down into the grass. "Where are we going?"

"The last explosion was a car bomb. We should check the parking lot."

This time, Carly planted her feet, stopping at the top of the stairs. "No." She pulled out her cell phone again. "I'll text Captain Hendricks and have his men begin the search. You need to stay as far away as possible from anything that goes boom."

Ivan closed his hand over hers to stop her. "How many people in there do you think have cell phones?"

The last bomb had been triggered by a cell. Carly looked through the windows to the swaying mass of humanity inside the ballroom. She inhaled a steadying breath at the enormity of what they were up against. "You think there's anyone here who *doesn't* have one?"

"For the last time, leave me alone." Carly and Ivan both turned toward the shrill tone in the woman's whispered voice to see Galina tugging against the grip of Ralph Decker's hand on her wrist as the two hurried out the far door. "I am not going anywhere with you."

Decker released her and put his hands up in surrender. With a noisy harrumph and a nod toward Ivan, she hurried down the steps and disappeared along the walkway around the corner of the building.

Keeping Carly's hand in his, Ivan took a step toward the reporter. "Are you annoying the lady, Mr. Decker?"

The dark-haired man shook his head as if he was baffled by Galina's behavior. "She must have a hot date with somebody. And it isn't me."

"I don't think she's interested in seeing anyone right

now," Carly gently pointed out. "Did you know she was engaged to be married? Her fiancé was killed just three months ago."

Decker swore, his remorse evident as his cocky attitude disappeared. "I didn't know. I thought my charm wasn't working. I'll track her down later to apologize." He tapped the camera hanging around his neck. "Hey, since you're here, how about a picture of the two of you together? Dancing in the moonlight. With your permission, of course."

"Of course." Ivan turned Carly into his arms again and posed for the camera. She realized he was acting as if everything was normal—that there was no threat in his pocket, no bomb to be found—so that Decker wouldn't be suspicious and start asking questions.

He did, anyway. But not the ones Carly had expected. "Did you mean what you said in your speech, Your Highness? The materials Lukinburg is supplying the research team will revolutionize the way our country fights a war? Better technology? Fewer casualties?"

Ivan draped his arm around her shoulders for another shot. "There are also other, nonmilitary applications, but that is my hope."

"Then that's a good thing." With a rueful smile, Decker shook the prince's hand and nodded to Carly. "You two enjoy the rest of your evening. If you'll excuse me. I need to find Ms. Honchar."

"That was a weird conversation."

Ivan agreed. "I have a feeling Mr. Decker is a man of many secrets."

They were still standing at the top of the stairs when the glass door opened and closed, momentarily filling the air with strains of orchestral music. Carly leaned into Ivan's chest. "Is it wrong of me to think of the other nights every time I hear classical music playing?"

He laughed. "I think of it every moment."

"I wish…"

"I know. I wish we had more time."

"There are so many reasons why we would never work."

"And one very important reason why we would." He pressed a kiss to her temple and Carly hugged him around the waist.

Feeling the bulk of his protective vest instead of the warmth of his body reminded Carly how foolish she was to put her heart before the job at hand. She was pulling away when she saw the hooded figure moving near the hedge lining the wrought-iron fence. "Ivan."

Hiking up her skirt, Carly ran down the steps in pursuit. But the moment she stepped off the flagstone walk, her heel sank into the grass and mud, halting her momentum and pitching her forward. "These shoes!"

She would have landed flat on her face, but Ivan was there to catch her. "Carly, wait. We don't know what he's up to."

Leaning on his arm, she sucked the ruined heel out of the mud and stepped back onto the walkway. But when she looked to the hedges again, the cloaked figure had disappeared. She saw the guard several yards farther along the fence, heading in the opposite direction. He'd never even heard the figure to turn around. "Where did he go?" She turned toward the driveway and parking lot beyond that. "The guards will stop him at the gate, right? I didn't imagine him, did I?"

"I saw him, too." Ivan pulled her back up the steps,

hurrying toward the veranda doors and reentering the ballroom. "Where is Aleks?"

She had a more important question. "Where's your security team?"

"There." He pointed out Filip moving through the room toward the front hallway. He was talking to someone on his radio. "Hopefully, the guards outside will have detained the man in the hood and called it in."

She scanned the room for Danya, but he was nowhere to be found. "If the intruder was leaving, that means he's already put his plan into play. A bomb or whatever he intends to do tonight."

"You get to Captain Hendricks." Ivan nudged her toward the exit where Filip had disappeared. "I have to find Aleks."

Carly caught his hand and stopped him. "You aren't going anywhere without me. I'm your last line of defense, remember?"

"Fine. Then walk with me."

They circled the perimeter of the tables and guests, pausing to acknowledge someone when greeted, but otherwise moving as quickly as they could. The music that had sounded like a tender memory a moment ago now seemed inordinately loud, to the point that Carly raised her voice. "How many people do you think are here?"

"Two hundred? Three hundred?"

Galina appeared in the nearby archway, surveying the room until she saw them. She hurried across the dance floor, her dark eyes rimmed by tears, her tone panicked. "Your Highness. Officer Valentine. Please. I must show you something." Turning back several times to make sure they were following, Galina led them back into the quieter private hallway from where she'd appeared. She opened the first door just through the archway into a well-appointed office lined with walnut paneling and gold brocade drapes. "I needed a moment to myself to review the guest list and…"

"It's okay, Galina." Carly reached out and squeezed the other woman's hand. "I could tell Mr. Decker upset you. He didn't know about your late fiancé. I'm sure he didn't mean to dredge up any bad memories. Did you find a tissue?"

Instead of being grateful for the concern, Galina burst into angry tears and crossed to the desk in the center of the room. "I found *this*." She showed them a cube-shaped package wrapped in plain brown paper. *End Ivan!* was written across the top of the brown paper wrapping. "This is the guest office we worked out of this week. Is it…what I think it is?"

Carly caught her breath on a wary gasp and pulled the other woman away from the desk. There was only one thing that package could be. "We need to clear the room. I need to notify the bomb squad. Let's go."

Only Ivan was moving in the other direction. *Toward* the package. He circled the desk, studying it from every direction before he grabbed the letter opener from the blotter beside the package.

"Damn it, Ivan." She watched as he pulled the paper away from the plastic-coated wires wrapped around a brick of plastic explosive. "Careful."

"It is rigged with another cell phone," Ivan announced.

Galina wept beside her. "It's like St. Feodor again. All these people…"

"Galina," Ivan chided, coming around the desk to

take his chief of staff by the shoulders and gently shake her. "Pull yourself together. Do your job."

The dark-haired woman stared at him a moment before wiping away her tears and hugging her tablet to her chest. "What do you need?"

"I need you to find the ambassador. Tell him we have a situation. Have him make an announcement asking everyone to turn off their cell phones—make up some excuse about them interfering with the sound system. Then we need to calmly, without raising too much alarm, evacuate the building."

"Smoke from the kitchen," Carly suggested, rubbing Galina's back, trying to soothe her fear. "Tell them we need everyone outside on the veranda and the parking lot, so we can ventilate the building." She tilted her gaze to Ivan. "I can get to Chief Taylor. He can escort the mayor and some of the other dignitaries out."

Galina nodded. "Cell phones. Smoke. Calm evacuation. I'll have them use different exits so there's not a rush for the doors." Although it probably wasn't protocol for her to do so, she squeezed Ivan's hand before he pulled away. "You're the target, Your Highness. What about you? Shall I send Filip in here?"

"He's outside. He can help keep things organized out there."

"Danya? I haven't seen him, but—"

Carly turned to face her. "Ivan is my responsibility. I'll make sure he gets out safely."

"You don't want me to call anyone to help?"

"No." She walked the other woman out the door. "I want you to start the evacuation."

When she stepped back inside the office, Ivan was holding his glasses close to his temple, bending down to study the bomb again. "We need to get people out of this wing and evacuate the building." He pointed to the phone on the corner of the desk. "Call Joe on that landline. Bomb squad cannot come in with full gear or we'll have chaos. Someone could get trampled or have a heart attack."

Carly called Captain Hendricks and warned him about not using cell phones. She told him to put the SWAT team on alert, that she was bringing the prince out the back way through the veranda doors. She hung up and nodded to the door, expecting Ivan to follow. "Let's go."

"I am not going anywhere."

She tugged on his arm, pulling him away from the desk. "You're not staying here with this bomb."

"I can disarm it. It is not that complicated. Plastique. Wires. The cell phone is not counting down. I can disconnect it—"

"Just because you worked with explosives back in Moravska doesn't mean this is your job. You have a whole country you're responsible for. We need to close off this room and leave."

The music stopped abruptly, and, for a split second, Carly felt as though it was her heart that had stopped. Why was Ivan taking such a stupid risk? "Don't be a hero, Ivan. We have no idea when that bomb will go off."

He glanced up at the grandfather clock standing in the corner of the office. It was barely eleven o'clock. "I am guessing within the next hour. Today was the date on the picture he gave me."

The ambassador's voice coming over the sound system and the rising murmur of the guests responding to the unexpected interruption of their evening echoed the tension twisting through Carly. "Ivan, please."

Ticktock.

"Wait a minute…" Ivan slid the letter opener beneath a trio of wires and lifted them away from the plastique. "The phone is not connected to the explosive. There is no way to remotely detonate it." Blue eyes drilled into hers. "This bomb is a fake."

A fake? After all those threats? Naming the date of Ivan's death? Oh, hell. The hooded man moving through the hedge outside? A bomb inside the embassy? Guests evacuating to the parking lot? "Does that mean…?"

He was already running to the door. "There's another bomb."

They dashed down the hallway and stopped when they saw the orderly mass exodus leaving the building. Just like the scene at the Plaza, when they were being herded toward the parking garage. Toward the bomb.

"A car bomb killed Eduard," Carly said.

"They are taking them out to the parking lot," Ivan muttered at the same time.

Carly ran back to the phone. "I'll tell the captain."

Ivan hovered in the doorway. "We need to find Aleks."

"He's probably on his way outside with the others."

"We have to find him. Priority one is saving Aleks."

"Priority one is saving you." Carly hung up the phone and lifted the hem of her skirt to get to her weapon. She tugged on the lapel of Ivan's jacket and turned him so that she could enter and clear the hallway in front of him. "I have to get you to the SWAT van. That's what we agreed on."

Ivan pulled her hand away and backed into the office. "Go. Stay with Aleks. Get him someplace safe. I need to take this bomb apart."

"You said it wasn't a real bomb."

"Connect it to a trigger and it will take out this wing of the embassy. If we leave it alone, anyone could sneak in and do that."

"Then I'm staying with you."

Ivan pushed her out the door. "Save the prince!"

"But you…" Her back hit the opposite wall and she stood there long enough for confusion to segue into understanding. Then anger sent her charging across the hall. "Damn it, I knew something was off." She swatted his arm. Although, she wasn't sure if her anger was directed at him or toward herself for not guessing the truth. "You're not Prince Ivan. When I read those files… When I see the two of you together, you're so protective of him."

The man of purpose, the man of regal power and supreme confidence suddenly seemed unsure.

"Carly…" He reached for her, but she shrugged off his touch.

Her anger turned into a hurt she felt right down to her bones. "Aleksandr Petrovic?"

He nodded. "I tried to tell you the other night. When we were…in bed."

"But I didn't want to talk." She raked her fingers into her hair, knocking loose some of the upswept curls. She'd been a naive idiot. "I got so carried away."

"*We* got carried away." Ivan's hands were on her shoulders again. His sure, familiar hands. Only, they weren't Ivan's hands. "I should have tried harder. When you said you *felt* the truth about me, I thought—"

"That I knew you were fake? That you were lying

to me?" She pulled away and paced across the room. "I meant I knew what was in your heart."

"You do. I have never lied about that. Not about this chemistry between us. Not about my feelings for you." He caught her by the hand and turned her to face him. "You must have sensed something. You are too good a cop not to have at least suspected."

She nodded. She had suspected something. But she'd been so caught up in her feelings, compounded by the time limit on this affair, that she'd ignored what the clues had tried to tell her. "The scars. Losing your parents. Growing up poor. None of that happened to Ivan. That was *your* story you were sharing. You slipped up."

"Because you were so easy to talk to. You understood me. The real me. We have much in common. I have been living the lie for so long, I did not realize how much I needed someone who cared about me, not the role I was playing."

"If I could read Lukin, I would have discovered the truth. The details in Aleks's file are yours." She pulled away and lifted her skirt to reholster her gun. She didn't have to save this man. "What are you, Ivan's bodyguard? His friend?"

"Both. I am the geeky computer guy, as you say, who runs tech for the prince's security team. We have switched places before—years ago when we realized how much we look alike, covering duty shifts, going to class when one of us overslept, stupid stuff—nothing recent, and never on this grand a stage before. But after the bombing in St. Feodor—"

"You threw yourself over him when that bomb went off. That's how you got those scars—protecting the prince. You're protecting him now."

He nodded. "We switched places seven weeks ago, as soon as the doctor cleared me to return to duty. I'd been away recuperating—it was easy enough to change our hair, our glasses."

She touched the bruise that had been dimmed by makeup on her jaw. "The doctor knew?"

"He was familiar with my injuries—and Ivan and I both thought it was prudent for him to know the truth, in case any health issues cropped up for the real prince while we traveled."

She was silent, not sure what to say. She'd given this man her heart, her body. And he'd lied.

"I did not tell you because I promised Ivan I would not. I wanted to. I wanted you to know the truth. But my sworn duty is to my future king."

"I understand duty. I understand why you lied. The more people who know who an undercover operative is, the harder it becomes to keep it a secret."

"Yes, *dorogoy*. You understand, but do you forgive me?"

Dorogoy. Darling. Did he really love her? She pressed her hands to either side of her head, wishing she could make the hurt and mistrust go away. But she couldn't. Not in this moment. Not when she wasn't even sure what *she* was feeling anymore.

She pointed to the desk. "We have bigger issues to deal with right now. I'll get Aleks…" She shook her head, clearing her thoughts to at least one thing. Duty. "I'll get Prince Ivan out to the van. You see what you can do about that bomb." She paused in the doorway and turned back to those piercing blue eyes. "Do not blow yourself up. We have more to talk about."

Then she ran to join the exiting crowd.

Chapter Twelve

His one fear had been that he would hurt her. He hadn't realized how much seeing that look of betrayal in Carly's beautiful eyes would hurt him.

Aleksandr—had he really gotten so used to thinking of himself as Ivan?—couldn't shake the sense of loss he felt when he saw Carly running away from him. But he could compartmentalize his feelings and deal with the job at hand. The military had trained him to do that. His oath to his future king demanded it.

While the grandfather clock ticked away in the corner, he searched through the desk to find tools he could use. A small pair of scissors. Tweezers. Although this explosive wasn't rigged to blow, he worried that any spark from the cell phone might set off the C-4 accidentally. That meant untangling his way through these wires and removing the phone without building up any kind of static charge as he worked.

He pulled off his glasses that did more to distort his view of the world than correct his slight astigmatism. But they'd been a necessary part of his disguise to pass as the prince, who was nearsighted. He clipped the first few wires and unwound another to pull the phone free of the explosive. Then, he pried the phone apart and removed the battery.

Crisis averted. He breathed in a sigh of momentary relief. Time to make sure the prince was safe.

In that deep breath, Aleksandr caught a whiff of faint perfume lingering in the air. Carly didn't wear perfume—she smelled like the delicious foods she cooked. This was more exotic. Was that Galina's scent? She'd been gone for nearly fifteen minutes. Shouldn't her perfume have dissipated by now?

Sniffing the air, he followed the scent to the drapes at the window and pulled them aside. The window was unlatched, hanging open a fraction of an inch. All the windows on this side of the building had the same floor-to-ceiling design as the veranda doors. Had the bomber come in this way? Or gotten out?

His gaze dropped past the excess folds of the heavy gold brocade to a swatch of dark, dusty material stashed behind the curtain. Aleksandr knelt to grasp what was clearly a sleeve. A collar. A hooded coat. He lifted the coat to his nose, breathed in the overpowering perfume and residue of sweat from a hot summer afternoon, and then he cursed.

Galina had worn this. Tonight. On the Plaza. A replica of the coat worn by the rebel bomber in St. Feodor. Her perfume was expensive and distinct.

Why? Why would the prince's chief of staff want to kill him? Galina Honchar wasn't a political rebel. She had no ties to criminal families. Aleksandr shook his head and pushed to his feet. The whys didn't matter. This was over. He knew who had murdered Eduard Nagy, who had poisoned Frank Valentine, who had tried to kill the prince.

"Carly!" She'd be out of earshot by now, but he called to her, anyway. They were a team. Together, they'd found the answers he needed. "Carly!" He whirled around to see the dark-haired woman standing in the doorway. "Galina."

She held her tablet in one hand and a gun in the other. A gun she pointed squarely at him.

"The building is clear, Your Highness." She eyed the dismantled device on top of the desk. "You took apart my little toy." She strolled toward him. She set the tablet on the corner of the desk and typed in a number on the screen. "But I have another."

He tossed the coat back into its heap, wondering if she had any kind of skill with that gun and just how badly he'd get hurt if he charged her. But more than the gun, he worried about what the numbers and the blinking prompt on her tablet meant. So he stood his ground. For now. "We know about the car bomb, Galina. KCPD and embassy security are searching for it right now."

She trailed her finger around the frame of the tablet. "Yes, but will they find it before I press this button and kill, I don't know, seven innocent people? Just like St. Feodor? Maybe more? All I have to do is send this message."

If she'd been crying earlier, there was no sign of those tears now in her cold, dark eyes. This woman was beyond feeling anything but the rage that consumed her. "You've taken apart many things that were mine. You've destroyed so much."

Aleksandr took a step forward, testing her reflexes. The gun never wavered. He put up his hands in a placating gesture, pretending that understanding made a difference. But he wasn't about to retreat. He had to get that tablet away from her. He had to get past that gun first. "This is about Konrad, the man you loved. This is all about revenge."

Galina nodded. "I simply wanted to poison you—to see you die a painful, horrible death. The Loyalists would have taken the blame for the threats and your death, and all of Lukinburg would understand the pain that I have suffered because of you. But the apples got away from me. You wanted to give them to your girlfriend. Your stupid girlfriend! After that mistake, I realized I would have to be more clever. My Konrad taught me many things. How to love. How to build a bomb. How to fire a gun. But he didn't teach me how to live without him. How to live with his senseless death. He died protecting you."

"Konrad's death is no excuse for this." He channeled every imperial syllable of the prince's tone he could. "You will kill many innocent people. Kon would not want that."

"I want that!" She stepped toward him, using the gun to direct him away from the window while she picked up the coat. "My world was perfect until you came along and started changing everything. What was wrong with the old ways? I was happy. In love. Konrad was alive." She tossed the coat onto the desk. "That stupid reporter nearly caught me in here. Otherwise, I'd have cleaned up after myself. Just like I've always cleaned up after your messes. Everything had to be just the way His Royal Highness the Prince of Lukinburg wanted it." Aleksandr countered her position, inching closer to the tablet. She motioned him into the chair beside her and ordered him to sit. Feeling the barrel of the gun pressing against his skull gave him no choice but to oblige.

"*You* made enemies, and *he* paid the price. Now you're going to pay." She circled the desk again, turning the tablet to face her. "What a tragic, humiliating end to your visit to Kansas City. You will die. Your people will die. Your regime will fail. You can't stop me."

Carly Valentine's kick-ass tone sounded from the doorway behind Galina. "I can."

The color drained from Galina's face before Aleksandr saw the flash of sparkling turquoise behind her. Galina raised both hands, including the gun, as Carly circled around her, her own gun trained on the back of Galina's head as she reached for the weapon to disarm her.

"KCPD. You are under arrest—"

He saw the grim determination flatten Galina's mouth. "Carly!"

Galina ducked and swung around, cracking the gun against Carly's arm, sending Carly's weapon flying. Galina lunged toward the desk.

"Keep her away from that tablet!" Aleksandr shot to his feet, but it really was no contest.

There was a fistful of hair, a kick to the knees and Galina was pinned to the floor. Carly kicked one gun out of reach beside the door and twisted around to locate where her gun had landed. Galina tried to roll away from her, and she was forced to put a knee in Galina's back and hold her in place. "Really, lady? You want to keep fighting me?"

Aleksandr picked up the tablet. "Will turning this off set off the bomb?" he demanded.

"Go to hell," was Galina's answer.

"I will take that as a no." Good thing he knew a little bit about computers. He disabled the tablet's Wi-Fi connection, closed down the screen and pried open the back to remove the battery, just as he'd pulled apart the phone.

He heard footsteps running in the hallway as he set down the tablet. He was pulling off his belt to give Carly something to bind Galina's wrists with when a trio of men burst through the door. He was not a happy man. It didn't matter that Ivan was flanked by both Filip and Danya. He shouldn't be anywhere close to this traitorous witch. "What are you doing here?"

"Are you all right?" Ivan asked. "Carly?"

Filip and Danya must not know they had the real prince with them. "Get him out of here."

The two bodyguards rushed forward, pulling Aleksandr to his feet and flanking him. But Ivan wouldn't listen. "Galina Honchar, I accuse you of treason. Danya, take her into custody."

"Shut up, party boy." Galina was beyond reasoning now. "You're a waste of my time."

The prince stepped forward. "How dare you speak to your future king like that?"

"Future king?" Galina repeated.

"What?" Filip and Danya stood there agape.

Danya released Aleksandr first and moved to stand beside Ivan. "You are the prince?"

Ivan grinned. "Surprise."

Danya turned on Filip. "Did you know this?"

Filip glared at Aleksandr. "I did not."

"What are you saying?" Galina seemed more stunned than either of the men. "You? With all your sightseeing and flirting... I could have killed you a dozen times. Those nights we worked late at the hotel while he was with her?" Galina's roar of frustration was almost feral. "I will kill you!"

Carly hadn't spotted her gun yet, but Galina had. Fueled by whatever grief and anger was driving her, she twisted away from Carly and grabbed the gun from beneath the desk. She rolled, fired.

Aleksandr leaped in front of the prince and felt the bullet strike him in the chest. Pain blossomed on the right side of his rib cage as if he'd been struck by a rocket.

"No!" Carly shouted, her concern followed just as quickly by a curse. And then she switched her focus entirely and took Galina down again. She wrestled control of the gun and jammed it against Galina's neck before the woman finally stilled. "Is he hurt?"

While Filip and Ivan helped him sit up, Danya went to Carly. He picked up the discarded belt and wound it tightly around Galina's arms above her elbows. "This will hold her for now."

Carly shook her head. "She's not getting off another shot. I'm not letting go. Is he hurt?" she demanded.

"I am all right," he reassured her, breathing through the bruising pain. He unbuttoned his shirt and peeled it back to reveal the flattened bullet that had lodged in his protective vest. The shot might not have cracked a rib, but it sure did feel as if it had. He wished he could read the message in Carly's green eyes. Worry? Anger? He still reassured her. "The wind is knocked from my chest. I will be all right."

And then he turned his attention to the prince, who helped him to his feet. "What are you doing here? You're supposed to be safe in the SWAT van."

"Galina wasn't with the rest of the entourage. Neither were you. I was worried. I may be a prince, but I am also your friend. Your very grateful friend."

"Yeah, this is touching," Carly groused. "I need handcuffs." Joe Hendricks and two members of the SWAT team entered the room. She glanced up at him and saw him holding his side. "And a medic."

One of the officers immediately knelt and pulled out his cuffs to take Galina into custody. The other went to the desk to examine the explosive.

"You okay, Valentine?" Joe asked, helping Carly to her feet. That's when Aleksandr noticed that Carly had taken off her shoes—or lost them in the mud outside. "We found the second bomb in the royal limo. Bomb squad is taking it apart now."

Aleksandr moved to the desk. "This one has been dismantled, but they will want to dispose of the components properly." He handed Joe the tablet. "Take this, too. Any good computer tech in your crime lab should be able to trace when she used it to set off the bomb that killed Eduard."

"I'll send someone in to clear the room. SWAT Team Two is doing a full sweep of the building. We'll debrief later." He nodded to the two SWAT officers. "Get her out of here." He turned to the real prince. "Your Highness. If you would kindly stay where we put you this time. It'd be a hell of a lot easier to keep you safe."

Filip agreed. "We will make sure he remains secure. Danya?"

Suddenly, the room was empty except for him and Carly. He got a glimpse of one gorgeous leg as she pulled up her dress to holster her weapon again.

She didn't seem affected by his obvious attraction to her. "You need to be checked by a medic."

When she headed for the door, he blocked her path. "We need to talk."

"Ivan... I mean, Aleksandr. Aleks? What do I call you?"

He took a deep breath. This wouldn't be easy, but he had to make this right. "My friends call me Aleks."

Her lips warped into a frown before she extended her hand to shake his. "Nice to meet you, Aleks. I'm Carly Valentine. I have issues with people who lie to me."

"And you are always honest with me." He tightened his grip and held on when she would have pulled away. "I am sorry I have hurt you. That was never my intent. But I had to keep my word to the prince. I became him to keep him safe."

"You just took a bullet for him. Good job. You're a man of your word. May I have my hand back?"

"No." He pulled her into his arms. She put up a token fight but stopped the moment he winced at a shove against his bruised ribs. "I wanted you to love me. The man whose parents were murdered, the man who served six years in the army." He lifted her hand to his face and held it where she had touched him so many times before. "The man with the scars. Is there any way you would give Aleksandr Petrovic a second chance? One where I do not lie to you?"

The grandfather clock chimed midnight.

Carly rested her hands on his chest for a moment, then busied her fingers rebuttoning his shirt and straightening his tie. When the chimes stopped, she pulled away, as if that was her cue to leave. "You have to go back to Lukinburg. Today. We survived the deadline. Your traitor has been identified. No more bombs.

You have to protect Ivan. I don't even have a passport. We'll probably never see each other again."

"Carly—"

"I'm glad for the time we had. Truly. I felt special. It felt…real."

"Aleksandr." Danya called to him from the doorway. "His Highness would like to speak to you."

"You'd better not keep your boss waiting." Carly put on a brave smile that made him feel as if he'd taken that bullet to the heart. "You said one week. You never lied about that." He retreated to the door but wasn't ready to leave her. "I knew about the time limit on this assignment. I understood I was never going to have a prince of my own—no matter how much I loved him."

Everything inside him went perfectly still, then bloomed with hope. "You love…?"

Danya grumbled a curse. "Petrovic. We must make a statement to the police and then get the prince back to our hotel."

Carly waved him away. "Go. Duty calls. We both know how that is."

Duty. How many times in his life had he chosen duty over love?

How many times had he even been given the choice?

Aleksandr cupped the side of Carly's neck and tipped her face up to cover her mouth in one last hard, passionate kiss. *"Obicham te, dorogoy."*

Then he drew his finger across her cheek and followed Danya down the hallway.

Chapter Thirteen

"Carly! Rise and shine. You have a visitor."

Carly pulled the pillow over her head to muffle the noise of her brother knocking on her bedroom door. When it didn't stop, she threw the pillow across the room and sat up. "I was up late, Frank. Fix your own breakfast for once."

"I ate three hours ago."

She glanced over at the clock. It was nearly noon. Maybe he was looking for lunch. She didn't have much of an appetite herself. Possibly because she was still full of the pint of coffee ice cream she'd eaten when she'd gotten home from the ball. Or maybe because after that self-pity pig-out, she'd cried in the shower until the water had run cold. Then she'd put on her sweats and had run a couple of miles around the neighborhood to clear her head, falling into bed as the sun was coming up. She might have a better grasp on everything that had happened this past week—she might even have a sense of acceptance over the way things had ended with Ivan, no, make that Aleksandr. But she was still too emotionally drained and exhausted to be hungry.

Or social.

Or nice to her brother.

"Go away, Frank!"

"No can do, Carly Barley. It's official police business. He says he needs to talk to Officer Valentine."

Carly tipped her head back and groaned. "Give me five minutes to get presentable."

"Okeydoke."

She was out of bed and freshening up in the bathroom before she heard him head back upstairs. The stack of condoms she'd stolen from Jesse's old room sat on the counter beside the sink, taunting her. Before the memory of that special night overtook her and left her sobbing again, she opened a drawer and dumped them inside. She pulled on a pair of cutoffs and tank top, twisted her hair into a braid and hurried up the stairs, barefoot.

"Who is it, Frank? I'm on vaca..."

"I brought you a present." She froze at the deep, accented voice she found so sexy. Aleksandr Petrovic, once known as His Royal Highness Prince Ivan of Lukinburg, handed her a large, rectangular box with a turquoise ribbon tied around it. He set it in her hands and she nearly dropped it, partly because of the unexpected weight, and partly because she was in shock at seeing him here. He caught the box before it hit the floor and held it out to her again. "I see that you can use a pair of shoes."

Carly couldn't look away from those blue eyes. "What are you doing here? Aren't you supposed to be on a flight to Lukinburg right now? It'll be a long walk home."

"Perhaps not."

"Okay, a long swim."

"I am staying in Kansas City."

Carly blinked. He was staying? She blinked again. "But…" She dropped the box to the floor and closed the distance between them, wrapping her arms around his waist and snuggling in to the place she liked best. "I'm sorry."

His arms folded around her and he whispered against her hair. "For what, *dorogoy*?"

"For getting stuck in my head and not listening to my heart. I felt stupid that I hadn't seen your deception. But then I realized you had to be really good at your job to pull that off, and I admire you for that. You said we would fake a relationship, but every bit of it was real except for your name. I didn't want you to go last night. I don't want you to go now. Wait. Why are you staying?" She pushed against him to see into his eyes and immediately apologized when he grimaced in pain.

"You're hurt?"

"Some bruising and swelling. The doctor says I will be fine."

"Carls, my dear." Her father had gotten off the sofa to join them in the foyer. "The guy's been wounded in action. Ask him in for coffee. Frank? Let's go out back and inspect that work you've been doin' on my deck." He reached out to shake Aleks's hand. "You know she's got two big brothers and me lookin' out for her if you don't treat her right."

"Dad!"

But Aleks grinned. "I would be more scared of her than any of you if I screw this up."

Her father laughed. "Then you do know her. You're okay, Mr. Prince. I like you." He ended the handshake to hug Carly to his side. "Is this what you want?"

She hugged him back. "*He's* what I want."

He kissed the top of her head. "Then go for it. We'll give you two some privacy."

"Thanks, Dad."

Several minutes later, Carly was wearing the burgundy boots she'd admired when she'd been shopping for evening gowns, and she was sitting in Aleks's lap on the couch. "They're beautiful. I love them." She gave him a quick kiss. "Thank you."

Aleks wore another suit and crisp white shirt, but this time without the tie. He looked downright casual and infinitely handsome. He skimmed his hand up and down her leg, from the cuff of her shorts to the top of her new boots and back. The friction of his gentle caress warmed her skin and heated things up deeper inside. "I did not think you would like another pair of those sparkly heels. These make you smile."

"You make me smile." She stroked the fine silk of his beard along his jaw. "You're sure you aren't in any danger from Galina Honchar? Or Lukin rebels? I'd rather not play bodyguard again if I don't have to."

"Galina is being extradited to Lukinburg where she will stand trial. Danya..." Carly tightened her fingers against his skin when he hesitated. "He was not happy to have his brother's death be the excuse she used to assassinate the prince. He is taking some time off. But I advised Ivan to ask him to take over as security chief, and encourage Filip to retire."

"Sounds like a smart plan," Carly agreed. "Now tell me again why you're not going home to St. Feodor with Ivan?"

He pressed a kiss into her palm and smiled. "I asked to be assigned to Kansas City to represent Lukinburg's interests here. There may be a time when I go back to my country. For a visit. But by then, you will have a passport. There is much I would like to show you, just as I have seen much of your beautiful city." He nuzzled the shell of her ear, then kissed his way down her neck until he found the bundle of nerves that made her squiggle in his lap. He smiled against her skin as it heated beneath his touch. "I cannot make you a princess, but perhaps you would be content to be a geeky computer nerd's wife."

"I already said yes." Carly captured his jaw between her hands and kissed him again. "Do you really love me?"

"That is what *obicham te* means."

The guttural expression of his feelings warmed her as thoroughly as his touch. "I want to learn more of your language."

"I will teach you."

"Will you take me dancing?"

"Every night if you wish." He smiled. "Since we are laying down the ground rules of this very real relationship, I know that you wish to continue your work with KCPD. They are very lucky to have you. But you will still have time to bake me a pie?"

"What flavor would you like?"

His smile faded, but the intensity of those blue eyes never dimmed. "Will you love me for who I really am?"

"Aleksandr Petrovic—I didn't fall in love with a prince. I fell in love with a man." She traced the scar that cut through his beard and then touched her lips to the brave, vulnerable spot. "I fell in love with *you*."

* * * * *

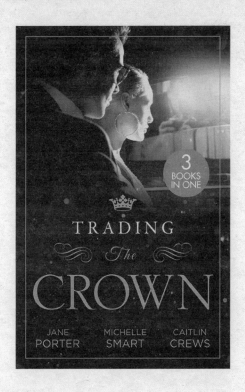

LET'S TALK

Romance

For exclusive extracts, competitions and special offers, find us online:

- **f** MillsandBoon
- **t** @MillsandBoon
- **○** @MillsandBoonUK
- **♪** @MillsandBoonUK

Get in touch on 01413 063 232